# ASH OCK

## Christopher Hinz

A TOM DOHERTY ASSOCIATES BOOK
NEW YORK

This is a work of fiction. All the characters and events portrayed in this book are fictitious, and any resemblance to real people or events is purely coincidental.

ASH OCK

Copyright © 1989 by Christopher Hinz

Cover art by Kevin Murphy

A Tor Book
Published by Tom Doherty Associates, Inc.
175 Fifth Avenue
New York, N.Y. 10010

Tor® is a registered trademark of Tom Doherty Associates, Inc.

ISBN: 0-812-53078-0

First Tor edition: October 1995

Printed in the United States of America

0  9  8  7  6  5  4  3  2  1

For Kate, Ann, Bill, Gerry,
Barb, Elaine, Sue

*for their support*
*for their friendship*

# Prologue

Ghandi stood with the Captain on the flight deck, their hands gripping the sway bars, their bodies rocking back and forth. Outside the shuttle, the fierce Colorado winds screamed across the thick hull, blasting wads of snow against the narrow band of windows, buffeting the craft as if it were a freefall toy in the hands of a child. The pilot, strapped tightly in his acceleration chair in front of them, kept his eyes riveted to the instruments. Sight navigation was useless in such a storm.

"Well?" demanded the Captain.

The pilot, maintaining his vigil on the control board that half encircled him, shook his head. "Gone again, Captain. It's a weak signal . . ."

"I don't care what kind of signal it is," growled the Captain. "I'm not spending the whole day flying through this crap. If you can't lock on in sixty seconds, get us the hell out of here."

A particularly violent updraft banked the craft thirty degrees. Ghandi lost his balance. He lunged sideways, mashed his face into the Captain's shoulder, inhaled the stench of a freshly spirited odorant bag. The smell alone almost knocked him back in the opposite direction.

The Captain glared. "If you can't stand a bit of turbulence, Ghandi, then strap yourself in!"

Ghandi exhaled slowly, turning away to hide his anger. This Captain had a nasty temper, but corresponding displays from his crew were not tolerated. Even a mild grimace from Ghandi could gyrate the Captain into a full-blown tantrum.

And the man had a smell that would frighten children.

Ghandi wore an odorant bag too; most pirates kept a hybrid of foul scents looped around their belts—a symbol of their particular clan, a badge of the true Costeau. Still, Ghandi removed his odorant bag once in a while . . .

"It's back!" yelled the pilot. "And I've got a fix."

The Captain grunted.

"Six or seven miles to the southwest," said the pilot, "right where Denver squeezes itself against the mountains."

"One of our ships?" asked the Captain.

"No."

"E-Tech?"

The pilot hesitated. "I don't know. I've never seen a beacon like this before. A sporadically pulsed cardioid pattern. Extremely low power. I doubt whether anyone beyond a twenty-mile radius could even pick it up. I'm sure it's a distress signal, but whether or not it's E-Tech, I couldn't say."

"What could you say?" grilled the Captain.

The pilot shrugged.

The Captain's eyes drifted shut, a retreat into deep thoughts. Ghandi knew what those thoughts were.

*If it's an E-Tech ship, it could be a trap. Sucker us down to the surface with a phony distress signal, then arrest us for illegal trespass. We're on a dirty flight—unlisted with E-Tech's orbital control—and we're in restricted airspace to boot.* Lately, the bastards were getting tougher—penalties for such intrusions were becoming harsher. Whatever moral qualms E-Tech had once boasted regarding entrapment had vanished years ago. Pirate captains, caught on the surface without permission, were being levied heavy fines. Some Costeaus had even been stripped of their vessels.

Good reasons for not responding to distress calls.

*But maybe this ship isn't E-Tech. Maybe it's Colony-bred treasure hunters, just as dirty down here as we are. Maybe they had engine failure and can't lift off.*

An E-Tech outpost existed in Texas, seven hundred miles to the southeast. But if the Captain of this shuttle was on a dirty flight, probably he would not risk contacting that base, at least not until things got desperate. A short-range, low-powered distress beacon offered a fair shot of reaching one of the numerous Costeau flights that constantly scavenged the planet. And pirates, whether down here legally or otherwise, provided the best chance for getting rescued *and* staying out of trouble with the Colonial authorities. Boost the power of your signal—shout HELP over a ten-state area—and E-Tech Security patrols would be crawling all over you within the hour.

The Captain opened his eyes. "I think it's a dirty flight."

The pilot nodded. "Engine problems, maybe."

The Captain's mouth twisted into the vaguest hint of a smile. "They might need our help."

In the proper circumstances, *help* could be a very expensive commodity.

"Let's take her down."

Ghandi smiled too. This asshole Captain did have his good points.

"What do you make of it?" asked the pilot.

"Hell if I know," muttered one of the others.

The five of them stood silently, in full spacesuits, in twenty inches of snow, on the western edge of Denver, Colorado, where the flat sprawl of the mile-high city began to undulate as it squeezed itself against the front range of the Rocky Mountains.

Six-and-a-half million people had lived here once, had breathed this air, had made this place into one of the great metropolitan centers of the twenty-first century. Now it was dead, no different from the other Earth cities, lifeless for almost a quarter of a millennium, the air still saturated with organic poisons, practically unbreathable. Just another icon to planet Earth: another of humanity's junkyards, decimated by the nuclear-biological Apocalypse of 2099, two hundred and thirty-nine years ago.

The storm had subsided a bit, or else the mass of skyscrapers rising a few miles behind them somehow limited wind intensity at ground level. Even so, a fair amount of fresh snow swirled through the air, blowing down from the western peaks. Ghandi touched a sensor on his control belt, notched his faceplate thermal wiper into a faster mode.

In front of them, an eight-lane highway—probably once a major interstate thoroughfare—bisected this particular development, truncating the deserted streets and dividing the staggered rows of eight- and ten-story condos into two separate arenas. Ghandi thought it likely that the highway had also served as a governmental dividing line; an official boundary permitting the once-extravagant condo-dwellers to consider themselves as denizens of discrete subcommunities. The idea fit well with what he knew of pre-Apocalyptic history.

On the far side of the highway, about a hundred yards to the north, in a vacant lot beside a car refueling station, rested the unfamiliar shuttle. The interior lights were lit and the main airlock stairway was down. There was no sign of life.

Their own shuttle squatted behind them, in the center of an exit ramp—one hundred and fifty feet of white metal and plastic, a pair of stubby wings angling upward, the blackened heat shields testifying to frequent atmospheric incursions. Beneath the craft, the ice and snow had been melted away by the intense heat from their vertical landing jets; plumes of gray smoke still drifted from the sextet of exhaust tubes. Cracked yellow paving—the exit ramp's original surface—lay exposed, extending outward in a twenty-foot arc from the vessel.

"Should we leave a guard behind?" asked the pilot.

"You scared?" the Captain retorted.

Ghandi said nothing. The asshole *should* leave someone behind, just in case they ran into problems. No backup . . . that was begging for trouble.

The other shuttle was roughly the same size and shape as their own. There were no large markings visible on the stubby body, but that was not unusual. Anyone on a dirty flight ran the risk of being visually sighted by an E-Tech ground unit. Without ID markings, there was no way for E-Tech to positively identify the craft and bring official charges against the crew upon their return to the Colonies.

The Captain turned to one of the other pirates. The man wore a shoebox-sized device strapped to the front of his spacesuit: a rhythm detector—standard hunt-and-search gear for ground expeditions.

"Picking up anything?"

The crewman checked the digital readout and shook his head.

"Nothing, Captain. No movement within three hundred yards. Either they're out of the neighborhood or they're still inside the shuttle."

*Not necessarily*, thought Ghandi. *They could be shielded.* It was not extraordinarily difficult to block the scanning waves of a rhythm detector; some of the surrounding condos—like the shuttle itself—might have walls thick enough to inhibit the device's tracking sensors. And AV scramblers would also foul a rhythm detector, though Ghandi acknowledged the remoteness of that possibility. AV scramblers were still on E-Tech's restricted technology list and even black market models cost a fortune, providing you could find one.

He said nothing, however, knowing it would be a wasted effort to broach any of his concerns. This was only Ghandi's third flight with this Captain and crew, but already their weaknesses were obvious. They were too clan-confident, relying on their reputations as Costeaus, rather than applying sound logic and judgment to potentially dangerous situations. Macho idiots usually died young. Ghandi thought it miraculous that this crew—and the Captain in particular—had survived for so long.

The five of them stepped carefully over a section of crushed guardrail and trudged across the snow-covered highway, toward the shuttle.

As they approached, Ghandi noted that the craft had a thick covering of fresh snow all around it. And the stairway was virgin white—no footprints. Beneath the vessel, two- and three-foot icicles hung from the end cones of the vertical landing jets. Whoever these people were, they had been here for a while—at least several days. Or longer.

"Maybe they're dead," remarked the pilot.

Ghandi hoped so. That was certainly the best possible scenario. A dead crew meant that the shuttle was theirs to plunder. If the crew was still alive . . . well, that opened up several options.

The standard arrangement for helping a downed crew—other than fellow pirates—called for an *assist fee*. In advance. But if the Captain saw evidence that this crew had plundered valuable antiques or other treasures from the surface, then a more lucrative partnership arrangement might be demanded. And whatever was demanded would be granted. This Captain might lack qualities as a tactician but he was a Costeau.

Of course, those possibilities assumed that this shuttle crew was willing to bargain. But maybe this bunch would not want to cut any deals.

Ghandi dropped a palm to his belt and fingered the butt of his thruster. All five of them wore the powerful hand-guns strapped to their belts. And the pilot carried a deadlier version of the weapon—a modified, and highly illegal, thruster rifle, with enough pulsed energy in its blast to blow a hole through an unshielded spacesuit at close range.

Ghandi hoped things would not degenerate into violence. He had killed before—a clan fight in his youth, a sandram cracked against the head of an opponent with too much force. Watching the other boy crumple into death had not been an entirely unpleasant experience. But wiping out a shuttle crew down here on the surface could lead to serious consequences. Up in the Colonies, E-Tech might start asking questions.

And these days, E-Tech was not the only potential source of trouble. It was entirely possible that other Costeaus would bring them grief.

There was a growing movement over the past few decades, throughout the Colonies, to mainstream the Costeau population; an effort with unofficial origins thirty-one years ago, the year of Ghandi's birth. In that year—2307—a rival clan, the Alexanders, had helped rid the Colonies of two Paratwa: Codrus, the Ash Ock mastermind, and his servant, the liege-killer. Since that time, more and more pirate clans had begun to cooperate openly with E-Tech and the Irryan Council. However traitorous and despicable Ghandi might perceive such collaboration, he could not deny the overall effects. Being hunted for murder by E-Tech would be a serious problem. But being hunted by other Costeaus ... well, that was something else entirely.

They were less than twenty feet away from the shuttle now, and Ghandi suddenly realized that there were *no* markings visible on the faded paint, not even the standard tiny warning emblems, clustered around the heat shields, engines, and airlocks. Someone had taken the time to blot out even the slightest hint of an insignia. That was overkill—long-range E-Tech video tracking gear was not *that* good. Small markings would surely escape detection.

The lack of markings made Ghandi nervous. He was about to chance the Captain's wrath by mentioning the anomaly when a female voice cut into their suit intercom circuit.

"Thank you for coming."

The voice was young and husky, but decidedly feminine.

"I've had a major engine shutdown," the voice continued. "The main cooling system, I think."

They froze as a spacesuited figure strode out onto the airlock ramp. The pilot raised his thruster rifle.

The woman stared down at them, her face almost completely hidden by the helmet visor. Ghandi could just make out pale skin and a mass of curly blonde hair. She gave them a tentative smile.

"I need a ride and . . . I'll be glad to pay for it."

The Captain moved to the bottom of the stairway. "Where's your crew?"

"I have no crew."

The pilot kept his rifle trained on her.

"This is my own shuttle," she explained slowly. "I'm down here on a research project. I'm preparing a paper on the psychosomatic ailments of pre-Apocalyptic condominium dwellers."

One of the pirates chuckled.

The woman smiled. "You know how it is. *Everyone's* fascinated by pre-Apocalyptic lifestyles."

The Captain mounted the snow-covered stairway. The other crewmembers followed. Ghandi hesitated at the bottom of the ramp.

*Something's wrong. A rich Colonial princess, with her own shuttle, down here on the surface, all by her lonesome self. That didn't fit. She's obviously been here for days. She says she's doing research. Fine. But why mess around with a short-range distress beacon when you're facing a major engine failure? Why not simply blast a HELP signal across the spectrum?*

"You must be having some serious power problems," Ghandi challenged. "Your beacon was very weak. Of course, I see that you still have enough electricity to run internal lighting."

She hesitated. "I didn't want to attract any . . . major attention. Come inside. I'll explain."

Ghandi kept a hand on his thruster as he followed the others up the ramp.

The six of them squeezed into the airlock, waited silently for pressurization. The inner seal opened and they followed her into the shuttle's main corridor.

Bright walls.

That was the first thing Ghandi noticed. The corridor had been painted with an incredibly gaudy mixture of colors. Fiery red stripes crisscrossed a deep violet background and the whole mess was splotched with random patches of green and gold. The arrangement lacked any sort of harmony. The colors were so intense that at spots they seemed to be pulsing.

She led them down the long corridor and through an open air-seal, into the shuttle's midcompartment, a large central space boasting a scattered arrangement of chairs, tables, and zero-G hammocks. Ghandi was relieved that the obnoxious color scheme had not been repeated in here. Soft, eye-pleasing pastels were highlighted by the dim light from a ceiling grid.

The woman unsealed her helmet and laid it on a table. Carefully, she removed her spacesuit.

Ghandi was thirty-one years old and had had his share of women: pirates, smugglers' wives, barely pubescent Colonial girls, tantalized with the idea of romping with Costeaus. Once, he had blown almost his entire profit from a two-week artifact hunt during one extended visit to a silky palace in Velvet-on-the-Green. Still, for the most part, he prided himself on a modicum of self-control.

When the woman stepped out of her spacesuit, Ghandi got an erection.

There was nothing blatantly erotic about her and it had not been *that* long since he had last been with a woman. Yet there was no denying her effect on him.

Her clothing was very plain; a faded blue vest tucked

into loose-fitting white trousers. Bare arms displayed well-defined biceps. The skin bore a light tan. All five foot five of her looked to be in prime physical condition. She could not have been a day over twenty-five.

"Up your lookers," she chided gently.

Ghandi, realizing he had been staring at her breasts, elevated his attention to her face.

She smiled. "Like what you see?"

The voice was soft, sexy, straining at invisible leashes. The face: a perfect oval framed by that mass of golden curls, pale cheeks rouged with tiny dimples, aquamarine eyes, dancing . . . drawing him closer, into a throbbing sea, gentle waves, caressing . . .

His throat went dry. Without turning away from her face, he toggled a sequence on his control belt, felt the suit's thin waterhose extend itself from the underside of his helmet, sensors probing for his mouth.

His lips closed on the hose's nipple and he suckled, drawing a tiny stream through his mouth, across his tongue, letting it flow to the top of his throat, now swallowing, but allowing the cold liquid to trickle effortlessly down. He imagined that the nipple was her breast.

"Look around you," he heard her say. "Do any of you like what you see?"

The Captain answered. "Yes. We like what we see."

Ghandi tore his eyes away from her and stared at the delicate pastel walls of the midcompartment. But immediately he began to get a headache.

"Sit down," she instructed Ghandi. "You look ill."

With his tongue, he pushed the waterhose away from his mouth. "My head hurts."

She smiled and laid her palm on his shoulder. Even through the thick padding of his suit, her touch felt electric. His pulse quickened.

She motioned him to one of the utilitarian chairs. "If you get out of that clumsy spacesuit, you'll be more comfortable."

He sat down. *Undress.* Yes, that made sense. They certainly could not make love with Ghandi wearing this armor. And his groin was starting to bother him. Spacesuit crotchplates were not designed for great expansion.

"I'll be right back," she whispered. "I'm going to give your friends some chores to do."

Ghandi could only nod.

His spacesuit—a rumpled mass of bendable plastic—lay in a heap beside his chair. He had been sitting in the midcompartment for what seemed a long time, alone, staring at the floor because whenever he tried to look at the walls his headache worsened.

He was trying desperately to remember something. Something important. A facet of pre-Apocalyptic history. But the idea of making love to the woman kept interfering with his thought processes. He simply could not concentrate.

*I need her.*

That was important.

*I need her. Yes!*

The conscious acknowledgment brought him back.

He roared to his feet, grabbed the thruster from the belt of his crumpled spacesuit, and ran to the nearest window. He kept his eyes focused directly ahead, away from the pastel walls.

*I need her all right. Son-of-a-bitch! I need her like I need a second asshole.*

She had caught them, drawn them in like bees to honey. She was using an almost mythical device of pre-Apocalyptic origin—a needbreeder—state-of-the-art technology from over two centuries ago, when Earth science had reached undreamed-of heights.

He recalled what he had read about the device, about the invisible beams that tracked eye movements, insinuating their curious pattern of radiation, skirting the brain's cerebral judgement centers to overwhelm the less rational safeguards of the emotion-oriented limbic system. The hypnotic effects of the needbreeder enabled the user—in this case the young woman, who was probably using special contact lenses to shield herself—to emotionally manipulate any and all victims. Needbreeder trances could last anywhere from hours to days.

Ghandi assumed that the midcompartment's pastel walls housed the needbreeder's actual hardware—the tiny subliminal televisors, flooding the room with their deadly hypnotic radiation. That made perfect sense, and accounted for the extraordinarily vibrant walls in the corridor. The optic assault of those walls had prepped Ghandi and his mates for entering the needbreeder compartment. Simple psychology. Their eyes had been automatically drawn to the soothing pastel walls, finding relief from the spectral madness outside. Subconsciously, they had been indoctrinated into looking more intensely at the hidden needbreeder.

"I'm impressed," said the woman.

Ghandi whirled. She stood there in the open airseal, hands on hips, smiling.

He aimed the thruster at her chest. "Don't move!"

"I won't." She did not appear upset by his action.

"I could kill you for what you've done."

"Yes," she agreed. "But you won't."

"What makes you so sure?"

"You're not a talker, Corelli-Paul Ghandi. Talkers *never* resist—let alone escape—my needbreeder. You're a doer. If you intended to kill me, you would have done it by now."

"Pretty sure of yourself."

"Yes."

Anger surged through him. "Who the fuck are you? How the hell do you know my name?"

"Don't be weak," she chided. "Getting mad can be effective in many situations, but not in this one. Anger's a tool. Use it well or don't use it at all."

"Answer my question, bitch."

The aquamarine eyes seemed to study him for a long moment. Then:

"My name is Colette. And I know *your* name because I scanned your shuttle's computer when it was still a hundred miles away from Denver."

Ghandi frowned. "That's not possible. We have a shielded computer."

She looked down at his crotch. "I notice you lost your erection." She smiled. "That's too bad."

"Don't change the subject."

"I haven't."

Ghandi felt his pulse beginning to quicken. "Where's my crew?" he demanded.

"Outside."

Keeping his thruster pointed at the woman, he moved to the midcompartment window. The glass bore a light dusting of snow, but Ghandi could see through it well enough to make out their own vessel, resting on the exit ramp beyond the eight-lane highway. The main loading hatch was down. The Captain and the pilot were using a portable winch to lift a seven-foot-high, pale ivory egg into the cargo bay.

It was a stasis capsule—a genetically manufactured living cocoon, surrounding and protecting someone being held in suspended animation.

*Son-of-a-bitch!*

And in the middle of the highway, Ghandi spotted a second stasis capsule, fastened to a small powersled, being guided toward their shuttle by his other two crewmates.

"Do you know why you escaped the needbreeder?" the woman asked calmly.

"Shut up! Who the hell are you? Where did you come from? Who's in those stasis capsules? And why the fuck are they being transferred onto my ship?"

"You escaped," she continued effortlessly, "because you're smarter than your mates. *You* should be the Captain, Corelli-Paul Ghandi. Why do you waste your time, serving lesser men?"

Anger surged. "Don't push your luck, bitch!"

She sighed. "Stop being dense, stupidity doesn't become you. You escaped from the needbreeder because you have a certain inner control, a quality that few humans possess. And I need someone with such an attribute. I have plans . . . and you are the man who may be able to help me carry them out.

"I could have killed you, Ghandi, as you sat here help-lessly for the past hour, fighting the needbreeder. But you overcame—you've proven your worth.

"I *need* your help. I wish to . . . emigrate . . . to the Colonies. I wish to learn about Colonial life—you could become my teacher, my guide. I need someone with intelligence to function as my business partner—someone who understands the dynamics of intercolonial commerce, someone who understands the value of marketing certain products . . . shall we say, technological items that are presently officially prohibited." She grinned. "The needbreeder is merely a sample of what I have to offer.

"And so, Corelli-Paul Ghandi, I hereby offer this proposition: assist me—and I will make you wealthy and powerful, beyond your dreams." She peeled open the blue vest and let it fall to the floor. She wore nothing underneath.

Her breasts were perfect. Ghandi felt his heartbeat accelerating. His palm grew sweaty. The gun wavered.

Laughing, she unsnapped her white pants and let them fall to the deck. "I don't like underwear."

His erection returned. His throat went dry again. "Who are you?" he whispered.

Dancing eyes, sparkled with joy . . . amusement. "I told you—my name is Colette. But I have a secret name. Come closer, and I will whisper it to you . . ."

Ghandi heard a sharp noise. He looked down. He had dropped the thruster.

Either she moved to him or he moved to her—Ghandi

was not sure which. But abruptly they were together. Arms encircled him. Hot breath tickled his ear.

"I am a human needbreeder," she whispered. "And my secret name is . . ."

"Sappho."

*Sappho.* A name out of history. There were two of them: one a poetess of ancient Greece, and the other . . .

The other was the name of a Paratwa of the royal Caste. An Ash Ock.

*Two of them.*

Ghandi understood. For one timeless moment, he considered trying to tear himself away from her embrace.

"I want you, Ghandi."

And then it was too late.

To Susan Quint, there was nothing at all remarkable about the four-mile-wide, eighteen-mile-long space community of Honshu. Like the other two hundred and seventeen floating cylinders that comprised the Irryan Colonies, Honshu orbited the devastated Earth at a perigee of over one hundred thousand miles. Like most of the other Colonies, the cylinder's inner surface was divided into six lengthwise strips—alternating land and sun sectors—the latter three arcs composed of thick slabs of cosmishield glass. Honshu's citizens lived on the inside of the vast cylinder, on the three land sectors, under a gravitational pull of 1G induced by the cylinder's slow and carefully regulated rotation rate. For a medium-sized Colony with a service economy, Honshu's population fit the normal curve; slightly more than five million people breathed the air of its self-contained ecosystem. Most of those citizens lived in this capital city of Yamaguchi.

In almost every respect, Honshu was an ordinary Colony. In almost every respect, Susan Quint was glad to be leaving it.

She took one last look at the triple image of the noon-day sun, reflected through the three cosmishield glass strips by rows of mirrors, and then entered a glittering red arch-way between two office buildings. The archway, typical of shuttle terminal entrances in Yamaguchi, was shaped like an ancient pagoda. Inside the portal, the pagoda arch collapsed into a luminescent tunnel: a glowing ramp descending into the bowels of the city.

Susan squinted. Shuttle entrances were notoriously over illuminated and this tunnel had to be at least twice as bright as the filtered sunlight out on the street. A monumental waste of electricity, she thought, but then everybody wasted electricity. Few Colonies ever had to worry about the cost of energy; community power needs were adequately satisfied by keeping the northern ends of the cylinders aimed at the sun. Solar power was cheap and abundant and Honshu, like many other midsized Colonies, flaunted its electrical wealth.

But no matter how well Honshu lit itself, no matter how exotic its shuttle port entrances appeared, this Colony, like all others, faded into the shadows when contrasted against the light and decor of Irrya.

Susan could hardly wait to get back home. She certainly enjoyed her job and the fantastic travel privileges it afforded her. But on this trip, she had been away from Irrya for almost a week, and to be out of touch with the Capitol for that length of time did nothing to help her career, to say nothing of her social life. Maintaining status was not an easy task in Irrya; the crown jewel of the Colonies demanded constant attention and the competition for that attention was intense.

Susan allowed herself a smile. Of course, she *did* have a rather unfair advantage. Not everyone could boast that their great-aunt was an Irryan Councillor—one of five human beings whose decisions determined the political course of the Colonies.

Aunt Inez was the Chief Executive of La Gloria de la Ciencia—the Science/Technology advocacy group—and it was in that capacity that she had gotten Susan this job, as a Progress Inspector for the organization.

The brightly lit entrance tunnel continued curving downward. A few hundred feet later, it opened into the equally well-illuminated underground concourse. Five other inlet ramps poured into the terminal from ground level, depositing multitudes from Yamaguchi's various street entrances. In addition, there were six ramps to handle outbound traffic as well as a plethora of escalators and elevators leading to the actual shuttle docks a hundred feet below. Susan sighed. Honshu did share one unfortunate characteristic with Irrya. Like shuttle terminals everywhere, it was overcrowded.

At least she would not have to wait in line at any of the automated ticket machines that rimmed the concourse. Susan's shuttle pass, issued by La Gloria de la Ciencia, enabled her to move from Colony to Colony with minimal delay. La Gloria de la Ciencia took care of all travel arrangements and Susan consciously thanked them for that little perk each time her duties necessitated plunging into a corpulent terminal like this one.

Gripping her transit bag tightly, and with a glance upward at the color-coded ceiling grid, she began squirming her way through the mass of people, heading for the departure gates. She walked briskly, eyes straight ahead, ignoring the usual profusion of social fatix and outcasts who seemed to gravitate to shuttle terminals throughout the Colonies.

There were beggars and barterers. There were hordes of silkies, male and female, wearing every imaginable style of enticing garment, their eyes alert for bored travellers with enough time—and money—to afford a sexual romp at one of the nearby hotels. Missionaries garbed in flowing blue-green robes solemnly handed out invocation disks, seeking converts for their Reformed Church of the Trust. Even today, the Church remained a powerful institution, albeit a pale shadow of its progenitor, the original C of the T, which had splintered following the debacle of fifty-six years ago, when its Bishop had been exposed as the tway of an Ash Ock Paratwa.

Dealers and traders drifted through the crowd, offering every sort of merchandise, from rare Earth coins and holo games to scrap antiques, aural encyclopedias, and authentic Costeau odorant bags—the fumigated variety. Phony C-ray ignors stumbled back and forth, eyes vacant, message plates strapped to bare and dirty chests, neon words begging for enough cash cards to provide them with a meal. A few years ago, Susan might have been taken in by these helpless-looking creatures, but these days she was too much the experienced traveller to be fooled. Authentic, genetically retarded individuals, whose ancestors had suffered overexposure to cosmic rays, were a rarity in 2363. Susan found it amazing that people continually stooped to such depths to make money.

She passed by a quartet of Costeaus—the mainstreamed variety—two men and two women, sans odorant bags. They were dressed in stunning purple leisure suits of a style that Susan recognized as being designed by the high fashion house of *A-la Pa-pa-la* in Irrya's North Epsilon District. But Costeaus remained Costeaus, and this bunch was not about to let anyone forget the fact. One of the women wore a miniature thruster housed in a silver and pink belt strap. Legal, but extremely unorthodox. And the taller of the two men had his shaved skull implanted with staggered rows of detoxified beryllium spikes. Susan flinched. That was positively *grotesque*. No matter how well mainstreamed into Colonial society they might appear to be, and no matter how much everyone seemed to brag about the "Grand Infusion," pirates remained pirates.

"That's a fine ass, silky," uttered a male voice, from directly behind her.

Susan did not turn. She instinctively knew that the man was talking about her and she also knew that it would be a mistake to even acknowledge his existence.

"Let's trade, silky. Fresh bread for fresh white-meat."

She sighed. He wasn't going to let it go, either—one stupid remark would not be enough.

"Hey, silky—today's payday, if you'll only take a chance."

Not just an ordinary hustler, she thought, but a dumb one as well. Silk trading was technically illegal in many Colonies, although authorities everywhere tried to ignore the cylinders' oldest profession. Still, a little subtlety was called for when propositioning in public places. Local patrollers *did* police shuttle terminals and if Susan was bold enough to formally complain, the patrollers would at least have to give the bastard a citation.

But her tormentor doubtlessly realized that Susan—along with most other sexual quarries—would be in too much of a hurry to make an issue out of a few noxious remarks.

Having been mistaken for a prostitute enough times in the past, she had gotten used to it. Still, the lewd remarks were annoying. She sighed. *Nothing to be done about it.* She was twenty-six years old and naturally attractive and those advantages were too important to disguise by dressing herself like some sort of pre-Apocalyptic nun. And it certainly wasn't Susan's fault that many of the high-priced silkies also seemed to have adopted the latest fashion in Irryan bunhuggy slacks.

The voice tried again. "Hey, silky! With an ass like that you should . . ."

The words degenerated into a loud, obscene gurgle. Susan twisted her lips in disgust. Enough was enough. Just because she would not involve patrollers in the matter did not mean that she had to put up with this sort of blatant harassment. She spun around, fully prepared to throw the bastard a few choice words.

He stood three yards behind her—an older man with a pudgy face and deep-set brown eyes. He looked astonished. A full-circle white cape flowed outward to cover an obvious potbelly and the front of the cape bore an odd design of large red splotches. For just an instant, Susan thought that his startled expression had to do with her turning around. But then he opened his mouth and gurgled again, and huge globs of blood poured out and splattered onto the front of his cape, creating a fresh arrangement of gross red stains.

Susan retreated in horror.

The man shuddered and collapsed face down onto the terminal floor. The back of his cape was torn and shredded; he had been stabbed from behind.

A woman shouted. Off to Susan's left, a rapid series of thruster blasts thundered above the din of the terminal, and then the entire crowd seemed to erupt into a screaming mob.

Someone shoved her from behind and she stumbled forward, almost tripping over the body of the caped man. Pivoting at the last moment, she avoided touching the bloody corpse. But she was thrown off-balance, and she had to run several feet forward to regain equilibrium, and then suddenly there was no crowd, but there were bodies littering the floor—*everywhere*—and she was tripping over arms and legs and some of them were no longer attached to anything, and then her toe smacked into the back of a woman's head, and the head went rolling across the deck—an attractive young face with smiling eyes . . .

Susan froze. A scream erupted from deep down inside her chest, but it just seemed to blend into the other screams, as if Susan were just one miniscule fragment of some total entity, one huge creature, overwhelmed by terror.

But the force that maintained Susan Quint as a discrete

being erupted to life, and that inner spirit whispered into consciousness.

*Run! Get away from here!*

And then she was leaping over bodies, head twisting wildly from side to side, simultaneously looking for the killer and scanning the leading edge of the retreating crowd, knowing that she would be infinitely safer as a part of a group, rather than out in the open like this . . .

Everything seemed to slow down for her; the slightest micro motion became perceptible. She could feel muscles tensing and compressing as her legs carried her through the air, over still-writhing torsos and flopping append-ages—a video ballerina, operating at some heightened level of awareness, more alert than she could ever re-call . . .

*Noise.* A shock wave of insane melodies, blasting into her head: the endless mass scream of a thousand terrified peo-ple, the deep bass roar of thruster fire, and high above it all, the shrill echoes of fresh victims. And Susan suddenly realized that she was moving closer to those primal cries, closer to the source of death.

And there he was, not more than ten feet away from her, a madman with a pair of flashing daggers. Susan felt abruptly unreal, as if her *body* had gone blind, as if this were all just a bad dream, happening in some other place, some other time.

He looked like a typical ICN banker, wearing a sharply creased gray suit, with a stylish sunshield visor circling his forehead, draping a pair of faintly polarized disks across his eyes. He had short-cropped blond hair, a hooked nose, and a slate-colored blade in each hand.

And there was something bizarre about the daggers.

Susan could not focus on them, could not actually see the knives clearly. It was as if she were looking at a kinetic holo projection with the beams out of alignment, creating blurred edges. A crazed killer with three-dimensional car-toon images clutched in his fists.

But those images were administering death—real and final.

He spun to face her and for a fraction of a second, their eyes locked. And then Susan experienced the strangest shock of all, for she saw a spark of recognition play across the killer's face, and she knew—in one infinitesimal moment—that somehow, somewhere, they had met.

But even as her eyes confirmed the acquaintance, her mind tried to deny it. *I could not know such a monster.*

The moment of recognition passed. His face returned to a blank stare. With frightening speed, he lunged forward, right hand extended, an indistinct blade coming at her, a gray blur seeking her chest. It was too late to react—her forward speed would thrust her straight onto the dagger.

And she thought: *I'm going to die—away from Irrya.*

The Costeau saved her life.

He lunged at the killer from behind, his beryllium-spike hairdo glimmering weirdly under the terminal's intense lighting, a serrated dagger poised at his side, ready to strike.

The killer whirled, and Susan experienced a sense of confusion, for the madman's movement was unnatural, overly delicate—liquid speed—precise beyond what should have been humanly possible. One of the killer's daggers seemed to leap forward, as if the blade itself had somehow doubled in length.

A flash of red—a blur piercing the pirate's chest. The Costeau fell. The madman spun back to face Susan, but the crowd had changed direction again, and she was enveloped by a wave of screaming people—a primal force with its own sense of orientation.

She caught one last glimpse of the killer, indistinct knives cutting into new prey, and then the crowd mercifully carried her away.

The thundering roar of thruster fire came to an abrupt halt. Rising above the wails of the panicked mob, a man yelled:

"The Paratwa must not return! Long live the Order of the Birch!"

It was the killer with the knives. Susan was sure of it.

And from further away, from the source of the thruster fire, came a second male voice: "Long live the Order of the Birch!"

The horrendous thruster erupted again and the crowd instantly reacted. Susan felt herself being squeezed on all sides, almost lifted into the air by the enormous pressure of the terrified mob. She fought to stay upright, maintain her balance, flow in the direction of the mob, knowing that if she should fall, or attempt to fight this human current, that she would be trampled to death.

The crowd funneled insanely into one of the exit ramps and she experienced another episode of distorted time. But this time, awareness seemed to descend into some incredibly ancient pathway of body knowledge, and it was as if she had suddenly gained access to a place beyond ordinary memory, a primal environment where only physical rhythm carried meaning. She felt herself struggling for life in that place and she had the sense that she was being squeezed through a womb, fighting to be born. In some strange and inexplicable way, Susan knew that she was actually reliving a fragment of her own birth experience.

And then the lights dimmed and the pressure relented and there was space to breathe again as the screaming mob plunged out through the pagoda archway, onto the Yamaguchi street. Birth memories dissolved under Honshu Colony's noonday sun and she was in the present again—*alive*. The golden light of Sol, repeated in triplicate through the three strips of cosmishield glass, splashed across her face, burning away the madness and fear.

*Alive!*

Susan did not stop to savor the emotion. She kept running, until she was far from the terminal.

It was an ancient chamber, a twenty-sided room built in the days of the pre-Apocalypse, when Irrya was still new and the colonization of space still a challenge to technological ingenuity. In the waning years of the twenty-first century, few realized that the Colonies would become a final sanctuary for the survivors of a devastated planet; the Council of Irrya, a governing body for all who remained of the human race.

Yet even then, the designers had infested the chamber with tradition. Each leather-veneered wall held a grouping of old Earth paintings, artworks so valuable that they had been sealed behind glare-free humidity partitions over a quarter of a millennium ago. In the center of the chamber, a massive prism chandelier, supported by wire mesh, hung from the darkness of the high arched ceiling, pouring soft golden light onto the polished round table which dominated the room. Ten chairs encircled the thick oak slab. Five of the chairs, intended only for temporary occupancy, had been constructed with deliberate austerity; ritual complements to the other set, the five lushly padded seats that supported the Councillors of Irrya.

The lion of Alexander had tenured one of the permanent seats for the past two years. But still, after all that time, this chamber—on the heavily guarded sixteenth floor of the Irryan Capitol building—remained alien to him. It was as if he was a guest in some rich Colonial home, where the trappings were so valuable, so important in and of themselves, that they dared not be touched. Although the lion had not been born a Costeau, he had lived most of his sixty-eight years as one, and a Spartan lifestyle appealed to him in a fundamental way. He feared that this Council chamber, reeking of wealth, would forever seem unnatural.

But it was not merely the royalty of this room, the sanctified dispassion, that made him feel like a stranger. More so, it had to do with the basic fact that he was a Costeau.

Although pirates were officially welcomed throughout Colonial society, and although this very Council strongly supported the mainstreaming of Costeau culture—the so-called Grand Infusion—subtle bigotries remained, some so ethereal that only a complete outsider could hope to identify them. Someday, the lion realized, a new generation of Councillors would sit in this chamber, totally free of prejudices. But he did not think that he would be alive to witness that achievement. The Costeaus had remained beyond Colonial culture for too long—over two centuries of isolation. Much more time would have to pass before a pirate could truly feel at home here.

He suspected that Inez Hernandez felt the same way, though for different reasons.

She sat across from him, her delicate fifty-year-old face aglow with bacterial skin toners. She had thick black hair styled in a pageboy, dark pupils nearly overwhelmed by massive eyebrows, and white fluff earrings that appeared ready to fly from her lobes if she turned her head too quickly.

She caught him staring, and looked up from her monitor.

"Inez," the lion offered, "did you know that a young Costeau once asked me why La Gloria de la Ciencia behaves so arrogantly?"

She smiled. "He must have been very young."

"He was. But the answer I gave to him perhaps betrays my own age. I said that La Gloria de la Ciencia acted that way because society allows them the privilege."

Inez laughed. "Just as it allows the Costeaus the privilege of remaining outlaws to Colonial society."

"True enough. But I wonder why it is that our two institutions are permitted the liberty of arrogance while the rest of society must conform to more rigid standards of behavior?"

That got Doyle Blumhaven's attention, as the lion had intended. The E-Tech Councillor glared at them, his babyfat face slowly shaping itself into a frown.

"No one is *permitted* to wear the mantle of arrogance. Certain individuals—and organizations—choose to crown themselves with it."

"But only in self-defense," prodded the lion.

Blumhaven bristled. "Defense against what?"

"Social inequities . . . what is perceived by some as a lack of justice, a dearth of fair opportunities."

The E-Tech Councillor raised his hand and pointed a finger to his head. "Up here," he said, tapping the finger against waves of cleanly styled brown hair. "Here is where these so-called social inequities exist—in the minds of Costeaus."

*And there,* thought the lion, *there lies the core of anti-Costeau bigotry.*

Many shared Blumhaven's attitude. They simply blinded themselves to the existence of the problem, as if by refusing to recognize that prejudice still existed, it would somehow disappear.

The lion also realized that his own gentle provocations toward the E-Tech Councillor did nothing to bridge the wide gap between their beliefs. On one level, the lion's provocations remained insignificant; they would never alter Blumhaven's attitude. Still, it was not good politics to constantly taunt the man. Yet the lion seemed unable to control himself.

*We are all servants of our passions.* Despite its counterproductiveness, the lion knew that he would continue to antagonize Doyle Blumhaven. The only alternative would be to release his true feelings, his wrath—a *Costeau's* wrath—to lash out at the stupidity of those who failed to perceive the outlines of the world around them. But he could no longer afford such displays. He was the lion of Alexander, chief of the United Clans, but he was also a Councillor of Irrya, a role in which he was expected to bring harmony and understanding to the billion-plus citizens of the Colonies.

It remained difficult.

Maria Losef, the fourth and final person seated at the table, brought the session to order.

"Council of Irrya, August 2nd, 2363," she spoke for the computerized recorders. "Confidential database, standard access."

Maria Losef was the Council President. More important, she was the Director of the ICN—the Intercolonial Credit Net—the powerful banking and finance consortium that totally controlled the Colonies' monetary system.

"First order of business will be the Van Ostrand report."

The lion stared at the petite woman for a moment, trying vainly, as usual, to see into those cold blue eyes, to read some display of emotion on her pale elfin face.

Eminent individuals usually presented a careful public image, using their style of dress or their manner of speaking or the very expressions on their faces to put forth a gestalt that the so-called average citizen could identify with. Maria Losef ignored such inanities and the lion grudgingly respected her for that. But Losef carried lack of pretension to extremes. She dressed plainly, spoke plainly, and kept her blonde hair unfashionably shaven in an ancient male style known as a "DI." Freelancers dubbed her "the ice dyke," in reference to both her public and private lives. She did not seem to care.

Losef turned to the center of the table, to the five-sided metallic box that squatted there in obvious contrast to the rest of the room. "Van Ostrand . . . are you ready?"

The small pentagon dissolved into a quintet of monitor screens. An instant later, the screens themselves dissolved into multiple images of Jon Van Ostrand, the fifth Councillor, Supreme Commander of the Intercolonial Guardians. Hidden speakers supplied a deep voice to complement the handsome and distinguished face.

"I'm here, Losef. Clean video at my end today. No interference problems. However, I'm afraid I can't stay at the FTL for more than a few minutes. Admiral Kilofski and I are preparing for lift-off—we're doing another security inspection. Have to make sure everyone keeps on their toes."

The lion repressed a sigh. He liked Van Ostrand and the man was certainly competent enough. Yet the Guardian Commander seemed to have deliberately crippled his effectiveness as an Irryan Councillor by establishing his floating base of operations out beyond the orbit of Jupiter. It would have made more sense for Van Ostrand to command his people from these chambers.

The Commander had left the Capitol five months ago, headed for the massive network of detection satellites that the Colonies had installed along the outer reaches of the solar system, a network slowly put in place over the past fifty-six years, in preparation for the return of the Paratwa.

The Paratwa—the genetically engineered creatures who had been in no small way responsible for the decimation of the Earth, the mind-linked killers and assassins who had escaped from the solar system over two hundred and fifty years ago, seeking sanctuary amidst the stars. The Paratwa—bred for destruction, created by homo sapiens in the madness of the final days, that terrible thirty-year period preceding the Apocalypse. And among those presumably hundreds, perhaps thousands of assassins who had escaped in the great starships, would be their leaders, the two surviving members of the royal Caste—Sappho and Theophrastus of the Ash Ock.

The lion corrected himself. Actually, *three* of the Ash Ock still survived. But no one at this table, and perhaps no one alive today in the Colonies, knew about the third

member of the royal Caste. And the lion had no intention
of divulging that particular secret.

The gray-haired Van Ostrand went on. "Actually, I
have nothing new to add to Wednesday's report. We are
now two hundred and four days into the FTL window—
only five weeks remain." He paused. "We should detect
something soon. Unless, of course, our calculations are
wrong."

"Our calculations are correct," insisted Blumhaven.
"Fifty-six years ago, when E-Tech captured the FTL from
Codrus, those calculations were initially performed. Since
then, they have been repeatedly checked and double-
checked—thousands of times over the past half century.
You know that."

Inez Hernandez agreed. "Our scientists have an excellent understanding of FTL technology, Jon. I wish we
could convince you of that."

"Linked pairs," proclaimed Blumhaven. "With these
FTL transmitters operating as two parts of a whole, it becomes possible to calculate certain ratios of each particular
linkage. We can't know *where* this other Ash Ock transmitter is located, but we can know *when* the two transmitters
will be in physical conjunction with one another. And we
are absolutely certain that the Star-Edge transmitter will
enter our detection grid within the next five weeks."

Van Ostrand offered a skeptical shrug. The lion
understood—and to some extend shared—the Guardian
Commander's misgivings. To those without advanced
training in protophysics, superluminal science remained a
very puzzling concept; a working technology brimming
with contradictory theorems and bizarre notions. FTLs, for
instance, did not *receive* information—using correct scientific nomenclature, they only *transmitted*, even though individuals at each end of an FTL linkage could communicate
back and forth with one another. To the lion, such incon-
gruities remained maddeningly elusive.

Among the Councillors, only Blumhaven and Inez possessed enough training to truly grasp FTL theory. Yet even Inez admitted—privately—that some aspects of faster-than-light technology still confused her.

And the lion knew that Jon Van Ostrand harbored another grave doubt: namely, that the Colonies possessed such meager information about Paratwa technology in general that *any* firm conclusions had to be suspect. The latest opinion polls hinted that such uncertainties lay deep in the minds of many Colonists.

*We should detect something within the next five weeks.* But that entire line of reasoning—their very rationale for the massive and outrageously expensive detection/defense grid— assumed that Paratwa science had remained essentially comprehensible.

*Unknown technology.* That was humanity's greatest fear, a fear that had been propelling this Council and the supporting Irryan Senate for the past fifty-six years.

When the Paratwa had escaped from Earth at the end of the twenty-first century, in those dark years of runaway technology which had led to the Apocalypse of 2099, E-Tech—the organization that now existed to control the pace of scientific growth—had been a fledgling group of citizens concerned with the unhealthy effects of unlimited technological progress. E-Tech had succeeded, over the years, in gaining and maintaining firm control over the advancement of science within the Colonies. This worthy goal had provided two centuries of relative peace for Earth's survivors: a chance for humanity to rebuild, rejuvenate itself.

Then, fifty-six years ago, it was learned that two of the Ash Ock Paratwa, and hordes of their minions, had survived the Apocalypse by retreating from the Solar System in a great fleet of spaceships—the Star-Edge Project. The Colonies had been forced to acknowledge the possibility that the returning Paratwa might be, technologically, two hundred years advanced.

And there were real grounds to support such fears. This

FTL transmitter, the guts of which were housed in a large room below street level, allowed the Council to instantaneously communicate with Van Ostrand. FTLs, it was assumed, had been invented by Theophrastus—the Ash Ock whose great talents lay in the realm of scientific research.

And no one had the faintest idea what else Theophrastus might have invented.

The lion glanced at Inez, noted her frown. It was Inez's organization, La Gloria de la Ciencia—the once radical outlaw group, which had preached for a return to the great technological achievements of the twenty-first century—which was today officially responsible for "catching up" with suspected advancements in Paratwa science. The lion did not envy her the task.

"Jon," began Inez, "have you tried the new scanners yet?"

On the FTL screens, Van Ostrand's multiple images nodded vigorously. He seemed relieved to escape yet another Council rehash on the subject of unknown Paratwa technology.

"Yes, Inez. We have a prototype up and running, and to date it has expanded our detection capabilities by almost six percent. My compliments to your research group. My people tell me that we should be able to begin production and distribution within the coming week."

"Excellent," complimented Blumhaven.

"We're certainly pleased," added Van Ostrand. "But frankly, Inez, I'm not sure these new scanners are going to mean much in the long run. We're already probing for vessels as small as a number five shuttle, and have our defenses aligned accordingly. I can't imagine the Paratwa returning in ships any tinier than that."

Inez nodded.

"How are your people holding up?" asked Losef.

Van Ostrand shook his head. "We've had three more committed to psychplans in the last two days. The tension—*the waiting*—is atrociously unhealthy, according to my personality specialists." He shrugged. "But the scanners say there's nothing out there. Until that status changes, we'll just have to maintain vigilance."

For a moment, no one spoke.

*Is there a massive argosy of starships poised at the boundaries of our detection network?* the lion wondered. *Are they armed with weapons two centuries advanced over what the Colonies consider state-of-the-art? Are these ships preparing to overwhelm our defenses? Are we faced with an enemy that we have no hope of defeating?*

Not knowing. That was the worst part.

Blumhaven broke the silence. "On the positive side, my people still maintain that the Paratwa could not have developed FTL travel. Our latest projections indicate, with ninety-seven percent certainty, that their culture, with its limited resources, would not have been capable of developing a faster-than-light drive."

*Ninety-seven percent certainty?* The lion kept his doubts to himself. Computer projections often took on an absurd quality when substantial data was lacking. How could they really be certain of anything regarding the returning Paratwa?

On screen, the Guardian Commander turned sideways and motioned to someone off-camera. "I have to go," he said. "Admiral Selleck has orders to fire up the FTL and contact you immediately if there's any news while I'm gone. Otherwise, you'll hear from me at Wednesday's session. Van Ostrand out."

"Thank you, Jon," said Blumhaven graciously.

As the FTL screens went blank, Losef's eyes panned the Council chamber. "Any comments before we move on to other matters?"

No one spoke.

"Very well," replied Losef. "The next order of business will be a discussion of yesterday's massacre in Honshu. E-Tech has a report on the incident."

Blumhaven glanced at his monitor and nodded. "As all of you know, the fanatics struck again yesterday. The main shuttle terminal in Yamaguchi, Honshu Colony, was attacked during a peak travel period. The death toll is currently at one hundred and fourteen, with another thirty-five seriously or critically injured. Out of the five known Birch attacks over the past four months, this one is by far the worst.

"Once again, the killers proclaimed that the Paratwa must not be allowed to return. Again, they announced their affiliation with the Order of the Birch."

*And again they escaped,* thought the lion.

"We have already interviewed numerous witnesses," continued Blumhaven, "and are currently looking for others who fled the scene. As in the previous attacks, there were two killers involved. Their modus operandi closely matches the style of the Alpha Ostrava massacre, twenty-nine days ago.

"Again, the first killer attacked with the daggers. A few moments later, with the crowd beginning to panic, the second individual opened up with the other weapon . . . this spray thruster."

"Anything new on these weapons?" asked Inez.

Blumhaven nodded. "We still believe the spray thruster is virgin technology. We have nothing like it, nor can we find any mention of such a weapon in pre-Apocalyptic archives. I was hoping La Gloria de la Ciencia could provide us with more data."

Inez shrugged. "I wish we could. I have an entire task force assigned to investigating the technological aspects of these Birch killings, specifically the weapons. Unfortunately, my people essentially agree with your conclusions. Virgin technology. In fact, we can't even duplicate the effects of the gun. Normally, thrusters require about a one-second recharge interval between blasts—that's a law inherent to the nature of the weapon. The only method known to circumvent this recharge cycle essentially involves putting multiple thruster tubes in tandem—a process that quickly increases the gun's mass. Yet according to the witnesses, this spray thruster is apparently no larger than a small rifle, and is even thinner than a regular thruster. And the estimated firepower rate is somewhere in the neighborhood of twenty blasts per second."

"How about the other weapon?" asked Losef.

"There we've had a breakthrough," announced Blumhaven, with a hint of triumph in his voice. "Flash daggers—pre-Apocalyptic devices, believed to have been developed by the North American CIA in the mid-twenty-first century. Basically, a flash dagger is an energy weapon—a physical blade surrounded by an induced field, which, by means of transformations within the metal, allows a hot particle stream to flow down the length of the knife, effectively doubling or tripling the weapon's reach. This particle stream will cut through anything, short of a crescent web."

Inez nodded thoughtfully. "Flash daggers ... weren't they from the same technological line of development that ultimately led to the Cohe wand?"

Blumhaven nodded. "Flash daggers were indeed a precursor to the somewhat deadlier Cohe. Unfortunately, although E-Tech possesses some documentation on the history of both these weapons, we have been unable to locate archival blueprints for either one. We do possess the pair of Cohe wands that were taken from Reemul, fifty-six years ago. But, for better or worse, the Colonies no longer have the sophisticated manufacturing techniques necessary to reproduce these weapons. More specifically, we cannot duplicate the power units—the extraordinary wetware batteries that enabled such tremendous energies to be contained within such tiny devices. Such organic technology is long-lost."

The lion kept silent. On one level, it was certainly important to examine all aspects of these heinous murders, including the type of weapons. But whether virgin technology, developed by hi-tech outlaws, or ancient technology, lost hundreds of years ago in humanity's mad escape from a dying planet, the fact remained that two vicious killers were on the loose.

*Two of them.* That fact worried the lion more than anything else.

"Any new leads on the Order of the Birch?" inquired Losef.

Blumhaven shook his head. "E-Tech Security has *thoroughly* infiltrated the structure of the organization." The Councillor smiled. "Some of the Birch's newly elected officers are even E-Tech operatives. Yet, we've found nothing to indicate that the Order is anything other than what they proclaim: a minor political party, totally legal, whose members happen to oppose any compromises or concessions to the Paratwa. The Order of the Birch believes that any returning starships that attempt passage through our defensive network should be destroyed. The Birch's leaders make no bones about the fact that they would prefer outright war with the Paratwa to any sort of peaceful solution. Yet these same leaders flatly deny any affiliation with the killers. Most of the organization's senior officers publicly and privately abhor the massacres being done in the Birch's name. My Security people are convinced of their sincerity.

"However, there *are* radical members within the organization who appear, at least privately, to support the terrorist actions. It's very possible that we're dealing with a secret faction within the Birch itself—fanatics, willing to kill innocent people in the misguided belief that it will bring support to their cause."

"Any concrete evidence to indicate such a faction actually exists?" asked Inez.

"Yes. But not enough to link them directly to the killers." Blumhaven paused. "However, we're hopeful that a connection will soon be uncovered."

"All well and good," said Losef. "In the meantime, what can be done to stop these killers?"

"Or *killer*," added the lion.

They all stared at him. Blumhaven's jowls twisted into a stout grimace.

"I thought we had disposed of that nonsense at the last Council meeting," muttered the E-Tech Councillor.

"Have we also disposed of open minds?" challenged the lion.

Losef ran a hand through her close-cropped hair. "Any new evidence to indicate that these two killers could actually be a Paratwa assassin?"

"None whatsoever," insisted Blumhaven. "We've done full profiles of each attack in order to specifically study that possibility. The parameters obtained at the Yamaguchi massacre site support our earlier data. E-Tech archives contain a wealth of information about Paratwa attacks and we've applied sophisticated analysis techniques to each incident. If these two killers were actually one mind-linked creature—a Paratwa—our tests would have uncovered certain characteristics relating to the way the killers operated. If they were actually *one* consciousness with a telepathic link between the two bodies, a certain modus operandi would have been revealed.

"But the results prove just the opposite. There is nothing to indicate that we are dealing with a Paratwa."

The lion was not satisfied. "What about the speed of the killers? Survivors of these massacres have claimed that the killers exhibited superhuman movements."

Blumhaven sighed. "It is well known that people exposed to incredible stress often perceive events with time-altered awareness. In some cases, movements appear to be occurring impossibly fast; with other individuals, time seems to slow down, as if everything is occurring in slow motion. These temporal alterations—these tricks of the mind—have been well documented."

Inez nodded her head in agreement. "Also, there are ways to actually increase the speed of the human nervous system, ways that mimic the genetic enhancements that the Paratwa were blessed with. Retinal implants, coupled with minor surgical alterations, enable 'pictures' to be sent from the eye to the brain at speeds beyond the normal ten-per-second average that limits human reaction time. These retinal modifications have been available on the black market for years."

"Quite true," said Blumhaven. "And it's likely that the killers have access to the black market—these unknown weapons would seem to substantiate such a possibility. And the Birch assassins could also be using microtransceivers to communicate with each other, coordinate their attacks. Transceivers would explain some of the witnesses' accounts that the killers seemed to be able to see what was going on *behind* them. Paratwa assassins generally arranged the two tways so that they could cover each other. Often they fought back-to-back. Yet with some training and the use of implanted transceivers, two men could essentially mimic such combat positioning."

Losef bored into the lion with her cold blue eyes. "And in addition to technical reasons, why would a Paratwa commit these ruthless murders in the name of the Birch—an organization dedicated to assuring that no Paratwa ever returns to the Colonies?"

"Subtle human reconditioning," proposed the lion. "Even if the Order of the Birch officially denies involvement in these massacres, the Birch's cause is adversely affected. Citizens who might agree with Birch ideals become uncomfortable with the thought of supporting the organization. A certain psychological advantage is thereby granted to opponents of the Birch, who favor a peaceful solution to the Paratwa return."

Losef shook her head. "It's true that Birch membership has declined slightly since these massacres began four months ago. But the latest opinion polls have found no corresponding increase in support for allowing the Paratwa to return peacefully to the Colonies."

"And we don't even know whether the Paratwa *want* to return in peace," suggested Blumhaven. "For all we know, they fully intend to make war on us as soon as they arrive."

"Possible, but unlikely," said the lion. "Our destruction will bring them nothing. Everything we know about the Ash Ock suggests that they're conquerors, not destroyers.

"And in regard to psychological advantages, there are subtle facets which do not always manifest themselves in public opinion polls."

"True enough," agreed Losef. "But I simply cannot accept that these massacres are being done by a Paratwa assassin for such subtle psychological reasons."

"We're dealing with madmen," said Blumhaven angrily.

"Madmen?" wondered the lion. "Let us not forget the events of fifty-six years ago. The assassin Reemul was on the loose for almost a month, and even by Paratwa standards, he was quite mad. Yet most of Reemul's killings were done at the bequest of his Ash Ock masters."

Blumhaven rolled his eyes, a gesture that said: *We've heard all this before and do not wish to hear it again.*

Losef spoke calmly. "All of us are more than familiar with the events of fifty-six years ago. We have all read the history texts, though naturally our knowledge cannot compare with the intimacy of your own experiences.

"Even so, you must admit that your case is weak. If this is a Paratwa assassin, where did it come from? Who awakened it from stasis? Granted, some attributes of these massacres resemble Paratwa attacks. But if this is a binary killer, murdering innocent citizens in order to alter public opinion polls, then why even take the chance of being mistaken for a Paratwa? Isn't it much more reasonable to assume that we are dealing with killers who are attempting, for whatever reason, to mimic the actions of a real Paratwa assassin?"

"Watch our glorious newscasts," growled Blumhaven. "The freelancers love the idea that we could be dealing with a Paratwa. They've even named the tways!"

Inez gave a weary smile. "Slasher and Shooter."

"Slasher and Shooter," repeated Blumhaven. "Now I ask you, Councillor, to consider a pair of fanatic madmen, hungry for publicity. Would not the idea that they are being mistaken for a dread Paratwa seem more tantalizing? Would not these killers be able to feed their warped egos upon such public fears?"

The lion nodded. "Maybe I'm wrong—you've all offered valid rebuttals to the idea that we're dealing with one of the assassins. But be that as it may, we should at least *consider* the possibility that I'm correct."

He turned to Blumhaven. "I'm not asking for a full-scale investigation. You know that. I'm not asking that we feed public passions by announcing my suspicions. What I'm asking for today is the same thing I've been asking for during the past four months, ever since these massacres began."

Blumhaven stiffened. The lion sighed, knowing it was no use, but determined to press on anyway.

"Awaken the two men that E-Tech holds in stasis," he pleaded. "Awaken the two men who've been asleep in your freezers for the past fifty-six years, the only two men who could dispel our doubts once and for all."

"*Your* doubts," pointed out Blumhaven coldly. "For the last time, the Council of Irrya does not share these ideas of yours. Gillian and Nick, however useful they might have proven themselves in the past, are nothing more than contract killers. These two men made their livelihood hunting down and destroying—quite brutally, I might add—Paratwa assassins."

The E-Tech Councillor turned angrily to Losef and Inez. "I request that the Council censure, once and for all, this endlessly repeated argument which the lion leads us into at these meetings. E-Tech does not intend, at the present time, to awaken Gillian and Nick. We do not feel that their particular talents will prove advantageous to the current situation. I reiterate that we have not blinded ourselves to the possibility that they may prove useful at some point in the future. We are certainly keeping our options open. But if and when Gillian and Nick are brought out of stasis, it will be E-Tech that makes the decision. On this matter, we will not bow to Council pressures."

"Understandable," said Losef. Inez gave a thoughtful nod.

Blumhaven turned back to the lion. "And may I respectfully ask you, sir, once again, to examine deeply the roots of your own overwhelming belief in these two individuals. And may I also respectfully suggest, and with no denigration whatsoever intended, that at least some of your passionate faith in Gillian and Nick remains the faith of a twelve-year-old child."

The lion found himself glaring at Blumhaven, and he could feel the rage bubbling up inside him. Doyle Blumhaven was a fool—a bureaucratic imitation of the kind of man who had ruled E-Tech fifty-six years ago. And Doyle Blumhaven was dead wrong about Gillian and Nick—they *would* prove useful.

But Blumhaven had also touched a nerve. The lion could not deny that some of the Councillor's words were right on target.

*I want to see Gillian again.*

It was a simple feeling, and one that the lion had carried iniside him for the past fifty-six years. It was a longing, totally irrational, an emotion that had grown in stature over the years until some days it almost seemed to dominate his thoughts.

*I want to see Gillian again. I want to walk beside him, talk to him, better understand the man who saved my life, as I saved his.*

The memory returned, as clear now as it had been for over half a century.

The Colony of Lamalan, where the lion had been born. The most terrifying day of his young life. A twelve-year-old boy, trapped with his mother in their own home, facing certain death at the hands of that insane Paratwa assassin, servant of the Ash Ock—Reemul, the liege-killer.

And then Gillian had appeared. And the two incredible warriors had plunged into a battle to the death, their genetically enhanced muscular systems operating at inhuman levels, three twisting blurs, hi-tech energy weapons shrieking, the lion and his mother frightened beyond all reason, hoping against hope that Gillian would endure.

But Gillian was one tway, and Reemul was two—Smiler and Sad-eyes, two telepathically linked bodies fighting under the spell of one consciousness—the very essence of the Paratwa assassin. And slowly, as if in a surreal milieu, the liege-killer had forced Gillian to the edge of death.

But at that moment, the lion, with a courage he had not realized he possessed, acted. And that action upset the balance, turning the tide of the battle in Gillian's favor. And when the madness ended, the lion and his mother and Gillian were alive, and the reign of the liege-killer was over.

As clear as if it had happened yesterday.

He looked up from the Council table, met the disinterested stares of Losef and Blumhaven. But Inez favored him with a warm smile. She was the only one who even remotely understood what the lion was feeling.

She said: "The past is a powerful thing, Jerem."

The lion nodded. Even his real name brought back memories of those days, of that strange and all-too-short period known as childhood, and of those even stranger and impossibly precious days he had spent with Gillian.

Blumhaven cleared his throat. "I believe we were discussing what could be done to stop these killers. The E-Tech Tactical Division has outlined some tentative plans regarding heightened security at all public gathering places. Please key A63 on your monitors."

The lion touched his keyboard and Blumhaven's video presentation appeared on the monitor. He followed it with ease. But the maps and digits on the screen occupied only a small portion of awareness, whereas a whole other part of him remained centered within places and times long gone. It was always like this. To think about Gillian was to

open up his entire personal history for introspection. It was
as if those days with Gillian served as some sort of magnet,
attracting the events of his life, molding them into
patterns—polarized effigies of an entire human existence.

Fifty-six years ago, the random events in the life of a
young boy had taken on clarity. Fifty-six years ago, the
lion had become obsessed.

*I must see him again.*

It was vital that Gillian and Nick be awakened.

Susan Quint lay on her back, on the mat floor of her day
room, head propped slightly forward on a cushion, eyes
staring vacantly upward through the angled glass wall.
Outside her apartment, Irrya's blue skies were beginning
to change: an invasion of dusk. In the vacuum of space,
huge rows of mirrors were slowly rotating, altering the angle of the northern sunlight entering the cosmishield glass
strips, bending solar rays through a complex series of
prisms and refraction modules. From centersky—the
gravity-free core of the rotating cylinder—pink clouds were
issuing forth as the weather processing machinery, operating in tandem with the Colony's preprogrammed day/
night mirror-cycle, added its contribution to the com-
mencement of evening.

Over a full day had elapsed since the massacre in the
Yamaguchi terminal, yet Susan had only managed to return to her apartment a few hours ago; it had taken a tremendous effort just to get off Honshu. Following the
attack, all of the Colony's terminals had been temporarily
closed as E-Tech Security forces poured into the city. Cit-

izens wishing to leave the cylinder had been forced to go through rigorous interviews, conducted with heavily armed squads of patrollers standing by. Only after Susan had assured her detainers—several times—that she had been nowhere near the massacre site had they allowed her to leave.

She felt a bit guilty about having lied to the Security people. Still, sometimes you had to "tan the strip," as Aunt Inez was fond of saying—cut a straight line between where you were and where you wanted to be.

One of her reasons for being untruthful was purely selfish: She had no desire to be grilled for hours by E-Tech Security, and have to fill out endless statements, and probably appear again at a later date to answer more stupid questions. Besides, there were certainly more than enough witnesses to the massacre. They did not need her.

But the primary reason concerned that madman with the daggers, and the way he had looked at her, his face melting into familiarity, as if he *knew* Susan Quint. Just thinking about his expression made her pulse race and her hands grow sweaty against the mat floor.

*I could not know such a monster.*

A triplet of hazy silhouettes took shape on the skyscrapers that surrounded and soared up past Susan's lower-level apartment complex. Twenty stories above her, false brickface darkened as a trio of burnt ochre shadows crept slowly downward across the sides of the structures.

She stared at the shadows, feeling her body beginning to drift away, mind easing itself down into a gray fog. With all the excitement, she had been unable to catch more than a few hours of rest on the shuttle flight back to Irrya. A long night of uninterrupted sleep would be wonderful. She considered expending energy to trek into the bedroom, but the mat floor felt just fine, and she was already stripped down to her underpants. Why move when you didn't have to?

She continued gazing at the shadow patterns, trying to

imagine she was a little girl again, playing with a tri-angaton, composing intricate faces and forms with one of her treasured childhood teachtoys. But for some reason, the shapes refused to be molded, refused to follow Susan's will. And then, abruptly, all of the shadows plunged together, mutated into a pale sphere which rolled across the wall of the skyscraper: a decapitated head with smiling eyes.

A tiny cry escaped her. She bolted upright.

*Just great! Nightmares, and I'm not even asleep yet!*

It was obvious she had to talk to *someone* about the events in Yamaguchi. Someone who was concerned about how Susan Quint felt being a witness to such horror.

Aunt Inez.

And Susan also remembered hearing her aunt once discuss a line of pre-Apocalyptic drugs used to help disaster victims. If she pestered enough, Aunt Inez could probably dig up something through La Gloria de la Ciencia—a pill or snort tab that took away your torment without depriving you of your feelings. Nothing too strong—just a little knockout to assure a couple of nights without dreams.

Tomorrow she would take a taxi over to La Gloria de la Ciencia's headquarters. She wished she could call Aunt Inez right now, but today was Sunday, and Sundays and Wednesdays were Council meeting days—occasions when it was nearly impossible to reach the woman.

Besides, Susan was still physically tired. Nightmares, or not, she had to get some rest.

Above her, the sky continued its programmed dissolve, the clouds melting into fluffs of gold against a background of deepening blue, triple shadows continuing their relentless march across the soaring walls of the Irryan buildings. Lights began to come on; vivid white bands outlining each floor, multicolored peepholes marking individual apartments. As the sky turned a rusty shade of black, Susan felt herself again drifting away, but peacefully this time. No headless images intruded upon her diminishing awareness.

She smiled. Everything was going to be all right. Just thinking about Aunt Inez had helped.

The doorbell chirped.

With a sigh, she pushed herself up on her elbows. A sudden thought: *I didn't make a date for tonight, did I?*

The possibility wiped weariness from her mind. Quickly, she struggled to her feet and crossed to the desk.

God, if she had to break a date ...

You just did not do that sort of thing in Irryan circles, at least not lightly. If word got around, the top liners would demote you. Irryan social rankings were subtle, but rigorously enforced. Someone who strove to reach the upper circuits through dating had to shine constantly. One broken date with the wrong person, for *whatever* the reason, and word might get around that you were unreliable.

The desk calendar ignited with a wave of her hand. She breathed a sigh of relief. *Thank god—nothing tonight.* Tomorrow she was seeing an ICN programmer. And Saturday, of course, was her most important engagement ever—the new Marketing VP from Clark Shuttle Service was taking her to a freefall ballet above the Calais Emporium. The Marketing VP was a 10G screamer—word had it that he was next in line to head the company.

The doorbell chirped again.

She grabbed slippers and an orange wraparound from the bedroom closet, and whipped a comb through her long auburn hair. A squirt of mouth spray and a three-second grip on the barrel of a fleecer eliminated any possible body odors.

The bell chirped a third time.

*I'm coming, dammit!*

She moved to the portal and switched on the inset monitor screen. The default setting displayed the view from her apartment's main hallway camera. Two men, neatly dressed in dark business suits, stood in the corridor.

She toggled the two-way audio. "Yes?"

The taller of the pair, a bald man with polished gray sideburns, took a step forward. "Susan Quint?"

"Yes?"

"Ma'am, we're from E-Tech Security. I'm Investigator Donnelly and this is Sergeant Tace."

The men held their palms up to the camera, showed Susan their ID slabs. She examined the holos for a moment, then swallowed nervously.

"What do you want?"

"We'd like to speak to you concerning your presence yesterday at the Yamaguchi Shuttle Terminal in Honshu Colony."

Susan frowned. "Honshu Colony? I . . . uhh . . ."

Investigator Donnelly smiled. "Ma'am, you had reservations for a twelve-thirty-five departure from Honshu."

God—how could she have not thought of that? Her shuttle ticket—such a simple way to trace her.

"Ma'am—may we please come in?"

She sighed. She could lie again, say that she had never made it to the Yamaguchi terminal, but somehow she did not think that these men would believe her. Oh, well— nothing to be done now except tell the truth, and admit that she had lied to the authorities in the first place. Still, it was no big deal. She'd tell them that she had been scared witless—which was certainly the truth. What could they say?

She undid the mechanical lock and waved the door open. The officers entered. She led them into the living room and offered them seats.

The bald one with the sideburns—Investigator Donnelly—settled himself comfortably in her antique recliner. Sergeant Tace, a heavier, black-skinned man, remained standing at his side.

"Something to drink?" Susan inquired.

Investigator Donnelly shook his head. "No, thank you, ma'am. And we won't take up much of your time either. Just a few simple questions."

Susan sat down in the room's prime chair—a chrome-piped, backless *Rogel*, which she had gotten at a good price through a distributor friend. She crossed her legs and balanced her palms delicately on her knees and asked:

"How may I help you?"

She thought she sounded pretty good. "Look confident and you'll feel confident," her body motion instructor often proclaimed.

"You were at the Yamaguchi terminal during the massacre?" inquired Investigator Donnelly, in a manner that suggested he already knew the answer.

"Yes," said Susan calmly.

"And you saw the killers?"

"Only one of them—the man with the daggers. The one with the spray thruster seemed to be on the other side of the concourse."

"And did you recognize anyone at the terminal?"

"No." She frowned. Should she tell them about the way the killer seemed to know *her*?

Investigator Donnelly hunched forward. "Miss Quint, we must be perfectly clear on this point. Did you recognize—or even think you recognized—anyone? In the terminal? On the entrance ramp? Outside, perhaps, as you were coming down the street? Or immediately following the incident?"

"I did not see anyone who looked familiar." She decided not to tell them about the killer's expression. If she did, things would become needlessly complicated for her; a disadvantageous codicil to her social life. She would be publicly linked to the killers. God, some of the more blatant freelancers would have a three-week-run with news like that. At Susan's expense.

The officers stared at her for a moment. Then Investigator Donnelly gave a nod. He appeared satisfied that she was telling the truth.

"Just one more question, Miss Quint. We must know if

you've spoken to anyone else since the massacre. This is very important."

"No one," she said firmly. Then she frowned. Why would they ask such a question?

The answer came to her in a flash. *Aunt Inez.* Susan was no ordinary witness—she was the grandniece of an Irryan Councillor. These officers would certainly be aware of Susan's special status.

Even though E-Tech and La Gloria de la Ciencia were historically at odds with one another, Aunt Inez had said that the two organizations had been much more cooperative in recent years, mainly because of this business about the possibility of the Paratwa starships returning. Probably these men had been given special instructions to avoid, if possible, any public embarrassment to Susan's aunt.

Inspector Donnelly stood up. "Miss Quint, thank you very much for your cooperation."

She walked them toward the door. But suddenly they stopped, and she almost ran into the back of Sergeant Tace.

Inspector Donnelly turned with an apologetic smile. "Excuse us for a moment, Miss Quint. Instructions coming through."

Susan nodded and backed away a few steps. Most officers wore transceivers in their ears. Some even had implants. The men were probably receiving instructions from their headquarters.

She wondered if they also had microcams sewn onto their suits. Probably. Susan's interrogation had surely been seen and heard by other E-Tech authorities.

The Inspector compressed his palm over his mouth and muttered something into a ring microphone. Then he lowered his hand and turned around to address Susan. He had a sad expression in his eyes.

"Miss Quint, I'm terribly sorry, but I'm going to be delayed here for just a moment." He pointed to his ear. "Vital communications coming through. We have to maintain our positions."

Susan nodded. Probably, interference messed up their transmissions in certain buildings, especially if they moved around. Still, they could have acted a bit more politely and waited *outside* her apartment. Then it occurred to her: *Their instructions must concern me.*

Sergeant Tace spoke, in a clear soft voice which belied his appearance. "Ma'am—may I use your bathroom."

She held back her impatience. "Down the hall to the left." *God, I hope they don't plan on making a night out of it.*

The Sergeant brushed past her. Susan stood there for what seemed like several minutes, watching the Inspector's face go through a series of apologetic expressions.

From the day room, a high-pitched beeper broke the silence.

Susan frowned. "What's that?"

The Inspector shrugged.

She walked back through the hallway. Sergeant Tace was slowly circling her day room. The beeping noise emanated from a small box which the officer clutched in his palm.

She folded her arms tightly across her chest. "What are you doing?"

"Ma'am, this is a bug-checker. I'm trying to ascertain whether any surveillance devices have been planted in your apartment." He smiled at her. "Do you know of any?"

An uneasy feeling took hold. "Of course not. Why do you want to know that?" she demanded.

"Procedure in special cases." He put the bug-checker in his pocket. The beeping stopped. "Ma'am, you'll be glad to know I've found nothing. Your place is clean. Nothing but the standard door/window security sensors."

"We're ready," called the Inspector.

Sergeant Tace motioned to her. "We're through now, Miss Quint. Thank you for your patience."

Susan turned and led the Sergeant back out into the hall. But now the Inspector was gone. And on the other side of the hall, the previously closed door into Susan's bedroom was open.

Her guts clamped together; that same sickly feeling she had experienced yesterday in the terminal raced through her body, like an electric current unable to find its ground. She wanted to open her mouth and demand that the men leave her apartment at once. But words would not come. The best she could accomplish was a quivering lower lip.

The Inspector appeared in her bedroom doorway. For a moment, cold eyes stared at Susan. Then: "Bring her in here, Tace. We'll do it on the bed."

And suddenly, from behind her, the Sergeant's thick hands were gripping her shoulders, propelling her forward.

She didn't even think. She simply reacted.

Whirling. Knee up. Full force into the Sergeant's groin.

If he had been expecting any resistance, he could have stopped her easily. She could almost see the look of surprised regret on his face, mixed with sheer pain, as he dropped to his knees on the carpet, arms snapping across his chest, body folding into a fetal pose to fight the agony.

She spun around. Inspector Donnelly charged forward, right hand fumbling under the breast of his jacket.

Time decelerated, like in the terminal yesterday. In slow motion, the barrel of a thruster emerged from beneath the Inspector's coat.

The Inspector was within three feet of her when she punched him in the mouth.

It was not a hard punch, not enough to knock him over. He just sort of stopped coming toward her. He stood there, a pace away, a peaceful expression on his face. Then his eyes began blinking rapidly, as if he were trying to refocus them.

Susan did not wait for his reflexes to come back. She ran down the hallway, waved the door open, and hurtled out into the corridor.

A mile from the north pole, in the middle of a forest of pines, the lion of Alexander knelt at the edge of a clearing. He was planting his third rose bush of the morning, carefully tamping the mud between a stunted fern and a clump of braced red daffodils. Intoxicating smells filled the air: freshly cut albino grass, truetone violets, the surrounding pines. The faint scent of barbecued meat derivatives, emanating from the huge A-frame tucked under a nearby lonely oak, clashed with the pungent aroma of dead fish.

A smell of home. A smell that could be trusted.

The dead fish odor came from the dozens of Costeaus who milled around the house and throughout the acres of surrounding woodlands. This was a Costeau place—more specifically, a park reserved for the lion's clanspeople: the Alexanders. Some of the pirates who came here were mainstreamed Irryans, but many were not; odorant bags hung from numerous belts.

Over thirty years ago, the Alexanders had purchased this entire tract, as one of the first official acts of the "Grand Infusion"—the mainstreaming of Costeaus into Colonial culture. It had been a purchase fought by many Colonials, the lion recalled, and the rationalizations of bigotry had abounded. Proper Irryans had been indignant. It was one thing, they had claimed, to ask pirates home to dinner, show that you were willing to beat down the walls of prejudice—it was quite another matter to actually invite Costeaus to purchase Irryan property.

Nevertheless, reason had prevailed. Naturally, the land had not been prime: anything within two miles of the north or south polar plates was considered poor real estate. Too much moisture in the air and a view that many considered unpleasant. But the Alexanders had ripped up the old streets and had torn down the crescents of dilapidated, mostly abandoned, buildings, and had made this section of the seventy-mile long cylinder into a peaceful arena of pines, roses, and carefully spaced habitats.

And when the lion of Alexander, as chief of the United Clans, rose to the Council of Irrya, this park grew into his second home, a retreat from the skyscraper pace of the Capitol district, thirty miles to the south. The park was a fine place to hold meetings. Surrounded by trees and flowers, people seemed to feel more comfortable.

The lion hoped that the environment would soothe whatever was troubling Inez Hernandez.

She had called him late last night, hours after the Council meeting had ended, and the strain on her face, and in her words, had been obvious. The lion had known Inez for many years, and not once in all that time had he ever sensed such worry. Nor had he ever known her to be so cryptic.

"We have to meet," she had said, "secretly and as soon as possible. I'll be bringing someone with me—it's vital that this person's identity be protected. Can you arrange it?"

He could.

"No one must know about the three of us getting together. This is an extremely delicate situation, for all involved. Security measures must be stringent."

He promised that they would be.

An odorless guard, armed with a thruster rifle, entered the clearing. "Sir, they're here."

The lion stood up and brushed a coating of damp earth from his knees. Behind him, on a slightly elevated ridge of shaven white grass, the servants had prepared a lawn table with three chairs. Pitchers of coffee and cognac-flavored

leaf tea highlighted a setting of walnut cookies, sliced car-
rots, and buttered perch wafers on toast.

Inez and her companion approached from the south, on
the stony path which wound its way down through the
pines from the main parking lot. La Gloria de la Ciencia's
Councillor wore loose hiking slacks and a purple bandana
with matching wide-brimmed sombrero. She greeted the
lion with a smile and a hug.

"You look well-disguised," he offered.

"I hope so. We took precautions to make sure we
weren't tracked." The smile faded as she gazed at her surroundings. "This place looks . . . very open."

The lion waved his arm at the canopy of pines. "The
trees shield us from observers." Even on a cloudless day,
no one could spy on them from the Colony's Alpha or
Gamma sectors—Irrya's other land strips—which hung
overhead, on trisected arcs of the six-mile-diameter cylinder. "We also have a special permit for an AV scrambler
system to deter remote surveillance, as well as a variety of
other toys that my security people beg that I keep silent
about. And the grounds are swept constantly for intruder
bugs."

Inez seemed satisfied. She introduced her companion.
"Jerem, this is Adam Lu Sang."

He was a tall and slender young man who appeared to
be in his late twenties. Oily black hair was cropped short
in front, long on the sides, and the gaunt hollow cheeks of
his Oriental face gave him a slightly undernourished appearance. For a moment, piercing brown eyes regarded
the lion with suspicion. Then Adam Lu Sang extended a
frail hand.

"Pleased to meet you, sir."

The voice was soft and controlled, the handshake firm.
The lion motioned his guests to the table and they sat
down.

"Now, Inez," said the lion, after drinks and food had
been served, "what is this matter of gravest urgency?"

Inez hunched forward. "Adam approached me several weeks ago—secretly—and asked for a meeting. Last night, I finally managed to find the time. We talked for several hours and when I realized the staggering import of his information, I called you immediately." Inez turned to the young man. "Go ahead, Adam, tell him everything you related to me last night."

Adam Lu Sang took a long swig of cognac tea and began.

"I work in the E-Tech vaults in our Irryan headquarters building. I'm a programmer; decryption and detoxification are my specialties. I'm one of about fifteen people in all of E-Tech who has full access to the data archives."

The lion was suitably impressed. The E-Tech archives was an impossibly immense warehouse of riches; information about thousands of the so-called lost sciences resided there, encoded into the computers—data from the pre-Apocalypse days, when science had run amok. E-Tech, working under its original five-hundred-year plan, was slowly reintegrating the immense wealth of information back into Colonial society, at a slow, restrained pace that hopefully, this time, would prevent humanity from self-destructing.

The lion knew that some alterations to that original reintegration plan had occurred, most notably the run on weapons data which had begun fifty-six years ago in response to the feared return of a scientifically advanced Paratwa culture from the stars. La Gloria de la Ciencia had been given almost carte blanche approval when it came to developing means to defend the Colonies from the possible invasion; over the years, E-Tech had permitted Inez's people to convert a great deal of archival data into working technology.

But even so, since the Apocalypse of 2099—two hundred and sixty-four years ago—only the barest fraction of the archives had ever been opened. And in each era, only a handful of trusted individuals were ever granted complete access to that vast melange of data.

Adam continued. "My main job is to break into heavily encrypted pre-Apocalyptic programs and detox them for analysis."

"Detox?" quizzed the lion.

"Yes—make them safe, remove any data roadblocks installed by the original programmers. Back in the final days, everyone was paranoid—even simple, innocuous programs had angels crawling all over them." He stopped, noting the lion's confused expression. "Angels," he explained, "are subroutines installed into the main program to prevent illegal entry. Angels guard the data from being improperly accessed, lost, or rerouted.

"Many of these old programs have soft perimeters, too—that means you can't guess your way in. In order to gain access to a soft perimeter program, you have to share your own knowledge with the program, feed it information. In simple terms, you have to open up your whole network and allow the program's angels to explore *your* data before it lets you have *its* data."

The lion nodded.

"Anyway, about three months ago, we started turning up some weird discrepancies in some of these pre-Apocalyptic programs. I was assigned to decrypt/detox a program which told how North American shuttle maintenance contracts were awarded for the fiscal year 2094. A university researcher was writing a paper—the specific data was requested—our normal procedures couldn't break into the program, so it was sent over to my department. Routine business—no big deal.

"But when I opened up the program, I discovered a rash of tumors—the worst case of terminal cancer I'd ever come across."

"Terminal cancer?" whispered the lion. He had a feeling that this was going to be a long meeting.

"The original data had been almost completely wiped

out. Only the program shell remained, along with the angels. But what they had been protecting was almost completely gone—data lesions everywhere. For all practical purposes, it was a dead program. It had been reamed of its content, and it had been reamed from the *inside*.

"So, I thought—fine, no big deal. The damage to the program had probably occurred centuries ago. Maybe someone wanted to hide information about how shuttle maintenance contracts were being awarded back in 2094. This person got into the program and wiped out the data, but left the shell intact, so that later programmers would not become suspicious unless they actually tried to access the information. From the outside, it still *looked* like a solid program.

"Anyway, that was three months ago. We all thought this shuttle contract program was a freak—an anomaly. But then we started turning up more cancerous programs. In fact, these tumor-infested programs started turning up *everywhere*—two or three new ones each week."

Adam leaned forward; his piercing brown eyes seemed to drill into the lion. "And over the past few weeks, the rate of cancerous programs has risen—as of yesterday, about one of every seven hundred programs we open is dead—reamed of usable data. And that rate is *increasing*."

The lion frowned. "You say that these programs become . . . cancerous. What exactly does that mean? How does it happen?"

"We don't know," admitted Adam, "not exactly. But there are two theories floating around the programming department.

"Theory one—which the heads of my department are in agreement with—claims that we are witnessing a natural process that was initiated back when these pre-Apocalyptic programs were actually created. In the late twenty-first century, E-Tech, and other organizations that were attempting to restrain runaway technology, started talking about creating programs with built-in terminators. In other words, rather than fashion a program that would theoretically last forever—or at least as long as the computers existed to support it—the designers would encode a self-destruction module into the fabric of the program."

"Why would they do that?" asked the lion.

Adam leaned back in the chair and shrugged. "I guess it fit in nicely with their idea of limiting science, limiting technology. And it was also a way to eventually cut down on the sheer bulk of data which was being encoded into the world's computer networks at a geometrically increasing rate. Self-destructing programs would eventually create more space in the system.

"Of course, no one wanted to lose crucial information overnight, so they talked about allowing generous time frames before these terminators would wake up and destroy the data. And the figures most often discussed were in the two to three hundred year range—exactly the period we're in now."

The lion nibbled on a carrot. "So what the heads of your department suggest is that these cancers were deliberately put into the programs, over two and a half centuries ago, and that today we happen to be witnessing the fruition of these ancient data-termination plans."

"Exactly."

"But you don't believe that."

"No. There's no hard evidence to indicate that the pre-Apocalyptic programmers ever implemented any of these self-destruction concepts. I believe it was all talk—just ideas that were thrown around. Programmers talk concept all the time, but little of it ever gets translated into working tech.

"I have another theory, which is shared by a few of my department co-workers. We believe that these cancers have a more recent origin. We believe that someone, somehow, managed to input a sunsetter into the archives. A sunsetter is a killer program, designed to destroy angels and pierce soft perimeters in order to wipe out targeted information."

"Like a data virus?" asked the lion.

"Yes, but far worse than a simple virus. And if my theory is correct, this sunsetter would have been put into the network approximately twenty to twenty-five years ago— that's about how long we calculated it would take a sunsetter to explore such a vast network and figure out where everything was—establish a base of operations, so to speak. When the sunsetter was finally entrenched in the system—which probably occurred a couple of months ago—it went to work, and began reaming programs."

"What about E-Tech's other data facilities?" asked the lion. "Aren't there a dozen colonies where the archives are duplicated?"

"That's right. But there's only one network—in terms of data flow, everything's linked together. This sunsetter simultaneously destroys program copies along with the originals."

"A powerful program," mused the lion.

"*Very* powerful."

"And you have no idea who would have put such a thing into the archives?"

"Not really. Anyone who had access to the system twenty-odd years ago could have done it. I mean, they could have input the program. Where they obtained it, I haven't the faintest idea."

Adam hunched over the table. "And this sunsetter is *very* particular. Mainly, it seems to be attacking very old programs—primarily those which contain classified scientific and technological information. We've calculated that if this sunsetter is not stopped, in under ten years, it will wipe out ninety-five percent of these old programs! And that's a liberal estimate, based on today's rate of attack. That rate could increase in the future."

The lion remained calm. "But your superiors do not share your belief in this . . . sunsetter."

"No," Adam said bitterly, falling back into his seat. "They'd rather cling to safer theories. They think we just

happen to be in the time period when a lot of these encoded terminators are waking up and destroying their
programs. They believe we're at the top of the curve—
everything will level off in a couple of years and we'll end
up losing no more than five or six percent of the archives.
They shrug their shoulders and say: 'Nothing to be done.
It's an unavoidable tragedy, just another legacy from the
pre-Apocalypse.' "

"They sound like a bunch of fools," the lion said softly,
with a glance to Inez.

"They are fools," muttered Adam.

"And what are you, Adam Lu Sang?"

The young man met the lion's gaze. Suddenly, his face
broke into a weak grin. "I know—I sound like a fatix. After all, I'm only twenty-nine years old and some of my superiors have been doing programming since before I was
born. What do the young upstarts like me really know
about programming? Maybe after we've been around a
few more years, we'll begin to gather a little wisdom?
Right?"

The lion said nothing.

Adam shrugged. "I happen to think that after you've
been around for a few years, something other than wisdom
takes hold. I think you begin to like your job so much that
you'll do *anything* to keep it. I think that you won't risk admitting that the entire data archives could be in jeopardy—at least not until it's too late."

"And what does Doyle Blumhaven have to say about all
this?" asked the lion.

Adam gave a cynical laugh. "He supports my superiors,
of course. In fact, he hardly seems worried about the
whole mess. He'll come down to the archives once every
few weeks, pat everyone on the back, and say: 'Handle the
situation the best that you can. I'm sure everything will
work out.' Blumhaven's a professional bureaucrat, and
that's about the nicest thing anyone's ever said about the
man."

Inez poured herself a second cup of coffee. "Adam, tell Jerem about the Begelman program."

"You know who Begelman was?" asked Adam.

The lion nodded. "Fifty-six years ago, he was one of E-Tech's finest programmers."

"Not *one* of the finest," corrected Adam. "*The* finest. Begelman was state-of-the-art, and probably one of the best computer hawks since the Apocalypse. He wrote half the standard material circulating today—hell, I cut my teeth on his work.

"Now fifty-six years ago, it was Begelman who was responsible for waking up Nick and Gillian—the Paratwa hunters. And after the liege-killer was stopped, when Nick and Gillian asked to go back into stasis, it was Begelman who created the program that was to be used to wake them up again."

The lion found himself concentrating intently. *Gillian.* It was as if Adam had used a magic word, lanced a fishhook into his spirit.

The young programmer went on. "Rome Franco, who was head of E-Tech back then, didn't want Gillian and Nick brought out of stasis until our era—the year when the Paratwa were supposed to return from the stars. So he arranged to hide Gillian and Nick amid the millions of other pre-Apocalyptic stasis capsules in the E-Tech vaults and he had Begelman create a soft-perimeter program to make sure that they stayed hidden.

"Now we all knew about this program, but we couldn't enter it until ten months ago—the beginning of the year when the Paratwa were scheduled to make their reappearance. Once the year began, we were able to detox and run the Begelman program. It gave us the location and access code for the stasis capsule that Nick and Gillian had been put to sleep in, fifty-six years ago."

"But Doyle Blumhaven won't allow you to awaken them," whispered the lion.

"Exactly. And that's ultimately why I'm here, why I've

taken the chance to tell you all this." Adam folded his arms and slumped down in his chair. "Do you have any idea what would happen to me if E-Tech learned I'd gone public with this information? Do you know what they could do to me? Hell, I signed my life over to them the day I was given a full security clearance to work in the vaults. For violating my oath, E-Tech could have me banished to one of the criminal strips. And that would be after they did some enzyme scrambling in my brain, wiped out a good chunk of my memories." He shook his head. "I must be crazy for even taking this chance."

He stared at the lion. "But someone has to do it. I'm certain—absolutely, positively certain—that my sunsetter theory is correct. We're going to lose a large part of the archives. We're going to lose sciences and technologies and philosophies that took humanity ages to reach. The pre-Apocalypse, for all the destruction it brought on us, for the Paratwa and all the technological evils it unleashed on society—those final years of the twenty-first century still remain the epitome of human achievement.

"And we're going to lose all that—for good. With the archives gone, we'd be forced to start from scratch in many fields. I can't allow that to happen. A way must be found to wake up Nick and Gillian."

The lion frowned. "And what can they do to prevent the decimation of the archives?"

Excitement flashed across Adam's face. "Gillian, I suspect, can do nothing at all—he's just a warrior, a Paratwa-hunter."

*He's much more,* thought the lion. *He's the third surviving Ash Ock Paratwa, a living anomaly: tway of the royal Caste—Empedocles of the Ash Ock.*

*And he's a shadow on my life.*

"Nick is the one we need," continued Adam. "Begelman met Nick, fifty-six years ago. Begelman claimed that Nick was the finest programmer he'd ever come across—a bona fide wizard from the days of the pre-Apocalypse.

"I suspect that Nick was even more than that. I've researched those pre-Apocalyptic programmers, especially the ones whom today we consider geniuses—the Asaki brothers, Gorman, Vittelli, a handful of others. They were the cutting edge of computer science. And there were others who worked secretly; shadow-figures, men and women whose names were never known. Nick, I believe, was one of these hidden geniuses."

Adam gripped the edge of the table. "The concepts they toyed with! The technologies they designed, of which only fragments survive today! Interlace core drives, hunt/seek inhibitors, wetware memories, mnemonic cursors . . . not to mention sunsetters. I could list a thousand inventions.

"And Nick could bring them back to us! If he is actually one of those pre-Apocalyptic geniuses—and I have little doubt that he is—he could teach us so much! And if there is anyone who has a chance to stop this sunsetter from wiping out the entire archives, it's Nick."

The lion gave a slow nod. "You've told Doyle Blumhaven about your belief in this man Nick?"

"Of course. But I get the same old response. Blumhaven doesn't believe Nick would be of any use to us. I'm convinced that Blumhaven is not going to allow Gillian and Nick to be awakened—ever."

"Why?"

Adam licked his lower lip. "I don't know . . . not exactly. But if I had to guess, I'd say that Doyle Blumhaven is afraid. Afraid of change. The first time Nick and Gillian were awakened from stasis, their discoveries turned Colonial life inside out. Blumhaven doesn't like that sort of untidiness. It doesn't fit in with his idea of the status quo."

Inez raised her eyebrows. The lion smiled. This young man had just expounded their own shared opinion of E-Tech's chief.

"So," the lion concluded, "you want Nick and Gillian to be awakened . . . illegally. And you have a plan to accomplish this. But you need our help."

Adam Lu Sang drew a deep breath. "Yes."

The lion stared past Adam and Inez, through the shadows of the pine forest and beyond, to the immense gray wall two miles in the distance—Irrya's north polar plate, the end cap of the cylinder.

*I want to see Gillian again. I want that more than I want anything else in the universe.*

He sighed, remembering an old Costeau saying. *When dreams come true, payment is due.*

Adam Lu Sang was delivering the dream. But what would be the cost?

He turned his attention back to the programmer. "You're a very trusting soul. You come here today to persuade two Irryan Councillors to break the law, involve ourselves in what could become a politically self-destructive sequence of events."

Adam swallowed. "I came to Ms. Hernandez because I thought La Gloria de la Ciencia would be the most likely source of assistance. She suggested coming to you . . ."

"And so you did—as a traitor to E-Tech, the organization that you swore an oath to. Why should we trust you? 'Once a betrayer, always a betrayer,' I've heard it said. Things would be much safer if we simply reported this entire incident to your superiors."

Slowly, Adam pushed back his seat and stood up. He pointed his finger at the lion. His hand was shaking.

"I came here in good faith. I came to you because I believe the archives are in jeopardy. There's a sunsetter in there and no one alive today has the remotest idea how to stop it. If you refuse to help, fine. All I ask is that you keep this meeting confidential. I'll find someone else to assist me."

"Sit down," ordered the lion.

With a red face, the programmer snapped back into his chair.

"You have the courage of your convictions," stated the

lion. "That's a good start. But it will take more than that."
He paused. "Do you have a family?"

The programmer drew a deep breath and swallowed.
"A wife and two girls."

The lion smiled grimly. "You risk losing a great deal."

"I know."

"And you've thought about the consequences . . . if
events backfire."

"I have."

The lion glanced at Inez. She nodded.

"All right. I assume that you can get the stasis capsule
containing Gillian and Nick out of whichever E-Tech vault
it happens to be in?"

Adam wagged his head eagerly. "I can do better. I can
have that stasis capsule transferred to any colony, and in
such a way that it won't appear to be missing from its
vault."

"How?"

"The whole storage system is numeric-based, which is
the only sensible way to deal with eighteen and a half million stasis capsules. You can access some capsules by name,
of course, but in this case, there are no records of any
names—the Begelman program merely contains capsule
ID data.

"I can enter that system and decode/recode without
leaving a trace. I can move the Nick/Gillian capsule as a
routine transfer and route a second capsule from somewhere else to occupy the missing numeric slot. Then, after
Nick and Gillian are brought out of stasis, I can transfer
their empty capsule back into the system. For a short period, there will be one less capsule than there's supposed to
be, but I can cover that discrepancy by making sure that
a routine capsule audit is occurring at the same time.

"Once they're awakened, of course, they'll have to be
hidden."

The lion nodded. "That could be arranged."

"I can provide Nick with an access code to get into the

archives. He can work directly on the sunsetter problem
from anywhere he chooses."

Inez frowned. "I thought you had to be physically inside
the archives in order to access them?"

"A myth, perpetuated by the E-Tech bureaucracy," said
Adam. "You can penetrate the system from a simple home
terminal. Of course, you must have the access codes and
a working knowledge of the layout—it is the security of
those aspects which maintains the secrecy of the archives."

The lion stood up. "When can we begin?"

Adam grinned. "I've already done the preliminary work.
The stasis capsule can be transferred tomorrow. All I need
is the delivery location."

"You'll have it by this afternoon. And now, Adam—
would you excuse us for a moment? I'd like to speak to
Inez in private."

"Certainly."

They left the programmer seated at the table while they
ambled up the grassy path toward the A-frame house.

"I assume you ran a thorough check on our young wizard?" asked the lion, when they were out of earshot.

"Absolutely," said Inez. "That's why I made him wait
several weeks before I even agreed to see him. It's not everyday that someone from the vaults requests a clandestine
meeting with me. I wanted to make sure I wasn't being set
up for any dirty tricks.

"I'm convinced that Adam Lu Sang is for real. His entire professional life—eight years—has been spent with
E-Tech, and he's had astonishingly rapid advancement. In
school, most of his teachers claim he was the best student
they ever had, with a natural aptitude for programming;
he was top of his class from day one until graduation. And
he's highly respected throughout most of the computer industry." Inez smiled. "Some are even calling him the next
Begelman."

"Do you have other contacts in the E-Tech archives?"
asked the lion. "Someone who can verify this story of his?"

"I have some people who supply me with information on a regular basis. And for the past month or so, they've been hinting about big trouble in dataland; something is terribly amiss down there in the vaults. But until last night, I had no real idea of what was happening. Adam's story filled in all the missing pieces; everything fell into place."

The lion permitted himself a faint smile. "If things go wrong, Inez, we're going to be most unpopular."

She chuckled and laid a hand on his arm. "Since when did that ever bother Jerem Marth?"

"Not recently," he admitted.

She released his arm. "Good. Then I won't feel so bad about burdening you with something else. Do you remember me telling you about my grandniece, Susan Quint?"

The lion nodded. "She's the one you got a job for with La Gloria de la Ciencia last year."

"Uh-huh. As a Progress Inspector. An occupation that I felt might give her some direction, some purpose. Susan has always been sort of . . . well, concerned with shallower things; nothing ever seemed to grab her, hold any real meaning. Being a Progress Inspector has helped somewhat, but I suspect Susan still believes that attending an Irryan banquet remains one of life's most important events."

Inez stared upward at one of the pines. "Susan did not have a very pleasant childhood. Her parents—my nephew and his wife—were devout members of the Reformed Church of the Trust, and rather . . . affected. If you remember, about fifteen years ago, the Council of Irrya signed that Senate resolution that placed a numeric limit on the Church's freedom to bury its devotees down on the Earth. When Susan's parents realized that it would become more and more difficult for them to be granted a planetary burial as the years went by, they committed ritual suicide in order to guarantee that their bodies would be immediately entombed on the Earth."

The lion shook his head sadly.

"Susan was eleven at the time; another nephew of mine

took her in, raised her as part of his family. Over the years, she's had extensive psychological counselling. But obviously, some severe damage had been done.

"Anyway, early yesterday evening, Susan came to my apartment building and demanded to see me. She was almost incoherent; between the tears, she kept babbling weird stories about being in Honshu and witnessing the Birch massacre and feeling as if she somehow knew one of the killers. Then she told me how she had just escaped from her own apartment; two E-Tech Security officers came there to interview her about the massacre. And then they tried to kill her."

Inez sighed. "To say that I was a bit skeptical would be an understatement. But I put an immediate call into our Progress Inspection department and it turned out Susan *had* been scheduled to pass through Yamaguchi Terminal—obviously, she had indeed witnessed the Birch massacre there. But the part of her story about feeling as if she recognized one of the Birch killers—a fleeting eye contact, she called it—and E-Tech Security officers trying to slay her ... well, knowing Susan's past, I concluded that these portions of her tale were pure paranoia. Probably, she had misunderstood the officers' intentions. I figured the terrible experience of Honshu had thrown her over the edge. I calmed her down as best I could, then called a doctor and arranged for her to be admitted to my hospital and committed to a short-term psychplan. With her personal history, it seemed the right thing to do ... she was so terribly confused and frightened ...

"We drove to the hospital and she was still in pretty bad shape the whole time, still crying uncontrollably, babbling out this same story, begging me to believe her. She gave the names of the two E-Tech officers and I promised that I would check things out. But by the time I got home, I was dead tired, and the next thing I knew the Colony was facing sun.

"Five minutes after I woke up this morning, I got a call

from the hospital. It seems that Susan managed to sneak out of her room sometime in the middle of the night. And she didn't show up for work." Inez shook her head. "The fact that she escaped from the hospital did not surprise me—Susan was always a very ingenious little girl, very sharp, a fast thinker. I wasn't really too worried about her running away—I figured she would calm down eventually and get in touch with me or return to the hospital.

"But then about an hour ago, on my way to the rendez-vous with Adam, I heard over one of the freelancer channels that two E-Tech Security men were murdered last night—some kind of an ambush in a parking garage."

The lion nodded. "Yes, I heard about that too."

"Their names were Donnelly and Tace. They were the same two officers whom Susan claimed tried to kill her last night."

The lion stopped walking. "You don't think she had something to do with the killings?"

Inez leaned against a slender pine and folded her arms. "No. Those two officers were ambushed and murdered during the time that Susan was at my apartment."

The lion rubbed his foot across a fallen pine cone, bury-ing it in the soft mulch at the base of the tree.

"And it gets more interesting," Inez continued. "I called one of my sources in E-Tech Security. Those murdered of-ficers weren't assigned to the Birch killings. There was no reason for them to be in Susan's apartment last night.

"After hearing that, I had no more doubts that Susan was telling me the whole truth. Poor girl—I feel so bad that I didn't believe her."

The lion frowned. "Then there must be a connection between Susan's witnessing the Yamaguchi massacre and the murder of these two E-Tech officers. Did Susan men-tion any other details about the massacre?"

"I can't recall her mentioning anything significant other than this feeling that she somehow knew one of the killers. But even that was pretty vague. She was in pretty bad shape the entire time I was with her. She wasn't making a whole lot of sense.

"At any rate, it's now vital that I find her as soon as possible. If someone tried to kill her once, they may try again. And the fact that her two murdered assailants were actually from E-Tech Security ..."

"You want outside assistance in locating her," finished the lion. "You want Costeau help."

Inez nodded. "And if your people can locate her, I'd like your clan to keep her in hiding—at least until I find out who can and cannot be trusted in E-Tech Security."

The lion gazed back at Adam Lu Sang, who was watching them intently from the clearing. "Anyone else you want me to hide for you today, Inez?"

She laughed. "No, Jerem—I think that will about do it."

They headed back toward the waiting programmer. Inez chatted about an Irryan Senator who was causing La Gloria de la Ciencia problems. But the lion heard little of what she was saying. His thoughts were on the future, on Gillian, and what he would say to the man whom he had not seen in fifty-six years.

Ghandi knew that someday the rage would consume him.

He could feel the muscles in his upper arms twitching, as if tiny creatures had come to life there, madly dancing microbes fighting the natural rhythms of his body, taunting for release. As always, he was able to contain himself, force muscles into obedience. Over the years, the fantasies of letting go—screaming out his anger—had gradually lessened, though there were still night incursions into a world where liberation was permitted. But most often, when mornings came and the real world beckoned, the fantasies retreated. All that remained to mark his rage were those tiny little microbes which, if given their way, would plunge Ghandi's whole body into uncontrollable seizures.

The elevator door opened. Tight-lipped, he stepped out into the executive suite of CPG, fifth largest corporation in the Colonies. CPG stood for Corelli-Paul Ghandi; legally, this was his corporation. But he had never truly controlled its destiny.

The microbes twitched.

"Good morning, sir," said the black execsec from behind her spacious desk.

Ghandi mumbled a greeting.

"Sir, your wife is here. She arrived about fifteen minutes ago. She said to tell you that she'd be in the board room."

"Is she alone?" he asked, already knowing the answer.

"No, sir. Your aide is with her."

*His aide.* Ghandi felt the little microbes shift ever so slightly, trying to jerk his muscles into a response. He took a deep breath, steadied himself.

Calvin, his so-called aide.

*That fucking maniac!*

The secretary keyed open the door to the inner offices and Ghandi stormed down the wide entrance hallway, past the onslaught of holographic bullets: ricocheting color logos of CPG's major publicly controlled corporations, each three-dimensional image exploding into etchings of major product lines. The hallway was ostensibly designed to impress visiting dignitaries, though its main purpose—known only to Ghandi, Colette, and Calvin—was to enable the hypnotic manipulation of specific individuals. The spectacular high-speed holos existed primarily to camouflage one of Colette's needbreeders.

The hallway expanded, branching into a series of gently rising ramps leading to the various private offices of CPG Directors. Ghandi continued on the straight path—the trunk of the tree—heading toward the solid platinum-colored door at the end of the corridor.

He placed his right palm against the door's ID sensor. The portal fragmented into thirty-two rectangles; each rectangle held its shape for a moment, then decomposed into a harmless pink gas. Ceiling fans sucked the gas up into the ventilation system. Ghandi stepped through the opening, feeling a draft across the back of his neck as the door reformed behind him.

It was an old-style board room, in stark contrast to the hi-tech door. Ghandi had designed the room from a photograph he had once seen on the anteroom wall of a facial palace down on the surface many years ago, during his pirate days. He could not even recall what city; somewhere in the Ukraine, perhaps. But the photo-image had stuck with him and his recollections had served as the architects' primary reference.

The room was long and narrow, with blue velvet walls and six evenly-spaced crystal chandeliers sprouting from the carved ceiling. The rectangular table was grained plastic—imitation mahogany—with eleven seating locations: five on either side and one at the end for the Chairperson. Shiny brass lamps with translucent shades cast dense circles of light on the highly polished surface. A second entrance—a manual door at the far end of the room—lay half-hidden by thick drapes.

Solemnity. That was the effect Ghandi had been after and he had succeeded. Even the inlaid data screens beneath each lamp did not disturb the tranquility of the room.

Only Calvin could do that.

Ghandi did not see his aide, only Colette. She sat at the head of the table, in Ghandi's seat.

Ghandi's wife had changed little over the past twenty-five years. Colette had the same golden curls, the same perfect oval face that he had first laid eyes upon in that shuttle, down in Denver, Colorado. A few lines creased her forehead now, but those were deliberately inscribed; plastic reformations designed to make her appear a bit older, make it seem as if she had aged.

She did age, of course, but at a fantastically reduced rate. She was the tway of Sappho, the tway of an Ash Ock Paratwa, one half of a mind-linked creature with a lifespan measured in centuries. Colette was almost three hundred years old. Barring disaster, she would still be alive long after Ghandi's body had turned to dust.

She smiled. "Hello, my love."

"Where is he?" Ghandi demanded.

"Right here."

Ghandi circled the table. Calvin knelt on the floor at Colette's side, his head resting on her left knee. His tongue was extended. He was licking her skirt.

The microbes twitched.

"Get up," ordered Ghandi.

In his own inimitable manner, Calvin obeyed. Neck twisting, arms slithering from side to side. Stilted legs wobbling, knees bending. The torso being lifted into an upright position. A snake being charmed.

He wore a sky blue jumpsuit overloaded with large zippered pockets. An insignia over his left breast read JET PILOT. Twentieth century occupational clothing—the very latest in Irryan fashions.

Ghandi moved to within a yard of the six foot tway. "Did we have fun last night, Calvin?"

A nod, followed by a delicate smile. The boyish face wanting to grin openly, but restraining itself. Calvin *did* understand the value of self-control, especially in the presence of Colette.

"Kill anyone else last night, Calvin?" Ghandi prodded. "I mean, besides the two E-Tech officers."

Calvin's mouth opened. Mock surprise. Me? Kill someone?

"Are we wordless today, Calvin? Or just stupid."

Calvin raised his left hand, palm outward. Green

holotronic letters took shape in the air above his fingertips, the thought-impelled phrase projected by microscopic inducers built into his false nails. WE ARE NEVER WORDLESS.

Ghandi hid his frustration. A vocal Calvin, although rare, was slightly easier to deal with. Slightly.

"Now, Ghandi," soothed Colette. "Don't be too hard on poor Calvin. He feels very bad about his mistakes."

Calvin turned to stare at his seated mistress. A frown took shape.

*Ream the bastard out,* willed Ghandi. *Make the scud feel like an idiot.* Colette/Sappho could do that, if she so desired.

"We must not dwell on past errors," Colette continued. "We must simply make a few adjustments."

"Adjustments?" snapped Ghandi. "Each time Calvin makes an *adjustment,* our problems are compounded."

"There's some truth in that," Colette admitted.

Calvin held up his palm. Another set of thought-induced letters sparkled above his fingertips.

CORRECTION/DOWNGRADING OF ORIGINAL ERROR REQUIRED SEVERE ACTIONS.

Ghandi scowled. "Original error? Yes, let's talk about that again. Let's talk about Calvin the assassin—the highly trained killer—the *professional* whom I've heard so much about all these years. Colette told me you were the deadliest Paratwa ever created, even better than Reemul."

The fingertips flashed. INCOMPARABLE.

"I suppose so," said Ghandi, "considering that Reemul's been dead for fifty-six years." He paused. "But I've heard it said that Reemul would never have been foolish enough to give himself away in public."

Calvin smiled, but it was the defensive smile of the chastised child. The face projected meekness; the eyes plotted murder.

Ghandi drove the barb home. "If you hadn't recognized that girl in the Honshu terminal—and allowed her to *know* that she'd been recognized—we wouldn't be faced with this mess."

WHAT MESS?

Ghandi laughed. "So it's denial today? Good, Calvin. I enjoy it even more when you entwine yourself in rationalizations. I'll be happy to untangle you.

"Let's begin at the Yamaguchi Terminal. Not only do you make eye contact with this Susan Quint woman, you fail to kill her on the spot. Errors number one and two."

EYE CONTACT WAS AN UNFORTUNATE COINCIDENCE. UNAVOIDABLE.

"And why weren't you able to kill her?"

SHE WAS VERY FAST. POSSIBLY SHE POSSESSES A GENETICALLY ENHANCED NEUROMUSCULAR SYSTEM.

Ghandi sighed. "That's pretty flimsy, Calvin. You know how rare such enhancements are in humans."

NONETHELESS, SHE WAS VERY FAST.

"So you send Donnelly and Tace to her apartment here in Irrya. They ascertain—to your satisfaction—that she's spoken to no one about the incident. Then comes error number three—you order those two E-Tech morons to kill her. 'Make it look like a rape/murder,' you say. Instead, Susan Quint disables your people and escapes!"

Colette reached out her arm, stroked Ghandi's shoulder. "Now my love, you're getting yourself a bit too worked up over this. Donnelly and Tace have paid for their stupidity."

PERMANENTLY DISABLED, said the fingertips.

"And what about Susan Quint?" demanded Ghandi. "She's out there somewhere, probably spreading her tale . . ."

"True enough," interrupted Colette. "But she has to turn up sooner or later. And when she does, Calvin will deal with her."

The tway smiled.

"And what if she identifies Calvin before we get to her?"

Colette shrugged. "That would be unfortunate. But it is

unlikely to occur. Susan Quint made eye contact with a tway she's never met. It is *this* Calvin—your aide—who actually knows her. Even assuming she deduces that Calvin is actually a Paratwa, there is no evidence to connect the tways."

Calvin wagged his head. I WAS ON THE OTHER SIDE OF THE TERMINAL FROM HER. SHE NEVER SAW ME.

Ghandi was still not satisfied. "And what if someone checks the travel records, gets a list of all the people who were passing through Yamaguchi Terminal that day. Calvin's name is on that list. And Susan Quint would recognize that name."

"Calvin's name *was* on that list," said Colette. "But I made certain adjustments early this morning. I sent our sunsetter on a little foray into the transit computers. The travel records have been changed. On the day of the Yamaguchi massacre, Calvin KyJy, your aide, has been officially listed as being in the Colony of Michigan Deuce—not Honshu. I even forged hotel reservations for him there, along with a few other flourishes that should fool any investigating team.

"And since Calvin KyJy's travelling companions were all killed in the Yamaguchi massacre—as planned—there will be no one to connect him with the tway that Susan made eye contact with."

Ghandi shook his head. "I thought you said it was dangerous to allow the sunsetter to work outside the E-Tech archives."

"Dangers are relative, my love."

DANGERS ARE FUN, said the fingertips.

Ghandi circled the table. "E-Tech Security probably got a full transit report immediately after the massacre, before the data was altered. And there are other ways to place Calvin in Honshu that day . . ."

"True on both counts," admitted Colette. "But E-Tech Security will not release that data, nor will they use it in an investigatory capacity. Doyle Blumhaven will do exactly as ordered. And it's unlikely that anyone else will take an investigation beyond a standard check of the transit records."

"Just for the sake of argument," said Ghandi, "what if Susan Quint does somehow connect Calvin with the tway she saw in Yamaguchi? What then?"

Colette was silent for a moment. Then: "If that occurs, we will have to alter our plans."

YOU HUMANS WORRY TOO MUCH, announced Calvin.

"Only when we're confronted with stupidity," snapped Ghandi.

The tway came forward a step, eyes flashing. His palm shot upward, tight against his chest, so that only Ghandi could read the sparkling green words.

YOU WILL SOMEDAY OUTLIVE YOUR USEFULNESS TO THE PARATWA. WHEN SAPPHO TIRES OF YOU, I WILL KILL YOU. I WILL ENJOY IT.

"Don't threaten me," growled Ghandi. "If you—"

"Stop it!" ordered Colette.

They turned to her.

"Ghandi, if you can't control your temper, then lock yourself in a room and release it. I'm tired of these childish displays."

Ghandi met the aquamarine eyes, felt some of his rage dissipate. She was so beautiful, so full of *herself*. Even when she was angry, even when her voice was filled with fury, he could feel himself being drawn to her.

*I am a human needbreeder,* Colette had proclaimed, on that day in Denver, twenty-five years ago. So true.

Yet still, the microbes danced.

"And Calvin," she warned, "if you shape words in my presence, then you make sure I see them. Understood?"

The tway became motion. Legs buckling, arms thrust back; a stick figure collapsing to his knees before her. There was grace to his movement, Ghandi admitted, but it was impossible to describe; no human corollaries existed. When agitated, Calvin moved like a machine coming apart.

He lifted Colette's long skirt to her knees. His tongue slithered out, licked at the bare flesh above her left ankle.

Ghandi turned away. He felt no jealousy when Calvin subjugated himself to Colette. Nor did he experience revulsion toward the tway's actions. But there was a feeling.

*I am human and they are Paratwa. I am singular and they are plural.*

There would always be that difference.

The microbes twitched.

Calvin moaned softly. Colette petted the tway, her hand caressing his short-cropped auburn hair.

It had been easier, Ghandi thought, before Calvin had been awakened from stasis last year. For almost twenty-five years, Ghandi had had Colette to himself. If he had known, on that day in Denver, what was contained in those stasis capsules that his Captain and crew had been hypnotized into loading onto their shuttle . . .

A sleeping Calvin—a Calvin in stasis—could have been destroyed. Ghandi could have found a way to accomplish that. But now it was too late. For better or worse, the maniac was awake.

And Ghandi was forced to admit that he had never *really* had Colette to himself. Colette was his lover and his wife, but she remained a tway, one half of the Ash Ock Paratwa known as Sappho.

The woman he had fallen in love with—the human needbreeder—that woman sometimes vanished, melding herself into her other half, forming a mental/emotional interlace: a dialectic convergence unique to the Ash Ock Paratwa—a singular consciousness that transcended the vast distances separating the two tways. Sappho never spoke, never attempted any form of communication with Ghandi. But he always knew when she had arisen. He would look upon his lover's face and realize that Colette was no longer there, that she had become a part of something else, something powerful beyond his understanding.

Colette never discussed her other tway, the one who still remained out in space, far beyond the Colonies. Yet when Colette interlaced—when the two consciousnesses melded into one—when the cold light of Sappho appeared in his lover's eyes, Ghandi felt that he could somehow see Colette's other half.

And what he saw occasionally terrified him.

The microbes would vault up his spine, sending uncontrollable shivers through his whole body. There was no basis for his fear, no rational source that he could pinpoint. Colette was Paratwa; that Ghandi had accepted from the beginning. Yet he dreaded the moment when he would have to meet Colette's tway.

Effortlessly, his wife eased Calvin away from her body. The assassin arranged himself on the floor beside her chair, his head drooping to his chest, his legs folding themselves under his body. Calvin in the lotus position—a contented puppy.

Colette spoke softly. "In a few days, there will be another massacre. The arrangements have been made."

Calvin's head rose slightly.

Ghandi nodded. He did not like these insane killings, but there was nothing he could do to prevent them. With or without his approval, Ash Ock plans would be carried out.

"Where?" he asked.

"Here in Irrya. It's time for the Order of the Birch to strike closer to home."

Ghandi decided that he did not want to know the details. He changed the subject before Colette could tell him.

"Any word on your long-lost relative?"

A strange glint appeared in Colette's eyes. For a fraction of a second, Ghandi thought that she was going to interlace—become Sappho.

The moment passed. "Gillian remains in stasis. Doyle Blumhaven is naturally cooperating."

Ghandi said nothing more. Officially, Sappho and the other Ash Ock, Theophrastus, did not want the only other surviving tway of their breed awakened, despite the fact that they had long ago learned—through the distant monitoring of intercolonial broadcasts—that Gillian was but a singular entity and theoretically no threat to their plans.

Yet when Ghandi brought up the subject, he always had the feeling that his wife was not revealing the whole truth. For some unfathomable reason, Colette/Sappho *wanted* to meet her traitorous breed-cousin.

He glanced at Calvin, unable to resist one more taunt. "It's good that we have Blumhaven in our pocket. Although Gillian was only one tway, he somehow managed to destroy Reemul." Ghandi shrugged, allowing his thoughts to trail off.

Calvin's mouth opened slightly and his eyes met Ghandi's. A hungry puppy.

Colette smiled and stroked Calvin's chin. "Gillian would be no match for the special abilities of my Ash Nar."

The tway raised his hand. NO MATCH.

*Perhaps,* Ghandi thought. Still, he found himself entertained by the perversely pleasant fantasy of Gillian reawakened. By all accounts, the tway of Empedocles was also very special. There was always the possibility that this Gillian could find a way to destroy the maniac.

Abruptly, the microbes retreated. Ghandi could feel some of the tension leaving his body.

*I must cultivate pleasant fantasies more often.*

The first thing Gillian felt was the dream.

A vast ocean. Gentle white-capped waves lapping at his sides. An inner light rising from endless waters, burning through him as if his body were some translucent membrane, a culture slice on the tray of a microscope.

And then the dream began to fragment, throwing off random pieces of thought, each hardening into word/images—mental constructs, rock-solid in comparison to that endless ocean from which he arose. Visions filled him. Ideas took shape.

*Reemul is dead. The liege-killer is dead.*

*The human who does not fear is the human who has lost his boundaries.*

*I move . . . I am. I want . . . I take.*

*Catharine, where are you?*

*Six hundred years. I can live for six hundred years.*

*Catharine?*

*A circle of five—the sphere of the royal Caste.*

A voice said: *You have a place in that circle, Gillian. You are Empedocles, youngest and fairest of them all, the child who will someday grow to be our protector.*

He argued with that voice.

*But two are gone. Two have perished. Aristotle and Codrus are dead. Only three of the Ash Ock remain.*

*You are Empedocles. You are one of them.*

*Yes. But I am also a single human being. I am Gillian.*

Another voice: *You were never married, Gillian. Catharine was not your wife. She was your tway.*

He recalled the pain of his tway's death—Catharine's death.

*I am being awakened from stasis.*

His body erupted, became a thrashing mass of arms and legs at the center of that vast inner sea. He longed to escape but there was no place to go.

He screamed with the agony of restoration.

The lion of Alexander had carefully prepared his study for the meeting. The oak desk had been moved outside and a comfortable white sofa put in its place. An array of refreshments covered the coffee table; cinnamon-glazed ice biscuits in a transparent cooler, a tray of synthetic bolognas, coffee, tea, and fresh orange juice—the oranges imported only yesterday from the tropical Colony of El Paso Juarez. The study's large vertical slabs of glass, looking out onto one of the gardens, had been curtained; the lion wanted all attentions to remain focused within this room.

He sat opposite the sofa, in a plain, high-backed chair, his hands folded uncomfortably on his lap. A tiny remote rested on the chair arm and every few moments, the lion found himself touching the keypad, altering the room's lighting. His choices ran the gamut from an indirect, hazy yellow glow, all the way to blue-white spotlighting, complete with shadow fillers. He simply could not decide.

Voices. Outside the door. Quickly, he tapped the keypad again, forcing the illumination circuits into yet another adaptation. Red-dish backlights, located at the perimeter of the floorboards, ignited, and a quartet of intense ceiling spots blazed across the center of the room.

The door slid open. The midget came in first, squinting. The lion resisted touching the keypad again.

The midget beamed. "Howdy, lion! I'm Nick."

He had slick blonde hair, a generously wide mouth, and alert blue eyes. He looked to be in his late forties.

The lion could not keep his eyes off the second man. He heard himself whisper, "Hello, Gillian."

Gillian stared at the white-haired old man, wondering at the tone of familiarity in his voice. *Do I know you?*

The lion stood up. He kept his hands pinned to his sides to stop them from shaking.

He felt like a child again. All the emotions came back, pure and unsullied by the passage of more than half a century. He was Jerem Marth, twelve years old, in the Colony of Sirak-Brath, where they had first met.

*Exactly as I remember you.* Not surprising, of course; Gillian had been in stasis; he had not changed in fifty-six years.

The same crinkled leather jacket, the dark brown hair cropped short on the sides and long in the back, the calm gray eyes. But he looked much shorter. It took the lion a moment to realize the nature of that discrepancy: Gillian's build had not changed. He was still six feet tall and a touch on the slender side.

But Jerem Marth had grown up.

The lion found his voice. "Do you know . . . where you are?"

"Irrya," said the midget. "Your wake-up technicians filled us in on geography. We're about a mile from the north polar plate. A private park, owned by the clan of the Alexanders." Nick grinned. "And you're the head honcho."

"The what?"

"Never mind."

Gillian took a step closer to the old man and frowned. There was something in the features, in the shape of the mouth, the cut of the eyebrows. The wake-up team had told them how long they had been in stasis. This old man could have been a teenager when Gillian was last awake . . .

He knew. "You're Jerem Marth."

The lion felt tears welling in his eyes. "It's been a long time." The words sounded stupid, inconsequential. Nothing he could say would make the moment more real than it already was.

He stepped forward, unable to stop himself, knowing that the emotion had to be fulfilled. He threw his arms around Gillian, hugged him tightly.

For an instant, there was no response, no acknowledgment of the lion's feeling. Then, awkwardly, Gillian returned the hug, and patted Jerem on the back.

The lion pulled away. "I know my actions must seem strange to you." He forced a smile. "I thank you for indulging an old man."

Gillian thought of Catharine, his long-lost tway. "No. Not strange at all."

The lion felt a warmth spreading through his chest, as if he had just consumed a carafe of hot liquors. The warmth spread, reddening his face. *I'm embarrassed.*

Jerem Marth, the twelve-year-old boy, felt no shame. But Costeaus rarely flaunted emotions with other men; the lion of Alexander felt encumbered by the display.

*It's strange how we live with such dichotomies. It's almost as if we carry multiple consciousnesses inside us. I am the lion of Alexander, yet a part of me remains a young boy, frozen in time.*

And he thought about how truly strange it must be for Gillian.

*This man carries within him the singular consciousness that is Gillian. Yet imprinted within the very cells of his being is the consciousness of the Ash Ock warrior, Empedocles.* Gillian could be either singular or plural. Within one physical body, he could be either a discrete human or a mind-linked Paratwa.

In comparison, the lion's own inner dichotomy seemed insignificant.

"Please," the lion gestured, recovering his composure, "sit down. Help yourselves to refreshments."

Grinning like a puppy, Nick poured himself a glass of orange juice and plopped down on the sofa. Gillian remained standing.

The lion remained standing, too.

The midget grimaced. "Guys, I'm going to get a sore neck staring up at you."

The lion smiled and sat down. Gillian seated himself on the edge of the sofa. Calm gray eyes panned the room.

*Alert,* thought the lion. *Always alert. That's how I remember him.*

Gillian felt . . . odd. It was hard to imagine that the boy he had once helped was now this old man. Gillian had been asleep for fifty-six years; before that, he had been in stasis for over two centuries. *Each time, a new world—full of strangers.* He thought of the people he had met more than half a century ago . . . Jerem Marth—this boy who was now a man; Jerem's mother Paula and the pirate Aaron; Rome Franco, head of E-Tech; Begelman the computer hawk, Pasha Haddad . . .

*All dead, probably.* But he had to know for certain. "Jerem . . . your family?"

"A wife, two sons, and a daughter. Several grandchildren." The lion smiled, abruptly comprehending Gillian's real question. "My mother and Aaron married shortly after you went into stasis. They moved to a Costeau Colony, where I was raised. Both of them died about four years ago, within a few months of each other."

Gillian nodded.

The lion shrugged. "They had a good life together. No regrets. And as Aaron's son, I grew up as a Costeau." He chuckled. "I experienced some rough teenage years; for someone who had been raised in a cylinder as peaceful as Lamalan, a pirate colony was quite a change. At that time, most Costeaus led more . . . rigorous lifestyles."

"But times changed," said Nick, finishing his orange juice and starting in on a frozen biscuit.

"Times changed," agreed the lion. "As for the other people you knew fifty-six years ago . . . I'm afraid they're all long gone."

Gillian's right hand began to itch. He stared down at the bandaged palm, remembering Reemul's firedart, the burned flesh.

The lion followed his gaze. "Our medical people must have a look at that. We've made some advancements since you were put to sleep. New techniques, salves and painkillers . . ."

"No painkillers," said Gillian quietly, staring straight ahead, past the lion.

There was an awkward moment of silence. The lion shrugged. "As you like. However, I must insist that you submit to some minor facial refabrication. I don't know that anyone today would recognize you and as far as we know, no pictures of you exist. But we must err on the side of caution. The refabrication techniques are very rapid—a few hours at the most. A recovery period is unnecessary."

Gillian nodded.

"If you desire," added the lion, "the refabrication can be reversed at a later date. You can have your original face restored."

*My original face*, Gillian thought. He could barely remember what that had been. His current face was a twenty-first century rebuild, courtesy of E-Tech. "It doesn't matter. It's not important."

Nick gazed sharply at Gillian. Then the midget shrugged and turned to the lion. "I assume that only Gillian gets a facial. Does that mean that you expect me to stay close to home?"

"I'm afraid so. Fifty-six years ago, someone managed to take your photo—at a private party for Irrya's elite, I believe. Since then, your likeness has been reproduced in numerous history texts." The lion smiled. "Over the decades, you have achieved a certain notoriety. And even with refabrication, your stature would make disguising you a difficult proposition."

"The price of fame," sighed the midget.

"I'm sorry. But you'll have to remain here in our retreat."

Nick shrugged. "So be it. At any rate, I assume we weren't awakened just because you're short a pair of bridge partners."

The lion settled back in his chair and began. He told them about the "Grand Infusion"—the mainstreaming of the many Costeau clans into Colonial society. He explained how the social fabric of the Colonies had been altered by the events of fifty-six years ago and how the makeup of the Council of Irrya had changed over the years. He outlined the responsibilities and perspectives of each Councillor, especially Doyle Blumhaven, who had refused to permit E-Tech to awaken them.

Minutes dissolved into hours. The lion spoke of the Colonies' massive detection/defense grid out beyond the orbit of Jupiter, and of the growing tensions throughout the past year as the cylinders anticipated the return of the Paratwa. He told them of the Order of the Birch, who wanted war declared on the assassins as soon as their ships were detected, and of the senseless massacres being done in the name of that political organization. He told them about his own suspicions regarding the killers; his fear that they could indeed be a Paratwa assassin. And he told the tale of Inez Hernandez's grandniece, Susan: her witnessing of the Yamaguchi massacre and her subsequent near-fatal encounter with the two murdered E-Tech officers.

"Have you located this Susan Quint yet?" interrupted Nick.

"No. But I have the Alexanders as well as some of our supporting clans, out searching for her."

"This Yamaguchi massacre," questioned Gillian. "It happened three days ago?"

"Yes."

"I'd like to go to Honshu . . . see the place where the actual killings occurred."

"And," added Nick, "we'll need all the data you can dredge up regarding these massacres."

The lion nodded. And finally, he told them about his recent visit from Inez Hernandez and the E-Tech programmer, Adam Lu Sang, and of the young man's suspicions that someone had put a sunsetter into the data archives. When he finished the story, Nick's cheery face had collapsed into a deep frown.

"If there's a genuine sunsetter in the E-Tech computer system, and if it's been digging in for more than twenty years . . ." The midget trailed off. "That's bad news. I mean, sunsetters eat data the way kids eat Cheerios."

The lion was not familiar with the analogy.

"I'm honored that this Adam Lu Sang has such faith in my abilities," continued Nick. "But a sunsetter . . . gee, I don't know."

"You'll give it a try?" prodded the lion.

"Naturally. I haven't had a good challenge in fifty-six years."

"No one must know you've been awakened," reiterated the lion.

"That's fine," said Nick. "But are you sure our presence is going to remain a secret? I assume you're familiar with what happened fifty-six years ago."

"I am. All I can say is that I have no reason to doubt Adam Lu Sang's sincerity. And I would trust Inez Hernandez with my life."

"Good. Gillian, what do you think?"

Gillian turned to the lion. "My Cohe wand—I took it into stasis with me, but it wasn't there when I awakened."

"My technical people have it," said the lion. He hesitated. "It's yours when you want it, of course, but bear in mind that the penalties for the possession of such a weapon are just as harsh as they were fifty-plus years ago."

Nick finished his cinnamon biscuit and leaned forward. "Any other Cohe wands turn up since we were put to sleep?"

"No ... there's only yours and the pair that Reemul had. Supposedly, E-Tech has those locked away in the vaults."

*Reemul—the liege-killer.* At hearing the name spoken aloud, a strange emotion touched Gillian. A memory: *the pleasure of the hunt.*

*We have tracked down many Paratwa assassins, Nick and I. Two and a half centuries ago, in those insane days preceding the Apocalypse, we were responsible for killing more than a score of them. And fifty-six years ago ... Reemul.*

As if it had happened yesterday.

Yet there was a difference.

*Today I have the power to be whole.* He could feel it deep inside: echoes of thought, the pattern of another consciousness poised just beneath awareness, waiting for the proper sequence of events, the fulcrum that would bring it to the surface, bring Empedocles back to life.

That fulcrum was the whelm—the dialectic of swapped consciousnesses unique to the Ash Ock, and even more unique to Gillian, whose tway, Catharine, had perished centuries ago.

*The whelm.* A thing simultaneously desired and feared. Desired because it brought to him a wholeness that he could never know as Gillian.

He was not sure why he was afraid.

The lion continued. "My people will be at your service; you may call on the Alexanders for transportation, technical assistance, a safe haven in any Colony—whatever you need."

*Whatever we need,* thought Gillian.

Nick hopped down from the sofa. A soft smile spread across his cheeks. "What we'll need is a lot of luck."

Susan Quint flattened her hands against the specially treated pinewood bartop. She began to vibrate.

On the oval stage, in the center of the bass cabaret, tonight's major act—the Elvis Tways—rhythmically gyrated their hips, in beat with the trio of delrin players seated on a wide sunken sofa off to the left. The delrin musicians, wearing matching leisure suits and opaque visors, brutally thumped the glowing black strings of their guitar-shaped instruments, producing the mushy conglomeration of notes that set the cabaret's wooden fixtures shuddering.

Susan pulsed along with the music, wishing for oblivion. But the reality of her predicament refused to retreat from consciousness.

*What am I going to do?*

The Elvis Tways danced vigorously, their movements in tandem—two hirsute, muscular young bodies bleeding sweat, tangerine boxers pasted across white skin. The majority of the crowd—mostly young men and women from the adjacent corporate office district—sat at the five floating horseshoe bars. Hands compressed vibrating wood, upper torsos rocked with the deep-bass echoes that transferred pulses from the treated pine into flesh and muscle.

The cabaret was jammed—a large crowd for a Tuesday night. Couples slow-danced in the ever-changing floor areas between the motorized bars. Each bar was mounted on plastic bearings, and each one moved haphazardly throughout the spacious room, its course influenced by delicate, ground-level air currents.

Susan forced herself to concentrate on the entertainment—the pseudo-Paratwa dance act, the Elvis Tways. She had seen better. Although most Irryans rated this cabaret a 9G screamer, this particular pair of tandem dancers lacked the really outstanding characteristics of the better acts. The pair danced well—plenty of fancy back-to-back moves. But they did not appear to be telepathically linked. Susan had seen top-of-the-line, 10G pseudos: fast-moving acts where the dancers accurately mimicked the actions of a real Paratwa. This pair lacked that professional intensity.

Nothing like the pair she had seen in Yamaguchi terminal.

*What am I going to do?*

The specially enhanced notes continued to pulse through her body, and it was as if soothing hands were buried deep inside her, massaging muscles. "Caresses of the spirit," advertised the bass cabarets, "streamliners of the soul." The rhythms felt good; panaceas for her discontent. She thought about picking up one of the available males; sex would feel even better.

But panaceas would not take away her problems.

*Could the freelancers be right? Could those two madmen in Yamaguchi terminal actually have been a Paratwa?*

All of the official sources—most especially E-Tech and the Guardians—continued to deny such a possibility. Susan was not so sure. Whatever she had seen in Honshu was fast and frightening. Worse yet, it had upset the carefully structured balance of her life. She had been on the run now for almost two days, since early Monday morning when she had escaped from the hospital. And now it was Tuesday night, and here she was, lounging in a 9G screamer cabaret on the outskirts of the North Epsilon business district. And Saturday evening, the new Marketing VP from Clark Shuttle Service was supposed to be taking her to a freefall ballet. There was no way she could risk keeping that date.

But you simply did not break a date with a 10G screamer. The repercussions could devastate her social life.

*What am I going to do?*

*A real Paratwa.* Her mind kept returning to the possibility. The freelancers could be correct. She might have come face-to-face with a real tway.

It was all so confusing. And the past two days had provided no answers. Since Sunday night, when the two E-Tech officers had come to her apartment, her life had become a blur of events. She remembered running out of the building, wearing only slippers and an orange wrap-around, dashing down the street, ignoring the curious stares of neighbors, thinking only of escape, of getting as far away as possible from the murderous Security men.

A hailed taxi. A high-speed ten-minute ride on the expressway adjacent to the Alpha strip; a ride to safety, to the home of one of the few people Susan had been able to count on over the years.

*And Aunt Inez didn't believe me.*

Instead, her Aunt had committed Susan to the hospital. To a psychplan.

*Why didn't you believe me? Why didn't you trust me?*

No way was Susan going to allow herself to be coerced into another psychplan. At the first opportunity, she had slipped out of the hospital.

She had not dared return to her apartment, figuring that E-Tech would have been swarming all over her building by then. Instead, she had walked to the nearest ICN terminal and quickly transferred her savings account into cash cards.

A short time later: another incredible shock. While trying on a pair of new bunhuggies in a fashionable Irryan clothier, she overheard a conversation about the murder of two E-Tech officers in a parking garage. Donnelly and Tace—the same officers who had tried to kill her.

Monday night . . . more blurred events . . . a deep troubled sleep in a nondescript hotel, her room paid for with cash cards, under an assumed name. Twelve hours of unconsciousness, but not a satisfying rest. When Irrya faced sun this morning, she had awakened feeling groggy, uncomfortable. Sleep had not solved any of her problems.

And it was only this morning when she realized she had forgotten about Monday night's date with the ICN programmer.

Well, at least *that* was not Apocalypse. The ICN programmer was not on Susan's social plane; she had only been going out with him as a favor to a business acquaintance. When things returned to normal, she would have to make a few calls, issue some apologies. All in all, it was no big deal.

But Saturday night's date with the Marketing VP . . . that was a different story.

She did not dare go out with him. E-Tech Security would have certainly broken all of her computer codes by now, initiated surveillance on friends or acquaintances she might be expected to contact. There was no way Susan Quint could keep that date.

But there was no way she could break it, either. Irryan social ethics prescribed certain principles; when you said you were going to go out with someone whose standing was above your own, you damn well went out with them. Excuses, with rare exceptions, were not acceptable. A serious injury, perhaps, or a death in the family. But if that were the case, and you had a genuine excuse, proof would have to be supplied.

That was the way it was.

A broken date for false reasons targeted you for immediate repercussions, including a demotion in status. And once demoted, it was very hard to climb back up again.

Very hard.

The Elvis Tways froze in midstride as the bass trio ended their song—a sizzling triplet of harmonic finger-slides down the necks of their instruments. The bartop stopped vibrating. Patrons throughout the cabaret raised

their hands above their heads and clapped wildly. Susan
kept her palms pinned to the bar.

*What am I going to do?*

"Costello and Presley—the Elvis Tways!" hooted the
MC, mounting the stage. He wore an emerald-sequined
jacket and a permanent smile. "Let's give the Tways another big round of applause!"

The crowd clapped and hollered.

"And now, Cabaret Luge proudly presents—straight
from his freefall engagement in the centersky of Colony
Prague—will you please welcome a creature that will certainly get things moving . . .

"Big Bird!"

There was a brief drum roll. Then a man in a gigantic
yellow bird suit, with extended mechanical wings flapping
vigorously, descended from a trapdoor twenty feet above
the stage. He dropped in a full-gravity plunge, totally out
of control, fluttering wings doing nothing to break his fall.
He hit the stage with a loud crash. Amber feathers flew
from his body.

The crowd laughed wildly. The bird man lay on the
stage, unmoving.

The MC shook his head and stared forlornly at the
downed creature. "Well, folks . . . I guess before we hired
Big Bird, we should have explained that this wasn't a
freefall engagement."

The cabaret erupted—shrieking laughter followed instantly by a growing wave of spontaneous applause. People
on both sides of Susan rose to their feet, clapping and hol-
lering.

The bird man staggered to his feet, folded a broken
wing in front of his chest, and gave a graceful bow. Bare
scrawny legs wobbled erratically as he exited stage right.
Thunderous applause continued.

The woman beside Susan turned to her with a wild-
eyed grin. "A ten-G snaker! Blasphemy personified!"

The MC chuckled. "Folks, I'd sure like to hire Big Bird

for a night of raw sex. The problem is, I don't believe in featherbedding!"

A drum roll was followed by a fresh round of clapping. The delrin trio came to life in an explosion of heavily reverbed bass notes. Pinewood started pulsing. Dancers hit the floor.

Susan remained motionless. The one-trick birdman had not amused her in the slightest. A few days ago, she would have been in hysterics along with the rest of them.

She lifted her hands from the bar. They were shaking. *I have to get out of here. I have to do something.*

But what?

She needed to talk with someone about this whole mess. Obviously, she could not go to E-Tech. Aunt Inez's betrayal made it impossible to contact any of her acquaintances within La Gloria de la Ciencia. And she really did not have any close friends—at least none that she could talk with about life-and-death situations.

That was depressing.

*All right, Susan,* she chided herself. *There's no sense in wallowing in self-pity.*

Years ago, when her parents had died, there *had* been a few individuals whom she had been able to open up to. There were many psychplan counsellors during her teenage years, and two or three of them had been pretty decent. But the problem with psychplan counsellors was that they usually demanded long-term commitments . . .

No.

She remembered some concerned career directors, too, from school. But her days of formal education were long behind her, and she had not bothered to keep in touch with any of those people.

The Reformed Church of the Trust?

At one time, the Church would have been an easy target for Susan's pain and rage: indirectly, they had contributed to her parents' insanity. But primarily because of a few people within the Church who had befriended her during those awful weeks following the tragedy, Susan had never felt cause to blame them. In particular, she remembered a young priest.

She tried to recall his name. Lester . . . something-or-other. He had been there, comforting her in those hours immediately following the suicide of her parents . . .

Lester Mon Dama.

She had not seen him for well over a decade, either. But he was Church, and Susan's parents had always maintained that the Church was there for you whenever you needed it.

*There for you whenever you needed it.*

The words revivified dull memories from her childhood; echoes of those days spent with her parents. They were sweet memories, but each had been layered over with a coating of pain. She bit her lip, fought back a wave of tears.

*No, dammit!*

Years ago, when things had been really awful, one of her psychplan counsellors had taught her to add up the good things in her life in order to maintain some perspective on the bad. It was more productive than crying.

*Number one—I haven't broken Saturday's date. Not yet. I still have time to work something out.*

*Number two—I'm still alive.* Normally, that one did not count. But she figured that two close brushes with death in the past week qualified it for inclusion.

She felt herself smiling.

*And my name hasn't shown up yet on any of the E-Tech telecasts. Number three.*

A frown wiped away the smile. She hadn't really thought about it before, but the fact that E-Tech was not officially searching for her was a bit puzzling. She had assumed that Donnelly and Tace had been operating under the authority of someone within E-Tech Security. But maybe not. Maybe that night, in her apartment, they had

been receiving orders directly from someone else—
someone who wanted Susan dead.

*Slasher—the killer in Yamaguchi Terminal.* The man who had
looked at her with recognition. That was, of course, the
only possible answer. Since the massacre, she had been
trying to convince herself that she could not know such a
monster.

*But I do know him.* That had to be the explanation. Either
she knew him, or she knew his tway, if he was indeed a
Paratwa. In the real world, that killer was someone whom
she could identify.

The assassins had professed to be from the Order of the
Birch and that crazed organization purportedly had many
influential friends. People with enough clout to corrupt a
pair of E-Tech Security officers?

She shook her head. Sitting here in the crowded cabaret, the whole thing seemed ludicrous. Nevertheless,
Donnelly and Tace *had* tried to kill her.

*Aunt Inez should have believed me.* A sigh escaped her. Looking back, Susan could understand why her Aunt had not
accepted her story at face value. Foolishly, Susan had allowed herself to go into hysterics the moment she arrived
at her Aunt's apartment.

A chill swept through her. For the first time, she consciously acknowledged what she already knew to be true.
*The assassin ordered Donnelly and Tace to kill me. And when the
E-Tech officers failed in their mission, the assassin killed them, in order to prevent any real investigators from learning who they were
working for.*

Worse yet, that meant that the assassin must still be
afraid that Susan could identify him. *He's going to keep on trying to kill me until he succeeds.*

A hand touched her shoulder. She spun violently. Her
arm lashed out.

Her elbow caught the man in the windpipe. He staggered backward, choking, and slammed into a live bar-
maid. Woman and drinks spilled to the floor.

A flood of laughter erupted from the nearest patrons.

"I think he just wanted to dance with you," said the woman beside Susan, grinning.

Susan stared at the surrounding faces, at their mocking looks of contempt, and she knew that they were rating her well below the line, down with the 1G's—the beggars and silkies, the fatix and unmainstreamed pirates—the sludge of the Colonies.

I'm not one of them, she wanted to shout. But her mouth would not open.

*He's going to keep on trying to kill me until he succeeds.*

She bolted from her stool and dashed from the cabaret.

*Something is not right.*

Gillian paced back and forth through the crowded Yamaguchi Terminal, ignoring the distractions of silkies and dealers plying their trades, trying to allow his awareness to make the connection between this physical place and the vivid images that had been recorded here four days ago, trying to conceptualize the flow of events that had led to the brutal murders of a hundred and fourteen people.

He had been wandering through the terminal for the past hour, mentally integrating the parameters of this huge space with an actual video record of the massacre's aftermath, purchased from a young freelancer who had arrived in the terminal only minutes after the attack. Nick had used those images of human decimation, combined with the transit computer records acquired through La Gloria de la Ciencia at Inez Hernandez's request, to generate a set of event sequence maps.

The midget had studied hundreds of Paratwa killings, had learned to translate mass murders into cold data: information-chocked tables, charts and grids. Such digital recreations were especially viable in the larger massacres, like this one, where the sheer number of victims provided for a statistical reliability impossible to develop from smaller attacks. Often in the past, Nick's data alone had enabled them to actually identify the breed of assassin involved. On Earth, during the final days over a quarter of a millennium ago, the midget's sophisticated techniques, combined with Gillian's unique Ash Ock understanding of binary interlink combat, often had led them to their prey.

Mounted on the inside of Gillian's left sunshield visor was a microcomputer grid with an enhancer to permit his eye to focus at close range. He tapped the sensorized edge of the visor and watched as another of Nick's charts dissolved onto the miniature screen. It showed the terminal as a gridwork of black lines, overlaid by one hundred and forty-nine multihued slashes of color, each slash representing the area where a dead or injured Colonist had fallen. Each line of color indicated the victim's suspected direction of movement at the moment of his encounter with the assassin.

Victims of killer one—the assassin with the flash daggers, the man that the freelancers had dubbed *Slasher*— were displayed in a mixture of warm colors: shades of red, orange, and yellow, each differing hue symbolizing the specific time that that Colonist had met his fate. The more numerous greens, blues, and violets marked *Shooter's* prey: men, women, and children whose bones had been shattered under the rapid-fire assault of that weapon of unknown technological origin—the spray thruster.

Utilizing Nick's quarry motion chart, and with near-perfect recall of the video, Gillian had been able to mentally reconstruct the events of the Yamaguchi attack.

Before his shuttle had even docked in Honshu this morning, he had been fairly certain that this massacre was not the work of a Paratwa. The patterns were all wrong, the methods inconsistent with the manner in which tways operated.

These killers had begun the carnage from positions on opposite sides of Yamaguchi Terminal. According to the officially released E-Tech report, the place had been—like today—swamped with travellers. At the beginning of the violence, the two killers would have been far out of sight of each other, and if they were a Paratwa, that factor alone would have neutralized their single greatest advantage: the binary interlink's ability to observe an identical scene from two separate locations, perceive the same situation through a dual set of eyes. Virtually all Paratwa, regardless of breed, went into combat with their tways as close together as feasible.

There were exceptions to that rule, of course. Products of the deadlier breeding labs, such as the KGB-trained Rabbits from Voshkof Laser and Fusion, and the North American Jeek Elementals, tended to take more chances. Members of those breeds would occasionally risk separating the tways for brief periods. But even a Jeek as unpredictable as Reemul had always made certain that his tways were in close proximity when the epitome of violence was at hand.

In this terminal, the two killers had been on opposite sides of a huge mob. A real Paratwa would not have attacked from such a position.

Gillian had arrived at that conclusion only minutes after arriving in the terminal. Yet here he was, an hour later, still wandering through the vast space.

*Something is not right.*

He could not put his finger on what was bothering him; uneasiness refused to be shaped into thought. For about the hundredth time, he ran his conception of the events through awareness.

*The two killers position themselves on opposite sides of the terminal, facing the center. Slasher begins the murderous rampage with his flash daggers. Maybe six to eight seconds later, Shooter opens up with the spray thruster. They begin moving toward each other, toward the middle of the huge space.*

*About halfway through the attack, the killers suddenly stop, and fill the terminal with their fanatic raving about the Paratwa not being allowed to return. "Long live the Order of the Birch!" they cry, one after another. The panicked crowd splits into a series of smaller mobs, squeezing toward the exits.*

*The massacre ends with the two killers close enough to be within sight of one another. At that juncture, they change directions, begin moving on perpendicular courses. Slasher heads toward one of the west exits, Shooter marches southward. They hide their weapons, hurtle themselves into the thick of the crowds, and are swept out of the terminal, escaping along with hundreds of terrified survivors.*

Gillian shook his head. The modus operandi indicated a pair of transceiver-linked human beings. Not a Paratwa.

And yet . . .

*Something is not right.*

He stopped pacing and closed his eyes, tried to shut off the sensory barrage of the terminal, force his mind to become a blank slate.

Images and sounds blasted through awareness, burrowing beneath cerebral conceptions of quarry motion charts and recorded death images—a gestalt seeking clarity within the deeper reaches of his subconscious.

But the trick did not work. When he opened his eyes and tried to integrate the gestalt with abstract awareness, he was left with the impression that this four-day-old killing scene was too cold for unconscious assimilations to occur. He needed a fresh murder site, where the bodies were still in place, where the heat of the violence could ease down into the deepest levels of his being, where the maelstrom of his unique Ash Ock subconsciousness could exhume a true picture of the brutality.

He needed to wait until the assassins struck again.

There was nothing more that he could learn here. He turned around, intending to head for the escalators that led to the shuttle docks, located far below the terminal. But suddenly, an array of golden light burst forth at his side, and within that light, he saw the elfin face of a young woman.

Catharine.

For an instant, the image of Gillian's long-dead tway seemed to overwhelm the halo of brilliance that surrounded her. Catharine metamorphosed into the beautiful creature she had once been, long brown hair flowing across her shoulders, the warm blue eyes locked onto his face.

*Catharine.* Gillian moved toward her, knowing she was not real, knowing that she was an apparition from his deepest subconscious. She was his other half, the entity who could interlace her mind with his. Catharine and Gillian—tways who together could become the Ash Ock Paratwa, Empedocles.

He stepped forward. She appeared to shift to the left, moving from his path. He changed directions to match her movement, but she angled to the right. He forced himself to stop.

*I can't touch her. She's not real. She's a memory-shadow from my own mind, a distillation of Empedocles.*

But he longed for her, nonetheless.

Her lips moved. She was trying to say something. There were no sounds, no voices in Gillian's head to match her speech. But he felt certain that she was trying to communicate with him.

He shook his head, confused. She could not talk. She was not real. She was an abstraction, a mental construct.

Her face grew darker, her expression more intense. She seemed desperately to want Gillian to understand what she was trying to say.

Instinctively, he stepped closer, hoping to fathom her silent mouthing. His body bumped into something.

"Watch out!" snapped a tall, black-haired man.

Catharine disappeared, enveloped by a collapsing flower of golden light.

"Watch where you're going," muttered the man again, but with less antagonism in his voice. He was staring at Gillian's face, and apparently something there was causing him to restrain his anger.

"Sorry," Gillian mumbled. He turned away from the man and scanned the terminal, looking for Catharine. But she was gone. He drew a deep breath, sighed.

*She was not real,* he reminded himself.

Abruptly, his right hand began to itch. As he stared down at the bandages, thoughts of Catharine retreated to that subconscious maelstrom from which they had sprung. Last night his burn injury had been treated by a team of Alexanders' doctors, and since then, the wound seemed to be healing abnormally fast. Fifty-six years had at least produced some strides in medicine. Soon, his hand would be again able to grip a weapon. Soon, he would be ready to wield the Cohe wand.

And the doctors had given him a different face as well: more fleshy in the cheeks, a re-angled nose, eyes pinched slightly closer and tinted a darker shade of gray with cornea oils.

He wondered what Catharine would have thought of his new looks.

With a sigh, he resumed his interrupted march toward the escalators, to the subterranean docks and the shuttle that would transport him back to the Colony of Irrya.

A realization struck him. *It does not matter whether the Yamaguchi massacre was accomplished by transceiver-linked human beings or a Paratwa.* Either way, there was a deadly enemy in the Colonies.

*There is someone to hunt.*

Hunting produced a pleasure that few other activities could rival. But Gillian knew also that his sudden desire for the hunt carried deeper meaning.

The intensity of a face-to-face battle to the death could bring on the whelm—the duality of consciousness that would force him and his memory-concentrate of Catharine to interlace, become Empedocles.

*Hunting can make me whole.*

Yet as before, he felt doubts about the arising of Empedocles. Becoming whole was something to be both desired and feared.

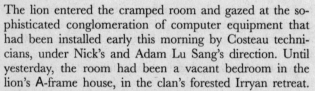

The lion entered the cramped room and gazed at the so-phisticated conglomeration of computer equipment that had been installed early this morning by Costeau technicians, under Nick's and Adam Lu Sang's direction. Until yesterday, the room had been a vacant bedroom in the lion's A-frame house, in the clan's forested Irryan retreat.

He squeezed a chair into a space beside the tiny programmer and sat down. "I'm sorry we couldn't get you a bigger room."

Nick grinned. "This isn't bad, Jerem. Besides, I don't occupy a whole lotta volume."

"Is the equipment almost ready?"

"Just about. Adam's with a couple of your techs right now, requisitioning more goodies. He seems a bit surprised that your people have been able to provide most of the gear we need."

"Intercolonial free trading can be a glorious thing."

The midget chuckled. "Is that how you refer to the black market these days?"

The lion smiled and motioned to a rotating 3D grid on the nearest screen. "What's that?"

"A graph of technological growth plotted against time and financial investment. It indicates to me that although the Colonies have increased their rate of technological advancement over the past fifty-six years in some areas—most notably weapons research—in terms of investment dollars, your society has a rather poor rate of return. You've accessed the archives for 'lost' sciences, sinking large sums into the redevelopment of working technologies. And you've also heavily financed virgin research. Yet overall, you haven't been spending your money well."

The lion nodded. "There's a very good reason for that. E-Tech still restricts large-scale dissemination of archival data. Very little scientific cross-fertilization occurs—spin-off technologies are almost unknown. In those circumstances, R and D is not cheap."

"Rome Franco must have done his job well," said the midget. "Even knowing that the Colonies were going to experience a growth spurt, he vowed that E-Tech would maintain stiff controls over the rate of that growth. I guess he succeeded.

"Still, in at least some areas, I would have expected the Colonies to be a bit further along. Most especially, I would have expected that the 'Ecospheric Turnaround' projects would have rendered large areas of the Earth reinhabitable by now."

The lion shrugged. "Over the years, the Council of Irrya, and most Senators, have felt that there was little sense in spending large sums of money on Earth revitalization projects until the threat of the Ash Ock was dealt with, once and for all."

"Makes sense, I suppose. I've also noticed something else about your society, by selectively examining certain parameters. Throughout the Colonies, crime rates are rising, political chicanery is on the upswing, and your major entertainment indexes are wildly out of control—popular diversions are at an all-time high." The midget hesitated. "Sort of reminds me of pre-Apocalyptic days."

The lion frowned. "We're living in troubled times."

"And so it goes," said Nick softly.

"I thought you were supposed to be working on the sunsetter problem?"

"I am. But first I'm trying to establish a background grid of your society, gain a clearer perspective of where things are headed. I have to be able to perceive the Colonies the way this sunsetter perceives them. I have to try and figure out the ultimate goals of our nasty little program."

"I thought its goal was fairly clear. It's trying to wipe out the data archives—specifically, older programs holding technical and scientific information."

"Maybe, maybe not. Sunsetters were often targeted to destroy only specific data. But they wiped out scores of other programs in order to disguise their actual intended targets. That process made it more difficult to discover the motivations of the sunsetter's progenitor."

The lion nodded. "Could this sunsetter have been put into the archives hundreds of years ago, by pre-Apocalyptic programmers? And for some reason awakened in our era?"

"A sleeper?" Nick shook his head. "It's theoretically possible, but I doubt it. Before the archives were transferred up to the Colonies, they were thoroughly detoxed. We came across no evidence of sunsetters, awake or sleeping.

"The fact that this program is in the archives *now* suggests two general possible scenarios. One: the program was entered for extraneous, albeit malicious, reasons. Perhaps a disgruntled programmer, twenty to twenty-five years ago, created or discovered the sunsetter and input it, perhaps as a kind of long-term vengeance on the organization. Or maybe a more innocent process occurred—an E-Tech experimental program, for instance, that got out of control.

"The second scenario is, of course, that the presence of the sunsetter is meaningful. Person or persons unknown have put it into the archives in order to achieve a specific goal or goals."

The door slid back and Adam Lu Sang marched into the room, his slender frame half-hidden by a large plastic box brimming with equipment. He nodded excitedly to the lion. "Genuine collusion-4 output desamplers—one of your techs got them for us. Your people must know the black market inside and out!"

Nick grinned. "Ahh, these Costeaus—fingers always in the cookie jar."

The young programmer hesitated, then squatted and set the carton on a low bench. He straightened slowly and faced the lion. "I didn't mean to suggest that all Costeaus are involved in criminal activities—"

Nick reached up and whacked Adam on the shoulder. The programmer flinched.

"Relax," chortled the midget. "Intercolonial free trading is a glorious thing."

Adam still looked uncertain.

The lion smiled. "It's all right, Adam. You have not offended."

"Yeah," agreed Nick. "If you *had* offended, the lion would probably ask you to take a walk in the forest with a couple of those large Costeaus you see roaming around the grounds. You know the ones I mean—they carry thrusters and look like they'd enjoy snacking on warm Christmas reindeer."

Adam managed an uneasy smile.

The lion asked, "How close are we to gaining full access into the actual E-Tech archival network?"

"Another day or so," replied the young programmer, nodding vigorously.

"We're still customizing the equipment," said Nick. "We're dividing this gear into two subnetworks. Adam will tie one of the systems into the vaults. But the second system will be separated by a special modem that will prevent

the sunsetter from entering. In fact, if it tries to gain access
to the second system, we'll know about it.

"We need a clean computer," Adam explained. "One
that can't be compromised."

"Right," said Nick. "An average sunsetter can foul the
data within any network it can make electrical or radio
contact with. And a really good sunsetter will actually be
on the lookout for enemy programs—ones designed to
track it down. If this sunsetter is really outstanding, then
it's going to go on the offensive once it discovers we're after it. But it won't be able to pass through that modem—it
won't be able to reach the system that's generating enemy
programs. At least that's what we're hoping will occur."
The midget grinned suddenly. "Gee whiz—this could be a
lotta fun!"

Adam headed for the door. "I'm due back at E-Tech
soon. Is there anything else we need?"

Nick squinted in thought. "Let's see . . . how about a
BLT?"

"A bore lithium tracer?" wondered Adam, shaking his
head in confusion. "What would we need one of those
for?"

"I was thinking more in terms of a sandwich."

"Oh." Adam grinned. "You had some funny names for
sandwiches back in the pre-Apocalypse."

"Funny sandwiches for funny times," Nick said dryly.

Adam waved good-bye and marched out the door.

The lion watched the young programmer through the
window as he headed up the twisting path toward the
main parking lot. "What's your impression of him?"

"A smart boy," answered Nick.

"Then you fully believe his sunsetter theory?"

"Unless he's a complete liar, then it's probably not
theory. A sunsetter on the rampage is the clearest explanation for all those cancer-eaten programs."

The lion hesitated. "If that's true . . . then why can't he
convince his senior E-Tech programmers? I believe I un-

derstand part of their reluctance to accept such a thing. But it seems to me that if Adam is so certain of this sunsetter's existence . . ."

Nick wagged his finger. "If Dickie doesn't know there's a toilet, then he's probably going to pee on the floor."

"What?"

"It's a matter of perspective. You gotta at least believe that there's a target before you can hit it. Highly trained programmers—technical people in many professions, for that matter—tend to get locked into belief systems that are totally based on their own experiences. A natural enough process—you absorb what you learn, and then apply that learning to all new experiences.

"But to be a really capable computer hawk, you have to transcend that process. You have to assume that there are no limitations to the machine, that anything can be accomplished. Adam's coworkers can't see this sunsetter because it doesn't fit into their belief systems." The midget grinned slyly. "They haven't been properly toilet-trained."

The lion chuckled. He liked Nick. In fact, the man's combination of fiery intellect and quaint expressiveness made it almost impossible to dislike him.

*But I must remember that this jovial little man is not merely a brilliant computer programmer.* According to what the lion had learned through classified Council records, Rome Franco had considered Nick to be one of the grand manipulators of pre-Apocalyptic civilization. Franco had warned that should Nick be awakened again, he might prove to have his own agenda for the Colonies: plans not necessarily in line with official objectives.

Franco also had been convinced that Nick was capable of being just as ruthless as the Paratwa. And although the midget had never taken part in the actual violence, he and Gillian had operated as a team, hunting down Paratwa.

*Like Gillian, he is a contract killer. I must never lose sight of that fact.*

Nick swivelled his chair, turned away from the computers. The lion felt bright blue eyes studying his profile.

"I have some questions for you, Jerem." The midget paused. "And I'd like your assurances that our conversations on these matters will go no further than this room."

The lion permitted himself a faint smile. "Questions about Gillian, I assume."

"Yes."

"You have my assurances."

Nick folded his arms across his chest and propped his short legs up on the console. "You've known the whole truth about Gillian all these years, about him being a tway of an Ash Ock, about his ability to actually *become* the warrior Empedocles. Gillian said he told you and your mother everything before Rome Franco put us back into stasis, fifty-six years ago."

The lion nodded.

Nick licked his lips. "Did he say *why* he told you all that?"

"Not really. I suppose he felt he owed it to us. After all, Gillian set the trap that Reemul walked into. My mother and I showed up there by accident. We were almost killed."

"And you saved Gillian's life."

"As he saved mine."

Nick stared at a blank monitor screen. "And in all those years, you've told no one about Gillian's . . . alter ego?"

"No one. He swore us to secrecy."

For a moment, Nick said nothing. He kept his gaze on the darkened screen.

The lion frowned. "What's troubling you?"

"During the pre-Apocalypse, when Gillian's tway— Catharine—was killed . . . when we of E-Tech kept Gillian alive, manipulated him to our own ends . . ." Nick hesitated. "I guess what I'm trying to say is this—back then, we were operating under the unquestioned assumption that Empedocles was dead, that his Ash Ock consciousness had perished in the instant of Catharine's death."

"A false assumption," said the lion.

"Yes. And back then we possessed—or we thought we possessed—a fairly complete understanding of the binary interlink phenomenon. Whatever the breed, the death of a tway automatically destroyed the telepathically bound consciousness ruling the two tways. The interlace collapsed and the surviving tway went mad."

The lion nodded. "You kept Gillian alive, and functioning, by hiding his past from him, by making him believe that he was a human being, not a Paratwa."

"We did what we had to do."

The lion sensed regret in Nick's words.

"Anyway," the midget continued quickly, "fifty-six years ago, our theories were proved wrong. Somehow, the consciousness of Empedocles still survives, imprinted within the very cells of Gillian's mind and body. In Gillian's final battle with Reemul, he found a way to bring back his Ash Ock monarch."

Images from that day, long ago, wafted through the lion's awareness: Gillian and Reemul locked in mortal combat, he and his mother trapped in the same room—the most terrifying day of his life.

*And the day I became obsessed.*

He realized that since seeing Gillian for the first time yesterday, much of the power of that obsession had been relieved. Yet he still acknowledged an urge to be with the man, to walk beside him, to discuss a vast range of subjects with him. *Will the part of me that remains a twelve-year-old boy endlessly long for his presence? Will that part of me forever seek out the man who was, for a short time, almost like a surrogate father to me?*

Questions, perhaps, that could never be answered.

"Gillian—the man—I know well," continued Nick. "He is a friend whom I have trusted implicitly for many years. But Empedocles ... him I do not know. *Him* I do not trust. He is Paratwa." The face hardened. "He is my enemy."

"But both Gillian and Empedocles opposed Reemul that day," argued the lion, even while understanding perfectly well what Nick was trying to express.

"That day, the needs of tway and monarch were probably identical," said Nick. "With Reemul, a personal score had to be settled.

"But now, in this era, with the other two Ash Ock—Sappho and Theophrastus—likely to return from the stars . . ." Nick shrugged. "The loyalties of Empedocles are in question."

"He could betray Gillian."

"He could betray humanity. And there's something else. I saw the report that Gillian's face-lift doctor filed, after giving him a full-med exam. I also recall the results of the exam that Rome Franco's doctors wrote on Gillian fifty-six years ago. Physiologically, there's an alarming discrepancy between then and now. Today, Gillian's reaction times are much slower—his reflexes are sluggish and he's not as mentally alert as he once was."

The lion paused. "I've heard that long periods of stasis can alter—"

"No, this isn't a stasis-sleep problem. I believe it's a process that began when Empedocles reawoke during Gillian's battle with Reemul. I believe that since then, Gillian has been engaged in a subsconscious struggle with his monarch. It is that struggle which is causing the deterioration of his response patterns."

The lion nodded slowly. "What can we do?"

"About his slowed reflexes, I don't know. But we have to keep any eye on him, that's for certain. I'd like you to give me a couple of your people: Costeaus who can't easily be traced back to the lion of Alexander, but whose allegiances to you are strong. I'd like to assign them to Gillian."

The lion shook his head. "The Gillian that I remember was adept at avoiding such attentions."

"You're right—he'll spot most any tail immediately. And he's very skilled at avoiding electronic eavesdropping. I doubt if we could plant a bug on his person without him detecting it."

"Then what's the point of assigning trackers?"

Nick offered a faint smile. "I'm not talking about trackers."

"I don't understand."

"Trust me. I have a plan."

Thursday evening, in the privacy of his office at CPG headquarters, Ghandi tuned to FL-SIXTEEN—the major freelancer channel. Earlier, Colette had hinted, in her cryptic way, that FL-SIXTEEN's eight-oh-five newscast might be interesting. If Colette said something was going to be interesting, then Ghandi knew he could not afford to miss it.

He sank into the lounger and watched a fair-complexioned, well-groomed young man take shape on the screen.

"AND NOW," croaked the man, his voice brimming with menace, "FOR THOSE WHO DEMAND THE LATEST IN INTERCOLONIAL NEWS COLLATION . . .

FL-SIXTEEN PRESENTS THE AWARD-DRENCHED FEEDBACK EXPERTS . . .

OUR PRIME COVERAGE ILLUMINATORS . . .

KARL ZORK AND THEANDRA MORGAN!

The announcer's face exploded.

Glittering streaks of ultrablue light shot to the right of

the screen, reversed direction, then reformed into a second computer-generated countenance: a beautiful older woman, ivory hair swirling behind her, angled checkbones rapidly changing color under the glow of an airborne auraflector.

"THE ZORK-MORGAN REPORT," the woman intoned smoothly, "IS TONIGHT PRESENTED BY CPG CORPORATION."

Another explosion of light; the woman's face disintegrating under a stream of chroma tracers, the exploding light augmented by a deep whirring noise, the sound reminding Ghandi of a shuttle docking.

Fade to black . . .

. . . Slow dissolve to a wide shot of a figure wandering purposefully beneath the massive gray steel leg of a profarming harvester/planter. Camera zooms to medium close-up.

The figure, garbed in a grimy plastic worksuit, removes his breather mask, revealing a weather-beaten face. His calloused hand backstrokes a ridged forehead, wiping away a layer of sweat. A real human actor—on the freelancer channels, E-Tech only permits computer-generated commercials for self-aggrandizement.

The ruddy face glares into the camera.

"My family's been farming since before the Apocalypse. We left Earth in ninety-eight, right near the end. Wouldn't have left if we'd had a choice."

He lays his hand against the massive harvester leg. The camera zooms in tighter.

"Twenty generations ago, my ancestors made a living on the Earth. Twenty generations ago, my people farmed the land, squeezing life out of the soil, working the fields fifteen hours a day. They struggled against the land, fighting to bring in every last bushel of wheat and every last ear of corn. But for all their struggles, they understood something: They knew they had to give back what they took.

They understood their role as caretakers of a great power. They understood the life force of the planet.

"When a good machine came along, they bent it to their wills and made it a part of their lives. And they expected from that machine no less than what they expected from themselves."

The farmer hesitates; his face breaks into the barest hint of a smile. "Well today, life's a lot different. Twenty generations ago, some grandpappy of mine wouldn't even have been able to dream of a machine like this." Dissolve to a wide shot. The farmer is firmly stroking the massive leg of the harvester/planter.

"The strength of the soil, the power of a good machine, and the fortitude to make it all come together. That's what it took my ancestors and that's what it takes today. And that's what it's going to take tomorrow.

"And do you want to know something? I've a feeling that when tomorrow comes, we'll be takin' ourselves back down there. Someday we're going to be using these machines to reseed the Earth. And the wounds of the Apocalypse will be healed, and we'll have real pastures again, and fields covered with wheat and corn, and forests of pine and oak extending for as far as the eye can see."

He gives the huge harvester leg a final pat. "Someday, these machines are going to help take us home."

He turns his back to the camera. The scene dissolves into a stunning crescent of Earth—a fragile arc of bluish green, bathed in white clouds, outlined by a shimmering haze of golden sunlight. From beyond the horizon, blurred script letters come into focus against the starless void.

CPG PROFARMING PRODUCTS.

SOMEDAY WE'RE GOING TO HELP TAKE YOU HOME.

Fade to black . . .

In the solitude of his office, Ghandi laughed.

The commercial was a cosponsor deal, with CPG split-

ting the production costs with E-Tech. The spot was running on all the major freelancer networks, as well as on
E-Tech's primary intercolonial channel. One of CPG's
wholly owned advertising companies had done the actual
shooting and editing and Ghandi suspected that the creators of the spot had been influenced by Colette, probably
via subtle hints and suggestions made during the editing
process. He knew his wife's style, and this spot reeked of it.

Ghandi had not previewed this particular inanity—there
were so many CPG commercials these days that he could
barely keep up with them anymore. But he suspected that
Colette had not asked him to watch FL-SIXTEEN this
evening just because CPG was debuting a new spot.

Then again, Colette was full of surprises. Perhaps it was
merely the new commercial that she had wanted him to
see, to later solicit his opinions on some subconscious manipulation technique that she had injected into its ambience.

Or that Sappho had injected.

He sighed. Colette alone remained difficult to fathom.
Her monarch had always been—and probably would forever remain—an enigma.

He returned his attention to the screen. Freelancer Karl
Zork, a gruff-looking ape of a man, half hidden by his
trademark zig-zag red beard, had just finished introducing
himself and his telecast partner—Theandra Morgan, who
was seated beside him. Zork's delivery was fast and
furious—an impassioned flow of words that suggested a
powerfully intelligent man of immense education.

"Theandra," he concluded, "rotate us into story one."

The two-shot cut to a close-up of Theandra: a tall attractive blond whom opinion polls consistently rated
among the most admired professionals in Irrya.

"Sliding with the sleaze factor—naked in Bermuda—
ridin' the clutch with flameouts in both engines." Her
voice was crisp, professional; the opening jargon fully

translatable only to those young colonials steeped in the latest craze of twentieth-century semantics.

"As everyone knows by now, Karl, dataland is in big trouble these days—E-Tech has problems galore. And this afternoon, at a press conference held at their Irryan headquarters, E-Tech has finally decided to do something about it.

"E-Tech Director Doyle Blumhaven announced the formation of an unlimited-duration action/probe to investigate numerous reports of corruption within their E-Tech Security division. This announcement comes in the wake of the latest E-Tech Security outrage—the unconfirmed reports that those two Officers who were murdered in an Irryan garage four nights ago had strong connections to the intercolonial black market."

Ghandi frowned.

"The two E-Tech Security men—Lieutenant Hector Donnelly and Sergeant Solomon Tace—" Their pictures dissolved onto the bottom of the screen "—are suspected of providing protection services to a Sirak-Brath-based gang of black marketeers, who've been operating here in Irrya for at least five years."

The close-up of Theandra snapped back to a two-shot. Karl Zork's bushy eyebrows flared in surprise. "Black marketeers? Theandra, I'd say that was a little more than sliding with the sleaze factor!" He stroked his beard. "I'd call it humping the humpback, maybe, or sleeping with the boss's wife."

"Call it what you like, Karl. Fact is, this is the fourteenth time in the past twenty months that E-Tech Security is suspected of being compromised by outside agencies."

"I'd say it's time for a major overhaul of their whole Security section," growled Karl.

Ghandi sighed. What was needed was an overhaul of the Irryan Constitution, which permitted these outrageous freelancers the right to publicly defecate on whomever they chose. This pair especially. Before Zork/Morgan had come to FL-SIXTEEN, they had worked together as steam 'n' scream theatrical instructors at a private body motion clinic in the Colony of Velvet-on-the-Green. Not exactly an occupation to qualify you for objective commentary on intercolonial affairs.

"Maybe you're right, Karl," continued Theandra breezily. "It certainly appears that E-Tech Security has an overload of dirty laundry these days. At any rate, there are some positive aspects to this new action/probe. The chairperson, introduced by Doyle Blumhaven at the press conference, is to be private prosecutor Edward Huromonus."

"Crazy Eddie?" quizzed Karl, his eyes widening with disbelief. "The man who successfully sued the Profarmers' Union for proprietary inflationitis? The man who publicly paddled that illicit centersky consortium in Brussels/Berlin? The man who—"

"One and the same," interrupted Theandra. "And Mister Huromonus has vowed that there will be no limits to his action/probe and that it will follow the trail of the investigation anywhere—even if it should lead to the highest echelons of E-Tech."

The screen returned to a tight shot of Karl. He was shaking his head in wonder. "Theandra—I'm impressed. For once, I salute E-Tech's integrity. If they have the guts to let Crazy Eddie loose in their organization, then maybe there's hope for us yet."

The bearded freelancer segued effortlessly into a second story, but Ghandi tuned him out.

A major E-Tech investigation? That raised disturbing questions. Where had E-Tech learned that Donnelly and Tace were connected to the Sirak-Brath black marketeers? It was true, of course—that was the lever Calvin had used to recruit the Security men in the first place, by threatening to expose their illegal acts unless they cooperated. Donnelly and Tace had been given no choice, although certainly they had been well-paid for their special services to Calvin. And if they had not fouled things up with that Susan Quint woman, probably they would still be alive.

Naturally, Donnelly and Tace had never suspected that Calvin—their employer—was Paratwa. And certainly they had never been given any information that could have connected Calvin and his plans with Ghandi, Colette, and CPG.

Still, it was unsettling to realize that an unbridled investigation would be probing into the lives of the murdered officers. Ghandi hoped that Calvin had not made other errors in judgment, mistakes that could lead the action/ probe right to their own doors.

Probably, E-Tech itself had linked Donnelly and Tace to the smugglers via their own internal sleuthing. Even though Doyle Blumhaven was the Director of the organization, his powers were not omnipotent. He must have been unable to derail the formation of this action/probe.

Still, Blumhaven should have done *something* to stop a full-scale investigation from getting started. And the freelancers were correct in their assessment of private prosecutor Edward Huromonus. Crazy Eddie was a tenacious old devil, unbribable, and from all accounts, utterly fearless.

Could Blumhaven be slipping? Was he losing his tight grip on the organization?

Twenty-two years ago, the E-Tech Councillor had been seduced by Colette. It was Doyle Blumhaven, operating from a mid-management position within the organization at that time, who had first provided Colette access to the E-Tech archives. It was Doyle Blumhaven who had made it possible for Colette/Sappho's deadly sunsetter to be set loose in the data vaults.

Ghandi recalled when he and Colette had first met Blumhaven, at a profarmers' convention in Pocono, back in the days when CPG was still a minor corporation. Following that first meeting, Colette had informed Ghandi that she intended to supervise Doyle Blumhaven's career and eventually make him the director of E-Tech.

Coming from anyone else, such an egomaniacal statement would have been cause for laughter. But by that time, Ghandi had been Colette's partner and lover for three years. He had accepted her statement at face value.

Doyle Blumhaven would prove perfect for her plans, Colette had explained. He was a man who lusted for power, but in ways that belied his mannerisms. He possessed most of the qualities necessary for a successful political life—the proper brew of projected strength, modesty, intelligence, and ambition. But he lacked one talent: he was not an originator. He needed direction, someone who could channel his prowess. Colette/Sappho decided that Doyle Blumhaven was a product looking for a consumer. She made plans to buy him.

Blumhaven's seduction into the Ash Ock fold had been much simpler than Ghandi's. For one thing, there had been no physical relationship between Colette and Blumhaven; his wife's particular wiles in that area would have proved ineffective with Blumhaven, a lifelong homosexual. And Colette needed a fully functioning, long-term ally—not merely a chattel to carry out a few specific commands. That negated the possibility of using a needbreeder.

Instead, Colette had offered Blumhaven money—lots of it. With CPG's growing success at producing and marketing small high-tech items, untraceable funds were becoming readily available for clandestine investments. A secret ICN bank account was set up and enough cash deposited to someday make Blumhaven—if he invested properly—a wealthy man. Later came Colette's shrewd advice for corporate advancement and candid support for Blumhaven-initiated programs; all in all, a steady stream of information that Blumhaven used to make his star shine brightly within the E-Tech hierarchy.

In return, CPG Corporation received preferential treatment when dealing with E-Tech. And later, when

Blumhaven became Director, CPG was allowed to circumvent many of E-Tech's basic testing procedures required for corporations introducing virgin or upgraded technology.

Like Ghandi, Doyle Blumhaven had sold himself for personal gain. But there remained one big difference between them. As far as Blumhaven knew, he had been bought by a man, a woman, and a corporation.

Ghandi had sold out to the Paratwa.

*And you're becoming harder to understand, my love.*

The microbes twitched.

"My plan will work!" roared O'Donahee, favoring his audience of over seven hundred loyal Irryan citizens with a look of angry reproach. "There is no other way! One of Neptune's micromoons must be vaporized!"

Murmured agreement filled Assembly Hall F of the Augustus J. Artwhiler Memorial Conference Center. Tonight's other six presenters, seated at a table beside O'Donahee's podium, clapped in wholehearted support. But it was not enough. O'Donahee needed more passion.

He gripped the sides of the oak podium and leaned forward. "We must teach the Paratwa that we mean business! We must show the invaders that they are not going to come squirming back into the Colonies like a gang of shuttle gypsies!"

"Yes!" a female voice cried out.

"You tell 'em, O'Donahee," someone else shouted.

"We must be the force that unites the Colonies!" he urged. "We must serve as the shock troops of our civilization. In these troubled times, the Order of the Birch must shine like a lonely shuttle beacon in that dark void between the stars!"

"Long live the Order of the Birch!" a group of young men in the left center of the hall shouted in unison. O'Donahee was pleased that his people were picking up their cues so well tonight. Practice paid off.

He snapped his left arm up level with his shoulder, then opened and closed his fist twice in rapid succession. About one hundred other left arms, scattered throughout the auditorium, erupted in imitation.

*Not enough,* O'Donahee thought. When a man such as himself—a full-fledged Rod Commander—proferred the royal salute, every true-hearted follower of the Birch should have raised his hand in exultation of their common cause. O'Donahee allowed bitter disappointment to show on his face.

"Is this a display of your loyalty?" he shouted. "Is this what you call united? Do the rest of you expect to limp *behind* the vanguard of the brave? Is the Order of the Birch to be a hiding place for cowards?"

"No!" shrieked the crowd.

"We're not cowards!" screamed a pair of preteens in the fifth row, drawing scowls from their parents.

"Well, I don't know," cackled a lone voice. "People who make this much noise usually turn out to be a bit on the weak-kneed side, if you know what I mean."

Angry murmurs swept through the hall. O'Donahee instantly targeted the heckler. *Probably another E-Tech plant.* These days, you could hardly run a decent Birch meeting without having to deal with such scud. E-Tech Security made sure that nearly every legal gathering of the Order of the Birch was hampered by professionally trained disrupters.

O'Donahee glared solemnly and aimed an angry finger at the heckler, a young man seated right of center in the fourth row. The disrupter wore a faded red jacket, Lennon-style eyeglasses, and an ear-splitting grin.

"And you, *sir*!" O'Donahee intoned, allowing the full fury of his righteousness to shine forth. "Do you speak your own tongue, or are you a mouthpiece for the corrupt conglomerate of traitors that imposes its cowardly will through the brute force of E-Tech Security!"

"Imposter!" the crowd shouted.

"Throw him out!"

The young man continued grinning. The crowd's reaction did not seem to bother him. "I certainly am *not* from E-Tech Security," he announced, when the audience had quieted down. "I serve a higher order." He paused, like a comic timing the delivery of his punch line for maximum effect. "My good people, I am the will of that great providence who controls the air above your heads." His voice rose to a powerful crescendo. "My good people, I am the will of the great Hot Head!"

Scattered chuckling filled the hall. O'Donahee permitted a scowl to show on his face, but inside, he felt relieved. It was doubtful that this young disrupter was an E-Tech plant after all. He sounded more like one of those crazed fatix who pestered decent citizens in shuttle terminals.

O'Donahee had experience dealing with *that* type. One simply talked over them, ignoring whatever nonsense spouted from their mouths.

He turned his attention back to the audience. "Fellow citizens of Irrya, and fellow citizens who have travelled here from the other great Colonies of our culture. The time has come."

"Yes, it has!" yelled the heckler, still grinning.

"We must show our support," O'Donahee solemnly proclaimed. "We must show the Irryan Council that we are united against the return of the Paratwa. We cannot afford to walk the easy path, and preach compromise toward an enemy who has vowed to crush us. And we must not surrender to the hedonistic addictions of our time, wandering aimlessly, our duty obscured by the momentary pleasures of the flesh."

"Don't like sex, huh?" the heckler shouted, and his words were followed by a hideous laugh.

O'Donahee continued to ignore him. "We must not allow ourselves to become weak while our enemy grows strong. We must let the Paratwa know that the Colonies of Irrya are a stronghold for a culture that rejects them utterly! We must send them a message:

"The Colonies of Irrya are sacred places! The Colonies of Irrya are shining lights of justice! The Colonies of Irrya will never give in to the tormented creatures of our dark past, these monsters of miscreation who have never even known the pleasure of living as solitary beings!"

"Yes!" screamed the crowd, coming to life.

O'Donahee thrust out his left arm, fisted his fingers twice. This time, almost the entire assembly followed his lead. Seven hundred left arms saluted.

"Long Live the Order of the Birch!" he shouted.

"Long Live the Order of the Birch!" screamed the crowd.

"Long Live the Great Hot Head!" shouted the heckler, and his voice seemed to drown out the entire assemblage. Necks craned toward the left front of the auditorium, seeking a better view of the disrupter.

O'Donahee glared. The disrupter had snapped a pair of miniature blast speakers onto his shoulders and a lip mic onto his chin. His voice now boasted enough amplification to overwhelm a sixty-piece queen-rock orchestra.

It was time to deal with this obnoxious fatix. O'Donahee signalled to a pair of his own security people standing in the rear of the hall. They nodded, and began moving toward the center aisle. O'Donahee turned his attention back to the heckler. "You, sir, are not welcome here. You must leave this auditorium! At once!"

"And you, *sir*, must shut your mouth. At once! For if you do not, the great Hot Head will descend upon you!"

O'Donahee started to respond, but hesitated when he noticed a plume of black smoke rising from an empty section near the back of the hall.

"Well, now you've done it!" warned the heckler. "Now the great Hot Head has arrived to burn up your meeting!"

The curl of smoke abruptly contracted into a dense ball, blocking O'Donahee's view of the rear exits. The people closest to that section began to rise from their seats, nervously eyeing the cloud. A wave of emotion swept through the hall: anger and surprise, tinged with fear. But no one vaulted from the hall in panic. As yet there was no fire, just the weird-looking smoke.

O'Donahee cleared his throat, stalling until he could think of something to say. He was relieved to see that his two security men were approaching the spot where the smoke had originated. Things would return to normal momentarily. The heckler—and his distraction—would be removed from the hall.

But suddenly, the black cloud—as if it had a life of its own—hurtled upward and splattered against the center arch of the high ceiling. A collective gasp of surprise and relief cut through the auditorium. It was now obvious to everyone that this was not real smoke. O'Donahee suspected that they were looking at some sort of very sophisticated holo projection.

The black cloud coagulated into a tight ball, assuming the shape of a distorted, evil-looking countenance. Burning red eyes emerged from its depths.

"Behold!" shouted the young heckler, his amplified words cutting through the hall. "Behold the great Hot Head!"

Everyone looked up, momentarily transfixed. And O'Donahee found himself following the crowd's gaze even as a sinking feeling nestled in his guts. He had lost control of the meeting.

Anger came over him and he tore his eyes away from

the ominous black cloud-face and aimed a finger of righteous reproach toward the heckler's seat.

But the young man's chair was empty. He had disappeared.

A wrenching scream cut through the crowd's confusion, casting a momentary silence over the assembly hall. A chill raced up O'Donahee's spine.

The wail had come from an elderly man, who was standing next to where the heckler had been seated. O'Donahee saw the senior's face twisting in torment and then the old man was jerked sideways, as if his feet had been yanked out from under him. He fell to the floor, vanishing behind the row of seats.

Before O'Donahee could even register surprise, a second hideous scream filled the auditorium. The next man in that same row shuddered violently and a frothy spray of blood erupted from beneath him, cascading high into the air. People in adjacent seats began screaming as the dark fluid splattered onto them.

The second man fell backwards with a gaping hole torn in his midsection—a bloody pulp of ripped membranes and severed ribs. Next in line, a skinny middle-aged woman wearing a fluorescent sunbonnet emitted a pitiful wail before she too slid out of sight behind the chairs.

The last man in the row made a desperate leap for the aisle, but the invisible force that was cutting through that rank like an angry domino swept the man's feet out from under him. His legs were sheared from his torso above the knees, and the screaming man crashed down onto the carpet, his blood-soaked stumps kicking at the floor, body writhing in death-shock.

In the back of the auditorium, people were pressing forward, actually trying to gain a better view of the screams and commotion up front. O'Donahee shouted into his microphone:

"Get out of here! Get out of the hall!"

But another voice contradicted him. Soothing words:

"Please do not panic. This is merely a test. You are experiencing the new anti-Paratwa weapon, designed to create confusion among our enemy. Long live the Order of the Birch!"

People hesitated, their attentions divided among the disturbance up front, the evil-faced black cloud overhead, and that soothing voice urging self-control.

O'Donahee knew that those pacifying words had come from the blast speakers mounted on the shoulders of the murderous heckler. Even as that realization struck, the assailant emerged from the devastated third row, on his hands and knees, crawling and hopping like some sort of wild animal, fists clutching twin caricatures—blazing knives—unreal, as if they were being painted onto the very air from instant to instant, dancing to the sharp jerky movements of his hands. O'Donahee recalled an ancient video, where vividly colored cartoon images were superimposed over real-life figures. And suddenly he understood what was happening.

It was *Slasher*—one of the killers terrorizing the Colonies in the very name of their Order. "Get out of here!" O'Donahee shouted. "Run! Get out of the auditorium!"

Panic finally took hold and the entire hall erupted into a mass of screaming human beings, racing for the exits. O'Donahee watched in grim horror as people fell and were trampled by the stampede.

On the stage beside him, the other six presenters had risen from their seats. All were shouting madly, adding their unamplified voices to the general bedlam.

Slasher was on his feet now, racing up the center aisle, flash daggers lashing out, slicing off heads and arms and hands—anything that came within range. And suddenly, from behind O'Donahee, another terrible sound erupted. It was the wail of a thruster firing with impossible speed, like ten guns going off simultaneously. The other six presenters beside O'Donahee jerked their heads forward and collapsed neatly into their chairs. The back of each man's skull had been crushed inward by multiple blasts from the high-powered weapon.

*I don't want to die!* prayed O'Donahee, turning around in dread, unwilling to face the killer, but unable to stop himself.

The second assassin—Shooter—emerged from stage right: a grim-faced man garbed in the regulation gray uniform of the conference center's maintenance staff. Shooter held his weapon in his right hand, at arm's length, a widemouthed stubby cylinder tapering into a spongegrip handle. It was the spray thruster—the virgin-tech weapon that even La Gloria de la Ciencia seemed unable to fathom.

O'Donahee could not move. He realized that he had begun to mutter to himself. "Why is this happening to me? I don't understand."

The spray thruster came to life again, drowning out his mumbling as Shooter fired into the crowd and O'Donahee knew without actually seeing that each single blast, each discrete packet of projected energy, had found a target. And he noticed that the thruster was emitting tiny puffs of white steam from beneath its barrel, and he felt fascinated by those discharges, those minute puffs that seemed to clash so oddly with the destructive fury of the weapon itself.

*So gentle,* he found himself thinking. *So very soft.* At that moment, he realized he was going to die.

Sparkles of red light erupted around Shooter. Someone from the crowd had managed to get off a shot, but the counterattacker's single thruster blast had dissolved harmlessly against the killer's defensive energy shield—Shooter's crescent web.

With unnatural movement, Shooter pivoted, his spray thruster belching invisible fury at the new target and O'Donahee realized, again without looking, that there would be no more counterattacks from that quarter.

And then Shooter's weapon was pointed at O'Donahee

and more delicate puffs of white steam were spurting out from beneath the barrel.

O'Donahee felt his guts compress together and then he was lifted into the air, and a brackish stream of liquid was pouring from his mouth, and he could not seem to catch his breath. There was no pain, just the odd sensation of not being able to inhale.

He was off the stage now, airborne, flying backward over the audience. *Why?* he asked himself, feeling that there must be a reason. *Why is this happening to me?*

And then a tremendous crash broke his concentration, and he felt his backbone snapping across some hard unyielding object, and he gave up trying to understand.

The lion met Inez in the corridor outside the Council chambers. She dashed from one of the elevators just as he emerged from the lavatory.

"Are we the only ones here?" she demanded, approaching breathlessly.

He shook his head. "Blumhaven and Losef are inside. We're waiting for Van Ostrand to come on line again."

"My god," she muttered. "This late in the evening. You would have thought that someone's timing would have been a bit better. Whenever I imagined it, I always assumed that it would happen during the day."

The lion managed a smile. "I used to imagine that it would happen in the morning. I'd be sitting at breakfast, discussing the finer points of auraflector artistry or some such thing with my wife. A call would come. My wife would answer. She wouldn't say anything. She'd just look at me, and I'd know."

Inez whipped off her hat—a wide-brimmed purple Carlisle—and twisted the front of the band. Internal ribs energized, quickly folding the headpeace into a one-inch slab. She stuffed the condensed hat into her pocket. "My god—what a night! First the Birch massacre, and now this."

"And now this," the lion murmured.

"Jerem, do you realize that we're probably going to re-member this night for the rest of our lives—what we were doing at each moment, what we had to eat, where we were . . ." She shook her head. "At least I'll remember. Ev-erything's going to be engraved on my mind, like one of those ancient wooden plaques that people used to present as awards. And the plaque will say: 'Friday morning, Au-gust 7th, 2363, three A.M.—the night we detected the re-turn of the starships.' "

"I'll always remember how tired I was," offered the lion.

Inez sighed. "Fifty-six years ago . . . I wasn't even born then. And for all those years, the human race has been preparing itself for this moment."

"You sound tired, too."

"Yes, Jerem," she said, favoring him with a sad smile. "I am." She threw her arms around him and crushed him in a surprise bearhug. "But it's more than being just tired. I usually don't babble when I'm tired. I babble when I'm scared."

He squeezed her tightly.

"Oh, Jerem! I feel like I've been waiting for this moment since I was a little girl . . . waiting my entire life to find out what it all means."

The lion understood. "Waiting your whole life to find out whether you—and the rest of the human race—are destined to become slaves to the Paratwa."

"Yes. And the waiting . . . it changed me, I think. I

never told anyone this before, Jerem, but . . . the reason I didn't marry, the reason I chose not to have children . . ."

She stopped, and suddenly buried her face against his chest. The lion rubbed her back reassuringly.

Just as quickly, she pulled herself away from him. "I'm sorry," she mumbled, wiping a palm across a wet spot beneath her left eye. "You know I'm not usually like this."

"We've had a few hectic days." The lion recalled his own intense emotions brought on by seeing Gillian again. He shrugged. "There's a Costeau saying: Either feel the fool, or fool the feel."

Inez forced a smile. "I don't think I could even say that without stumbling."

"Most can't."

She swallowed. "I suppose there's still no word on Susan."

The lion shook his head. Inez now called him at least three or four times each day to ask for an update on the search for her missing grandniece. "Nothing, yet. But that shouldn't be cause for despair. My people still maintain that Susan probably went into hiding. Given her psych background, and all that she's faced over these past few days, that certainly would be an understandable reaction." He hesitated. "Does E-Tech know about her disappearance yet?"

"No. I've been covering for her. As far as I can tell, no one's yet making any fuss. I informed La Gloria de la Ciencia's Progress Inspection department that Susan has been temporarily transferred to a new position. They should accept that story, at least for a while."

The lion nodded thoughtfully. "Why don't you leak the details of Susan's disappearance to Edward Huromonus's action/probe."

Inez raised her eyebrows. "Do you think that's wise? I mean, this isn't exactly the first major investigation into the questionable doings of E-Tech Security. For all we know, this will turn out to be another whitewash—

Huromonus could be working hand-in-hand with the very people he's attempting to investigate. Informing them could very well place Susan in an even more dangerous position."

"That's possible, but I tend to doubt it. I know Edward Huromonus. Years ago, he served as a temporary counsel for the United Clans." The lion smiled. "There's a reason that they call him 'Crazy Eddie.' I don't believe he can be bribed, or threatened. His integrity is unimpeachable. And he has many formal connections that the Costeaus lack. He may be able to locate Susan. And he's certainly smart enough not to involve E-Tech Security people in his action/probe. He'll recruit investigators from outside the organization."

"If that's all true," said Inez, "I wonder why Doyle picked him to head up this action/probe?"

The lion shrugged. "E-Tech Security—and Doyle Blumhaven—are coming under a lot of fire lately, and from many different directions. Doyle probably felt that he had to give this action/probe some teeth, or else everyone would assume that it was just another cover-up."

Inez nodded slowly. "All right. I suppose your idea makes sense. I'll arrange for a data leak later today."

"But don't give Huromonus too much information," warned the lion. "I would let him know only that Susan vanished on the night that Donnelly and Tace were slain and that there could be a connection. Give Crazy Eddie too many leads and he's liable to end up investigating us."

"That wouldn't do," said Inez, biting her lower lip.

*No, it wouldn't,* thought the lion. He did not even want to consider the furor that would arise if Edward Huromonus—or anyone, for that matter—learned that they had illegally brought Gillian and Nick from stasis.

Inez took a deep breath. "Things are getting scary, Jerem Marth."

"I know. I'm a bit frightened myself."

She regarded him strangely for a moment. Then a cynical smile swept across her tanned face and dark pupils regarded him with amusement. "But Jerem—you're a Costeau. You're not supposed to get scared."

"I'll try to remember that."

At the end of the corridor, the huge black door slid open. On the other side, within the Council chambers, stood Doyle Blumhaven; a solemn figure perfectly framed by the rectangular portal.

"Inez—just in time." His voice seemed rigid, more controlled than usual. "Admiral Kilofski has reported that Jon's specialists have completed the first phase of data analysis. Jon himself will be coming back on line momentarily, with a full report."

They followed Blumhaven into the chamber and took their seats. The E-Tech Councillor began typing rapidly into his terminal. The lion imagined that most of E-Tech must be awake by now, each department standing by, ready to do their duty. The lion wondered idly whether Adam Lu Sang had been swept into the turmoil yet.

Across from the E-Tech Councillor sat Maria Losef, calmly trimming her DI haircut with a suction razor. She did not appear tense like Blumhaven, nor emotionally agitated like Inez. If anything, she looked bored.

In the center of the polished round table, the five-sided FTL displayed the blocky countenance of Admiral Kilofski, one of the Guardians' fleet commanders. He was carrying on a conversation with someone off-screen.

As the lion gazed at the Admiral, he found himself reflecting on the Guardians: on the great changes that had occurred within that organization since the time of his youth, since the cylinders had first learned that the Paratwa had also survived Earth's Apocalypse.

When the lion was a boy, he remembered seeing Guardians, impressive in their crisp black and gold uniforms, patrolling the cylinders; a military/police force nearly a million strong, responsible for maintaining intercolonial law and order. But over the years, the Council of Irrya had gradually altered their duties, assigning to them the formidable task of defending the Colonies against the returning assassins. Today, few Guardians remained in Earth orbit. E-Tech Security, in cooperation with various local policing authorities, currently enforced justice within the cylinders. Almost the entire Guardian force was now scattered out beyond Jupiter: over two million men and women, a rotating contingent of volunteers, the main force sequestered in miniature support colonies, the vanguard diligently poised in defense satellites and nuclear-armed attack ships. All were waiting for the possible invasion, waiting for the day when they might be ordered to go to war.

That day might have arrived.

On the FTL screens, the image switched to another camera shot. Jon Van Ostrand, Supreme Commander of the Guardians, appeared, seated behind a console.

Losef stopped shaving her skull. "Council of Irrya, Emergency Session, August 7th, 2363," she spoke for the recorders. "Confidential database, confidential access." She nodded to Van Ostrand. "We're all here. You can begin your formal report."

The Guardian Commander stared straight into his camera. "Approximately ninety minutes ago, remote sensors along our outermost detection perimeter picked up an incoming spacecraft, on a direct bearing toward the Colonies. Velocity of the intruder was a little under point two percent lightspeed at the moment of detection and has been dropping steadily, indicating a consistent rate of deceleration.

"Our first phase data analysis indicates that the intruder is approximately the size and shape of a medium transit shuttle, three to four hundred feet in length. Definitely of Earth design. If the intruder maintained its present course and rate of deceleration, it would arrive at the Colonies in about three weeks.

"The intruder is not broadcasting—at least nothing that we can pick up. We are still too far away for our penetration gear to be activated. Likewise, we're still too distant to ascertain the parameters of the intruder's computer shielding."

"ETA to intercept?" quizzed Losef.

"We should be able to intercept the intruder with a fleet of our manned attack ships in approximately five days."

"A ship the size of a transit shuttle," muttered Inez, "Not only travelling at point two psol, but decelerating as well?"

Van Ostrand grimaced. "Yes, the latter was a bit of a surprise. All of the Star-Edge technology we're aware of suggests that the pool-fusion propulsion systems that powered the original fleet needed the large mass of the starships to contain them. If, in fact, this intruder was launched from that fleet, then its high velocity is understandable. Up to twelve percent lightspeed was within the known limits of Star-Edge science. Point two psol is a relatively unsurprising figure if we assume that this small intruder is merely cruising toward us at its initial launch rate. But that doesn't explain how it's managing to slow itself down. As yet, we've detected no evidence of propulsion reactions, either accelerative or decelerative. Our best guess now centers around the concept that the intruder vessel is somehow being remotely controlled from their main fleet. Perhaps the bigger Paratwa ships have the ability to retard the velocity of their auxiliary craft."

"How would they do that?" Blumhaven wondered.

"Some sort of obverse laser sail technology?" Inez speculated.

"That's possible," said the Guardian Commander. "But we've detected no evidence of a sail."

Losef faced Inez. "Does La Gloria de la Ciencia have any research projects along those lines?"

She nodded. "Yes. But purely theoretical. And our current understanding of laser sail spaceflight calls for the presence of a very large metal sail in the immediate vicinity of the vessel itself."

"There's no sail," Van Ostrand reiterated. "What we've got is one small ship, heading straight for us. And that's it. Our projections suggest that we're dealing with an advance scout, sent ahead of their main fleet."

"To test our defenses," said Inez.

"Possibly."

"Can we destroy this intruder?" Losef questioned.

The Guardian Commander shrugged. "According to projections, a craft of this size would be no match for one of our attack ships. But that's just computers spouting data. Who really knows?"

The lion nodded. Van Ostrand did not have to spell things out. They were faced with the same apprehension that had faced the Council of Irrya for over half a century. *Unknown technology.* This intruder could be carrying weapons and defenses beyond their understanding.

Inez finished keying something into her terminal, then brought her attentions back to the FTL. "Jon, what about the vessel's course? Where's it coming from?"

"That's another surprise. Our primary detection systems have remained in solsynchronous orbit, concentrated along the axis of the Star-Edge fleet's original direction of departure from Earth. But this intruder is approaching from an entirely different angle, about seventy-five by thirty-five degrees polar from the original departure coordinates—way out of alignment."

Inez nodded thoughtfully.

"Is there any evidence," began Losef slowly, "to indicate that the intruder may not be travelling in a straight line?"

"No," replied Van Ostrand. "Current projections establish a rectilinear course. Naturally, it's possible that the vessel altered direction before we picked it up."

The lion frowned. The original Star-Edge ships had departed from the solar system—as a group, pooling their fusion drives—on a compromise heading that would take them in the general direction of the three targeted star systems: Epsilon Eridani, UY Ceti, and Tau Ceti—all suspected of bearing planets. A final destination was not to have been decided until the ships were nearly forty years out; by then, it was hoped that closer astronomical observations would reveal their best choice, or choices. A method of alternating stasis had been employed by the Star-Edge crews, so that at any one time, only a fraction of the explorers remained awake.

But at that forty-year juncture, the Colonies had later learned, the human crews had been overwhelmed by the Paratwa who had apparently infiltrated the entire Star-Edge project. Messages had been sent back to the Colonies suggesting that open revolt had broken out among the crews and that nuclear detonations had destroyed some of the ships. Today, it was known that those messages had been a ruse, transmitted back to civilization for two reasons: to hide the basic fact that the Ash Ock and their loyal breeds had assumed control as well as to allay suspicions that any stellar adventurers, whomever they might be, could someday return as enemies of the Colonies.

And now, at long last, a ship was returning. *But from a completely different direction?*

Blumhaven leaned forward, rested his elbows on the polished table. "Jon, assuming for a moment that the Paratwa fleet is following this advance scout on a direct line toward the Colonies, where would they be coming from?"

"From deep space. There's nothing in the neighborhood—in that particular direction, the nearest star is over half a million lightyears away."

"Then we'll have to assume," began Inez slowly, "that the intruder's approach coordinates are meaningless in terms of their fleet's location."

"Agreed," said Van Ostrand. "We're going to continue operating under the assumption that their fleet could come at us from any direction. I'm certainly not committing our main forces to that particular grid, aside from the intercepting attack ships."

"That sounds expedient," offered Inez.

Van Ostrand gave a weary smile. "*That* remains to be seen."

"Anything else?" grilled Losef.

"For now, I'm afraid not. I wish I had twenty bricks of hard data to send you, but we're still too much in the dark. My people estimate that it will be another two to three days before the intruder comes close enough for our main penetration gear to be activated. Until then—until we get a crack at this vessel's computer—I don't think we'll be able to substantially upgrade our information. Unless, of course, we detect something else."

An uneasy silence fell on the chamber.

The lion spoke: "Do we break this news to the Colonies as planned?"

Losef's cold blue eyes seemed to burn into him. "You are all aware of the ICN's views on this matter. No information should be released until a clear data base is established. We're just going to inspire needless confusion if we release this report now."

"Confusion for whom?" quizzed Inez sharply.

The two women locked gazes. The process of releasing information had been a point of dispute between La Gloria de la Ciencia and the ICN for the lion's entire two year reign as a Councillor, and probably well before that. To a degree, the lion understood some of the ICN's reluctance; the banking and finance consortium strove to maintain the status quo, to keep the intercolonial marketplace as stable as possible. Abrupt releases of major information tended to inflict microchanges on all facets of the cylinders' economies, affecting the trade flow between Colonies as well as disturbing long- and short-term investment strategies.

But there remained a fine line between maintaining economic well-being and depriving citizens of information that could deeply affect their lives. In this instance, the lion felt that the free flow of information took ultimate precedence.

Blumhaven said, "E-Tech believes that all data regarding the returning ship should be released as soon as possible. The Colonies must be kept fully abreast of the situation."

On the FTL screens, Van Ostrand nodded.

Losef's shoulders rose—a barely perceptible shrug. "The ICN is well aware of the Council's feelings on this matter. We will not dispute the decision."

Maria Losef remained the most eminently practical member of Council, thought the lion. Outvoted four to one, she would waste no time on additional debate. But other than her pragmatic skills, there was little to admire in the woman; at times the lion even acknowledged a vague feeling of animosity toward her. Of the four Councillors, she was by far the least accessible to the billion-plus people whom she helped govern. Even Blumhaven, with his demanding bureaucratic nature, espoused more obvious human considerations.

She typed something into her terminal. "I suggest that we release the Van Ostrand report—subject to the standard security deletions—simultaneously to all major intercolonial data networks and licensed freelancers. Would later this afternoon be acceptable?"

Everyone nodded in agreement.

"And with that report," added Blumhaven, "I believe that the Council should transmit a special note to the Order of the Birch, expressing our sympathies toward their loss."

Van Ostrand frowned. "Doyle, is that wise? I can't begin to count the number of times that the Order of the Birch has publicly criticized each and every member of this Council for our supposedly weak stand on the Paratwa issue. I see no reason to offer special patronage to them."

Inez broke in. "Jon, I agree with your feelings. But in

the coming months, I suspect that we're going to need all the public support we can gather. I think Doyle's right."

"A special sympathy note will be tagged onto our official release," said Losef, ending the discussion.

Inez turned to Blumhaven. "Has the Birch murder site been cleaned up yet?"

The E-Tech Director shook his head. "Not yet. We're shuttling a special investigation team in from Napoli. The murder site will not be disturbed until they arrive later this morning."

"I was wondering," Inez began casually, "whether a special team from La Gloria de la Ciencia would be permitted access to the scene as well?"

Blumhaven regarded her suspiciously. "For what purpose?"

"This team has done some remarkable plasma necropsy work, using experimental techniques. Possibly these techniques could locate evidence that might be overlooked by regular methodology."

For a moment, the lion thought that Blumhaven was going to refuse. But then he shrugged. "All right. Send them over in about six hours."

"Thank you," said Inez graciously.

*And I thank you, too,* thought the lion, keeping his smile to himself. Inez's ploy had worked.

Gillian, in disguise as a plasma necropsy researcher from La Gloria de le Ciencia, would be allowed to examine a fresh murder site. The lion was not sure whether such an investigation would actually uncover anything new, but Gillian and Nick had seemed to think it was extremely important, and the lion had convinced Inez that their eagerness was genuine.

This latest massacre, the sixth one in four months, and coming only five days after the Honshu tragedy, was likely to provoke a tremendous outcry throughout the Colonies. The Council would be put under heavy pressure to stop these insane killings. That was probably why Doyle

Blumhaven, normally reticent in allowing outside agencies
to directly intrude upon E-Tech Security investigations,
had relented to Inez's request. It was Blumhaven, in the
days ahead, who would come under the most fire to bring
an end to the massacres.

The lion acknowledged a fresh concern. The Order of
the Birch massacre at the meeting hall had occurred
within hours of the Guardians' detection of the returning
Paratwa starship. Coincidence? It had to be. He could not
imagine what possible connection there could be between
the two events.

"Is there any other business to attend to?" questioned
Losef.

No one responded. Losef ended the session with a
formal remark to the recorders.

"It's going to be a busy day," muttered Inez, as they
prepared to exit chambers.

The lion did not doubt it.

"Identification, please?" challenged the guard, raising his
thruster rifle to chest height.

Gillian whipped out his fake ID slab, supplied by Inez
Hernandez at La Gloria de la Ciencia, and extended the
holo. The young E-Tech Security man examined it for a
moment, then nodded. "I believe they're expecting you,
Mr. Dynassa. Your assistants have already arrived."

Gillian smiled. He had never met his so-called "assistants," had no way of even identifying them. He was not
a plasma necropsy specialist from La Gloria de la Ciencia
and his name certainly was not Amphos Dynassa. One

more prevarication and this whole fragile plan was liable
to collapse into a rubble of disconnected lies.

He made his way past the guard, through the rear service entrance to the Augustus J. Artwhiler Memorial Conference Center. There was a certain irony to the fact that
this huge building had been named after the deceased
Guardian Commander. Fifty-six years ago, Artwhiler had
been a real hindrance to Gillian's and Nick's search for
Reemul.

*The passing of time often rebuts the passing of the individual,*
Aristotle had once remarked. Gillian found himself smiling
at thoughts of his long-dead Ash Ock proctor, the Paratwa
who, along with Meridian, had been ultimately responsible
for Gillian's training. Aristotle had taught Gillian and
Catharine well, filling them with subtle knowledge, preparing their monarch Empedocles for some future role in the
Ash Ock's grand scheme of conquest.

*The circle of five—the sphere of the royal Caste. We were created
to unite the Paratwa and rule humanity.*

But the madness of the final days—the coming of the
Apocalypse—had interrupted the great plans of the royal
Caste, and the five monarchs of Gillian's unique Ash Ock
breed had been swept toward other destinies. The tways of
Aristotle had perished in a freak disaster in South Africa.
Gillian, still undergoing training, had lost Catharine in an
attack on their Brazilian base.

It was then that Sappho and Theophrastus had secretly
gathered up many of the surviving Paratwa, gained control
over the Star-Edge project, and extricated themselves from
the madness that was engulfing the planet. The fifth Ash
Ock, Codrus, had emigrated to the Colonies and set out to
cripple the technological growth of Earth's survivors, an effort that had been successful until he was caught and killed
fifty-six years ago.

*And now Sappho and Theophrastus are coming back.* Despite
the fact that the Guardians had detected only one small

ship, Gillian felt certain that a Paratwa fleet would not be far behind.

At the entrance to assembly hall F, two more guards demanded ID. Satisfied that Gillian's holo closely matched his appearance, one of the men whispered something into a hidden transceiver. The wide door hesitantly slid back, forming a slender opening. Gillian slipped through. The door slammed shut.

The sides of assembly hall F converged toward the front; the floor descended slightly, then rose into a stage. If viewed from overhead: a pie slice, with the pointed end lopped off by a dark burgundy wall—the stage backdrop—textured with enough holo-rivets to ignite and sustain a dozen simultaneous 3D projections.

On the stage itself, the main presenters' table bore a sextet of slumped-over bodies. The remainder of the massacre victims were scattered throughout the hall. Most looked grotesquely posed, as if they had been rigged from above by some crazed puppeteer who had suddenly cut their lines, permitting them to fall haphazardly into theater seats or collapse into misshapen bundles in the aisles. Less than ten feet in front of Gillian, resting perfectly on an armrest, lay a severed human hand, its fingers still gripping the plush fabric.

*Death:* a filmy layer of static, an overload of information penetrating sensory pores. It was as if he had stepped into a high-pressure whirlpool, where each droplet of water carried an electrical charge.

He drew a sharp breath. The air reeked of tissue preservative and a vaguely unpleasant odor that reminded him of stasis capsules. Probably the corpses had been sprayed by E-Tech immediately following the massacre. Nevertheless, it was a fresh murder site. Here he could do what could not be done in the terminal in Honshu. Here he could allow his mind to structure a gestalt of the violence. Here the unconscious assimilations could occur.

But first, purely cerebral demands had to be addressed.

He could not simply wander through this room in a semitrance, trying to metabolize and integrate the brutal deaths of dozens of people. Not without creating suspicions.

Too many *living* human beings, most garbed in E-Tech Security uniforms, were swarming through the huge space. Some examined bodies, others transferred equipment up and down aisles or stood together in small isolated huddles, whispering. From one of those huddles, a short potbellied man, wearing a lab smock stained in blood, spotted Gillian. He gave some orders to his group, then marched across the hall.

Tiny eyes in a jowled face appraised Gillian for a moment. Then the man stretched out his hand. "I'm Inspector Xornakoff, E-Tech Security. You're Mr. Dynassa?"

Gillian gave a nod and shook the extended palm, noting that there were only four digits. The Inspector's little finger was missing; the hand was shaped to encompass only a thumb and three fingers. Not surprisingly, the man's other palm boasted an identical arrangement.

"An accident of birth which my parents chose not to correct," smiled Xornakoff, taking notice of what Gillian had assumed to have been a subtle glance downward at the other hand. The Inspector kept his eyes riveted to Gillian's. "I've been assigned as your liaison. I hope you and your people can give us some help. This is the fourth Birch massacre I've personally investigated. Frankly, E-Tech could use a fresh perspective."

Gillian did not believe that his last remark was entirely sincere. "How many dead?"

"Only eighty-three this time." The Inspector shook his head. "Sickening. I'd sacrifice another set of fingers for just one clean shot at these bastards with a thruster rifle."

Gillian nodded solemnly.

"Of course, I suppose you're more accustomed to seeing this sort of thing than I am. Before the Birch killings began, I was assigned to one of our tactical divisions. Homicide was never my specialty." He paused. "I believe, however, that one of your assistants mentioned that you've been doing plasma necropsy research for a very long time."

"Eight years," replied Gillian, recalling the data profile of the fictional Amphos Dynassa that he had been supplied with earlier this morning. He hoped that his "assistants" had also done their homework.

The Inspector raised his eyebrows, as if doubting Gillian's answer. But that trick was an old one. Gillian said nothing and maintained a calm expression. Xornakoff continued smiling pleasantly.

*I'll have to be careful here.* Xornakoff projected the aura of a man skilled at detecting falsehood.

"Amphos!" The word cracked loudly through the silence of the hall, capturing glances from half the people in the room. Two lab-coated technicians, examining a decapitated body near where Gillian and the Inspector stood, frowned in dismay, as if to suggest: *This is a place of silence. Please show more respect for the dead.*

Gillian turned. Two women, one tall and pale-skinned, the other stocky and black, were approaching up the far left aisle. Each carried a red medical pouch.

"Quite a pair," said the Inspector. "Do the three of you work together often?"

Gillian did not have an answer for that one so he remained silent, keenly observing the approach of his two "assistants," pretending that he had not heard Xornakoff's question.

If these two women were not experts in the field of plasma necropsy, as promised, all three of them were going to be in a lot of trouble. Gillian had a fair understanding of postmortem examinations, especially where Paratwa victims were concerned, but about this specialized field he knew next to nothing. The data profile of Amphos Dynassa had contained a complete outline of the science, but there had been time to absorb only a few basic terms and definitions.

Nick's plan—to allow Gillian to examine this fresh murder site—had been conceived only last night, after they had learned of this latest massacre. Hastily executed plots always bore rough edges and this Inspector was doing his best to snag some splinters, catch a lie. Gillian wondered whether something in particular had made Xornakoff suspicious. Had the two approaching "assistants" been careless with information? Or was the Inspector merely exhibiting a natural distrust between E-Tech Security and La Gloria de la Ciencia?

Originally, Gillian had wanted to meet with the two women before coming here, and then arrive at the murder site together. But Nick had worried that Gillian's dearth of knowledge would be more sorely tested that way. Better to have the "assistants" come first, pave the way. That made a certain kind of sense. Still, arrangements could have been made for a prior rendezvous.

"Hello, Amphos," drawled the taller woman, sounding bored. She was a slim ponytailed blonde, wearing a gray blouse with a pair of tiny blue sapphires sewn across her nipples. Gillian stared at her, intrigued. And he found himself swept unexpectedly into an ancient memory.

He and Catharine were very young, perhaps ten years old. Meridian had taken them onto a South American air club: one of those cavernous low-atmosphere ships able to periodically simulate zero-gravity for their customers via rapid ascensions and dives. A dancer in bikini pants—a wing nut, Meridian had called her—had been the air club's star performer that day. The wing nut had had her nipples surgically altered into high-powered holo projectors and each time the air club travelled the arc, treating the passengers to a brief foray into weightlessness, she would somersault violently across the glassed-in performance chamber, spilling intricate holograms of her breasts in all directions. Catharine, transfixed, had giggled with delight at the exhibition, but Gillian had found himself more interested in the reactions of the air club's mostly male patrons.

Silent austere faces; eyes flashing back and forth, following the wing nut's gyrations with the rigorous intensity of tracking lasers. Awarenesses exclusively focused, to be sure, yet Gillian sensed that those possessed faces sought to fractionalize the moment even further, to cut through the density of spiralling holos, fragment the wing nut's performance until each instant was somehow transformed into something of value, like a series of treasured video stills. But even that conceptual pattern did not capture the essence of what he was witnessing. He left the air club feeling deeply confused by the experience.

Later that evening, as always, Gillian and Catharine had been asked by Aristotle to vocalize their impressions. Catharine stated that she had found the trip amusing, but ultimately silly and a waste of those few precious recreational hours that they were permitted. When it was his turn to confess, Gillian had stood in front of Aristotle's brutish-looking male tways, vainly attempting to explain his perceptions of the bewitched men in the air club, stumbling for words and images to clarify his feelings.

The tways of Aristotle had assumed identical frowns. "Why did you and Catharine not interlace? Is it not likely that the arising of Empedocles could have distilled your confusion?"

"Coming together did not seem . . . proper," Gillian had replied, feeling certain that such a vague response would anger his master, who would perhaps punish him for his lack of clarity. But Aristotle had merely smiled, and sent him on his way without so much as a word of disfavor.

And that same night, Gillian had experienced his first wet dream.

"Buff and I were telling the Inspector all about you," proclaimed the tall blonde with the sapphire nipples.

Gillian's awareness flashed back to the present. "Nothing bad, I hope."

"Oh, no," replied the second woman, Buff, a compact bear with skin the color of light fudge. Buff stood only a few inches taller than Nick, yet she looked capable of hurtling a Sumo wrestler through the netting of a freefall pen. "You know that Martha and I would never talk bad about our hero."

Martha and Buff. Gillian hoped that Nick knew what he was doing.

Xornakoff's smiling gaze remained pinned to Gillian's face. "Mr. Dynassa," he began, "I must admit to being professionally curious about your methodology. Plasma necropsy, after all, is still a fairly new field. I was wondering—do you plan to initially integrate the fluid linkages among victims or would the Vallochian transfer method be a more appropriate starting point?"

*Yes*, Gillian wanted to answer. He restrained himself.

"We'll utilize data from both methods," replied Buff, saving the day and locking a thick, well-muscled arm around Gillian's waist in the process. "We'll cross reference on a Kay-grid and index tissue anomalies separately."

Xornakoff raised his eyebrows. "I don't understand how that can be accomplished. Mr. Dynassa . . . could you elaborate?"

"It's very technical," uttered Martha.

The Inspector smiled politely. "I believe that Mr. Dynassa could make himself understandable."

Buff squeezed Gillian tightly and laid her head on his chest. "Inspector, I'm sure that Amphos can answer all your questions. But later, okay? Maybe we can go to lunch and trade work-tech." She stared up into Gillian's eyes and sighed with pleasure. "Amphos M. Dynassa, I can't wait to get my mouth on you again. After we finish here today, I'm hauling you straight over to my apartment."

Xornakoff's eyebrows arched another half-inch.

"It's not what you think, Inspector," sighed Martha, affixing Xornakoff with a bored gaze. "Buff's not interested in simple orasex."

"Martha, please!" snapped the heavy black woman, abruptly crushing Gillian against her side. "Don't be crass. Admit it—you're just jealous cause tonight it's my turn."

"Galvanic dentures," Martha revealed. "A little crushed ice, a set of acu-pins straight into the balls—some serious power-sucking."

Again, Buff released an exaggerated sigh. "Really, Martha. The voltages are regulated. You know that."

Martha rolled her eyes. Xornakoff cleared his throat and took a cautious step backward, his pasted smile fading beneath an ascending frown: a man doubtlessly considering the ramifications of electrified needles in the testicles.

Gillian held back a grin. "Inspector, I'd like to be alone with my assistants for a few minutes. Would you excuse us?"

Xornakoff nodded slowly, still uncertain of whether Buff and Martha were joking. Gillian led Buff toward the back of the assembly hall. Martha followed.

"Not bad," he offered, after the three of them were facing the rear wall to prevent lipreading. "Needles in the balls?" Gillian chuckled. "I've never heard of that one."

"It takes some getting used to," offered Martha, not smiling.

Gillian decided to change the subject. "At any rate, you saved me from an impending jam. Another few minutes with our Inspector and my cover would have evaporated."

"You're very welcome," chirped Buff, releasing his waist from her iron grip.

"Are you both wearing scramblers?"

"Extra yes!" spouted Buff. "Are you kidding? This is E-Tech Security. They probably have enough surveillance gear in this hall to open a factory."

"Bug heaven," agreed Martha, toying with one of her blonde ponytails.

"How good is your shielding?"

"As good as it comes," said Buff. "How's yours?"

Gillian nodded. "I think we're safe enough. What have you found out so far?"

"Not much," said Buff. "Other than the fact that Inspector Xornakoff is one suspicious puppy. Bend over and he'd sniff your ass for a week."

Martha wagged her head in agreement.

"What we got isn't much more than what's already been released to the freelancers," continued the black woman. "This was a local meeting of the Order of the Birch, advertised and open to the public. About seven hundred people attended. Up on the stage, the meeting's special guest—a low-level Birch screamer named O'Donahee—had just finished a ten-minute rant about why we should vaporize one of Neptune's micromoons with a few thousand nuclear devices. Mister Neptune believed that such a vivid example of our atomic destructive capabilities would provide a noticeable warning to any returning Paratwa: 'The Colonies are not playing games, *we mean business,*' et cetera, et cetera.

"Anyway, the crowd loves this kind of nonsense, so at the end of Mister Neptune's speech, they're all agitated and up out of their seats—"

Gillian interrupted. "And that's when this heckler starts carrying on."

"Yeah," Buff continued, "bad man one—Slasher. And then Shooter appears on the stage with his thruster and it's boom-boom time.

"Our guest speaker—sweet Mister O'Donahee—is blown right off the stage and lands in the third row of the audience, probably dead even before his spine broke across the back of a chair. And the other Birch presenters, seated at the table, were killed execution style—one shot each to the back of the head." Buff paused. "We think that might mean something."

"I doubt it," said Gillian, closing his eyes, trying to intellectually piece together the images. "Shooter was probably just eliminating his nearest threats, and as quickly as possible. I'll bet the next thing he did was to turn his thruster on the people going for the side exits."

Buff turned to him with a surprised look. "I'm impressed. That's the way that E-Tech figures things happened."

"Keep facing the wall," Gillian urged. "Xornakoff is bound to have lipreaders watching us."

"Maybe the Inspector was even smart enough to have inserted microcams in this wall," suggested Martha.

"Wouldn't matter. What I'm wearing will scramble even passive gear."

"Jesus," muttered Buff. "Just how illegal are you?"

Gillian smiled. He had asked for the best and Jerem Marth's people had provided it. The meshwire shirt and tracking gear were not as potent—nor as detectable—as a genuine AV scrambler, but they were banned hardware nonetheless. If Xornakoff knew what Gillian was wearing, the three of them would probably be arrested on the spot.

He still felt exposed, however, and he knew why. His Cohe wand remained with Nick. The midget had considered this foray to the murder site risky enough without the illicit energy weapon—trademark of the Paratwa—on Gillian's person.

"Do you two really know about plasma necropsy?"

"Some," said Buff. "I mean, we can get by as research assistants. We took a couple of crash courses back around the time the massacres began, four months ago. And we've been plugging into sleep modules at least two or three nights a week. As a matter of fact, I just recently completed La Gloria de la Ciencia's advanced forensics course."

"But this isn't your regular occupation," Gillian concluded.

"No."

"What is?"

Martha, grinning, fingered the sapphire on her right nipple.

Buff answered slowly. "We don't actually work for La Gloria de la Ciencia. We're sort of . . . security consultants."

"Who *do* you work for?"

"We're sort of freelance."

Gillian sighed. Nick was playing games again. The midget had claimed that the two women were experts from La Gloria de la Ciencia. Half-true, perhaps. *I'll have to sort things out later.*

"Did Xornakoff give you any information about what E-Tech thinks about the massacre? Any conclusions?"

"Same story as before," said Buff. "E-Tech believes that we're dealing with two crazed killers, who are imitating the actions of a real Paratwa. About the only notable difference in these killings was that the assassins didn't utter any of their 'Long live the Order of the Birch,' or 'The Paratwa must not be allowed to return' crap. I guess, under the circumstances, our bad men felt that such statements simply would not have been proper." Buff grinned. "At least we're not dealing with hypocrites."

"Any obvious connections among the victims?" Gillian asked. "Some facet that makes any of those eighty-three stand out from the hundreds who survived?"

Martha shook her head.

"Anything at all?" Gillian prodded.

"Well," said Buff slowly, "you're always going to find some connections when you have this large a sample. I mean, we've got six victims who were born in the same Colony. We've got fifteen who worked in the shipping industry, thirty victims who were males between the ages of twenty-six and twenty-nine, seven people with minor communicable diseases—colds, mostly, plus a couple of different strains of flu.

"We've got fourteen who've been in psychplans at least

once in their life—not surprising when you consider the crowd. We've got thirty-seven confirmed pet owners—"

"I get the picture," said Gillian. "How many injured this time?"

"Eighteen were hospitalized," said Buff. "Most of them suffered minor injuries—grazed by thruster fire or banged up in the dash for the doors. All expected to recover."

Gillian nodded. "How did the killers escape?"

Buff shrugged. "The same modus operandi as in the other Birch killings. Apparently, they put away their weapons and blended into the mass of people squeezing through the exits."

"Which exits?"

"Witnesses disagree on that point," said Buff. "But the majority seem to believe that Slasher moved toward the front of the hall, then made his way through the door below stage right. Shooter jumped off the stage and headed for the back exits."

*Same pattern as in Honshu,* Gillian mused. *They head toward each other and when they're close, they change directions and start moving away from each other, on perpendicular courses.* And as in Honshu, the same shadow of confusion fell across awareness.

*Something is not right.*

A sudden question occurred to him. "Slasher and Shooter—were they wearing crescent webs?" Gillian recalled that at several of the previous massacres, the killers were believed to have used the near-invisible defensive energy screens.

Buff shrugged. "Hard to be sure. A couple of the survivors who were close to Slasher reported hearing a low hum—that could be evidence of an active crescent web. And several people said that a man in the front row managed to get off a blast at Shooter with a low-powered thruster. They said that it looked like this man scored a direct hit, but that Shooter wasn't bothered in the slightest. That might indicate a strong energy shield. But we'll never know for certain. The man who fired the shot was killed an instant later."

"Slasher fights with a dagger in each hand," Gillian mused. "But Shooter uses only one weapon—the spray thruster—holding the gun in one hand." He hesitated, unsure of where his thoughts were leading. "Is Shooter right-handed or left-handed? Or is he ambidextrous?"

Buff gave another shrug.

"He's right-handed," said Martha firmly.

"How do you know?" Gillian probed.

"'Cause after the first massacre, Buff and I managed to question a couple of witnesses after E-Tech got through with them."

"The first massacre," recalled Gillian. "That was the restaurant slayings in Brilicondor Colony?"

"Yeah," chirped Buff, "that's right. About four months ago. Now I remember. One of the witnesses described how Shooter came marching into the restaurant through a robotized service tunnel—one of those ultraskinny corridors used by the mech waiters. Anyway, Shooter had to squeeze through there sideways—he could barely fit. And this witness said that when he came out of the tunnel, he was leading with his right—the weapon was in his right hand."

A vague excitement coursed through Gillian. "And the other massacres?"

"All the same profile," said Martha.

Buff nodded vigorously. "Yeah, now that I think about it, Martha's correct. Shooter's a rightie."

Gillian's excitement grew. "You're sure? I don't remember any mention of this anywhere."

Buff shrugged. "No one thought it was important. But I recall a bunch of witnesses saying the same thing. The killer with the boom-boom gun is right-handed."

*He's right-handed and he wears a crescent web*, thought Gillian. An energy shield was almost impenetrable at the front and rear, but it was weak at the sides to allow air circulation and to permit the arms to extend weapons. Nevertheless, a man with an active shield sacrificed full range of movement when utilizing regular line-of-motion firearms. No matter how fast Shooter was, he would not be able to wield his thruster as freely with an active web. Consequently, he would always enjoy a distinct combat advantage toward the side where he carried the weapon. If he was marching in a straight line, he would possess greater firefield coverage to his right.

When the killers were marching toward each other, they were roughly balanced—Shooter, leading with his right, Slasher, able to wield the flash daggers in both directions. Supporting firefields, meshing together to sweep across nearly a 360-degree combat radius. But in each of the massacres, when the killers came within sight of one another, their pattern changed. Shooter continued marching in a straight line. But Slasher *always* cut left, began moving on a perpendicular course.

And at that moment, they sacrificed the advantage of supporting firefields. When Slasher cut to the left—Shooter's right—all of their weapons were concentrated to one side. In terms of firefield coverage, they had shifted from a 360-degree to a 180-degree combat radius. Slasher should cut to the *right*, not to the left, in order to cover that huge blind spot. But instead, Slasher moved in the one direction that made both of the men—or both tways—more vulnerable to attack from the rear. In this instance, more vulnerable to enemy action from the right side of the hall.

Gillian knew that this was the uncertainty that had been bothering him since his trek through the Yamaguchi terminal, three days ago. At that time, he must have subconsciously sensed that Shooter was right-handed, and that Slasher's change of direction created a senseless tactical situation. If the killers were transceiver-linked humans, it was perhaps possible that such an anomaly was simply the result of poor planning that had eventually metamorphosed into a bad habit. But even that seemed remote. And if this were a Paratwa . . .

A fluidly ambidextrous Paratwa, operating without a crescent web, might adopt such a peculiar attack pattern. But if Martha was correct—and Gillian sensed that she was—Shooter was *not* ambidextrous. And he *did* wear a crescent web, which limited his full range of arm motion and attached extra significance to the fact that he was right-handed. No Paratwa that Gillian knew of would ever operate in such an unnatural way.

*Then what are we dealing with here?*

From deep within his body an answer beckoned: a hot rhythm—pure stimuli—originating at the base of his spine, pulsing upward, trying to penetrate the translucent mask separating physical sensation from the cold logic of cerebral consciousness. Like water on a glass window, the hot rhythms condensed, transformed themselves into a wet sheen on the face of awareness. Clarity whispered. And Gillian knew that it was time to open that window, allow the unconscious assimilations to occur.

He turned to Buff. "I want the two of you to walk me through the room—quickly. I don't want any distractions. Keep Xornakoff and anyone else away. Tell them that I'm concentrating. Don't talk to me unless it's absolutely necessary."

Buff regarded him curiously for a moment. Then she shrugged. "Lead the way."

He marched down the center aisle with the women on either side of him, following a trail of dried blood meandering from the back of the hall to the base of the stage. They passed small groups of E-Tech personnel; men and women studiously examining corpses or parts of corpses: lopped off arms and legs, a head wedged between two chairs, an ear resting on the lap of a lifeless female. Gillian ignored them, tuned out all distractions, allowed concentration to follow its own path, freeing himself of intellectual constructs and assumptions, with one exception:

*Why does Slasher always cut to the left?*

And then the gestalt was upon him, overwhelming the

limitations of normal analysis. Distractions disappeared; consciousness was swamped by a raging stream of raw data. The window opened and for one timeless instant he perceived the body-ridden assembly hall as a congestion of opposing forces. He saw the movements of the killers and the victims and he began to understand the dynamics of what had occurred. And he felt his head pivoting to the right, scanning the right side of the room—the killers' blind spot—searching that 180-degree arc with unbridled intensity, searching for the missing fragment of the puzzle.

But at the preinstant of clarity, when comprehension beckoned from the deeper reaches of his mind, when the wild stream of data was about to be damned by a wall of logic—at that instant, Catharine appeared.

The familiar bubble of golden light. Her elfin face shimmering within that cloud of brilliance, the wild brown hair dancing across her narrow shoulders, the blue eyes gazing at him . . .

She stood a mere fifteen feet away, between two upraised seats. *So close.* Longing overwhelmed him. He stumbled forward, thoughts adrift, unfocused. His arms reached out for her.

She moved away. Rejection. Her denial restored mental clarity.

*She's just a memory-shadow,* he reminded himself sternly, even while desperately wishing that it were not so. *She's just an apparition—unreal.*

Her lips moved; as in the Honshu terminal, she was trying to speak to him. He squinted, unable to comprehend the silent mouthings. Her face darkened with anxiety and her eyes seemed to cry out to him, begging to be understood. The pain on her face mirrored his own.

*What are you trying to say?* he pleaded. *What is it that you want me to know?*

Even as Gillian's beseechments echoed through his own mind, the golden bubble began to shrink in upon itself, dissolving Catharine's countenance into a pale cloud of lurking energies. But before she vanished completely, before the golden light faded into nothingness, some fragment of her consciousness seemed to thrust itself outward, straining mightily to bridge the vast canyon that kept them apart.

And in that fragile moment, Catharine's voice soared through him. Her words pulsed with clarity, as sharp and potent as if she were alive.

*You must bring on the whelm, Gillian. We must be united—forever.*

And then she was gone, the golden light reinternalized—a fading memory. His gestalt collapsed; the data stream became a raging waterfall, plunging back down into his subconscious. He was alone again, his functions delimited to the logic of ordinary intellect. But feelings remained . . .

A stirring in his guts: part hurt, part anger. The hurt was obvious; the reality that Catharine was no longer living flesh remained a wound that he knew would never completely heal. And the anger . . .

He felt as if he had been made the victim of some cruel joke. It must be their monarchial consciousness—Empedocles—who wanted them to be together again. It was their Ash Ock, from the lost nether regions of Gillian's soul, who desired the whelm, and who voiced his desire through Catharine. But even if Gillian could find the proper fulcrum to again create the whelm—that dialectic of unity/duality—he sensed that Empedocles could not be sustained for any length of time.

Certainly not forever.

*Don't you understand,* he projected bitterly. *Catharine is gone. She's dead.*

There was no response.

"Are you all right?" a man's voice whispered.

Gillian turned his head, saw Buff's dark face, her solemn eyes pinched with concern. Martha stood a pace away, wearing a frown.

"Are you all right?" asked Inspector Xornakoff again.

Gillian was surprised to find himself hunched over one of the auditorium chairs. He straightened, took a deep breath.

"I'm fine."

The Inspector regarded him silently, the heavy jowls camouflaging suspicion.

"Sometimes," Gillian lied, "all this—" he spread out his arms, encompassing the array of bloody corpses "—gets to me." He allowed a weak smile. "I should know by now not to have such a heavy breakfast. I believe necropsy work is better performed on an empty stomach."

Xornakoff nodded in sympathy, but his eyes remained skeptical.

"Why don't we get out of here for a while," suggested Buff. "A walk might help you feel better, help you regain your balance."

Martha, playing with one of her blue sapphires, agreed.

—from *The Rigors*, by Meridian

*Once, when my master Theophrastus had completed a particularly challenging research effort and allowed that he was in the mood for open discourse, I asked him to speculate on a puzzling facet of Ash Ock existence.*

*What brought about the great division among the royal Caste? Why did these five super-Paratwa, created to function as a unified group—like a quintet of exquisitely trained singers—fail to reach this ideal?*

*My master settled his tways into the invisible web of a zephyr seat—just one of the numerous self-inventions that littered his private chamber*—*and leaned back, his somber faces lost in thought. The zephyr's powerful airjet streams, rising from the floor to suspend his collocating bodies, whined gently, automatically adjusting to micromovements. But other than the lilting melodies from these invisible geysers, suspending his tways on an unseen fountain of bridled air, the chamber remained cloaked in silence.*

*Theophrastus finally replied, speaking through the tway whose public name was Port. Naturally, no one knew the real designations of his Ash Ock tways—the secret names. But somehow, Port and Starboard had always served to delineate his stature and define his curious humor.*

*"Imperfections, Meridian. The royal Caste was a flawed crystal from the outset, a conglomerate of entities too unique to ever truly function as a unit."*

*I permitted both my tways to smile. "Imperfections within the child suggest imperfections within the mother."*

*"True, of course. But that conclusion, Meridian, I would be wary of quoting too freely. The Ash Joella have sharp ears."*

*I acknowledged Theophrastus's percipience. This newest breed of Paratwa—the Ash Joella—when not involved in their primary duties of shepherding mature Os/Ka/Loq plant life, tended to wander through the Biodyssey, overhearing all manner of conversation. Some assumed that such Ash Joella attentiveness provided diatribes for Sappho's ears.*

*"Nevertheless," I continued, "my root question remains unanswered. Granted the Ash Ock were, as you say, 'a flawed crystal,' they also collectively possessed the ability to grow, to learn, to correct that flawed structure."*

*"In theory, perhaps," conceded Theophrastus. "But in practice, very real differences existed among us. Codrus, for example, simply lacked the intellectual fortitude to make the great leap of understanding into the larger sphere of perception. As Sappho has frequently suggested, Codrus was simply too planetbound in his thought to ever truly comprehend the second coming. It was not merely his financial skills that made him the perfect choice to leave behind in the Colonies."*

*I could not help but agree with Theophrastus in this regard. Ultimately, it was probably fortuitous that Codrus had perished during the Gillian/Reemul debacle. The Codrus that I remembered from the days of the pre-Apocalypse would have been shocked by the true magnitude of the second coming.*

"But a lack of intellectual fortitude does not account for Aristotle," I pointed out.

"Correct. Aristotle was an intellect of rare power." Theophrastus paused. "Obsessions, Meridian—obsessions also account for the imperfections within the crystal. I, for example, am quite obsessed. The research I engage in, the inventions I produce—even if it were not Sappho's will, I would still spend every spare moment in the laboratories.

"But my obsession with the purity of science can flourish, in one form or another, within a wide spectrum of political systems, chiefly because it can remain apart from those systems. Aristotle's obsession—with the political process itself, with the interaction of disparate, emotion-driven entities—did not grant him such freedom. He began to involve himself too closely in the very processes he was studying."

"The dangers of emotional entanglement," I mused. "They ultimately brought about his downfall. But what about the fifth Ash Ock?"

My master's faces melted into sly grins. "Ahh, Meridian. We now begin to approach your true target. It is not the overall failure of the royal Caste that fascinates you. The imperfection of the whole is merely a path to lead you to the imperfection of the one. Your own emotional involvement drives this discussion."

I laughed. As always, Theophrastus was able to cut to the heart of the matter. "You're right," I admitted. "Ever since we learned that a tway of Empedocles still lives, I have found my thoughts returning to bygone days."

For a time, my master regarded me with calm gazes. Then Port broke into a smile while Starboard's face assumed a dark scowl. Theophrastus had split into his separate tways.

"Gillian survives," said Port.

"And so does Empedocles," added Starboard, his voice grim. "The consciousness of an Ash Ock monarch can perish only when both tways are killed."

*"But although tway and monarch are still alive,"* continued Port, *"their days are numbered."*

Starboard shook his head sadly. *"Arrhythmia of the whelm."*

*"Sappho says that there is a way to save him,"* I replied carefully.

*"Yes,"* admitted Port. *"There is a way."*

*"But Gillian/Empedocles remains a traitor,"* uttered Starboard. *"The Ash Ock will not rescue him. He will be allowed to perish."*

*"The arrhythmia of the whelm,"* I whispered, feeling a sense of dread at the mere thought of that unique Ash Ock affliction.

*"A fitting end,"* said Starboard.

"Are you still a child of the Spirit of Gaia?" inquired Lester Mon Dama.

Susan, standing with him just inside the entrance to the tiny chapel, shook her head. "I gave up the practice . . . a long time ago." She was not about to lie to this man, certainly not if she expected his assistance.

The bearded priest removed his robe, and hung the garment on a hook beside the hand-carved wooden door. Underneath, he wore casual attire: a white cotton shirt and baggy beige trousers. Not very stylish, Susan thought. But then true believers did not have to be.

Smiling, Lester Mon Dama rammed the door's thick mechanical bolt into place. "The Reformed Church of the Trust tries hard to live up to its name, Susan. But unfortunately, Southern Irrya still awaits the blessings of neighborhood rejuvenation. It is best to keep the locks secured."

She nodded, feeling awkward now that she was actually here, now that she was ready to spill her guts and request help from a man who was almost a total stranger.

He led her toward the front of the chapel, past the hanging curtain of thin misk hoses upon which worshipers suckled during formal ceremonies. Misk was the Church's holy sacrament—a strange, milky-white liquid which once had been distilled from fault chemicals created on Earth during the original Church's burial ceremonies. But with the cessation of Earth entombments, the Church's misk storehouses gradually had been depleted. Susan recalled reading somewhere that this new variation of misk was being manufactured and processed in low Earth orbit.

She followed him through a side door, down a dank and narrow hallway, and into an office. A scarred oval desk with embedded monitors, four aging chairs, and disorderly stacks of boxes had been crammed into the tiny space. Walls were peppered with antique telephone directory covers, all individually sealed in translucent preservation envelopes. Most of the faded yellow covers were labelled: BELL OF PENNSYLVANIA, SOUTHWESTERN BELL, NEW ENGLAND BELL. Among the pre-Apocalyptics, "Bell" must have been a very powerful man to control such a vast communications empire.

"I've a weakness for twentieth-century telephonic materials," the priest admitted. "I've been collecting this sort of thing since I was a boy."

He motioned Susan to a chair, then sat down across from her. "And I do apologize for the furnishings. Unfortunately, my parish is not among the larger ones. And it is no secret that our Church as a whole grows poorer with each passing year."

*Poorer since the time of the Great Trauma,* Susan mused. Back around the turn of the century, before the original Church of the Trust had been betrayed by the Ash Ock Codrus, the religious order had wielded great power and influence throughout the Colonies.

"I must say, Susan, that I was quite surprised to receive your call the other day. I'm sorry I couldn't see you sooner, but the Church can, at times, be a demanding institution." He ran a hand through his long straight hair. There were speckles of gray there, she noticed. Lester Mon Dama was no longer the young man she remembered from fifteen years ago.

"You say that you're in some kind of trouble . . . something that you can't go to the authorities with?"

She nodded rapidly, feeling more stupid by the minute. But she did need help, and she needed it right away. Besides that, she had to talk to *someone* about the events of the past week.

She blurted out the whole story: the Honshu massacre, the feeling that she somehow knew the assassin, the E-Tech Security men trying to kill her, and their own murders later that same evening. She told Lester of Aunt Inez's betrayal. And at last, she told him of her persistent feeling that the killer still wanted her dead.

For what seemed a long time, the priest said nothing. Then Lester Mon Dama shook his head. "You should be thankful that you're still alive. It's . . . miraculous . . . that you escaped."

She nodded.

"In the Spirit of Gaia, Susan . . . how may I help you?"

"I need a favor. I need you to go the North Epilson office district for me, to the Clark Shuttle Service building. I need to get a message to someone there."

"This message cannot be delivered via phone?"

"No." She hesitated. "I'm afraid that this assassin . . . he might trace the call. Those two E-Tech Security men . . . they probably saw my desk calendar, passed on that information to the killer."

Lester pursed his lips. "Even if that is so, it would seem unlikely that this assassin could be capable of operating telesurveillance on everyone—"

"These assassins are killing people with high-tech weapons," Susan reiterated. "The freelancers claim they're using virgin technology. If that's true, then who knows what they're really capable of."

The priest shrugged. "Could you not call from a public place—"

"No. They could trace it. I don't want to leave them any leads. I know that I probably sound paranoid. But I'm . . . very afraid."

"All right, Susan. Under the circumstances, I can certainly understand your extreme caution." He shook his head in wonder. "Two brushes with death! Twice you escaped the Conversion of Souls. It could be claimed that you had been spared by the Gaian Spirit itself!"

Susan said nothing. She had come here to elicit the help of a man who had once befriended her. His religion meant nothing to her. Hopefully, Lester Mon Dama would keep in mind that Susan Quint was not a worshiper.

"Of course," Lester continued breezily, "a bodily existence such as your does not suggest the simplistic rejoinder that spiritual intervention saved your life." He smiled warmly, in a way that suggested they shared some deep confidence with one another. "The roots, after all, remain beyond the touch of us mortals. And in life—within the human sphere—we must cherish those things which grant us our strength. Doubtlessly, your special experiences have taught you this."

She shifted uncomfortably in her chair. She had no idea what he was talking about.

For a moment, Lester seemed to gaze at her with unrestrained intensity. Then his face drifted into a weary smile. "I'm sorry, Susan. I'm . . . not making much sense, am I?"

"Not really." She cleared her throat. "And as I said, I'm not even a member of the Church anymore."

"Of course."

"But what did you mean about my special experiences?"

He hesitated. "I was referring to the demise of your parents. I guess I was trying to say that children—like yourself—who lose their parents at an early age . . . children in those circumstances tend to be more . . . survival-oriented."

"I suppose we do," she answered uneasily, hoping that this was the end of any discussion about her parents.

He changed the subject. "Susan—this message you want me to deliver. This person at Clark Shuttle Service will be able to help you with your predicament?"

She hesitated. "Not exactly. You see, I'm supposed to meet this person . . . tonight. But the killers will certainly know about our rendezvous. They may be watching his offices and home, waiting for me to show up. I can't risk contacting him, even to cancel.

"That's why I need you to get a message to this man, postponing our rendezvous. No one will be suspicious of a priest going to his office. You probably know as well as I that many Church people regularly solicit in North Epsilon."

Lester Mon Dama's cheeks lifted into a delicate smile. "We prefer the term 'supplication' for our fundraising activities. But tell me, Susan—this rendezvous—is it of vital importance? Please correct me if I'm wrong—or tell me its none of my business, if you prefer—but it sounds as if you're asking me to break a date for you."

She sighed. "Yes, it's a date. But you must understand that this is a high-end matchup, not just an ordinary night out. I've never scored at this level before. This man is being groomed to be the next head of his corporation. I've spent years working toward such a goal. At this stage, I can't afford any setbacks."

The priest stared at her.

She swallowed, continuing rapidly. "I was thinking that if you went to this man, and explained that you were my priest and that I was involved in a deeply personal matter that required that I be out of circulation for several weeks . . . well, the Church still remains a very important institution—"

"—And because I'm a priest, my explanation would carry greater weight. Your status with this man would not be jeopardized."

"Exactly."

Lester gave a noncommittal shrug. "Susan . . . I realize now that you didn't come here for advice. But I feel bound to speak frankly. I think that you should contact your Aunt Inez, work things out with her. Give her a second chance.

"And as a practical matter, in terms of breaking a date, I would suspect that your Aunt, being an Irryan Councillor, would be better suited to smoothing out your prospective relationship with this Shuttle Service man."

She shook her head vigorously. "No. You don't understand! Aunt Inez didn't believe me! And even if she changed her mind . . . things just wouldn't be the same between us."

The priest frowned. "Susan, people make mistakes. And most often, given the opportunity, they will go out of their way to correct those mistakes. I do not know your Aunt personally, but I've always found her political strains to be calming, and laden with intelligence. She has always struck me as a woman of great compassion."

Susan felt herself becoming angry. *I shouldn't have come here. This was a mistake. Priests have a distorted view of the world.*

She raised her chin. "So you won't help me?"

He favored her with a soothing smile.

*Arrogant,* she thought. *And so condescending.* She rose from the chair. "I have to go now. Thank you for listening to me. I trust that you will keep my visit here in strictest confidence—"

He raised his arm. "Susan, please. I understand your anger. But you must listen to your own words. What you're saying to me makes very little sense."

She clenched her teeth. "Don't tell me about making sense! In a lot of different ways, being a priest doesn't make much sense! So don't sit here in judgment—"

"Please sit down," he pleaded. "And just listen to me for a few more minutes. If you're willing to do that, then you have my word as a Priest of the Trust that I will deliver this message for you, and with no further 'judgment.' "

She sat down, still fuming.

He sighed. "Susan, I remember when you were a young girl, running around in your parents' parish following sacrament. You always had so much energy, so much . . . *life-force*." He hesitated. "And I'm not speaking strictly in religious terms here, either. What I mean is, you were a very active little girl; demanding, but not rude; opportunistic, but not selfish. You couldn't know it at the time, but many in your parish were in awe of your parents, for being blessed with such a child.

"After their death, we didn't see much of you—your father's elder brother took you into his family, and they were not members of the Church." Lester gave a sad smile. "In all fairness, I don't believe anyone could blame them for wanting to get you as far away as possible from the influences of the Trust. But even though we didn't see you any longer, you were well-remembered."

"Of course I was," Susan cracked bitterly. "Everyone was bound to remember the poor little girl whose parents killed themselves so they could be immediately entombed on Earth."

"True," Lester admitted. "Their demise naturally brought out the most profound sympathies in people. But Susan—and I tell you this truthfully—you were deeply missed by many, myself included."

Susan bit her lip, holding back tears. *Don't do this to me. I can't take all that hurt again. It's too hard. I don't want it!*

Lester nodded with understanding. "I know, Susan, I know. That sort of pain is no easy thing. And probably it will never go away, at least not completely. But I think it's important that you remember those feelings.

"You dealt with your parents' deaths remarkably well, considering the fact that you were eleven years old and had no siblings." He hesitated. "I always suspected that you would be able to handle your loss . . . more easily, perhaps, than most other children would have been capable of handling it."

He shook his head. "Susan, I have not seen nor heard from you in fifteen years, not since the day your aunt and uncle removed you from our influence. And suddenly, today, here you are in front of me again—a grown woman, and a remarkably beautiful one at that. But Susan, and I say this to you with all my heart, perhaps you have dealt *too* well with that terrible loss."

She clenched her hands together on her lap. *No matter what you say, I won't cry. I don't want to feel those feelings—not ever again!*

"I'm not speaking to you as a psychplan counsellor, Susan, nor as a priest. I'm speaking as one human being to another. And I say to you that right now, you are making very little sense.

"You are worried about breaking a date. You are worried about how a certain man, whom I gather you as yet share no real relationship with, will react to your failing to spend an evening in his company. In almost the same breath, you claim that a pair of vicious killers want you dead.

"I would say, Susan—and I'm putting this as gently as possible—that you have your priorities confused. Your life is more important than the repercussions of a broken engagement."

Susan rubbed a tear from her cheek.

The priest stared at her for a moment, and then he unsealed the protective cover from one of his telephonic directories and began thumbing through the book, absently glancing at large advertisements competing for attention on the fragile, preservative-treated pages. For a time, he seemed completely lost in thought. Then:

"Frankly, Susan, I don't know exactly how I'd react if I were faced with your particular dilemma. I can certainly understand a reluctance to return to your aunt, given your strong feelings that she betrayed you." He shrugged. "Maybe such feelings will lessen over time. Given that, perhaps an alternate course of action would be for you to stay out of sight, at least temporarily." Lester paused. "You could seek sanctuary within the Church."

An awful feeling rose within her, a hopeless despair. And that phrase: *Seek sanctuary*. The words seemed to carry an emotional charge totally out of proportion to their simple phonetics, touching some delicate nerve deep inside her, triggering a long-buried set of memories. Susan heard her mother's voice, that soft lilting tone that she had learned—much later in life—to equate with religious fanaticism.

*The Trust demands our constant obedience, young lady. And someday, Susan, our duty will be rewarded and the glorious Earth will be ours forever, and we will dwell within the Gaian Spirit. Never forget that the Earth is the place of all beginnings, our true homeland, the very roots of our passion.*

Susan found herself lowering her head, as she had been forced to do as a child when mother recited the prayers of the Trust.

*Blessed are the rootmakers, for they maintain the sands of time. Blessed are the dustmakers, for they surround the roots and give them strength. Blessed are the rainmakers, for they pour from the heavens and deliver the dust unto the place of all beginnings.*

"I am a child of Gaia," Susan whispered in response.

*We are all the children of Gaia. On Earth, dwells our eternal spirit. The path of our mortal journeys leads forever downward, to the roots, to the soil from which life sprang. Do you understand, Susan?*

"Yes, mother."

"Susan?"

"Yes, mother?"

"Susan! It's Lester Mon Dama. Susan, wake up!"

She raised her eyes and stared across the desk at the priest, seeing him as he was many years ago: the long straight hair thicker and darker, the trimmed beard free of gray and white speckles, the Lester Mon Dama of Susan's childhood.

And then the pain erupted: the old feelings of her parents' suicide, the agonies that she had vowed, long-ago, never again to allow full release.

"I don't know what to do!" she cried, and a congestion of endless sobs overwhelmed her. Lester came to his feet and Susan hurled herself into his embrace, holding onto him as if he were the only real thing in the universe.

"Help me," she wailed. "I can't do this again!"

"It's all right," murmured the priest. "You can survive it. You're a strong person, stronger than you give yourself credit for."

"No! Not again! I can't!"

"Shhh." Large strong hands patted her gently. "It's all right, Susan. Everything will be all right."

For a time she stood there in his arms, quietly sobbing. Eventually the cascade of tears slowed, reaching some fundamental threshold where conscious choice again became an option. *Enough.* Her decision ended the tears; it was as if a switch inside her snapped shut, closeting the pain, injecting a wall between Susan Quint and her emotions, a translucent barrier protecting the present from the past.

She stared over Lester's shoulder at his scarred office walls, suddenly alive with the priest's ancient collection of preserved telephonic covers. She wiped her wet face across Lester's shirt sleeve and pulled away from him. A lone tear trickled along the edge of her mouth and she smeared it onto her lip.

Lester Mon Dama favored her with a warm smile.

"Why do you keep these old communication books?" she asked. Somehow, it seemed important to know the answer.

The priest answered carefully, his words infinitely solemn. "Bell of Pennsylvania, Pacific Bell—these are things that once were. Representations of time before time. They serve to constantly remind me that I have been preceded by another existence. I guess I feel a little more secure realizing that these very useful tools were around long before

I was born, long before the Apocalypse, long before there was such a thing as the Church of the Trust.

"Ultimately, however, I suppose that these covers remain fetishes, and as such, unexplainable." He chuckled. "In fact, if I could explain them, I suppose I'd have no need for them."

One of Susan's psychplan counsellors had once intimated that antique collecting was a refined form of pain relief: If you surrounded yourself with enough historical symbols, then your own internalized suffering was repressed, effectively diminished. Maybe Lester also suffered from deep childhood pain.

He handed her a slice of tissues from his desk. Susan dabbed at her still-wet cheeks. "All these things," she said, "make you feel as if you . . . belong."

Lester pushed aside some of the clutter and sat down on the edge of his desk. "Perhaps they do." His fingers toyed with the smooth spine of the directory. "Or perhaps they simply remind me that the world was once a much simpler place. More secure."

They were silent for a moment. And Susan found herself wondering if Lester Mon Dama had, like many of the other priests of the Trust, taken a vow of chastity.

"Susan," he began slowly, "maybe I have a real alternative for you—at least a temporary answer to your troubles."

She forced a smile. "You have my attention."

"Have you ever been to Earth?"

"No," she said warily.

"The Church maintains several facilities down on the surface. Nothing like we had in the old days, of course. The Great Trauma wiped out most of our bases. But E-Tech permits us to maintain a few Cloisters, places where our brethren can go when they need to reinvigorate.

"At any rate, I've been planning a trip down to our facility on Lake Ontario for some time now. As a Priest, I am permitted to take along any number of my parish; in

fact, the Bishops' Conclave encourages priests to recruit
visitors. There are usually many empty bedrooms within
the Cloisters. Surprisingly, most of our flock have no great
desire to set foot on the planet."

"At least when they're alive," Susan muttered.

Lester stared at her, his eyes impelling silence.

She sighed loudly. "I'm sorry. I've dwelt on my pain
enough for one day. But still . . . I don't know if I want to
travel to Earth. And I'm *not* a member of the Church."

"*That* is a problem with an easy solution. You recall the
sacrament of misk?"

"Of course."

"I could reinitiate you into the Trust; a simple private
ceremony. That would satisfy the requirements for taking
you to the Ontario Cloister."

"How long would I have to stay down there?"

"A transit shuttle arrives every other day. You could
leave whenever you desired."

"How long are *you* planning to stay?" She was surprised
to feel herself blushing slightly as she asked the question.
Her interest in Lester was becoming more personal, and
she was having trouble consciously admitting the presence
of those feelings.

*Steady, Susan. He's a Priest of the Trust. And even if he didn't
take a vow of chastity, nothing's going to happen between us.*

Nevertheless, the feelings remained.

If Lester was aware of her reddening face, he did not let
on. "I hope to stay at the Ontario Cloister for at least four
or five days, perhaps longer." His face erupted into a guilty
smile. "Even a priest deserves a vacation from time to
time."

"I'd be . . . fairly safe down there," she offered, trying to
convince herself.

"Away from the Colonies, away from all the danger. Believe me, Susan, there's an openness down there, a spa-
ciousness that many visitors find infinitely soothing. A
great many of our brethren later claim that they felt a

sense of inner peace on the planet that they had never known in the Colonies. And the Church still enjoys a certain degree of transport freedom. We have our own private shuttles. And E-Tech pays little attention to standard passports. I am absolutely certain that your departure from the Colonies could be handled with total discretion."

He took her by the hand. "The more I think about it, the more I truly believe that this would be your best course of action. Get away from this madness that seems to be pursuing you. Allow yourself to relax with me at the retreat until your problems in the Colonies are brought to their own conclusion. Eventually, these killers are going to be stopped. Then you can come back as a free woman and make peace with your aunt. And, if at that time it is still of some importance to you, I am certain that this man from Clark Shuttle Service will still be available."

She swallowed. "I don't know . . . it's a high-end matchup, the kind of date that doesn't happen without—"

"Trust me, Susan."

She squeezed his palm, feeling his strength. She found herself smiling.

"You've convinced me."

"Keep your eye on the main screen," urged Nick.

The lion hunched forward, watched the monitor dissolve to black as Nick typed in a CLEAR command. He hoped the midget was not going to take too much of his time. It was late Saturday afternoon and he was due to leave the Alexanders' retreat shortly. He had to be at the other end of Irrya in an hour to address a special session of the United Clans concerning the just-announced detection of the returning starship.

Nick typed rapidly. Some of his information printed across the bottom of the screen.

FB-330-3367-T569. *IRS AUDIT 1991*

"The first set of numbers," Nick explained, "is part of today's E-Tech security code for that portion of the archives I'm trying to access. Courtesy of Adam Lu Sang. The second set—IRS Audit 1991—is my own custom program. It's an infinite repeat scanner, and a fairly powerful one. I coded it into the data vaults back around 2095, but even that was about a hundred years too late. I always wished that I'd had this program back in the days when the real IRS was trying to audit me."

"The real IRS?"

"Never mind."

Nick typed: OPEN FILE GX-P34711-FY7-582HH-095D. Above his command, a green rectangle appeared on the dark screen. Within its borders, twin response lines printed.

OPENING FILE GX-P34711-FY7-582HH-095D.

CLOSING FILE GX-P34711-FY7-582HH-095D.

"Cute, huh?"

The lion shook his head. "I don't understand."

"The file I just ordered to open is pre-Apocalyptic, circa 2078. It contains technical specs and suggested design parameters for refraction tubing—the stuff that they weave into cosmishield glass to control what particular wavelengths of the electromagnetic spectrum can pass through. Now this file, in terms of size, contains about eight hundred megabytes—a pretty fair amount of data. It's also nicely protected—nothing as sophisticated as a soft perimeter, but still with enough standard safeguards to discourage illegal entry.

"I discovered this program about two hours ago, during a random search. I notified Adam. He's down in the data vaults right now. He worked up the physiograph—located the file's actual position within the network. Like most of the old files, it's a cascading floater, with geriatric sequence patterns. Finding its exact location, at any one moment, was no simple task, not when you take into consideration the fact that the program has duplicates and backups scattered in a dozen other subsystems throughout the Colonies. We're talking multidimensional vectors. But Adam's a smart boy; he figured it out. He knows his network."

"I'm sure he does," muttered the lion.

Nick grinned. "Sorry, I forgot. You're not real heavy into computers."

"A sound conclusion."

"Okay—in simple terms. What we have here is a program that is being opened and closed at the same time, a contradictory situation. That particular type of illogic constituted the basic target parameter for my initial search. I went looking for just such an anomaly. I created a set of tangent cruisers and gave them multi-stage access to the E-Tech archives. They turned up this program.

"I believe that our sunsetter is inside this file right now, doing its dirty work. That's why we're getting the contradictory message. I'm ordering the program to open, and a fraction of a second later, the sunsetter is ordering it to close, so that the sunsetter can carry on with its data erasure. But as soon as the sunsetter closes the program, my little IRS orders it to open again. And so it goes, ad infinitum. The net effect is that file GX-P34711-FY7-582HH-095D has been caught in a logic loop. It's going to keep on opening and closing itself until one of two things occur: Either I call off the IRS, which I'm not going to do, or the sunsetter decides it's had enough of this opening-closing bullshit and decides to do something about it."

"What will it do?"

A faint grin spread across Nick's face. "I really don't know. But whatever action it takes should tell us something about our enemy. Give us a bit of a psychological profile, so to speak."

"You make this sunsetter sound almost . . . humanly conscious."

"Really powerful programs mimic the thought patterns and even the emotional temperaments of their creators. Assuming our sunsetter's presence in the archives is no accident, then we have to conclude that there's a guiding hand behind its actions. It has a mommy."

The lion frowned. "Would this 'mommy' be controlling the sunsetter right now?"

"Probably not. Most likely, the program's mommy arranged for regular rendezvous. On a scheduled basis, perhaps once every few weeks, the sunsetter will deliver a status report to a specific terminal, somewhere in the Colonies. At that time, the sunsetter would also be able to receive new or updated orders from its mommy."

"Could you trace the sunsetter to one of these rendezvous points?"

Nick shook his head. "Not to the regularly scheduled rendezvous, not unless its mommy was extraordinarily careless, which under the circumstances, seems unlikely. But we may be able to create a situation where the sunsetter is forced to run to mommy for added input. Or mommy might have to make an unscheduled contact, give the sunsetter some new orders. In those scenarios, if we're lucky, we might be able to trace the program to its rendezvous point."

"And then?"

"And then maybe we catch a bad guy. But let's not get ahead of ourselves. I doubt if our sunsetter's going to run home to mommy just because my IRS is giving it a hard time. Right now, I'd settle for—"

The screen turned blue and white; the rectangle housing the opening and closing commands disappeared into a streaky white haze. The lion was instantly reminded of one of those rare earth skies, video documented by E-Tech ground crews, where the atmospheric pollutants were temporarily swept aside to reveal cottony fluffs against an endless blue backdrop.

"I'll be a son of a bitch," muttered Nick. "Freebird."

"What?"

"Freebird, a rescue program, the prototype of which was designed by the Koreans. Pre-Apocalyptic, late twenty-first century—from the same era that gave rise to sunsetters. A very, *very* powerful program."

The pastoral scene began to change; the clouds started to disintegrate as if violent winds were ripping them apart. The lion stared intently, not understanding, but fascinated by the ephemeral display. In another few seconds, the clouds were gone. Only a blue screen remained.

Nick typed: OPEN FILE GX-P34711-FY7-582HH-095D. In response, the screen faded to black.

A deep frown rippled the midget's forehead. He gazed silently at the blank monitor.

"Not what you were expecting?" quizzed the lion.

"About the last thing in the world I was expecting." Nick looked agitated. "A rescue program. Now where in the hell did that come from? And not just any old rescue program, but Freebird. Jesus Christ!"

"How do you know it was . . . Freebird?"

"'Cause I've seen this program work before. I recognized its signature—the clouds, the blue skies, the patterns on the screen. Freebird is a defender. In the event of an attack against one of the programs it's assigned to protect, Freebird alters that program's physiograph—changes its location within the computer. That's what occurred here. Freebird moved File GX-P34711-FY7-582HH-095D to a new location, probably to remove it from the logic loop that my IRS was creating."

"Can you find this file again?"

"Sure. Adam can work up another physiograph. It'll probably take about an hour. But by that time, our sunsetter might be done reaming out the file's data and have vacated the premises. And if not—if the sunsetter's still inside the program, and I go after it again with my IRS—then Freebird will probably reappear and snatch the file away again."

"Ad infinitum," said the lion.

"You're beginning to catch on."

"Is there anything you can do?"

"I don't know. I'm going to have to give the problem some serious thought. What worries me the most is that it appears that our sunsetter and Freebird are working together. I never heard of such a collaboration. I mean, rescue programs were originally designed to *thwart* sunsetters and other data destroyers. If the sunsetter's the bad guy, then the rescue program is supposed to be the good guy. In this case, they appear to be working for the same side."

"That's not very fair," quipped the lion.

Nick grinned fiercely. "I'll say. It's sort of like King Kong being protected by a guardian angel."

The lion had heard of guardian angels.

Blue letters appeared across the top of the dark screen. WHAT HAPPENED? I HAVE LOW-LEVEL DISTORTIONS AND A COMPLETELY ALTERED PHYSIOGRAPH, PLEASE EXPLAIN.

"That's Adam," said Nick, recovering his composure. The midget typed:

EVER HEAR OF FREEBIRD?

There was a pause. Then: YOU'RE KIDDING.

I WISH I WAS.

WHAT ARE WE GOING TO DO?

Nick smiled grimly. I GUESS WE'RE GOING TO HAVE TO LEARN TO FLY.

Gillian thought the near-empty Irryan restaurant bordered on garish, with its array of helium-filled imitation animals floating against the ceiling: panda bears, German Shepherds, mini llamas, a host of gray squirrels with massive tails and bucked teeth. At first glance, the monochrome walls—in stark contrast to the aerial menagerie—appeared almost elegant, with their tiny black-on-white stripes blending together in a linear fog of pearly ash. Only when he returned from the lavatory and sat down in their corner booth did the walls take on a more oppressive quality. At close range, the soft graying effect was lost; the black and white stripes leaped out at him, exposing themselves as a wild conglomeration of twentieth-century supermarket bar codes, each one meticulously checker-boarded into prominence. He would probably have developed a headache if he had not had one already.

"Feeling any better?" asked Buff. She sat across from him in the booth, her bare black elbows propped on the white tablecloth, her chin resting in upturned palms. Eyes followed his every motion.

"Just getting away from that auditorium helped," he lied. "Where's Martha?"

"Outside. Making sure that Xornakoff didn't have us followed."

"I doubt whether our Inspector was *that* suspicious."

Buff frowned. "I don't know. You were acting pretty weird back there. What happened to you?"

"I told you. I ate too much for breakfast. Necropsy work is better performed—"

"You didn't look sick," she interrupted.

"I was."

Buff shrugged. "Look, if you don't want to tell me what all that weirdness was about, then don't. But please, Amphos, don't spoon me shaft oil and tell me it's grape juice. They don't taste the same."

"I know what you mean. I've had a funny taste in my mouth since we met."

She straightened and regarded him coolly. "What do you mean?"

He mimicked: "We're sort of . . . security consultants . . . freelance . . . sort of."

A hearty chuckle filled the restaurant. "Yeah, I guess we weren't as straight with you as we could have been. But it's basically true. We are in the security business."

Martha ambled in from the doorway, her long blonde ponytails flopping from side to side. Again, Gillian was reminded of one of those ancient air club dancers. The taller woman shared more than jeweled nipples with wing nuts; there was a certain casual grace—if that was the phrase for it—in the way that Martha carried herself. Yet it was more than that, more than mere self-confidence and feminine allure, although she possessed those attributes in abundance. Martha was one of those women who, if she were stark naked, could appear to be fully dressed, wearing her flesh as if it were an exoskeleton, a removable framework. But she wore it well, like seasoned firewood wore the flame.

She eased into the seat beside Buff. The black woman regarded her with a questioning gaze.

"We weren't followed," Martha answered.

Gillian studied them both now, side by side, this oddly different pair, Buff warm and friendly, Martha cool and distant, and he knew that the women belonged together, and had probably been together for a very long time. Less than lovers, but more than partners.

A male waiter, who could not have been older than fourteen, emerged from the back of the restaurant. He rested his thighs against their table and leaned forward. "Sorry," he said, crooking a finger at their menu keyboard mounted on the wall side of the booth. "Your terminal's busted. You'll have to tell me what you want."

"No," said Martha calmly. "That won't do."

The boy looked at her for a moment, then frowned. "The menu terminal's busted," he repeated.

"Can you fix it?"

"I . . . don't think so." He grinned at her, but she did not return the smile. He swallowed nervously. "I . . . uh . . . have to take your orders manually." He held up his tiny keypad. "With this."

"What if that's not acceptable?" probed Martha.

"Uh . . . you can move to another booth—"

"We're comfortable here."

"Then . . . I don't know what else I can do." The young waiter shrugged his shoulders in exaggerated fashion, accenting his confusion. "I have to take your orders—"

"Manually," finished Martha. "Yes, we know. You've already told us that. How long have you worked here?"

"Uh . . . about a month."

"Any customer ever give you a hard time before?"

He shook his head vehemently. "No. Never."

"So I'm the first?"

The boy didn't know what to say. He just stood there, leaning against the table, his attention pinned to Martha.

"Bet you weren't expecting someone like me when you got out of bed this morning?" she quizzed.

"Uh . . . would you like to talk to the manager?"

"I'm talking to you."

Again, he swallowed nervously. "Look ma'am, I don't know what you want—"

"I want coffee," said Martha sweetly. "And put in a dash of vanilla."

The boy programmed her order, then turned quickly to Buff.

"Nothing here."

Gillian asked for seltzer water.

The boy practically ran back to the kitchen.

Buff grinned and slapped her partner's arm. "Really, Martha, he's just a child. You try taking him to bed and his mommy will probably come after you with a hot blade."

"She'll never know."

Buff sighed. "He'll probably *tell* her."

"I like him. He's got a cute downside."

"You're Costeaus," announced Gillian, surprised that he had not realized it sooner.

Buff raised her eyebrows, countering him. But Gillian knew he was right. As if in acknowledgment to his deduction, the headache—a final reminder of his recent hyperalert state—vanished. He was himself again, fully engaged in the present, unfettered by remnants from the past. For now, Catharine and Empedocles had returned to the shadows.

"What clan?" he pressed. "The Alexanders?"

Buff stared at him silently. Martha looked away.

"Look, you want me to be straight with you, I will. But you have to return the favor. Now what clan are you from?"

Buff glanced at Martha, then nodded. "We're originally from the Cerniglias. But now we serve the lion."

"And what do you do for Jerem Marth?"

"We work on special assignments."

"And what was your assignment regarding me?"

"We're supposed to assist you—"

"And keep an eye on me too, no doubt." Gillian shook his head slowly. Suddenly, it was all so obvious. "You have orders from Nick, as well as from the lion?"

No response.

"Did they tell you who I really am?"

Buff hesitated for a fraction of a second. Then she shrugged. "You're Gillian. You hunt and kill Paratwa."

The boy returned with their coffee and water, setting

the table quickly, avoiding eye contact with Martha. As he turned to go, Martha reached out and pinched his right buttock. The boy jerked his hips forward, then broke into another fast jog toward the safety of the kitchen. Martha smiled.

Buff chuckled. "I'll bet you he has a stiff cock."

"Maybe," said Gillian. "But I'll bet you he doesn't do anything about it."

Martha sipped her coffee and said nothing.

Buff hunched forward. "Look, Amphos, or Gillian, or whatever the hell name you want us to call you—"

"In private, Gillian will suffice."

"Look, Gillian, we're just supposed to help you. Naturally, we're to keep an eye on you. But only to keep you out of any trouble."

"You're lying," said Gillian.

Buff scowled. "You're not a very trusting person."

"You're lying," he repeated.

Buff shook her head angrily. "Believe what you want, then."

"No," said Martha calmly. "Enough crap." She stared at him. "You're right, there's more. Nick warned us that you might become . . . unstable . . . lose control . . . sort of like what occurred back at the auditorium. Nick said that if that happened, it was all right, just so long as you came out of it okay. But he said that it was also possible that you might come out of one of these episodes with a different personality."

"Oh, shit," muttered Buff. "We're not supposed to be telling you any of this."

"If that happens," Martha continued, "we're to contact Nick immediately." She set her coffee cup down and wiped a napkin across her lips. "But if this other personality of yours becomes aggressive, we're to take action."

Gillian felt a tight smile creep across his face. "What kind of action?"

"Subdue you, if possible."

"And if I can't be subdued?"

Martha met his hard gaze and a cool smile twisted her lips. "Then maybe we'll have to kill you."

"Oh, shit," groaned Buff.

And Gillian knew that Martha—and probably Buff as well—had killed before.

*I should be furious at Nick.* But he felt no rage. The midget had done what Gillian would have done under the same circumstances. Nick would not have told these Costeaus about Catharine, nor about the Ash Ock who lurked in Gillian's cells. Enough had been revealed, however.

Empedocles remained an unknown factor, and a potentially dangerous one. *I'm afraid of you, myself,* he admitted. *I'm afraid that if you arise, Gillian will be changed.*

Nick had done the right thing.

Gillian felt the tension leaving his face. He smiled openly at Martha.

"Why are you telling me all this?"

Martha shrugged. "I don't like bullshit assignments."

Buff rolled her eyes. "Oh, the lion's going to *love* that excuse."

"Let's hope," said Gillian calmly, "that the need to take action against me never arises."

Buff glared at Martha. "Let's hope that we don't get fired."

"What happened to me back in the auditorium," Gillian explained, "is called the gestalt—a hyperalert state that allows me to process information in a very special way. It was not one of my episodes of . . . changed personality." He hesitated. "At least it didn't start out that way. What I mean to say is, what happened to me in the auditorium was not exactly what Nick warned you to watch for."

The Costeaus stared at him, Buff grim and uncertain, Martha faintly curious.

"I realize that all this must sound very strange to you," he added quickly. "But it's important. And there's one more thing you should know. If my altered personality does emerge, it may prove to be . . . helpful. A friend, not an enemy."

"Maybe we *should* be fired," suggested Buff. "I don't think we're going to like this assignment."

"Speak for yourself," said Martha.

Buff was silent for a moment. Then she grinned. "I guess you're stuck with us."

"I could have done worse," Gillian admitted.

The black Costeau's face sparkled. "Can we take that as a compliment?"

"I wouldn't," said Martha.

Gillian met her cynical gaze, saw blue eyes tinged with anger, and in that moment he learned something else about Martha: She was a woman who burned inside, a woman with a morass of barely contained furies and desires. Such emotions were almost Costeau trademarks, perhaps, but like everything else about Martha, they were much more pronounced. She reminded him of Grace, the pirate who had been slain by Reemul fifty-six years ago. Both women lived fiercely, sheltering their agonies, but in Martha the hidden pains danced even more wildly across the surface, like non-concentric ripples from a raging waterfall, creating indefinable perimeters, blurring her edges. Extreme caution was necessary around such a woman. You could disturb those ripples—intrude upon her—without knowing it. She would be unpredictable. And that made her extremely dangerous.

He changed the subject. "This plasma necropsy business—did it provide you with any important information about the victims of this massacre? Or any of the other killings?"

Buff shrugged. "Not really. We did fluid linkages at all the previous murder sites, as well as this one. It allowed us to determine precise times of death—down to the second, even. We were able to chart the order in which the victims died, to about a ninety-nine percent accuracy. And we picked up a wealth of extraneous health data: who was

keeping their teeth clean, who had a cold, who was pro-
miscuous, who was not." The Costeau smiled. "Important
stuff, right?"

"Nick may be able to make use of it," replied Gillian.
"But we're still missing something important about these
killings. I almost had it back there . . ." He shook his head.
"A facet that's being overlooked. Shooter and Slasher . . .
they're not positioned right. Their attack profile makes no
sense."

He outlined his analysis: Shooter's right-handedness, the
360 degree combat radius that shrank to 180 degrees at
the end of each of their attacks, opening up that huge
blind spot, making both killers more vulnerable to attack
from the rear. He explained, as best he could, the
hyperalert state that he was able to put himself into, the
gestalt that allowed him to subconsciously examine a murder site.

"Maybe we should go back to the hall," offered Buff.
"You could put yourself into this hyperalert state again."

"It's not that simple. The gestalt . . . takes a lot out of
me. And trying to do it a second time—trying to absorb
the same images, the same scene . . ." Again, he shook his
head. "It usually doesn't work. A murder site has to be
fresh; I must perceive it as a brand new sensory experience. Otherwise, the gestalt becomes cluttered by earlier
sensory data." He did not tell them that he was also wary
of another encounter with Catharine.

And it was not Catharine per se who brought on his
fear. He knew that. It was what his lost tway represented:
the possibility of the whelm, the possibility that
Empedocles could arise, assume control against Gillian's
will . . .

*This is crazy. I shouldn't be frightened of you—my own monarch.
A part of me desperately desires to make you real. I need to feel the
duplicity of existence that once seemed so natural. I need your wholeness, your clarity. I need to feel like a tway again.*

But conflicting emotions remained: desire and fear.

"So what do we do now?" asked Buff.

"I don't know."

They were silent for a moment.

Buff asked: "Do you think we're dealing with a Paratwa assassin?"

"I'm not sure," admitted Gillian. "It doesn't feel quite like a Paratwa. But it doesn't feel like human killers, either. What do you think?"

"I think that if it were a Paratwa . . . I think that there'd be more victims."

"The number of victims can't be taken as a sign. Some Paratwa killed very few people, priding themselves on assassinating only specific targets. Others were outright mass murderers. A few were so effective that they never left any witnesses." He hesitated. "But you're right, there could have been more victims in these current massacres. I think that our assassin, whether Paratwa or human, is not operating to the fullest level of its abilities. The death tolls in these massacres could have been much higher."

Buff nodded. "But this combat radius . . . that's what's really bothering you?"

"Yes."

"You say that it creates a big blind spot, makes them terribly vulnerable. But Martha and I have studied all the massacres and as far as we could ascertain, no one has yet attempted to make use of this blind spot of yours. I mean, this lessened combat radius doesn't even come into existence until near the end of their rampages. But by that time, everyone's too terrified and panicked to even think about trying to counterattack. So maybe the killers realize that; they know that no one's going to give them any trouble."

"I considered that possibility," said Gillian. "But remember, these killers are very methodical. Look at their escapes: In all six massacres, once the killers have exited the immediate combat area, they simply vanish. You would expect at least *someone* to have a vague idea in which

direction they had fled. But no one sees anything. That
sort of disappearing act doesn't happen naturally. They
must have transportation waiting—cars parked nearby.
Probably the killers change their appearances as they're
running; maybe they duck into an alley for a moment.
They use reversible garments and minor cosmetic alterations; they remove a face mask or slap a new one into
place. Whatever the case, ten or fifteen seconds later,
they're unrecognizable.

"These massacres are carefully orchestrated, from beginning to end. But one sour note spoils the whole performance: the opening of that blind spot. It doesn't make
sense. It doesn't fit."

Martha rubbed her thumb across the sapphire over her
right nipple. "Maybe they had backup."

Gillian frowned. Deep down inside him, a weird sensation took hold, a vague pulsing beginning at the top of his
spine and slowly spreading outward to cover his whole
body. His skin felt electrified; goosebumps tickled the back
of his neck. Either he was about to suffer another headache or he was on the verge of a revelation. He hunched
forward. "What do you mean?"

"Just what I said," answered Martha, sounding a bit annoyed that she had to repeat herself. "Maybe they had
backup. Someone covering their rear."

"Yeah," added Buff, "someone who stayed hidden, but
who was there just in case they got into trouble."

Gillian gripped the edge of the table. The gestalt—the
same one that had been interrupted in the massacre hall
by the appearance of Catharine—abruptly returned. A
raging stream of raw data closed in on him, blinding exter-
nal senses. The stream took on a life of its own, circling
ever tighter until it transformed itself into a whirlpool, a
vortex possessing its own sights, sound, and odors, and
with proportions that threatened to overwhelm his conceptual understanding. But he concentrated on the center of
the whirlpool, delimiting awareness to one cold question:

*Why does Slasher always cut to the left?*

And then the whirlpool collapsed in upon itself, condensing into something solid, condensing until only a speck of hard logic remained. And that speck was the answer to his question, the missing piece of the puzzle.

Awareness returned abruptly to the present. Buff was staring at him with a deep frown. Martha's hands had dropped beneath the table and Gillian had the vaguest feeling that the blonde Costeau had procured a weapon from her medical bag, and that it was trained on his guts. He held up his hand. "It's all right. It's not what you think. It's not my . . . altered self."

Martha raised her eyebrows slightly. But her hands remained hidden.

Buff spoke hesitantly. "Was that . . . the gestalt?"

Gillian nodded. "Yes, the conclusion of the gestalt that began at the massacre site." He smiled grimly. "In a way, the answer to the puzzle was a simple one. But it was an answer that I was not prepared to accept. It goes against all that I know, all that I've been trained to understand. But it's a truth, and I can't deny it.

"I know what we're dealing with. Something new . . . something totally different. I've never even considered something like this before, and that's why it's been so difficult for me to comprehend.

"These killers are not human beings. We're faced with a Paratwa assassin. But no ordinary Paratwa."

"There are three of them," concluded Martha.

"Yes," said Gillian, a bit awed to actually hear it expressed in words. "Three of them. Slasher, Shooter, and a third tway—a backup—waiting in the shadows, ready to cover that 180-degree blind spot should the need arise. A Paratwa assassin consisting of three tways."

Martha laid her left hand back on the tablecloth. A tiny needlegun was clutched in her palm.

Buff gave a weak smile. "Just a little something to put

you to sleep. Just in case. Harmless, really. An anesthetized dart, too. You'd hardly even feel it."

Gillian smiled. Both of Martha's hands had been under the table. More than a mere needlegun may have been trained upon him.

He stood up. "We're going back to the lion's retreat. I have to meet with Nick." The midget might be able to shed some light on this strange new threat.

The Costeaus rose. Martha nestled the needlegun back in her medical bag and slapped five cash cards down on the table.

It was a much larger tip than Gillian would have left.

Philippe left Mister Cochise's office thinking: *I believe that this is a really good thing that I am doing.*

He gripped his new suitcase tightly and smiled throughout the elevator ride back down to Venus Cluster's spacious lobby. The Irryan street was uncrowded; the late afternoon sunlight was just beginning to lose its fierce midday brightness and the shuttle terminal was only a few blocks away. Philippe decided to walk. He arrived at the docking bay in short order, and with prepurchased ticket in hand, he and his suitcase passed unchallenged through the contraband/weapons detection grid and boarded the express shuttle bound for home—the Colony of Toulouse.

As the transport fell away from the seventy-mile-long Irryan cylinder, Philippe experienced that familiar sensation of disappearing gravity. A small girl, seated across the aisle with her parents, wiggled in excitement, pointing through the portal as the magnificent view of the Capitol shrank to full perspective. Philippe smiled with understanding. Even though his job required frequent intercolonial travel, he often experienced similar invigoration when his shuttle departed from a cylinder. But not today. Today there was something more important on his mind: the really good thing that he was doing.

Flighttime passed quickly and soon he was gravitized again, and disembarking upon the soils of Toulouse. Mirrors had rotated into darkness hours ago and it was well after midnight before the taxi dropped him at his single unit Alpha-sector apartment. After he had secured the door and lowered the shades and scanned his rooms with the tiny bug-checker that Mister Cochise had given him, the next instruction abruptly popped into his head.

*The suitcase must be opened in a very special way,* Mister Cochise had said. *Place it on a firm surface with the lock strip facing you. Set the bug-checker upright near the center. Wait for the bug-checker to blink three times before opening the suitcase.*

Philippe laid the hardframe carrier on his desk, feeling happier by the minute. The suitcase was not very big—maybe eighteen inches by twelve, and no more than five inches thick—but it was big enough to bestow upon him an odd kind of pleasure just by gazing at its burnished bronze surface. He followed Mister Cochise's precise directions, knowing that he was doing the really good thing. The tiny sensor atop the bug-checker flickered brightly—three times in rapid succession.

Philippe popped open the suitcase and unsnapped the protective sealtite cover. Inside lay a translucent mass of protoplasmic material, pulsating with life, and wreathed by a conglomeration of bluish white superconductor circuitry. The membrane appeared to be about the size of a human heart, but Philippe knew that this was no human organ. He had no idea what the purpose of the suitcase was, but that was not important. Only the really good thing that he was doing mattered.

He smiled as Mister Cochise's next set of instructions entered awareness.

*Fastened under the lid you will find a tiny edible injector. Insert the injector directly into the membrane and withdraw fluid until the injector reads full.*

Philippe continued to smile with pleasure as he located the device and pushed the slender needle into the soft red membrane, carefully observing the readout on the injector's trunk. When it indicated a full dose, he withdrew it from the protoplasmic mass. Almost immediately, he recalled fresh mandates.

*Place the edible injector on your tongue and close your mouth. In three or four minutes, the injector will melt. Swallow the liquid and then wash it down with a large glass of water.*

Mister Cochise was right—the injector melted very quickly and Philippe washed it down with his best imported mineral water, straight from the dispenser hose. Swallowing the cool liquid seemed to trigger yet another set of instructions.

*Under the lid of the suitcase, at the spot where the injector was fastened, is a strip of fabric different in color from the rest of the material. Lick your tongue across this strip until it is soaked.*

Philippe felt inordinately pleased with himself for locating the strip—it was bright white, while the remainder of the smooth fabric was matte black. He gently licked the light-colored band. It tasted sour.

*Sour.* That reminded Philippe of a phone number: BC84-162F. Excited, he sat at his terminal and quickly typed the code. A recorded message appeared on his screen.

STATE NAME AND COLONY

"Philippe Boisset, Toulouse cylinder," he answered proudly.

PLEASE WAIT.

Philippe sat before the blank screen for at least five minutes, but he did not feel bored. On the contrary, he felt that deep sense of satisfaction that came with accomplishment. He knew that he was doing the really good thing to the best of his abilities.

Finally, his terminal speaker began to emit a deep hum. Philippe recognized the sound. A line scrambler had been activated. A moment later, a strong male voice came over the line. "Mister Boisett?"

"Yes." The voice was unfamiliar to Philippe. It was certainly not Mister Cochise.

"Are you alone?"

"Yes, I am."

"Good. Go to the suitcase and check the strip. You should see two colors. Tell me what they are."

Heart pounding with excitement—caught up in the wondrous mystery of this game—Philippe ran to the open suitcase and checked the white strip. The voice was correct. The white strip that he had licked had changed colors. He raced back to the terminal.

"Blue and orange," he replied eagerly.

"Excellent," said the voice. "Now, Mister Boisset, here are your next instructions. Place the bug-checker inside the suitcase and reseal the unit. Put the suitcase inside a waste bag. Next, you are to hide the suitcase in that special secret place that you and Mister Cochise discussed. And after you have properly hidden the suitcase, Mister Boisset, remember: You must take the fastest route back down to street level. Do you understand?"

Philippe remembered. "Yes, I understand." He was to carry the suitcase over to the Au Fait Recycling Towers. In great detail, he and Mister Cochise had discussed numerous potential hiding places for the suitcase, before agreeing that this one was the best.

"And remember, Mister Boisset," said the voice. "You are doing a really good thing."

Philippe almost sobbed with joy. He felt ... *wonderful*. Resealing the suitcase, and making sure that the bug-checker was locked securely inside the unit, he placed the suitcase inside a plastic waste bag and hurried out the door.

It was four blocks to the Au Fait Recycling Towers, and Philippe walked briskly. The night air felt good; nocturnal breezes, generated by the Recycling Towers themselves, tickled his cheeks, although he did find himself pausing occasionally to cough. The back of his throat was beginning to feel swollen. Perhaps he was catching a cold, or one of the rare mutating flu viruses that still managed to outwit the latest vaccines created by modern medical technology.

"Rock 'n' roll with the best of 'em, Mister Boisset," one of the young evening maintenance workers called to Philippe as he stepped onto the main ramp leading into Tower One. Philippe smiled and gave the lad a hearty wave, not understanding the semantics of the friendly greeting, but happy that the boy was happy. The youth was slowly circling the perimeter of Tower Two on the saddle of a noiseless trimmer, using his combination of microlasers and sweep brushes to keep the decorative hedges at a respectable height. Philippe could not resist.

"That's a really good thing you're doing, Noel."

The boy smiled. Philippe smiled too.

At this late hour, Tower One was nearly empty—most people did their recycling during the day or in the early evening. Philippe entered an open elevator and was whisked straight to the top. He felt very pleased to be doing his citizens' duty and accomplishing the really good thing at the same time. *Two for one*, he thought. *How fortunate I am!*

The elevator deposited him onto the main gridfloor, a wide balcony encircling the hundreds of disposal bins. Each disposal bin, by means of spiralling ramps, fed the trash bags through a series of sorters and analyzers until finally—if accepted—they were deposited into the massive primary core of the tower for thermal breakdown and recycling. Along the outer ring of the balcony, evenly spaced doors led to the outside veranda, a unique sightseer attrac-

tion recently added to the facility by one of Toulouse's recreational bureaus. Tourism was very important to the Colony's economic base and even a simple recycling tower
was expected to contribute to the attractiveness of the
community.

According to a holotronic sign, projected down from the
high vaulted ceiling, Philippe was now two hundred and
fourteen feet above street level. A host of standard imagers
also littered the walls, some explaining the operation of the
Recycling Towers, others serving as teaching aids for
youngsters who were perhaps just learning their legal responsibility for proper waste disposal. Philippe smiled. The
signs were very thoughtful.

The balcony was deserted. That was good. Philippe recalled. Mister Cochise did not want anyone to see where
the suitcase was hidden. Clutching the waste bag tightly,
Philippe proceeded directly to one of the special bins reserved for dangerous materials. A sign flashed to life as the
thick metal door slid open.

WARNING: THIS INPUT CHUTE RESERVED FOR MATERIALS
CLASSIFIED AS CATEGORY THREE BIOHAZARDS UNDER THE
E-TECH SANITATION LAWS. IF YOU HAVE QUESTIONS CONCERN-
ING THE USE OF THIS CHUTE, OR ARE IN NEED OF ASSISTANCE,
PLEASE CALL TW76-909K.

Philippe threw the bag containing the suitcase into the
bin. The doors closed automatically. He smiled. According
to Mister Cochise, category three biohazards all went
through a six week automatic detoxification sequence before being routed into the central core for incineration.
That meant that the suitcase would remain hidden for six
weeks. After that, Mister Cochise had said, its fate would
be irrelevant.

Philippe acknowledged a thrill of triumph. His special
deed had been accomplished. *I have done the really good thing.*

Suddenly he felt tense, uncertain. And then he remem-
bered: *I have to take the fastest route back down to street level!* Mister Cochise had explained that this facet of his duty was

extremely important. And the voice on the phone had re-iterated the necessity.

Philippe raced back toward the elevators. But even though he was running fast, it seemed to be taking forever to get there. And then a horrible sensation ripped through him; his mouth went dry and he tasted the onslaught of a wave of unmitigated fear.

*I'm not going to make it in time!* he thought desperately. *The elevators are too slow!*

There was only one thing for him to do. He changed direction slightly and headed for one of the doors leading to the outside veranda.

*Quickly!* he urged himself. There was no time to waste. He *had* to get back down to street level.

Through the door, out onto the open balcony, the cool night air sweeping across his skin, the dazzling sweep of the cylinder fully visible from this great height, and he thought:

*I'm going to make it! I'm going to make it to the street in time!*

He leaped onto an observation bench, compressed his legs, and with all his might, dove high into the air, easily clearing the six-foot transparent barrier. His body continued to ascend for a moment before gravity overcame the initial thrust of his upward dive. Then he began to fall: down the side of Tower One, accelerating rapidly, the ground racing up to meet him with incredible swiftness. And in that final instant before he plowed into a ringlet of hedges, Philippe experienced a dark shadow of doubt.

*Perhaps this wasn't such a good thing after all.*

The steps leading to the three-story chalet—frozen blocks of ice lined with abrasive edge grips—snaked their way up the snow-drenched hillside, winding thrice beneath the shadow of the lower suspended porch before yielding to linearity, terminating in a gently sloping ramp hugging the right side of the forty-foot-square structure.

*I'm getting old,* thought Ghandi, breathing deeply as he counted the steps, *one hundred and fourteen, one hundred and fifteen,* on the final helix now, well above the level of the rough gray road and the garage where they had housed their treaded snowrover, and almost directly beneath and parallel to the railing of the overhanging second-floor balcony. He glanced upward, wary of falling icicles. But weather programmers had created no recent ice storms and polished teak floorboards shone cleanly against reflected snowlight.

"Hurry, my love," teased Colette, pausing twenty steps in front of him, twisting her neck around, blessing Ghandi with a bright smile, her slow, steady exhalations of frozen gray breath wafting upward to blend with Pocono Colony's permanently overcast skies. He glared unpleasantly, but that only made her grin.

"More aerobics, Corelli-Paul," she scolded warmly. "You need an enhanced exercise program, something with a little more bite to it. You should spend a few weeks in a muscle cone." Colette wiggled her bottom playfully then continued her effortless dash up the ice block stairway.

Ghandi grimaced, wondering if his wife was serious about his visiting an exercise cone. The miniature self-supportive facilities hung outside the Colonies, connected by long cables. They offered physician-supervised power-G workouts—anywhere from 1.2 to 3 times normal gravity—and turned weaklings into hearty, over-muscled supermen.

"Hurry, my pup," she urged again, laughing merrily as she vanished around the corner of the chalet, and he knew, from the sound of her voice, that she had been joking about the exercise cone. But it bothered him that he had not immediately been able to deduce that she was being playful.

*I* am *getting old. And you, my love, you* are *becoming harder and harder to understand.* Ghandi's two omnipresent demons, both growing more powerful with each passing day.

Twenty-five years ago, he had still been too young for the reality of Colette's extended lifespan to bother him. He could not have imagined what it would be like to grow old, to feel muscles languish ever so slightly, the vitality of youth beginning to blister from the incandescence of too many years, while Colette remained as strong and lively as the day they had met. And twenty-five years ago, comprehending the often mysterious schemes and intrigues of Colette/Sappho had not seemed so imperative. Life had been far simpler then; he had been willing to acknowledge that this tway of the royal Caste possessed an intellect far exceeding his own and that she would remain youthful long after he had degenerated into a bed-ridden old man. Back then, with their differences less extreme, he had willingly acquiesced to the twist of fate which had melded him to an Ash Ock.

But today he was paying for those sins of youthful insouciance. Today he sometimes felt like a tagalong stepchild, tolerated but essentially unnecessary.

A sound, behind and above him—a high-pitched echoing whine, increasing rapidly. He knew what it was, but he turned around anyway, pleased to focus on the sanctitude of the moment, pleased to find a reason to chase demon thoughts from awareness.

Speed Slope Fourteen—one of Pocono's fastest—was a nine-mile-long, twenty-foot-wide floating ice trough effortlessly suspended in midair by thin cables trailing upward and vanishing into the gray fog of centersky. There, the speed slope began, as an enclosed tube spiralling gradually outward from the Colony's central core, assuming greater mass as it receded from the gravitational convergence. And here, close to the end of the run, where the slope was a mere twenty-five feet above ground level, the greatest velocities were achieved.

This leisure Colony offered most variations of skiing: downhill, cross country, low-gravity aerobatics up near the weightless core. But the speed slopes—and the men and women who risked the two-hundred-plus-mile-per-hour runs—remained Pocono's primary tourist attraction.

Ghandi waited expectantly, hearing the whine of the skier's rocket engines growing louder and louder, and he could tell from the rapidly increasing pitch that this was no ninety-mile-per-hour rookie, gingerly learning the delicate relationship between jetpak thrust and where to position him or her self on the steep banks of the trough, but a seasoned pro at competition speed, perhaps even pushing for a record-breaking run. And suddenly the whine rose to a vile shriek—the nerve-bending hiss of a fighting tomcat—and the skier appeared, high on the opposite bank of the floating trough, a low crouch easily maintained by mutually repelling energy webs mounted on the back of the skier's thighs and ankles, swept-back Giger-helmet spring-buckled to the heel of the boots, a streamlined sexless form travelling at close to one-third the speed of sound.

From Ghandi's position at the base of the chalet, he was able to observe only three hundred or so feet of the actual inner raceway, and the daredevil flashed into view for but a brief instant. And then the skier was gone, the high-pitched whine falling rapidly in pitch as the Doppler shift reversed. A few faint puffs of jetpak exhaust hovered above the slope for a few seconds before the Colony's gentle winds dispersed them into the misty gray skies.

Prior to the run, the skier would have spent hours triple-checking gear, aligning energy webs, coating the underside of the uniski with low-tension polyfreeze, scouring the jetpak tubes; a plethora of preparation distilled into one hundred and fifty-plus seconds of high-speed excitement. A few of the wealthier team-supported pros even utilized seekers—ski-mounted robots that they sent down the course ahead of them—the seekers' sophisticated laser measurement systems analyzing track conditions, compiling up-to-the-minute schematics that located the ever-present ice cracks, any of which could lead to a potentially fatal spill. A mountain of effort in order to spend a few brief moments of life on the edge.

Ghandi clearly understood such dedication of purpose. In fact he admired it.

Turning, he continued his trek up the ice steps. Reaching the corner of the chalet, he forced himself to jog along the final few feet of gently sloping ramp which led to the rear second-floor entrance.

Colette was inside already, plopped on a sofa in the day room, long legs outstretched, lean thigh muscles clearly visible beneath skin-hugging gray trousers, black boots resting on a hassock. She leaned back, slipped her hands behind her head, and blessed Ghandi with an amused chuckle.

He knelt in front of the hassock, unclipped her boots, slipped the thermals over her ankles. Toes wiggled beneath red cotton stockings, demanding attention, and he massaged her feet, rubbing his knuckles deep into her arches, knowing how much she liked that.

"My love," she whispered, sliding forward onto the hassock, wrapping her legs around his back, her small hands caressing his cheeks. He drew a deep breath, feeling the beginnings of an erection, her electric touch as exciting as the day they had met. Pleasures he could lose himself in.

Pleasures that served to counter the twin demons of growing old and growing stupid.

"I need you," he mumbled. The words seemed to bubble up from deep inside him, carried within a turbulence of deeper darker emotions. *I need you.* A desperate urge, a shoot struggling to split the peel of hard dry earth, touch air.

He felt himself gasp, as if the very utterance of such a feeling was too intense for his body to properly assimilate, and then Colette's palms closed on his face, drawing him down, burying his face against the thin fabric of her blouse, between her breasts.

"I need you forever," he heard himself moan, like a little boy, desperate for acknowledgment.

"My love," she soothed. "It's been harder for you of late, has it not?"

He rubbed his cheeks across her bosom.

She sighed. "So much harder, my love. I know that. I know this past year, especially, has been difficult for you. Plans are finally coming to fruition, decades of effort are yielding rewards. And I know what this has meant to us. We have spent little time together of late, and our intimacy has suffered.

"But consider the future, Corelli-Paul. Consider that soon the long-delayed plans of the Ash Ock will be complete. The Colonies will be ours. The Earth will be ours. And you and I will be together always."

*Always.* He buried his face deeper against the warmth of her flesh, wanting to shroud himself there. Forever.

"And I know, Corelli-Paul, that these days you are troubled by the spectre of growing old, and that the dichotomy of our aging patterns becomes more of a strain as the years pass."

*Yes.* She understood. For the first time since childhood, Ghandi felt on the verge of tears.

She sensed his emotion, and her voice dropped to a hush. "When I am a tway of Sappho," she whispered, "when this body is functioning as one half of an entity, there are times when the effort of maintaining two separate bodies in conjunction requires . . . deliverance. The interlace must be depressurized, purged of its poisons; an emotional cleansing must take place. I must be allowed to fall into the madness that humans call flexing.

"As an Ash Ock, I can experience the process internally, without the need to manifest outward madness. Yet the rigor of flexing remains the same."

She caressed the back of his neck. A stray finger tickled the lobe of his left ear.

"You've always known of my flexing urges. And I believe that you've always known, though perhaps unconsciously, that it is you, Corelli-Paul, who has provided me with an outlet for those urges." She lifted his face to hers. "It is you, my love, who has endured the cleansings of my dual spirit. It is you who has given me the strength to continue."

And then her fingers were probing beneath his shirt, palms rubbing his chest, rubbing so hard that he felt his skin would peel away. He reached up, framed her face in his hands, lunged forward, his lips enclosing her mouth, sucking hard. Her strong hands shaped his buttocks, squeezed; their bodies slammed together. Her fingers seemed to be everywhere at once, detaching his trousers, peeling away his shirt, pinching, caressing, and then they were on the floor, rolling across the carpet, manic wrestlers in a timeless round. And still her fingers explored, under his arms, between his buttocks, deep into his mouth, like tiny insects seeking nourishment.

A chill swept through him. A nameless dread hovered just below consciousness.

"My love," she hissed, raking nails across his bare back, blurring his fear into a maelstrom of overwhelming desire. Fingers continued their relentless probing, finding all crevices, worming their way beneath the minutest folds of his flesh. And Ghandi knew that it must be his imagination, but he felt as if he was being devoured by more than one set of hands.

When he awoke, she lay sprawled across the sofa on her back, one bare leg propped lazily over the leather armrest, the other hanging to the floor, silken-haired vagina exposed. Ghandi staggered to his feet, turned toward the bathroom, stopped when he heard a dull repetitive pounding emanating from downstairs.

He squirmed into his pants, opened the door at the back of the day room, slithered cautiously onto the small inner balcony overlooking the windowless first floor rec chamber.

It was Calvin, all three of him—the Ash Nar en masse—the maniac collected and confined to several hundred square feet of gym space, sweat-covered tways in matching red shorts, standing in a tight circle, hurtling six palm-sized hardballs back and forth with impossible speed. None of the tways looked up, but Ghandi knew that he had been seen the instant he stepped onto the balcony. Three sets of eyes missed very little.

Fortunately, Ghandi's usual reaction to Calvin's presence—animosity on sight—was tempered by spent lust. Microbes abstained from their little dance; he remained remarkably at peace. No uncontrollable twitches of anger, no physical manifestations of rage. Protracted pacification: Even after twenty-five years, making love to Colette remained a multifaceted joy.

Under such conditions, taunting the Ash Nar would be enjoyable.

"Playing with yourself again, Calvin?"

Tway Calvin—Colette's aide—namesake of the Ash Nar, withdrew from the circle. The other tways, the redheaded twins—Ky and Jy—permitted two of the sextet of hardballs to exit the game. The rubber spheres cracked sharply as they slammed against the padded walls. Ky and Jy kept the other four effortlessly suspended, their four arms vigorously pumping, a high-speed juggling act that would have been unimaginable if the same consciousness had not been controlling both bodies.

Calvin crossed to the underside of the balcony, directly beneath Ghandi's position. The tway leaned back so far that it seemed certain he would tumble to the matted floor. No such luck. The six-footer maintained his poise, frame impossibly bent, eyes glaring upward, full of malice, cheeks locked into a boyish smirk. Gingerly, his left hand ascended, like a schoolchild signalling for attention. Holotronic letters melted into shape above the fingertips, formed sparkling green words, laser-crisp even against the spotlight-illuminated rec chamber.

WANT TO SEE A NEW TRICK?

Ghandi forced himself to match the tway's malicious grin. "Not particularly. But I suspect that you're going to try to impress me whether I want you to or not."

Eyes opened wide, pretending to be hurt. BUT I LEARNED IT JUST FOR YOU.

Ghandi knew he should step away from the balcony; Calvin's tricks were generally unpleasant. But if he retreated now, the Ash Nar would have the satisfaction of knowing that Ghandi had been spooked.

"All right, Calvin," he sighed, affixing the tway with a bored stare. "Impress me."

Calvin leaned back even farther. And suddenly his arms flailed at the air and the smirk disappeared beneath an astonished gawk. He fell backward; his butt slammed against the mat. Ghandi let out a delighted chuckle . . .

. . . and in the same instant, realized ruefully that he had fallen for the Ash Nar's feint.

Peripheral vision saw it coming, saw one of the twins catapult over his brother, power doubling—two bodies functioning in tandem, using two sets of muscles to turn a tway into a guided missile—and Ky was vaulting ten feet into the air, arms outstretched like an air swimmer, coming straight at Ghandi.

A frozen moment, stamped by regret. *I should have ignored him. He knew that he could capture my attention by having one tway pretend to do something foolish, something that I would enjoy.*

A flash of red hair, a blast of warm breath across Ghandi's face as Ky hurtled past, inches away, the human projectile still ascending. Ghandi jerked backward, instinctively craning his neck to follow, wishing that the tway would crash against the ceiling, hurt himself, hurt Calvin.

A sharp thud. Ky hit the ceiling above the balcony, directly over Ghandi. But he did not fall. The tway hung there like an inverted spider, facing the floor, suspended by four points of his body—the back of his heels and the back of his hands—and Ghandi realized that he must have smeared on twistik, the rubbery adhesive paste that maintenance workers often used when doing minor repairs on the exteriors of tall buildings. But twistik was always used with heavy strap-on gloves; it was unpleasant to even contemplate applying the adhesive directly to the flesh.

Nevertheless, Ky hung there by his skin, maintaining a polite smile, revealing no evidence of pain. Ghandi remained beneath him, staring upward, watching for movement, waiting for the tway to snap wrists and ankles into a ninety degree pivot, break the twistik's bond with the ceiling.

*Fall on me, you bastard.* Ghandi braced himself against the balcony railing, trying to keep one eye on the rec floor below him, trying to anticipate additional tricks from the other two.

*Fall on me, now,* he prayed. *Do it and I'll throw you over the fuckin' edge!*

Ky's mouth opened into a deliberate yawn, as if to say: *You don't think I'd do something so stupid, do you?*

And Ghandi felt a sudden cramp of irrational fear tighten his stomach muscles, and he wondered if Ky was armed, if the tway had somehow concealed a weapon beneath his workout shorts. This one's muscles were adroit in the use of flash daggers. Ky was the tway that the freelancers called Slasher.

Ghandi's peripheral vision caught sudden movement, down below, and he saw twin Jy vault over a pommel horse, cartwheel twice in midair, land perfectly in a small painted circle ten feet away. Ghandi instantly focused his attention back on the hanging tway, but Ky had not budged. However, the crotch of Ky's shorts now appeared to be soaking wet.

Before Ghandi could think to move, before common sense warned him to get out from under the maniac, droplets of urine were falling on his face. He spluttered and wrenched his body backward, shielding his face with his arm, dashing out of Ky's spray path.

Anger rose within him; muscles twitched as the microbes began their furious dance.

*Mindless fucking maniac!*

A wild crescendo of laughter—in triplicate—rocked the gym. Brimming with rage, Ghandi leaned out over the balcony, not caring whether the Ash Nar had other pranks in store. Tway Calvin still lay on his back, chuckling with boyish delight. Jy had stopped jogging, was now hopping madly around the gym, screaming with amusement, his bare legs whipping through the air as if his feet were on fire.

DID YOU ENJOY? grinned Calvin.

Ghandi gripped the balcony railing, squeezing so hard that his wrists hurt. He forced control into his voice. "Too bad that you don't seem able to apply your *ingenuity* to solving our problems, Calvin. Why don't you see if you can find Susan Quint? Maybe she'd enjoy your baby games?"

YOU SOUND PISSED OFF. A fresh peal of laughter circled the gym, going round and round from tway to tway, three sets of vocal cords contributing to a melody of one.

An image filled Ghandi's mind: that day in Denver,

twenty-five years ago, his needbreeder-controlled crewmates transferring two stasis capsules from Colette's shuttle
to his own. Calvin asleep: twins Ky and Jy sharing one
capsule, tway Calvin, tallest and physically strongest of the
three, occupying the other.

*I could have destroyed you then. I should have blown those cap-
sules apart with the thruster rifle.*

And suddenly he felt himself stagger sideways, caught in
a wave of dizziness. He pinched his eyes shut. The agitated
microbes assumed a new level of frenzy as the physical
manifestation of his third demon threatened to overload
consciousness.

Demons one and two, growing old and growing
stupid—body leavened by the passage of years, mind becoming less attuned to Colette's intricate schemings—those
could at least be faced with a certain degree of fortitude.
But against demon three Ghandi possessed no defense. Demon three remained a brooding agony, a sin without any
hope for redemption.

He rode out the storm, the maelstrom of agitated microbes, a thousand tiny electric sparks snapping inside him,
relentlessly punishing a netherland of inner flesh. And he
found himself thinking: *This is how I flex; this is how Ghandi
the human being expunges an overload of pain.*

The microbes soared to an apex, reached their epitome
of agitation. And then a familiar metamorphosis: the
twitches decomposing into a series of shivers which raced
up his spine, spreading chills through the muscles of his
upper back. Finally came relief, a sanctitude of body silence. He sensed that this was how an epileptic must feel
after emerging from the cruelty of a fit.

Calvin still lay on the floor, smirking. Fingers flickered.
I'M SORRY. I DIDN'T THINK MY PISS WAS SO
STRONG.

Ghandi wiped his face. His anger had disappeared, had
again been repressed, transmuted from an outward manifestation to an inward tension. It was always like this.

When the twitching microbes were appeased, all strong emotions were neutralized, grounded by the body. The repression was the only positive aspect of these emotional fits. Sometimes it felt good to feel nothing.

He turned slightly, sensing movement. And there stood Colette wearing a silk robe.

"Be together," she ordered.

The Ash Nar obeyed instantly. Ky twisted his wrists and ankles, broke the twistik's tension with the ceiling. The tway fell gracefully, catlike, landing on his hands and feet on the balcony railing, pushing off, vanishing over the balustrade, dropping down into the rec chamber. Calvin and Jy were poised below and they caught him easily in their arms. A moment later, the three stood in a line, holding hands, tway Calvin in the middle, looking like a proud father posing with twin adult sons.

Colette laid her hand on Ghandi's shoulder. Her palm was cool to the touch and it made him realize just how overheated he had become. A good nasty twitch of the microbes always elevated core body temperature.

She spoke patiently. "Calvin, Ghandi has a point. I am disappointed that you have failed to locate this Susan Quint."

Calvin freed his right hand from Jy's grip. Fingertips rose, came to life. SHE HAS VANISHED. PROBABLY GONE UNDERGROUND.

Ghandi sneered.

SHE HAS NOT ATTEMPTED TO CONTACT HER AUNT, NOR ANY FRIENDS OR WORKMATES. SHE DID NOT KEEP HER OSTENSIBLY IMPORTANT DATE WITH THE MAN FROM CLARK SHUTTLE SERVICE.

"Are you certain?" asked Colette.

YES, I WAS WATCHING. AND LAST NIGHT I ALSO QUESTIONED A SECTECH FROM THIS MAN'S OFFICE. THE WOMAN INFORMED ME THAT SUSAN QUINT NEVER CONTACTED

CLARK SHUTTLE SERVICE TO CANCEL OR
POSTPONE. SHE SIMPLY DID NOT SHOW UP.

Ghandi released an exasperated sigh. "How do you
know this sectech was telling you the truth?"

Tway Calvin grinned broadly. I SEDUCED HER.

"Like you seduced Susan Quint?" taunted Ghandi. "Are
you trying to create more troubles for us?" He forced a
grin. "Or maybe by now you've acquired a bit of wisdom.
Maybe you killed this sectech right after you climbed out
of her bed."

Calvin's grin faded to a murderous glare.

"Enough, both of you," warned Colette. She leaned
over the railing. "Calvin, are you certain that she did not
attempt to contact her Aunt? I find it odd that Inez
Hernandez—Susan Quint's closest living relative—failed
to report her disappearance to E-Tech Security. Doyle
Blumhaven has confirmed this."

LA GLORIA DE LA CIENCIA HAS BEEN ONE OF
THE MORE VOCAL CRITICS OF CORRUPTION
WITHIN E-TECH SECURITY. ALSO, INEZ HER-
NANDEZ'S POSITION MAKES HER NATURALLY
SCANDAL-CONSCIOUS. THOSE TWO FACTORS
SUGGEST THAT THE COUNCILLOR WOULD
NOT TURN TO E-TECH SECURITY FOR HELP.
SHE WOULD BE MORE INCLINED TO GENERATE
A PRIVATE INVESTIGATION.

"Perhaps," mused Colette.

I HAVE RESEARCHED SUSAN QUINT EXTEN-
SIVELY. UNFORTUNATELY, SHE REMAINS HARD
TO PREDICT. SERIOUS CHILDHOOD TRAUMAS
HAVE LED TO A HISTORY OF ADULT EMO-
TIONAL PROBLEMS. SHE IS CONSIDERED TO BE
UNSTABLE, AND THUS, DIFFICULT TO LOCATE
ON A PROBABILITY GRID. HOWEVER, HER IN-
HERENT INSTABILITY HAS A POSITIVE AS-
PECT—IT IS UNLIKELY THAT SHE WILL BE ABLE
TO FULLY CONVINCE ANYONE TO BELIEVE

HER STORY, INCLUDING HER AUNT. I CON-
CLUDE THAT SHE POSES NO REAL DANGER TO
US.

Colette gave a slow nod. "You're probably correct. Still,
do not underestimate the importance of what Susan Quint
witnessed. If she should connect with the wrong people,
and identify you—Ghandi's aide—as being in Honshu, our
plans could be severely jeopardized."

THE SUNSETTER WIPED OUT MY PRESENCE
IN THE HONSHU TRANSIT RECORDS—

"—And Edward Huromonus's action/probe could place
you back at the scene." Colette wagged her finger. "Remember, Calvin, this action/probe could conceivably gain
access to the unaltered data from the original E-Tech Security investigation into the massacre, before I was able to
employ the sunsetter.

"Fortunately, Huromonus is not presently concentrating
on the Order of the Birch killings. Right now, he is more
interested in corruption within E-Tech Security. And
Doyle Blumhaven has been instructed to feed the action/
probe information along those lines. But Susan Quint must
not enter the picture. She has the potential to connect you,
the massacres, the slain Security officers, and ultimately,
CPG, together into one package. That cannot be permitted. Not now, not when our goals are so close to being
achieved."

I WILL REDOUBLE MY EFFORTS TO LOCATE
HER.

Colette stared upward, at the ceiling, her face momentarily blank, and Ghandi wondered if she was on the verge
of interlacing, becoming Sappho. But when she spoke, she
remained Colette.

"It was a mistake trying to dispose of so many couriers
at the same time in Honshu. My error, but one that will
not be repeated. We'll go back to our earlier pattern: three
or four targets per massacre."

I KILLED SEVEN COURIERS THURSDAY

NIGHT IN THE ARTWHILER AUDITORIUM. THAT ACTION DID NOT JEOPARDIZE US.

"Nevertheless, from now on, we will be doubly cautious. Three or four targets per massacre—no exceptions to that rule."

Three tways nodded in unison. THAT WILL MEAN AN INCREASED NUMBER OF MASSACRES IN ORDER TO MEET THE TARGET DATE.

"Yes. But now that the Colonies have been informed that a Paratwa starship has been detected, no one in the Colonies will be surprised if the Order of the Birch killers suddenly become even more violent."

THE PARATWA MUST NOT BE ALLOWED TO RETURN. Calvin smiled. LONG LIVE THE ORDER OF THE BIRCH.

Colette nodded. "And we'll try to cut down on the overall number of couriers disposed of through the massacres by increasing the number of individual murders and, where feasible, suicides."

Mild disappointment showed on the faces of the three tways. Ghandi knew that the maniac did not gain as much pleasure from a secret solitary killing or an arranged suicide as he did from a full-blown massacre.

"What is the latest count of infected Colonies?" asked Colette.

THE SKYGENE SUITCASES HAVE BEEN SUCCESSFULLY TESTED AND ACTIVATED IN ONE HUNDRED AND THIRTY-ONE COLONIES. SEVENTEEN MORE CYLINDERS ARE CURRENTLY BEING PREPARED.

"Good. We're over halfway there."

Ghandi shook his head. "Why not stop now?" he argued. "I still don't see the point of having these skygene machines hidden and activated within every single Colony?"

"You know the answer, my love. The Irryan Council must be absolutely convinced that every Colony is infected, that there is only one solution to their problem."

Gently, she rubbed Ghandi's back. "Out of their hopeless-
ness will grow the seeds of peace. The Ash Ock have been
planning the return for centuries. Believe me, our way is
best for both humans and Paratwa. The deaths that have
resulted thus far are but a fraction of the lives that would
be spent in all-out confrontation."

Calvin broke into a three-pronged smile, as if the
thought of an all-out war was extremely pleasing.

*Mindless maniac.*

"Don't worry," Colette soothed, reading Ghandi's tension. "Everything will turn out for the best."

Ghandi nodded. But he did not believe her.

The lion ordered his Costeau guards to remain outside,
then led the group into his private study. As the door slid
shut, preprogrammed illumination circuits ignited glow
panels, bathing the room in warm amber light. Opposite
the entrance, a wall of vertical slab glass, overlooking the
garden of the Alexanders' retreat, yielded a measure of
cool starlight from the transparent cosmishield strip nearest
the horizon, providing a wealth of luminous counterparts
to the soft artificial fluorescence. Irrya's mirrors had just
completed their rotation into darkness and most of the
daylight clouds had been vacuumed, permitting a clearer
view of the reflected heavens. Shortly before dawn,
centersky pumps would reactivate, create a fresh pattern of
cumulus vapors for the following day. The lion did not
know tomorrow's weather; he no longer paid much attention to the monthly schedule of ecospheric conditions.
Even if a rare thunderstorm had been programmed, he

would not have been aware of it until the first crack of thunder.

Servants had moved his oak desk to the corner and a rectangular table of compressed lunar shale laminated in plastic now dominated the center of the study. Five cushioned uprights surrounded the heavy construct. The table was fully functional, yet priceless because it was the only known artifact to have survived Ari Alexander, a shuttle pilot who had helped construct the Colonies over two and a half centuries ago, and who had later become one of the founding fathers of the Costeau movement.

As the lion sat at Ari's table, his fingers instinctively felt along its edge for the tiny inset animal heads that Ari had carved into the compressed lunar material. He traced the sharp outlines, the simple strokes that represented tigers and elephants and giraffes, as well as Ari's favorite, the lions. All were ancient beasts of the jungle. Most were extinct.

Inez Hernandez and Adam Lu Sang assumed the two chairs on the left side of the table, Nick and Gillian captured the opposite set. The midget deftly snatched his partner's cushion out from under him an instant before Gillian's bottom landed on it. Nick added the second cushion to his own, enabling his elbows to reach the top of the table.

Gillian forced a smile at the midget's action. *Always, you play games. Always there are tricks.* But then his thoughts turned to a more somber element of Nick's horseplay.

*Lately, my reflexes do not seem to be as sharp. With only a modest effort, I should have been able to stop Nick from snatching that cushion. Yet I literally did not see him reaching for it.* Gillian hoped that the midget had mistaken his slowed reaction time for simple disinterest.

Nick squirmed on the double cushion and balanced his stubby arms on the laminated surface. For a long moment, he stared at Gillian. Then his blue eyes brightened with delight and he turned to the others.

"Councillor Hernandez, it's good to finally meet you in person. The lion has told us so much about you. We're honored."

Inez Hernandez smiled at Nick's greeting, but Gillian saw the strain on her face: a delicate lifting of the shaggy eyebrows, tension lines beneath the pupils, an infinitesimal quiver of the lower lip. She laid her hands on the table, but the fingers quickly interlaced, tightening until bony knuckles protruded. Even the tone of her voice suggested the exertion of forced control.

"Please," she urged, "there should be informality among us. My name is Inez."

The lion spoke. "I appreciate that both of you were able to come here on such short notice. I trust that neither of you experienced any security problems."

"I'm covered for six hours," said Adam. "I programmed a false itinerary. Right now, I'm supposed to be doing hands-on research at a rotopulse facility twenty miles from here."

Inez responded with a delicate nod.

"To business, then," said the lion. "Gillian, Nick? It's your meeting."

"The good news," Nick drawled, "is that we've learned something about the Order of the Birch killers. The bad news is that there's only *one* of them. We're dealing with a Paratwa assassin."

Inez's eyes widened. "Are you certain?"

"Uh-huh. Yesterday, Gillian's investigation into the auditorium massacre led him to that conclusion. Shooter and Slasher are aspects of one consciousness. The evidence is incontrovertible."

Inez frowned at Gillian. "How can you be so sure?"

*She doesn't know who I really am,* thought Gillian. Back in the time of Reemul, the Council of Irrya had been told of his true identity. But they had never divulged that secret. In this era, only Jerem Marth knew that he was the tway of an Ash Ock, a tway capable of extraordinary insights.

"I've studied Paratwa my entire life," Gillian explained. "I was born into the era when they first arose. I know these creatures. I know their ways."

Inez still looked skeptical.

"Worse yet," continued Nick, "is the nature of this assassin. We're not dealing with an ordinary Paratwa. This interlink is composed of *three* tways, not two."

Adam scowled. Inez opened her mouth in astonishment. "I thought that only the binary interlace was possible."

Nick squirmed on the cushions. "You're right, according to our understanding of the Paratwa phenomenon. What we're faced with here is a creature that is theoretically impossible. Living cells from a singular McQuade Unity—the telepathic organism that was first grown in a Scottish laboratory back in 2052—can only be injected into a *pair* of human fetuses, enabling the two fetuses to evolve into a singular consciousness, telepathically interlaced for life. But that process only works with *two*—trying to inject three or more fetuses renders the McQuade Unity dysfunctional."

The midget sighed. "I'm not a scientist, and I've never totally understood the complexities involved. But I've talked to enough genetic engineers to know that the formation of the mental-emotional interlink can only occur in the binary form. Only two can be brought together."

"And yet," mused the lion, "in this case you say that there are three." He faced Gillian. "Any chance that you're mistaken?"

Gillian knew that Jerem entertained no real doubts; the lion played devil's advocate for Inez's and Adam's benefit. Jerem Marth seemed to accept most of Gillian's conclusions with an almost naïve sense of trust, an unshakable belief based on the fleeting relationship that had developed between them fifty-six years ago. Gillian found such trust enigmatic. The passage of over half a century should have dulled teenage passions, shorn this man of such absolute faith. But the opposite seemed to have occurred. Just yesterday, he had come to realize that Jerem must have lived out the better part of his life under the spell of an ancient obsession.

*He'll believe most anything I tell him.*

Gillian did not relish such powers of persuasion; he hoped that eventually his flesh-and-blood presence would begin to restore the lion's critical abilities. And he fervently hoped that Nick remained unaware of Jerem's obsession. All too often, Nick utilized the dynamics of a relationship to achieve his own ends.

*Like you used me all those years.*

He felt no bitterness toward the midget. But he no longer trusted him, either. Fifty-six years ago, the awakening of Gillian's true self had driven a wedge between them. And yesterday's encounter with Martha and Buff had widened the gap, however much Gillian respected Nick's idea of saddling him with a pair of Costeau watchdogs. Manipulation remained manipulation.

Nick stared at him; cheeks crinkled into the familiar easygoing smile.

*I will do what you want. But only so long as it serves my own needs.*

Gillian permitted himself to again recall yesterday's gestalt, the clarity of his subconscious comprehensions. "I'm not mistaken about this Paratwa," he announced. "I don't know how, or why. But I'm certain we're dealing with a creature consisting of three tways."

"Which leads us," said Nick, "into an entire realm of mostly unpleasant speculations. First of all, where did this assassin come from?"

"A sleeper, found on Earth?" suggested Adam.

"Like Reemul?" Nick frowned. "I don't think so. If someone had successfully engineered such a Paratwa prior to the Apocalypse, we would have seen evidence of it. Such a unique creature would have surely turned up on the world armaments market. A tripartite assassin would have been considered invaluable."

Gillian agreed. His teachers, Aristotle and Meridian, would certainly have told him if such a thing had existed.

"So where does that leave us?" asked Inez quietly. And the lion knew that her thoughts had turned to his missing grandniece.

"Second generation," proclaimed Nick. "The Colonies have been introduced to the latest advance in genetic engineering: a phase two Paratwa assassin."

"It's the only possibility that makes any sense," added Gillian. "A tripartite Paratwa has to be based on concepts that were not understood by the original pre-Apocalyptic creators. This creature represents a spectacular design advancement over the original assassins of twenty-first-century Earth. And that means that Paratwa research never ended; it was only interrupted."

"I see only two conceivable scenarios," offered the midget. "One, this assassin is the culmination of a long-term clandestine research project operating somewhere within the Colonies."

No one replied. The lion knew that none of them could envision such a long-term research project remaining secret.

Nick went on. "The second, and more likely, possibility, is that we're dealing with a creature who was created and trained beyond our solar system, a creature probably bred by the Ash Ock."

"Trust preserve us," whispered Inez.

The lion, even after a night's sleep, still had trouble coming to terms with Gillian's conclusions. Just days ago they had learned about the returning starship. Yet if Nick and Gillian were correct, at least one Paratwa was already in the cylinders. The ramifications of that were terrifying.

"So Susan witnessed a Paratwa attack," Inez murmured. The Councillor's fingers were now locked together so tightly that Gillian could see the muscles pulsing beneath the backs of her hands. "And this Paratwa sent those E-Tech Security men to murder her. And when Donnelly and Tace failed, the Paratwa lured them to a parking garage and murdered *them*."

Nick nodded. "By failing to kill Susan, Donnelly and Tace became a liability. Susan had disappeared. Susan could connect the Honshu massacre with the two officers, provide a direct link to the assassin."

"Would Donnelly and Tace have known they were working for a Paratwa?" asked Adam.

"I doubt it," answered Gillian, "even though they were probably dealing directly with one of the tways. However, in all likelihood, Donnelly and Tace never realized that there was a direct connection between their employer and the Order of the Birch attacks ... at least not until they were ordered to kill Susan Quint. And I have a feeling that Donnelly and Tace were doomed the instant they agreed to that assassination. Even if they had succeeded in killing Susan, I suspect that their lives would have ended the same way, in that parking garage."

"No loose ends," muttered Inez.

"In the Honshu terminal," said Nick, "Susan accidentally witnessed more than she should have." He turned to Inez. "Your grandniece told you that she felt she recognized one of the killers. That tway—the Paratwa—must also have recognized her. And the assassin considered it imperative that Susan not live to talk about what she had seen."

Inez's fingers tightened another notch. The lion leaned across the table and laid his palm on her wrist. He spoke gently. "We still don't know what's happened to Susan. My people are searching everywhere and they've still found no trace. But for the time being, Inez, you must consider no news to be good news."

The Councillor shook her head. "She's been missing for a week. No one's heard from her." Inez swallowed and forced her fingers apart, pressed her palms against the table. "Seven days ... by now, we should have heard *something*."

"You're right," said Gillian.

Inez locked eyes with him. "You think Susan's dead, don't you."

"It's possible," he admitted. "The Paratwa could have found her, killed her, and disposed of her body."

Inez flinched.

"But it's just as likely that she's gone underground," Nick said hastily. "She could turn up anywhere."

"Please, Inez," urged the lion, patting her hand, "don't jump to any conclusions. There's no reason to abandon hope."

An echo of immeasurable sadness lurked beneath Inez's words. "I should have believed her. She came to me for help and I turned her away."

No one spoke.

The Councillor's despondent tone turned bitter. "I should have helped her. I should have had the good sense to realize that she needed my support. Instead, I turned my back on her."

"You couldn't have known," soothed the lion.

"I *should* have known. I should have realized that I was helping to seal her fate."

Gillian sighed. "Yes, your poor judgment probably led to her death."

Inez stared across the table at him.

"You probably killed her," he continued calmly. "Ultimately, your lack of foresight was responsible."

The Councillor scowled.

"And before the assassin murdered your grandniece," Gillian said softly, "it probably tortured her as well—to learn for certain whether she'd talked to anyone ... or maybe it just tortured her for the fun of it. Some Paratwa enjoyed things like that. And now you're going to have to add another burden to your pyre of guilt, that Susan died a slow and agonizing death."

Inez gritted her teeth. Cheeks swelled with anger.

"Good," said Gillian. "You're angry. That's fine. Stay a

bit mad. If you want to grieve, then at least wait until you have something to grieve about. Right now, the only thing we know for certain is that your grandniece is missing. Correct?"

"Correct," she snapped, glaring at Gillian with barely repressed fury.

He ignored her anger. "Jerem says that you checked Susan's apartment?"

"You're a real bastard."

Gillian did not respond. The lion noted that Nick was gazing at his partner with an expression of intense curiosity.

Inez drew a deep breath, brought her emotions under control. "Yes, I checked Susan's apartment the day after she disappeared. I found nothing. Her desk calendar memory was wiped clean. I also talked casually with her supervisor and several of her co-workers in the Progress Inspection department. She never showed up for work, never called."

"And no one has inquired about her since she disappeared?" asked Nick.

"No. To allay suspicions, I told Susan's co-workers that she'd been transferred. And as far as I know, she had no close friends." The Councillor paused. "For the most part, Susan shied away from relationships that made any sort of emotional demands."

"Any sexual partners that you're aware of?" asked Nick.

Inez spoke slowly. "Susan was quite active in that respect. She once told me that she often had as many as a dozen different partners per week."

"That's active," quipped Nick, keeping a straight face.

The Councillor stared down at the table. "Susan suffered from many problems. She was overloaded with hurt . . . things from her past, things that wouldn't go away. In many respects, life was extremely difficult for her."

The lion sensed the deep control in Inez's tone. And he

could not help noticing that Inez kept referring to Susan in the past tense.

"Susan dealt with these hurts as best she could. But she required a lot of . . . attention. Sex was a catharsis for her; she often went to clubs, picked up a string of men over the space of one evening."

"Pain relievers," suggested Gillian, with complete understanding.

"At any rate," continued Nick, "no one knows about her disappearance except us, the Paratwa, and the investigators from the Edward Huromonus action/probe, whom you leaked the information to."

Inez nodded.

"What could Susan have witnessed in that terminal?" asked the lion. "Even though we're now certain it was a Paratwa, even though Susan made eye contact with one of the tways, I still can't fathom why this creature would want her dead." He turned to Inez. "Susan's job took her all over the Colonies. She must have known thousands of people. How would she be able to connect this tway with someone she knew? Why did this creature take the added risk of having Donnelly and Tace attempt to assassinate her?"

"Maybe the Paratwa overreacted," mused Adam.

"No," said Gillian. "Jerem's right, there must be more to this than merely a fleeting eye contact. Susan must have seen more than she realized. That's the only explanation I can think of that would account for this Paratwa wanting her dead. If Shooter and Slasher have real-world identities, then they would have been well-disguised during the actual massacre. I don't see them being so careless as to allow Susan—or anyone else—to see through those disguises."

"Could Susan have recognized this third tway?" wondered Adam.

Inez shook her head vigorously. "She claimed to have made eye contact with only one of the actual assassins."

Nick shrugged. "Maybe so. But if this third tway—the

backup—was there in the terminal, it's possible that for some reason he was *not* in disguise. Maybe Susan saw him and recognized him. Maybe the Paratwa was afraid that Susan would connect this third tway with the tway she made eye contact with."

"But only two tways participated in the massacre," argued Inez. "So even if Susan spotted this third tway—this backup—how would she know to link him with the two killers?"

"Good question," admitted Nick.

"There's one possibility," Gillian began slowly. "Let's suppose that we're on the right track. Let's assume that this third tway was in Yamaguchi Terminal undisguised and that Susan would know him on sight.

"But maybe it doesn't matter whether or not Susan saw this third tway. Maybe that's not the point." He paused. "What if the Paratwa was afraid that Susan would be questioned by the authorities—legitimate E-Tech investigators—and that she would reveal her 'eye contact.' An investigator with even a small amount of common sense— and with access to the transit records—would probably have asked Susan to examine those IDs to see if she recognized any other names or faces among those individuals who had prepurchased shuttle tickets." Gillian paused again, waiting for them to follow where he was leading.

The lion and Adam looked puzzled. Inez shook her head. "You're saying that this third tway prepurchased a shuttle ticket, using his own name and identity? But so what? I still don't understand—"

"A honeysuck!" cried the midget, rising out of his cushions. "Son-of-a-bitch! The third tway was not in disguise because he was acting as the honeysuck! Goddamn it, that's gotta be it!"

The lion frowned. "What are you talking about?"

"The honeysuck," Gillian explained, "is an old assassin's trick. The basic premise was to manipulate a number of targets into a public location by having one of the tways

serve as bait. For example, a tway contacts each intended
victim individually and sets up a meeting—in a large restaurant, let's say. Each target shows up for the meeting at
the appointed time and place and when they're all together, the second tway enters the restaurant, weapons firing. Tway two kills all of the honeysucked targets as well
as a large number of innocent bystanders; he also allows
an equally large number of bystanders to survive so that
suspicion won't fall on his other half—the tway who served
as the bait.

"This is just one possible example. The honeysuck had
a thousand variations, some infinitely subtle. But the idea
behind it remained the same: One tway tricked the targets
into congregating at a specific location at the same time;
the other tway disposed of them. And if properly carried
out, a honeysuck massacre left very little evidence to indicate that it was a premeditated attack."

The lion turned to the others. Adam looked a bit aghast.
Inez was slowly shaking her head. Jerem Marth accepted
Gillian's example calmly, even though he fully understood
the sense of revulsion that Inez and Adam were experiencing. They all knew what the final days had been like; they
had all studied the history texts. Back then, murder for
profit had been a common, everyday occurrence, and
Paratwa assassins were often employed as the instruments
of death. But Gillian was a man who had lived through
that era, and to hear him matter-of-factly describe such
brutal acts lent a particular horror to the tale.

For the lion, however, hearing of such pre-Apocalyptic
monstrosities no longer carried the weight of revulsion and
distaste. Not since he was twelve years old had such tales
bothered him. Not since Reemul.

Nick wagged his head eagerly. "In Honshu, this third
tway must have been the honeysuck. Maybe some of the
targets were accompanying him and maybe he was scheduled to rendezvous with some of the others. But his job
was to make sure they were all there so his other two tways

could murder them within the larger framework of the massacre. Afterward, the honeysuck tway was probably even questioned by the investigators. But they would have had no reason to be unduly suspicious. Tway three would be perceived as just another lucky survivor."

"But if Susan knew him," offered Inez, "then she probably would have told the investigators."

The lion shook his head. "That still seems a flimsy reason for trying to kill her."

"Maybe not," answered Nick. "Let's assume that this third tway cannot afford to have even the slightest suspicion cast upon him. Maybe if the investigating team really took a close look at our boy, they would see that most, if not all, of his companions died in the massacre."

"A group of targets," continued Gillian, "who are in some way connected. And that connection might lead us to whomever is ultimately responsible for these massacres."

"The Order of the Birch?" wondered Adam.

"I doubt it," said Gillian. "I believe this whole Order of the Birch business is simply a convoluted kind of smokescreen, designed to cast suspicions away from the real reasons for these killings. Namely, that there are specific individuals who have been targeted for assassination."

The lion frowned. "What about this latest massacre, the attack upon the Order of the Birch itself?"

"Just an attempt to spread more confusion." Nick spoke slowly, measuring his words. "The deadliest Paratwa thrived on remaining unpredictable. And many assassinations were planned for multiple effects. In addition to wiping out specific targets, perhaps the assault on the Order of the Birch contributes to some long-range social manipulation." The midget turned toward the slab-glass wall, gazed out at the distant stars.

"These massacres," continued Gillian, "could almost serve as archetypal twenty-first century Paratwa attacks. If you have to assassinate one person, kill ten others at the same time to disguise the real target. But in Honshu, and

perhaps in the conference center as well, there must have
been more than just a few intended victims. Tway three
must have honeysucked a large number of targets—always
a riskier proposition. And then Susan Quint came along
and fouled things up."

"A *lot* of targets," mused Nick. "That suggests that whoever is behind these massacres needs to dispose of a great
number of people in a relatively short period of time."

"Exactly," said Gillian. "They're taking chances. If there
were a smaller number of targets, the assassin would probably eliminate them one by one, arrange their murders to
look like accidents and suicides: far safer methods of disposal than a multiple-target honeysuck."

"Maybe," suggested Adam, "they're using these other
methods as well . . . killing people individually."

"That's possible," Gillian replied.

"What I still don't understand," said the midget, turning
his attention back to the table, "is why our Paratwa wasn't
able to kill Susan the moment they made eye contact? It
should have instantly realized the potential threat. It
should have gone out of its way to make certain she ended
up on the floor as a victim."

Gillian nodded thoughtfully. "And she escaped from
those two E-Tech officers as well." He turned to Inez. "I
believe you mentioned to Jerem that your grandniece was
always a very fast little girl, a very sharp thinker." He hesitated. "By any chance, was she adopted?"

Inez frowned. "No. Why do you ask?"

"If we're reading this whole situation correctly, it sounds
to me as if Susan might have some sort of genetically modified neuromuscular system. I assume that you would have
mentioned it if such traits ran in your family. But on the
other hand, if she was adopted . . ."

"She was not adopted," said Inez firmly.

"Did you witness her birth?"

The Councillor scowled. "Her parents—my nephew
and his wife—were at a Church retreat down on the sur-

face during the delivery. But I saw Susan's mother several times during the period she was carrying Susan. She was *certainly* pregnant."

"Did you know her doctor?"

"No. He was a private doctor, from the Church."

"Any medical records?" asked Nick.

"Of course. After her parents killed themselves, all medical documents were forwarded to her psychplan doctors. They certainly never mentioned anything about genetic enhancements."

Gillian shrugged. "That doesn't prove anything. From a practical standpoint, a genetically modified neuromuscular system only can be spotted using very sophisticated test procedures. And Susan might not have realized she was blessed with such modifications; without training, such abilities can remain latent throughout a lifetime. If Susan was an athlete, perhaps, pushing herself beyond normal physical limits, then such extraordinary abilities would have been revealed to her. Otherwise, her enhancements might only have been noticed during times of stress, like in Honshu, and when the two officers tried to kill her."

"This is ridiculous," snapped Inez. "Susan wasn't bred, she was born."

"In vitro fertilization," added Nick, "was not the best technique for a genejob. It was easier to develop the fetus completely in the laboratory. But Susan's embryo *could* have been implanted in your niece's uterus, or genetically modified while in the womb. Either way, normal gestation and delivery would have taken place."

Inez glared at the lion. "This entire discussion is becoming absurd."

The lion was not so sure.

"Remember what we're dealing with here," cautioned Nick. "A Paratwa assassin, and a very special one at that. Some of them were so fast and deadly that they never left witnesses—*ever*. Yet Susan survived, even though this assassin must have instantly realized just how imperative it was that she not be allowed to spread her story. And then she escaped from Donnelly and Tace as well."

"There has to be a reason she survived," said Gillian. "If Susan's a genejob, that might explain things."

The lion said: "Since the medical records do not indicate genetic modifications, and since we don't have Susan here, then this is all a moot point. Correct?"

Nick looked from the lion to Inez. "Yeah, I suppose you're right. Sorry, Inez. We're just trying to fill in pieces of the puzzle."

"Let's concentrate on the assassin," urged the lion. "What's our next step?"

Nick turned to Adam. "Can you get us access into E-Tech Security?"

The programmer looked doubtful. "Security's not a direct part of the archives, though of course there are numerous junctions. But the junctions are heavily guarded. Lots of defenses. Security's about the toughest system to penetrate."

"I won't take no for an answer," said Nick. "I want to see the E-Tech Security reports on all of these killings. If we're dealing with honeysucks, we're going to need every bit of data we can dredge up to make sense out of this mess. Plus I want a list of everyone who was scheduled to pass through Yamaguchi Terminal at the time of the massacre."

"Don't you already have that information?" wondered Inez. "The transit computer records?"

A faded smile crossed Nick's face. "Let's see if we can't get the E-Tech Security report as well. Just for a comparison. E-Tech Security is under a great deal of suspicion these days. Perhaps they're hiding something."

Adam shook his head. He looked very nervous. "It won't be easy. Breaking into Security is going to take time. Weeks, maybe. And even if I can penetrate Security, I might end up leaving a trail for someone to follow."

"I believe that it's worth the risk," urged Nick.

The lion favored Adam with a supportive smile. "You've gotten involved with more than you've bargained for here. I believe we would all understand if you chose not to cast yourself any deeper into these waters."

Adam swallowed. "If it's necessary, I suppose I'll help . . . in whatever way I can."

"Thank you, Adam," said Inez graciously. "And I want you to know that we do appreciate your efforts. As far as I'm concerned, you're an unsung hero for coming forward in the first place."

The young programmer looked ready to blush. "Thanks," he muttered.

"How are we doing with the sunsetter?" asked the lion.

Adam frowned. "We're still having some difficulties."

"What we're having," said Nick, "is a hell of a time. It's bad enough trying to crack the sunsetter. But it's even worse with this rescue program hovering nearby, always ready to foul our efforts. Just when we're getting ready to lock onto a program that the sunsetter is reaming of data, Freebird shows up. Bye bye, program. We've even tried sending my IRS audit program after multiple sunsetter targets simultaneously. It doesn't matter. Where the sunsetter goes, Freebird follows. When the sunsetter is even remotely threatened, Freebird saves its ass." The midget shook his head. "Hell of a thing."

Adam hunched forward. "Should we tell them about our theory?"

Nick smiled grimly. "I suppose we'd better."

"We're beginning to suspect," said Adam, "that no direct relationship exists between the sunsetter and Freebird. They both run freely throughout the system, and they obviously interact. But that interaction is based on externalized parameters—a one-way data pact. When the sunsetter is threatened, Freebird takes action to preserve the destroyer's integrity. But the two programs seem to possess no mutual hinge points."

"Hinge points," continued Nick, "represent the data

nexus between two mutually controlled programs. But in this instance there are none, at least none that we can detect. What that means is that this particular version of Freebird must have other functions besides guarding the sunsetter from outside interference. And I have a funny hunch. It's nothing I can really put my finger on—not yet, anyway—but something tells me that the sunsetter and Freebird are not being run by the same mommies."

Inez looked bewildered. "Two different controllers?"

"Yes."

Adam nodded his head vigorously.

"The sunsetter," explained Nick, "is about twenty-two years old. That's about as close as we can calculate, based on the size of the archives and the rate of data decimation. However, Freebird appears to be older. Again, this is just a hunch. But Freebird seems to have a quality about it . . . some facet that makes its actions seem so effortless . . ." The midget hesitated, groping for words. "It's more than the fact that it's an immensely powerful program. This Freebird seems so . . . sure of itself. I can't explain it much better, certainly not with any real clarity. It's just that I get the funny feeling that Freebird knows the archives inside and out. Like it's been there for a long time."

"Fifty years or more," clarified Adam.

Nick went on. "There is a slight possibility that Freebird's a remote—an automatic program, a sleeper— put into the archives hundreds of years ago for unknown purposes. Freebird's prototype *does* date back to the twenty-first century."

"And your IRS program," suggested the lion, "somehow caused this Freebird to be awakened?"

"Yes. Freebird's tactical command center seems to have been triggered when my IRS program made its first assault on the sunsetter. The program came alive and, for reasons we can't comprehend, began protecting the sunsetter."

The lion sighed. "We seem to be producing more questions than answers here. We still have no idea who's controlling the sunsetter. Nor do we know the real purpose behind these massacres. And now there's this Freebird program."

"True enough," said Nick, turning to Gillian. "But I'm beginning to get the odor of a particular stench hanging over all of this, an odor of massive manipulation."

Gillian nodded. He felt it too. Things were tied together somehow. Things were connected.

"Ash Ock," concluded the lion grimly. "And for all we know, Sappho or Theophrastus could already be in the Colonies."

"I wouldn't bet against it," answered the midget.

*Ash Ock,* Gillian mused, his thoughts focusing on his own strange reality.

*I desire wholeness. Yet I'm afraid to permit the arising of Empedocles. I don't know where my monarch will lead me.*

Desire and fear: a dialectic becoming more powerful with each passing day. Gillian knew that sooner or later, whether he wanted it or not, he was going to be thrust into a state of extreme tension, a state that could bring on the whelm—the forced interlace melding him and Catharine together. Eventually, the growing force of this particular dialectic alone, the yin and yang of desire and fear, could lead to Paratwa unity. And when that time came, Gillian might be powerless to stop Empedocles from arising.

There were other paths that could also lead to the whelm. His flexing urges—those brief intervals of biorhythmic upheaval, internal cycles peaking every four hours, fusing wild subconscious tempests with rational thought, serving to relieve the interlace of excess pressure—those too were times when the possibility of the whelm was enhanced.

*But I'm still in control.* For the time being, as long as he did not consciously attempt to summon his monarch, he felt reasonably confident that separation could be maintained. Yet there remained an even greater period of danger.

*A physical menace, a threat to my life. Just as it happened fifty-six years ago, the possibility of bodily harm could bring Empedocles to the forefront, bring on the whelm.*

"What's our next step?" asked the lion.

Gillian was not sure. He knew only that they had to remain vigilant.

A deep frown crossed Nick's face. "If we assume that the Ash Ock are responsible for unleashing this tripartite Paratwa, and that this assassin is indeed honeysucking multiple victims for some unknown purpose, then something else seems clear: Our enemy is in one hell of a rush."

The lion agreed. "Their goals must be accomplished with all due haste." He paused. "Before their starships return?"

"I believe so," said Nick. "And that may mean that the Colonies are running out of time as well."

"What do you mean?" asked Inez.

"I'm not sure," Nick answered grimly. "But I'm starting to get a really bad feeling about all of this. Like we're heading into a battle that we've already lost."

The lion found himself gazing at Gillian, thinking: *You'll find a way to solve these puzzles. You'll find a way to save us.* But he instantly recognized such thoughts for what they were: exercises in wish fulfillment, the vague hopes of a twelve-year-old child.

Inez turned to Nick. "You make it sound like we don't stand much of a chance."

A rueful smile crept across the midget's face. "Yeah, I suppose I do. But hell, I'm an optimist from way back. And when you're faced with a losing ball game in the ninth inning, it just means that you have to start bending the rules a bit."

On her third day at the Ontario Cloister, the sun came out from behind the clouds.

When it happened, Susan was sitting crosslegged beneath the old steel dock, her back to a smooth concrete pier, staring out across the faintly misted lake, watching a pair of imported sea gulls take turns splashing against the dull gray surface of the water. To her left lay the sprawling complex of the Cloister, a sextet of interconnected two- and three-story structures that had been built over a hundred and fifty years ago by the original Church of the Trust. To her right and slightly forward, at the edge of the water, a stark four-hundred-foot tower rose into the gloomy skies. It was a revivifier—one of two protecting the Cloister—a tarnished red plastic monstrosity responsible for circulating fresh air and maintaining the immediate area free of organic pollutants. Without it, Susan would have been sitting lakeside in a sealed breathing suit, not shorts and a halter.

To the north, the swirling clouds of slate suddenly parted. And brightness poured from the sky.

It startled her. The surface of the lake transformed, became a shining tapestry; the tops of the gently breaking waves looked like they had been sheathed by an undulating skin of white flame. One of the gulls, gliding across the water, sent up a frothy spray, and the trembling droplets seemed to hang in the air, sparkling in the new light. And the shadows . . .

In the Colonies, with their standard arrangement of three land strips and three sun strips, controlled tripartite

images of a dulled sun cast three shadows—one strong and
two weak, the more potent light source always directly
overhead. But here there was only one source, a fiery
golden ball far brighter than any light that was allowed to
pass through the glass of the sun sectors, a light so fierce
that she could not even look at it. Crisp black silhouettes
appeared everywhere: the buildings of the Cloister cast
down their images along the gently rising bare-faced hills
to the south. The outline of the revivifier darkened a huge
expanse of newly planted pines behind the dock.

Susan held out her arms, wiggled her fingers, fascinated
not only by the perfect shadows on the moist sand but by
the sudden warmth along her flesh, as if she were inches
away from a heating grid. She twisted her arms, rotating
them so that all flesh received an equal chance to experience the curious sensation.

"Sunbathing?"

It was a man's voice, directly behind her, and she turned
quickly, not startled, but surprised that someone had managed to sneak up on her. He stood beside the thick pier
that supported her back, enveloped in shadow.

"Sunbathing," he explained, in a deep melodious voice,
"was an old Earth custom. People used to actually coat
their bodies in protective gels and expose their flesh for
hours—"

"I know what sunbathing is," she interrupted quietly.
"There are places in the Colonies—"

"Not the same," he insisted, stepping forward into the
sunlight.

She frowned and turned completely around to study this
stranger.

He was an older man, and big—over six feet tall, with
a thick neck and broad shoulders, his oversized frame enclosed in a simple gray robe that hung to his ankles. Massive brown boots had sunk into the wet sand; he must have
weighed close to three hundred pounds. The round face
drooped below the mouth, indicating the beginnings of a

double chin; the skin had a dark, but healthy looking, complexion. Thin gray hair curled around his ears but the strands were carefully trimmed in front, permitting scalloped bangs to fall almost to the eyebrows.

He craned his neck and squinted up at the sun. "Ahh, we're going to lose it. Too many reversal layers on the Canadian side of the lake. Can't sustain a sunburst for more than a few minutes, usually."

As he spoke, the light dimmed. In another moment the sun was gone, blanketed by the swirling mists. Shadows vanished. The warmth disappeared from her arms. Susan felt a mild sense of disappointment.

The man sighed. "Once, a couple of months ago, we had a really good summer storm. On a Tuesday, late in the afternoon. The third week of June, I believe. Right after the storm, the clouds and smog blew away, hustled back out over the lake by some freak atmospheric condition. The sun came out and stayed out for nearly twenty minutes. Some of the high level pollution was even dispersed and a couple of patches of blue sky appeared. It was very nice."

Susan found herself smiling. "I imagine it was."

"Did you know that this lake is about fourteen feet below its original level, its pre-Apocalyptic level?"

"No. I didn't know."

"Did you think that they would have built this pier almost completely out of the water?"

There was no criticism in his voice. In fact, there was almost a gentle humor behind the words. She found herself chuckling.

"I guess I wasn't thinking."

"Earth can do that to you."

She stood up, brushed a patch of wet sand off her butt. She extended her hand. "My name's Susan Quint."

He looked at her hand for a moment, then smiled. "I don't shake hands. Please do not be offended."

She shrugged and lowered her arm. "No problem." Susan had read that some Costeaus did not believe in the handshake custom either.

"Did you know," he continued, "that even though Lake Ontario is still poisoned, there are some species of fish, imported from the Colonies, that have adapted to its waters. And the gulls, they are beginning to feed on these fish."

"I didn't know that."

"Did you know that the sunbursts are occurring with greater frequency? Statistically, we should get one about every five days. Do you know what that means?"

She felt like she was back in school, being quizzed. "I suppose that means that the Earth is restoring itself. Ecospheric Turnaround is working."

A tolerant smile played across his jowled face. "The Earth is restoring itself. But Ecospheric Turnaround has little to do with it. E-Tech's projects have been going on for a long time, but they remain too isolated to generate any notable climatic changes."

"That's not what E-Tech says," she pointed out.

"Do you always believe what you hear on the E-Tech telecasts?"

"La Gloria de la Ciencia agrees. And most of the freelancer channels believe that E-Tech's Turnaround programs have been responsible for the growing changes."

"Ahh, well. I suppose that disputing such universal opinions could become a life's work. No matter. The changes are occurring. That is what remains important."

"Do you have a name?" she asked.

"Forgive my manners. I'm Timmy."

"Pleased to meet you, Timmy. How long have you been visiting the Cloister?"

He chuckled. "A good part of my life. I was born here."

"Born here?"

"Ahh, yes. I'm the chief caretaker. I take stock of things around here, make sure that what's broken gets fixed. What's loose, gets tightened. What's twisted, gets straightened."

"And you were born at the Cloister?" Susan had heard of a few isolated instances of people being born on Earth. But she had never before met anyone.

Timmy gave a solemn nod. "I was born near here."

"When was the last time you were in the Colonies?"

"I was never in the Colonies."

She frowned. "That's not possible."

Another chuckle. "Why not?"

"Because. It's just not . . . I mean . . ." She stopped, confused. "There's a shuttle that goes up every other day."

"Weak heart," Timmy explained. "Probably couldn't take the acceleration. Doctors say it would most likely kill me."

"Couldn't you get a transplant?"

"Don't want to go to the Colonies. I like it down here."

She could not imagine. *A whole life, never setting foot in the Colonies, never seeing Irrya. And yet . . .*

There was something about the planet, something about the slow easy life of the Cloister. Since coming down here with Lester, three days ago, all her troubles seemed to have receded. The Honshu massacre, the murderous assassins, Aunt Inez's betrayal, even her lost opportunity to date the Clark Shuttle Service VP. Everything had acquired a new perspective, had been immeasurably distanced within consciousness. All those things continued to be important; she would not allow herself to be deceived into thinking that her stay on the planet was anything more than a temporary respite from the reality of her problems. But a vacation remained a vacation. She was glad that Lester had convinced her to come.

Her only real disappointment was that Lester Mon Dama had been called back to Irrya yesterday. She had hoped to spend more time with him, get to know him better.

But in the days following the announcement of the returning Paratwa starship, the Colonies had been thrown into a minor uproar. The Reformed Church of the Trust had required Lester's presence. Priests could help allay people's fears, Lester had explained. She had been bitterly disappointed.

*Oh hell, Susan, admit it. You wanted him as a lover. Or more than a lover.*

But not seeing him for a day had put that particular obsession into perspective. Lester was nice, but he was really not her idea of a sexual mate. At least that was what she had been telling herself.

"Are you a lifelong member of the Trust?" asked Timmy.

She laughed. "Hardly. Less than a week, actually."

"Just wanted a trip to the planet, huh?"

"I'm afraid that's basically it."

"I'm not a member either. Don't tell anyone, but I think the Trust is one of the silliest religions ever dreamed up. Of course, historically, most religions appear rather absurd when seen from the outside. The mythic content of a religion only becomes powerful when the individual projects his or her own needs, desires, or fears onto its template. As an example, if you're afraid of dying, then a religion that promises eternal salvation predicates spiritual awareness."

"Everyone's afraid of dying," Susan countered.

Timmy stared out over the water. "No. Not everyone."

"You're not afraid?" she challenged. "Even a little bit?"

He smiled. "Again, I'm afraid that disputing such universal opinions is time-wasteful."

Susan shrugged. *Try walking into the middle of a massacre someday, Timmy. Or try having a pair of E-Tech Security men attempt to kill you. And then tell me about being afraid to die.*

Timmy gazed solemnly at her. "You went away there."

"Pardon?"

"You just went away. You just lost touch for a moment. I saw it on your face?"

Susan found herself scowling. "What do you mean?"

"You've got good solid body-thought. You shouldn't allow yourself to lose it, at least not when you're in public."

She did not know what he was talking about. "This is not exactly a public place," she said slowly, spreading out her arms to encompass the lake and the Cloister. There were a few other people walking near the buildings. But she and Timmy were far enough away to be considered alone.

"Two is public. One is alone. You're in public."

"And what is body-thought?" she demanded, feeling a bit perturbed, but not knowing why.

Timmy reached down and picked up a plum-sized stone from the edge of the pier. He hefted it for a moment, then bounced it up and down a couple of times in his open palm. His fist tightened around it. He raised his arm.

From less than ten feet away, he threw it at her, aiming for her chest.

Her arm jerked forward, snatched the stone from the air. It stung her palm. He had thrown it *hard*.

"Are you crazy!" she spluttered. "Are you trying to kill me!"

"No danger," Timmy soothed. "Good body-thought."

She hurled the stone out into the lake. "You think that was funny?"

"No. It was an object lesson, in the truest sense of the phrase."

She felt some of her anger dissipate. "You still shouldn't have done something stupid like that. What if I hadn't caught it?"

He leaned over and picked up another stone. Again, he hefted it for a moment, gauging its feel. Again, the fist tightened.

Susan stepped back a pace. "You're out of your mind," she whispered.

His arm came up. The stone came at her.

She snatched it and hurled it back at him. It hit him in the chest.

"Ouch!"

She swallowed, abruptly distraught that she might have hurt him. "Are you . . . all right?"

He pounded his chest. "Don't worry, plenty of padding here." The double chin blossomed into a thick smile. "I used to have good body-thought, back when I was a younger man. But nothing like yours. You're mercury on polished ice. Smooth and fast."

Keeping an eye on him, Susan turned and glanced back toward the Cloister. "I . . . uhh . . . have to go back now."

"I understand your fear. It's a natural reaction. You feel that I attacked you. You feel that I might be crazy. But I know good body-thought when I see it."

She found herself nodding. Anything to keep him occupied.

He sighed. "Oh, well. I hope you don't hold this against me. I thought we were getting along rather well before I threw the stones at you."

"Yes," she said warily, "that did dampen things a bit."

He laughed. "Tell me, Susan: If I had thrown a cotton puff or a feather at you, would you have considered it an attack."

"You didn't throw a cotton puff or a feather at me," she pointed out. "You threw a rock. Two rocks."

"But for the sake of argument . . . had it been cotton puffballs, would you have felt like you were being attacked?"

"I suppose not."

"Good. Perhaps you should give that example some thought."

"Oh, I will," she promised.

He continued gazing solemnly at her. "No, I see that you won't. You're just saying that in order to get away from me." A mischievous grin filled his face. "You're concerned that I might throw more stones, perhaps rain you with rocks as you dash wildly back to the safety of the Cloister."

She felt herself grinning. "That doesn't frighten me."

"I should hope not. I could stand here and throw stones at you all afternoon and not a one would touch you. Your body-thought wouldn't allow it."

"What makes you so sure of that?" she challenged. "I mean, what if this body-thought of mine were having a bad day? What then? You could have killed me."

Timmy sighed. "You still don't understand. Oh, well. In time, perhaps." His right eye blinked suddenly, erratically, as if it were caught in a spasm. The rest of his face melted into an apologetic smile. "Excuse me, please."

His hands reached up to cover his twitching eye. Susan gasped as the hands parted. His eye was gone. Only a dark hole remained.

He held out his hands, palms up. The shiny white orb twitched violently.

She swallowed and turned toward the Cloister. "I have to go back now."

"Nothing to be afraid of," promised Timmy. "I guess you don't see many of these up in the Colonies, huh? I lost my real eye a long time ago. This is an organic microprocessor—true honest-to-goodness wetware. It gives me better vision than the original. Lots of special enhancements."

"Oh. That's . . . good."

"Lately, however, I have to take it out from time to time. There seems to be some sort of problem. A dying circuit, perhaps." He sighed. "These days, it's hard to fix these things. Not too many people around who can work on wetware anymore." As his cheeks crinkled into a smile, a tiny drop of fluid trickled out of his empty right socket, rolled down his cheek.

"Good-bye," she said quickly, turning away.

"I'll see you tomorrow," he called. "Same time, same place."

She kept glancing back at him as she made her way toward the Cloister. She had a wild thought that he was going to throw his eye at her, and body-thought or no body-thought, she was most certainly not going to catch it.

But he just stood there, immobile, watching her until she reached the sanctuary of the nearest building.

—from *The Rigors*, by Meridian

*On the day after we learned of Codrus's death, Sappho summoned me to a private council. The Biodyssey was still fifty-six years away from the Colonies and the sudden demise of a member of the royal Caste had sent ripples of uncertainty throughout both Paratwa and human populations. Other than the Apocalypse itself, no single event had ever produced such widespread doubts.*

*Sappho's public tway, the seductive creature that we Paratwa called Colette, greeted me at the edge of a forest, where experimental strains of Os/Ka/Loq flora fought for dominance amidst the sovereign variety of Earth vegetation. Sappho's other tway was there too; I sensed her presence behind a ragged thicket located between two stunted white birches, on a small rise, fifteen yards away. As usual, Sappho's other tway would remain out of sight, an observer observing herself.*

*Colette's arms reached out to me as I approached. Two hands gripped four hands in familiar greeting.*

*"A sad day," I began, but Sappho terminated my attempts to acknowledge our bereavement with a wave of her blonde hair.*

*"Codrus is gone," she said calmly, "and our future is in jeopardy. Alternate plans have already been made. A special starship has been prepared. Tomorrow, I go into stasis and the following day, my vessel departs for Earth. Os/Ka/Loq enhancements will enable an initial acceleration far in excess of our own psol."*

*"ETA?" I asked, surprised not only by her cool pragmatic re-*

*sponse, but also by the fact that I had not been asked to participate in such a major strategic decision.*

"The special accelerators will enable my ship to reach the Earth in thirty-one years," said Sappho.

I glanced at the tangle of bushes, where her other self lay hidden. "You will make the journey . . . as a whole?" I was not surprised by her answer.

"Just Colette."

"A great sacrifice," I offered, noticing that the bushes were moving, as if her other tway had suddenly become agitated. I could not be sure, however. Perhaps it was just the wind.

"A great sacrifice," Colette/Sappho agreed. "But I have endured long separations in the past. It will be bearable because it is necessary. The Ash Ock must have a presence in the Colonies prior to our full return. Someone must assume Codrus's duties. Since it would be impractical for . . . both my tways . . ." She trailed off. There was no need for further explanation in that regard.

"Will other Paratwa be making the journey with you?"

"Only the Ash Nar."

Deep frowns unsettled my features and I made no attempt to keep criticism from my voice. "I've warned you about him. He's more dangerous than even you allow yourself to imagine. Theophrastus has concluded that Calvin is extremely unstable—"

"Reemul lacked stability, too," countered Sappho. "Yet Reemul did as he was ordered. So will Calvin."

I recognized that practical arguments were too late; strategies had already been formulated. "Was there a specific reason why I was not asked to participate in these decisions?"

She sensed the anger beneath my words. "There was. You too, Meridian, will be asked to make a great sacrifice."

My tways stiffened. "Separation?"

"Yes. For a short time, you also will have to endure the bane of the Paratwa. And it was primarily because of this necessity that you were not asked to participate in last night's strategy discussion." Her cheeks lifted into an elegant smile. "Your diplomatic skills are formidable, Meridian. We did not wish to allow ourselves to be dissuaded from this vital course of action."

My diplomatic skills. *I now understood what they wanted me to do, why my tways would have to be separated. Naturally, I argued.* "There are other Paratwa—"

"The decision has been made. And you are obviously the best choice. Reflect upon this and you will understand."

"I could refuse," I said boldly, knowing that my threat carried no weight.

Colette/Sappho smiled. "Now who is the unstable one: Calvin or Meridian?"

We both knew that there was no room for further argument.

"Relax, my Jeek," she soothed, rubbing my arms. "After all, your separation will not have to occur for many years, whereas my tways have but mere hours of physical company remaining."

From behind the thicket, Sappho's other half enunciated this reality—a hideous bray disintegrated into a deep-throated whimper. In response to the grotesque sound, a pair of gray squirrels scampered madly out of the adjacent bushes, leaping for the sanctuary of a towering oak.

"All my heart with flutterings wild as terror," quoted Colette/Sappho, her gaze pinned to the distant treeline.

I said nothing. The pained cry of her hidden tway reminded me that with Colette gone, I would have to deal directly with her other half.

There was nothing to be done about that aspect, however; the will of the Ash Ock was to be carried out. And that thing in the bushes represented the future. Like it or not, I had to begin to accustom myself to its presence.

Still, I hoped that face-to-face contacts could be kept to a minimum.

Gillian surfaced from an uncomfortable sleep to find the two female Costeaus standing at the foot of his bed. He was lying on his back. Sometime during the night, he had kicked off the covers.

"I don't wear pajamas, either," announced Buff, grinning from ear to ear.

Gillian sat up and wrapped a sheet around his body.

"Bashful," suggested Martha, still staring at his covered crotch.

"How did you get in here?" Gillian challenged. He felt vaguely annoyed that someone had managed to get this close to him while he lay here sleeping. Unprotected.

Buff shrugged. "Nick gave us the combo to your lock. He told us to go in and wake you up."

Gillian glanced at the wall clock. 5:30 A.M. The Colony had not even faced sun yet. Something must have happened.

"You look like you could use some more sleep," suggested Buff. "Sorry, but Nick said to fetch you right away."

More sleep was not what he needed. Last night, flexing dreams had plagued him—strange flights into worlds seething with realistic visions of his youth, when Empedocles had been whole, when Catharine had been a separate living entity. In one of the rapidly sequencing dream images, he and Catharine had been walking through the jungle beside a narrow stream. Gurgling water and the noisy chatter of local animals had filled his ears; the intense heat of the noonday Brazilian sun beat down across his bare shoulders and sweat trickled from his brow. Yet despite feeling physically uncomfortable, he had the sensation of being emotionally free, unencumbered by the terrible pains and oppressions that would threaten to drown his spirit in later years.

Catharine, pausing beside an immense quebracho tree, suddenly turned to him. Her pale elfin face crinkled into a frown; her whole body seemed to twist into a grimace of pain, distorting her natural beauty. In that instant, the weight of the world resettled upon Gillian. Emotional freedom was snatched away.

Catharine's lips moved.

*You must bring on the whelm, Gillian. We must be united forever.*

It was not Catharine. It was their Ash Ock monarch, Empedocles.

He argued: *We cannot be united forever. Don't you understand? Catharine is dead. She's just a memory-shadow.*

*Bring her back,* ordered Empedocles. *Bring on the whelm.*

Gillian sighed, distressed that his monarch could not perceive the obvious.

"I think Nick really likes me," proclaimed Buff. "Last night, he told me I had a body that reminded him of a pre-Apocalyptic toilet facility constructed from hardened clay."

Martha clarified: "Nick said she was built like a brick shithouse."

Buff clapped her hands in delight. "That's it!"

Gillian stood up, wiped the last vestige of sleep from his eyes. "Next time," he suggested, "knock on the door first. Okay?"

"Yes," said Martha indifferently, running skinny fingers through her acorn-streaked blonde hair. She wore pale blue bunhuggies and an oversized black jacket. He wondered what weapons the jacket might be hiding.

"Nick said there's important news," added Buff, obviously trying to hurry him along.

"What news?"

"That returning starship . . . it's been intercepted by our defense network."

"Should we leave while you dress?" asked Martha, her voice brimming with challenge.

Gillian threw off the bed cover and stood up, naked. Buff grinned. "Not bad, huh, Martha?"

"I've seen better."

Gillian ignored their banter and slid into a pair of open-top black pants. By the time he snapped on a shirt, the trouser's autowaist had pulled snug. Buff handed him his boots.

"I suppose," he concluded, "that you two will be spending the day with me."

Buff smiled. "Nick thought it would be a good idea."

Outside the huge A-frame, the lion was pacing the length of the elevated ridge of shaved albino grass, his tall form silhouetted by the faint red glow of an Irryan dawn. Nick sat below him at the lawn table, sipping coffee. To their left, the huge end plate of the Colony rose majestically, its innumerable pinpricks of light diffused by a creeping fog; a shadow wall reluctant to accept the encroaching day. Most of the tiny lights emanated from homes located on the end plate itself—perpendicular chalets boasting spectacular views, yet undervalued in comparison to other Irryan real estate because of the end plate's unnatural gravitation and the perpetually damp air. The overabundance of moisture was a peculiar quality inherent to the end plates of all cylinders. The Costeau Santiago had recently mentioned the anomaly to Gillian.

*Recently?* Gillian repressed a bitter laugh. In his own frame of reference, Santiago's remark—and the pirate's subsequent death during their violent confrontation with Reemul—had occurred only weeks ago. But in the real world, a half century of stasis had served to rob the event of any social immediacy. Stasis-jumps required radical adjustments in perspective, and to excessively dwell on an event which felt like it had happened only weeks ago, yet had actually taken place decades earlier, could lead the mind into a melange of severe cultural shocks.

Gillian found himself arriving at a sudden decision, simultaneously realizing that the parameters behind his choice had been taking shape for a long time.

*I won't allow myself to go back into stasis. Not ever again.*

The lion stopped pacing as they approached.

"Mornin'," said Nick, grinning and holding up the coffee pitcher. "Want some?"

Gillian shook his head. Martha and Buff plopped down at the table, attacked a setting of egg-crusted flake toast.

Gillian moved close enough to Jerem to see the haggard look on the older man's face. "Up all night?"

The lion nodded. Being tired was a luxury he could not afford just now. "I just returned from another emergency session at Council. A few hours ago, the intruding starship was met by one of our attack fleets. The intruder opened a line of communication. The message was short and simple." The lion read from a hand prompter:

"I am the tway of a Paratwa, an emissary of the Ash Ock. I have come in peace, to help the Colonies of Irrya develop a mutually satisfactory solution to our fears, and to end these centuries of hate and mistrust. As a token of my good faith, I have dismantled my shuttle's defenses and have jettisoned my weapons. I am at your mercy."

Nick smiled. "It just so happens that this tway is an old friend of yours, Gillian."

"Who?"

"A Jeek Elemental," said the lion. "The same breed that Reemul came from." The lion found it difficult to remain stationary. His body insisted on moving, on releasing energy, a futile panacea for too much anxiety and too little sleep.

Gillian knew. "It's Meridian."

"It sure is," chortled Nick. "And naturally, they're going to let the son of a bitch through the network."

"There's no other real choice," argued the lion. "You know that."

Nick sighed. "Yeah, I know. Still, it's nice to engage in a little wish fulfillment now and again. And my intuition tells me that we ought to nuke the bastard while we have a chance."

The lion faced Gillian. "This Meridian . . . he was once your teacher, wasn't he?"

Gillian nodded. "And my friend."

Martha set down a slice of toast and stared at some fathomless point above Gillian's head.

The lion continued. "He is to be transferred to one of our fastest ships and ferried straight here, to Irrya. His vessel will remain at the bounds of the defense network until our technical people are certain that it is safe."

Gillian suspected that whatever might be hidden aboard Meridian's ship would prove less of a danger than this wily Paratwa in the flesh.

"How long till he arrives?"

"About four and a half weeks," said Nick.

"The Council has agreed to allow immediate public dissemination of this development," added the lion. "We thought that Meridian's peace offering might help allay tensions."

Gillian frowned. "You don't believe him, do you?"

"As an Irryan Councillor, I must keep an open mind." The lion shrugged. "As a Costeau, however, I wouldn't trust this Meridian to carry my odorant bag."

"Just *one* tway," mused Gillian.

"Yes," said the lion, "although our penetration gear has also detected two nonhuman lifeforms aboard Meridian's vessel. A pair of dogs. We're not yet sure of the species."

Nick shrugged. "One tway makes sense. That simply means that his other half will be able to report everything firsthand. As for the dogs, who knows? Maybe the bastard's become a pet lover in his old age."

*His old age,* thought Gillian. Meridian was a mere Jeek

Elemental, and not blessed with an Ash Ock extended life-span. "Do you think he's been in and out of stasis over the centuries?"

"That seems the likeliest scenario," said Nick, gazing at him oddly. "Then again, maybe his Ash Ock masters found a way to extend his lifespan as well."

"Questions that today cannot be answered," stated the lion.

"That's right," said the midget. "And we've got more than a month to worry about Meridian. Meanwhile, Gillian, we've got something more immediate for you to handle: a lead in the Birch murders. Adam Lu Sang still hasn't been able to penetrate E-Tech Security, but he did manage to collect a lot of raw data on the previous massacres, mostly unclassified stuff floating around the network.

"Anyway, Adam and I have been collating all the available information from the six Order of the Birch attacks, concentrating on victim profiles, looking for correlations. So far, there've been over four hundred fatalities. We've cross-indexed these names, dredged up every scrap of data we could locate, no matter how innocuous it might appear at first glance. We were scanning for common denominators, of course, connections that might lead us to the purpose behind these honeysucks." The midget smiled at Martha and Buff. "But lo and behold, it was the modern science of plasma necropsy that provided our first clue.

"From the fluid linkages that Martha and Buff performed, we discovered that a larger-than-expected number of massacre victims were suffering from minor colds or viral infections. In most cases, the degrees of infection were so slight that most of them would have gone unnoticed during regular autopsies. But the plasma necropsy tests found these infections and also indicated that most of them were recent.

"But we still couldn't prove anything; a bunch of victims were under the weather, and so what. Even the viruses weren't the same, although I realized that we could be dealing with a wild mutater—all the infections could still have a common source."

Nick rose from his chair, began pacing beside the table, obviously excited. "Playing a hunch, I had Adam work up a list of all the unsolved murders and suicides that have occurred in the past four months throughout the Colonies."

Gillian gave a nod of understanding. "Other possible targets of this assassin."

"Exactly. And guess what?"

Buff jumped in. "There were slightly more viral infections discovered during the autopsies of these murder and suicide victims than could be accounted for by population averages."

"Give this woman a medal," chortled the midget. "From there it was easy. Adam and I collated this new list of names—all of the massacre victims, suicides, and unsolved murder victims who showed positive viral infections—and scanned for common denominators. Bingo! Over seventy-five percent of our names had recent contact with a certain Irryan-based company called Venus Cluster."

"They're a large service corporation," explained the lion. "Venus Cluster provides custom-trained domestic employees for wealthy clients throughout the Colonies."

Nick continued. "Some of our victims worked as specialty servants for Venus Cluster, others represented their own corporations in trade business, a few served as intermediaries between their own employers and Venus Cluster, et cetera, et cetera. But whatever their involvement, almost all of them visited the company's Irryan headquarters within a week of their deaths."

The midget favored Martha and Buff with another grin. "You two look a little bored lately. How would you like to accompany Gillian on a nice friendly visit to Venus Cluster?"

"I can hardly wait," said Martha dryly.

"Who owns this company?" Gillian asked.

The lion frowned. "We're not sure. The complexities of

control and ownership have become much more convoluted since the last time you two were awakened from stasis. The ICN has loosened many of its regulations in this area and consequently, many large companies have shielded investors. We're not certain just who has financial control of Venus Cluster."

Gillian raised his eyebrows at Nick.

"I know," answered the midget, chuckling. "A secretly controlled corporation sounds as suspicious as a nun in black leather. But it's very common today. Fifty-six years ago, the ICN wanted to encourage more corporate investments. The idea was this: With the Paratwa destined to return, more seed money was needed for R and D, especially weapons development. Deregulating the investment process was just one of the ways in which the ICN sought to open the doors for new venture capital. And their strategy appears to have worked. As a result, an enormous amount of R and D has taken place over the last half century."

"Dirty money," suggested Gillian.

"Yeah," agreed Nick, "no doubt about that. The ICN practically encouraged cash laundering. If Mister X had some illicit funds, he was invited to buy into a legitimate corporation, and no questions asked. No one but the top execs of the corporation would ever have to know just where the money came from. All a legitimate company had to do was rake in the cash, keep their mouths shut, and pay nice dividends."

Gillian frowned. "*Someone* would have to know. The ICN wouldn't totally blind themselves."

"You're right," said the lion. "The ICN oversees the entire banking industry and at least to some extent, they're able to track the financial currents. But most of their sensitive data is kept in inaccessible archives."

The midget wagged his head. "Ultrasecret nonnetworks. No way to get at them. When it comes to divulging data, the ICN are real tight-assed sons of bitches. But at any rate, their loosening of the rules did get results. Today, the intercolonial economy is booming. Corporate R and D is at an all-time high. Ultimately, the Paratwa threat has led to an incredibly wealthy culture."

Buff released an audible yawn.

Gillian nodded slowly. "So you want Martha, Buff, and me to pay a visit to the Irryan headquarters of Venus Cluster."

"Inez Hernandez has already made the arrangements," said Nick. "You're to meet with one of the company's vice presidents. A Mister Cochise. False IDs have been provided."

Gillian acknowledged a sense of pleasure at the assignment. He had been sitting around the lion's retreat for the past few days, becoming bored. Too much free time led the mind toward introspective cycles, forced awareness to double back over familiar territory. Right now, remembrance of things past was about as desirable as walking into a thruster discharge.

"How about our missing witness?" he asked. "Any word?"

The lion shook his head sadly. Even Inez no longer called constantly, seeking updates on the search for Susan.

"She's gone," shrugged Nick. "Not so much as a trace."

*Susan Quint is probably dead,* Gillian decided. Inez Hernandez was correct in feeling the way she did. Most likely, the Paratwa had found and killed the young woman immediately following her escape from the hospital. "Did Susan Quint's duties ever involve her with—"

"First thing we checked," interrupted Nick. "But Susan never visited Venus Cluster. That company was not on her duty roster."

Another question occurred to Gillian. "How are the Colonies reacting to the news that a Paratwa ship is returning?"

"So far, so good," answered Nick. "No major upheavals

as yet, although there have been a few incidents blamed on the announcement."

The lion shook his head. "The ICN reports some unforeseen trade imbalances. The leadership of one of our bigger profarming Colonies rather arbitrarily declared that they would be cutting back on their exports of certain food shipments until the crisis has passed."

"Hoarding syndrome," suggested Nick, frowning. And Gillian knew that the midget was thinking back to the final days, when pre-Apocalyptic shortages and illegal stockpiling had created nightmarish problems.

"A small riot in Sirak-Brath," continued the lion, "but then there are always riots in Sirak-Brath. The intercolonial entertainment index has reached an all-time high; they say that getting a ticket to any of the major touring dramusical acts is next to impossible."

"Escapist syndrome," offered Nick, "and not exactly unexpected. Still, all things considered, the Colonies seem to be taking the news quite well."

*The calm before the storm,* thought Gillian.

The lion waited until Gillian and his watchdogs had departed before turning to the midget with a scowl.

"I'm still having doubts about this, Nick. Not telling them the whole story about this Venus Cluster vice president could be a bad mistake."

"It's the only way," insisted Nick. "Gillian has to be thrown into a situation where his natural abilities can take over. Right now, he's almost useless to us."

Not for the first time, the lion felt a swell of anger at the midget's callousness. "You could get him killed."

Nick shrugged. "Ever spin a child's top?"

"No."

The midget smiled. "An old Earth toy. You spin it with your hand and it rotates on its axis. As long as it's moving fast, it remains perfectly balanced on its point. But as its angular acceleration begins to degenerate, it becomes more and more wobbly. Out of balance."

"Get to the point."

Nick seemed nonplused by the lion's curtness. "I've been watching Gillian carefully over these past days. His sleep periods have been restless, disturbed. His reaction times are ridiculously slow. He asks questions that he should already know the answers to, questions that betray a sluggish awareness. And this morning I had to send Martha and Buff in to wake him up. Jesus, they could have rammed a knife into him before he even thought to open his eyes!"

The lion scowled. "You bugged his bedroom?"

"Hell, yes." The midget fished a tiny transceiver out of his pocket. "Audio *and* video. Which highlights another one of his shortcomings: He didn't even think to check his room for surveillance devices."

Nick shook his head. "Day by day, he's getting worse. Gillian's abilities are disintegrating. And I still believe that it's because he's engaged in an inner war with his monarch. Empedocles is forcing Gillian to use more and more of his energies to fight off the whelm—the forced interlace. It's simple: Empedocles is trying to take control and Gillian is struggling to prevent it. And that inner struggle is transforming a lightning-fast assassin into an unstable neurotic."

"Have you talked to Gillian about this?"

"I tried, I really did. But he doesn't trust me these days." The midget hesitated. "To be honest, I can't blame him for not confiding in me anymore.

"But the reality remains that Gillian is like that child's top after it's slowed down. It's unbalanced, ready to fall over at the slightest breeze. Right now, whether he realizes it or not, he's easy prey. He needs a shock to his system. He needs to be jolted back into his old warrior patterns."

"So we throw him into the water and see if he swims," muttered the lion.

Nick grinned. "That's a real nice twentieth-century analogy. You must be reading up on your history texts."

"This isn't funny, Nick. You could get him killed. If this Venus Cluster vice president is, as you and Adam suspect, directly involved with the Birch killings—"

"Then maybe Gillian will find that out. Right now, this is the only real lead we have in the Birch massacres."

The lion stared grimly. "But what if this Cochise is actually a tway, one of the Birch killers? What if he identifies Gillian?"

Nick's wide lips failed to hide a smile. "If this Mister Cochise does turn out to be a yuppie from hell, then we're certainly going to shake things up a bit, now, aren't we."

The lion tried to make some sense out of the midget's true intentions. *Plans within plans. Rome Franco was right about you. You're a ruthless manipulator.*

"We gotta pop a few lids, Jerem. If the Ash Ock are behind all this, then the Colonies are in a lot more trouble than they imagine. It's time to send in the offensive team."

The lion's anger focused. "And maybe get Gillian—and Martha and Buff—killed in the bargain."

Nick rubbed his hands together and stared grimly at the lion. "I've risked Gillian's life before and I'll risk it again. That's what I do. And if you, *Jerem Marth,* can look past Gillian for a moment and see him as something other than some lost surrogate daddy—"

"You bastard!" The lion felt a fury rise up inside him the likes of which he had not experienced in many years. "Don't tell me about *my* obsession! I've dealt with those feelings."

"Maybe."

He aimed a quivering finger at the midget. "We're talking about *your* obsession, now: your blind hatred of the Paratwa!"

Nick was quiet for a moment. Then he shrugged. "You're right, I do hate them. I hate them for what they did to my world. I *despise* the Paratwa."

"And you'll send Gillian to his death to destroy them."

"If necessary." The midget sighed. "If you feel so

strongly about this, then why don't you go and tell Gillian how things really are. Go ahead. Warn him that this Venus Cluster exec could very well be a killer tway." A fierce grin settled on Nick's face. "But if you do that, then you just remember that whatever happens is on *your* head, not mine."

The lion drew a deep breath, tried to force his anger into perspective, tried to act like a Councillor of Irrya rather than a Costeau.

Nick read his hesitation. "Look, I know how you feel. But no matter how insensitive and ruthless I sound, I'm still looking out for Gillian's welfare. And I'm telling you, he's in bad shape. This is *not* the Ash Ock tway that I went into stasis with. Physiologically and psychologically, Gillian's coming apart at the seams." Nick sighed. "I'm not trying to hurt him, Jerem. I'm just trying to put him into a situation where his natural reactions might enable him to overcome this inner struggle. I'm giving him a chance to wake up."

The lion stared out into the woods, watched the hesitant Irryan dawn creep across the top of the pines. "And what about Empedocles? What if he wakes up instead?"

Nick had no reply.

Ghandi, weightless, eased along the main corridor, his friction boots crackling softly on the grated deck. He passed the closed bedroom door, assuming that by this hour, Colette certainly would have yielded to a dormant condition.

At one time, he had referred to her rest periods as sleep, but over the years, that word had developed the quality of

a misnomer, failing to encompass the weirdly alert state
that she entered when her body needed recharging. Only
in surface details did Colette imitate the human sleep process. She lay on her back with eyelids closed. But a gentle
nudge at four in the morning would provoke an instant response: Eyes would open, full awareness would shine
through; no drowsiness, no emerging through layers of expanding consciousness, no time wasted on intermediary
steps. A part of her never slept.

He used to wonder if she dreamed. In his younger days,
he had often quizzed her on such mundane matters, wanting to know what it was like being a Paratwa, being an
Ash Ock tway. She would respond to his eager questions,
his intellectual lusts, and often she would speak at length
about what it felt like being one half of Sappho. But her
descriptions always produced in him a kind of frustration.

Eventually, he had come to understand that her long
talks rarely contained much substance. Numerous specula-
tive texts were available on the Paratwa phenomenon—
Ghandi had read a great many of them—and for the most
part, Colette's self-descriptive disclosures seemed mere variations of those texts, bubbling with data but revealing no
clear gestalt of her Paratwa personality. On those rare occasions when she did seem to be divulging some facet of
her true self, her words remained cloaked in thick meta-
phor, deliberately obscure.

And if he prodded her too much, seeking to clarify those
metaphors, she would become angry. "Penetrating orifices
where you're not welcome is a form of rape," she had once
responded, and the force of that particular phrase had
stuck with him. Eventually, Ghandi had been forced to
grudgingly accept her imposed boundaries of their relationship. Whether she dreamed or not, he would never
know.

At the end of the hallway, the thick airseal leading to
their combination study/dinette was open. Ghandi froze.
Someone was speaking; dull whispers drifted from the

room, echoing along the hard-surfaced walls of the corridor. It did not sound like Colette.

Cautiously, he eased closer, a step at a time, trying to prevent the heels of his friction boots from making even the slightest noise as they contacted the floor's perforated grates. At this hour, there should have been no one else in this section of the ship; the captain, crewmembers, and servants always remained on the upper decks, unless summoned. And Calvin had been sent back to Irrya; yesterday, Colette had ordered the maniac to return ahead of them on another of CPG's private shuttles.

The intensity of the whispers increased as Ghandi drew nearer. The voice was female, but it still did not sound like his wife, and some inner sense assured him that those particular tonal qualities were not of electronic origin. *Servants, poking around where they were not permitted?*

Ten feet from the door, the hushed whispers began to melt into word-shapes.

". . . adjust parameter see-one-ten . . . block sequence five-oh-five . . . climb one-eleven . . . mute line ratios . . . overall rejection on forty-four . . . see-two pressure . . ."

He took a deep breath and stepped into the study. She was seated in front of the terminal, her back to the door, her attention riveted to the screen. It was Colette, or at least it was her physical body. If she had sensed his entrance, she was not revealing it.

". . . break seven-one-four-ee-B . . . climb one-six . . . lace four-core upside . . . negate see-two . . ."

On the screen, Ghandi watched her verbal commands translate into swirling patterns. Pale streaks of orange light exploded into flaming red blisters and tiny graphic characters—x's and y's and z's mostly—emitted comet tails as they haphazardly blazed across the volcanic display. Ghandi had seen Colette working with this particular program numerous times over the years. It was the sunsetter.

"Sit down, Ghandi," the woman ordered, pointing to a chair six feet away. Her attention never left the screen.

". . . splice oh-eight-nine . . . reject see-two negation . . .
oversplice six . . . oversplice eight-one-oh . . ."

He tightened his robe and nervously pulled himself
down into the chair, thankful for the lack of gravity, thankful that they were still in transit, hours away from CPG's
Irryan docking station. In the past twenty-five years, he
had seen her on numerous occasions, but she had never,
*ever* spoken to him. In some unfathomable way, he was
glad that her first words had been uttered out here, in the
blackness of space, far away from what was comfortable
and familiar. If there had been gravity, he believed that he
would have fallen over.

". . . oversight z-three . . . condense all local fields . . .
condense field one-six-six . . ."

He waited, observing the hot screen over her shoulder,
watching the mad dance of angry symbols across bubbling
lava, and desperately hoping that she would not turn
around, not even for an instant.

"Reintegrate . . ." she abruptly ordered, and the monitor dissolved into darkness. Ghandi felt a muscle quivering
behind his left knee. He locked his arms around the chair's
sway-bar, feeling like some kind of cylinder-bound Colonist
experiencing zero gravity for the first time.

"Why are you up at this hour?" she quizzed. Her eyes
remained affixed to the terminal.

"Couldn't sleep," he answered quickly, hoping that she
would order him to leave. "Thought a walk might help, so
I went topside, looking for company, but everyone's asleep
but the pilot. I guess what I was really looking for was
some gravity, so I could feel—"

"Don't prattle," she instructed.

Ghandi snapped his jaw shut.

For a moment she was silent. Then: "On occasion, I've
heard you sing—when you're alone with Colette. Costeau
songs. From a long time ago, from when you were a child.
Those songs . . . they bring you pleasure?"

He wagged his head, confused by the odd question, then

abruptly realized that she could not see his motion. "Yes, they bring me pleasure." The back of his other knee began to pulsate, and he twined both ankles around the chair legs, trying to bring the spasms under control.

"Would you sing for me?"

"I can't do that," he mumbled, instantly concerned that this quick refusal might have offended her. "I can only sing if the mood is right," he explained.

She turned around. "What is it about me that frightens you?"

He swallowed, and riveted his attention to the three wands of a baking module projecting from the wall on the far side of the chamber.

"Can you at least say my name?"

He nodded, but said nothing.

"Helpless halts my tongue," she whispered, as if quoting from some obscure text.

Ghandi drew a deep breath, restraining an urge to bolt from the room. "You're Sappho."

"I am Sappho."

He forced himself to look upon her face, seeing the familiar lines and crevices, the minute alterations that Colette had performed upon herself in order to mimic the human aging process, make it appear that she too was growing old at the same rate as her contemporaries. He recognized the pale dimpled cheeks, the wave of golden curls, the immodest lips that could prance across his flesh with abandon. The creature that sat before him looked almost exactly like Colette.

It was the eyes that betrayed her.

Cold and distant. Not lifeless—something existed behind those aquamarine irises, some semblance of a consciousness shone through—but alien, like it had arisen from some other species, from some other space and time. A distant memory erupted: visiting a Colonial Preserve, seeing a magnificent striped tiger, poised on a rise, fifteen feet away, studying the limits of its terrain, filtering the world through perspectives that no human could ever totally understand.

Ghandi remembered being scared of that tiger, even while being surrounded by older boys of his clan, even while knowing that no harm could befall them, that the Preserve's controllers were watching, ready to knock the animal unconscious via narcoleptic implants should it become violent.

A chill raced up his spine. Here and now, he sat before a wild creature that had no controller. In many ways, Colette too displayed characteristics of the alien, yet his wife still maintained multiple references to the environment of the recognizably human. Sappho projected no such illusions. Her eyes exceeded human comprehension.

"You have many questions," she stated.

"Your voice ... it's different from Colette's."

"An alteration of timbre and pitch occurs naturally when my tways are interlaced. Tonal harmonics are introduced." She paused. "The result is a distortion of what is proper?"

"It doesn't bother me," Ghandi mumbled, feeling like she was trying to trap him into saying something he would regret.

She smiled. "Next question?"

"What were you doing ... with the sunsetter?"

"A special update. New instructions. After all these years, our data destroyer has finally made contact with an enemy. And this enemy has—inadvertently, I suspect—led our program to its real prey." She hesitated. "Did Colette tell you about the IRS program that's been trying to attack the sunsetter?"

Ghandi nodded and tried to hide his surprise. *Don't you know everything that Colette knows? Wouldn't you automatically be aware of anything she told me?*

Sappho smiled, as if she was reading his thoughts, as if she knew that she had just revealed some heretofore unknown aspect of her Ash Ock self.

*She* doesn't *know everything that Colette knows.*

"As you're aware, Ghandi, this IRS program showed up in the archives recently. Ostensibly, it's been attempting to penetrate the boundaries of the sunsetter and halt the destruction of the data banks."

"Can it?" he wondered aloud.

"No. It's potent, but it's no match for Theophrastus's program."

Ghandi raised his eyebrows. So Theophrastus, the Ash Ock scientific genius, had created the sunsetter. Colette had never revealed that.

"However," she went on, "this attacking program does present some curious facets. First of all, it announces its name, IRS 1991. In the year 1991, there existed a real organization on the American continent, a real IRS, that enforced taxation laws. This program gleams with historical tidbits from that era."

"It's that old?"

"No. Its operational parameters suggest a twenty-*first* century lineage. But its creator has a working knowledge of twentieth century America; he could even have been alive back then. Furthermore, he's sophisticated enough to realize that his IRS program has no chance of stopping the sunsetter."

Ghandi frowned. "Then why bother?"

"First of all, the creator of IRS 1991 wants to let me know that he's still around. You see, I recognize the handprint of this program. And after more than a quarter of a millennium, I believe I know for certain just who he is."

Sappho paused, as if debating whether to reveal this latest insight. Ghandi did not really care. He had an overriding question of his own. *Why, Sappho, after more than a quarter of a century, have you decided to talk to me?*

"During the final days," she went on, "E-Tech provided the greatest organized hindrance to the plans of the Ash Ock. And within E-Tech, there was a programmer who consistently thwarted our efforts. We never knew who he was. In fact, until much later, we were never even certain whether he was an individual entity or a consortium of sophisticated programmers. Nevertheless, the Ash Ock gave him a name: the Czar.

"Fifty-six years ago, Codrus warned us about a little man, a midget, whom the Colonies later learned was the companion of Gillian. Codrus, in what we now must acknowledge as one of his rare moments of insight, suspected that this man Nick and the Czar could be one and the same.

"We now believe that Codrus was correct. Nick is the Czar. And he has again been brought from stasis. IRS 1991 is his calling card."

Ghandi betrayed surprise. "Then Gillian is also awake?"

For just an instant, Sappho broke eye contact, her gaze flashing to some point behind Ghandi. When she spoke, her words seemed more intense.

"I believe that the traitor is awake."

Ghandi entertained a fleeting fantasy of Gillian the warrior coming after Calvin, destroying the maniac.

"The Czar," Sappho continued, "must have deduced that there is a connection between the sunsetter and the Ash Ock. And he wants Theophrastus and me to know that he is on to us. I am not completely clear on the Czar's reasoning here; perhaps he hopes that his emergence from obscurity will provoke some response on our part."

"Something he could use to track you down."

"Perhaps. Naturally, we'll take no action that could serve this purpose. But the real news is that the Czar's program—IRS 1991—has somehow served to bring the sunsetter's true target out into the open."

"Freebird?" wondered Ghandi.

"Yes, Freebird. After twenty-two years, we've finally found our prey."

"Are you certain that this is the same program you're after?"

"All probabilities indicate that this is the one. Our sunsetter has ascertained that no other versions of that particular rescue program still survive within the E-Tech archives."

Ghandi found himself again wondering just what was so important about this Freebird program. Throughout the years, Colette had refused to divulge an answer to that question.

He nodded. "So the sunsetter can now fulfill its function and destroy the data contained in Freebird."

Sappho hesitated. "There are still problems. Freebird has adopted a clever tactic. It has initiated a one-way data pact with our attack program, preserving the safety and security of the sunsetter whenever the Czar's IRS 1991 attempts an assault. In essence, the very program we're trying to destroy has now become our unwanted, and unnecessary, savior—an ironic twist of events. The net result is that Freebird currently remains one step ahead of the sunsetter."

Ghandi withheld a smile. There was something oddly pleasurable about seeing the Ash Ock faced with a challenging problem. "Sort of like having an itch that you can't scratch," he ventured.

"An appropriate analogy. And we suspect that the conflict between IRS 1991 and the sunsetter is what alerted Freebird in the first place."

"But wouldn't Freebird have been aware of the sunsetter's presence all these years?"

"That's possible," she answered slowly. "The truth is, we really don't know the operational parameters of Freebird."

And Ghandi thought: *You know only that the information contained within Freebird is a great threat to the Ash Ock plans.* Perhaps Sappho would be more open to supplying an answer.

"Just what is so important about this program?"

Again, Sappho broke eye contact, turning to stare at the far wall. Her shoulders tilted into a gentle shrug. "Things that never should have been revealed—Ash Ock strategies and the like. Ultimately, however, Freebird's information would prove irrelevant to humans." A soft smile touched her lips. "Let's just say that it is a matter of Ash Ock pride that Freebird's data remains lost."

Ghandi did not believe her. Part of the reason for corrupting Doyle Blumhaven in the first place was specifically to gain access to the E-Tech archives in order to input the sunsetter. And every few weeks, for the past twenty-two years, his wife—or Sappho—had arranged to update the sunsetter from this special terminal aboard their private shuttle. Such purposeful dedication transcended pride. Not to mention that the sunsetter was in the process of devastating every old program it came across in the hopes of finding and wiping out Freebird. *No, pride has nothing to do with it. The annihilation of the data contained in this rescue program is vitally important to the Ash Ock.*

"Just how long has this Freebird been in the archives?" he asked, assuming it to be another question she would not answer, but deciding to take the shot anyway.

Sappho surprised him. "Freebird is over two hundred and fifty years old."

Ghandi raised his eyebrows. "I always sort of assumed that Freebird came from the era of Codrus and Reemul— something that Rome Franco's E-Tech people created fifty-six years ago."

"No. Freebird existed before the E-Tech archives were ever transferred from the planet to the Colonies. It is of pre-Apocalyptic origin.

"Codrus, during his lonely two-hundred year vigil in the Colonies, often tried to gain access into the archives, to search for this mythical program. You see, we never even knew for certain whether Freebird actually existed. In fact, up until five years ago, we were becoming convinced that it was indeed mythical. But finally the sunsetter came across actual archival proof that Freebird is real."

A wary smile touched her lips. "But enough of this.

There are more important things that deserve our consideration."

Ghandi wagged his head, pleased that she had revealed so much. "If Nick and Gillian are awake, then someone in E-Tech must have betrayed us. Doyle Blumhaven?"

Sappho twined her fingers and daintily laid the folded palms on the lap of her gown. Ghandi stared intently. It was an action so reminiscent of Colette that for a moment, he thought that the interlace had dissolved, that his wife had returned. But the eyes remained distant, alien.

"Doyle Blumhaven did not betray us," said Sappho confidently. "Theophrastus has projected the most likely possibility: One of the programmers from the archives arranged for the Czar and Gillian to be awakened, and then perhaps helped the Czar gain access into the archives. Calvin has been attempting to learn just who this renegade might be."

"Will Calvin . . . deal with him?"

"Yes. But it's possible that great damage has already been done.

"We must assume that the Czar, and Gillian, have looked into the Order of the Birch massacres. The Czar is extremely shrewd. By now, he would certainly have examined all available data relevant to Calvin's forays. And if the Czar manages to cross-reference enough data from the six massacres, it's possible that his formidable programming abilities may lead him to the common denominator of Venus Cluster. Also, there is still the matter of the altered transit records to consider. Assuming that the Czar's secret helper is an archival specialist, they may attempt an actual penetration of E-Tech Security. And if they should succeed in that endeavor and compare the transit records from the Honshu massacre with the classified E-Tech Security report, they will see that Calvin's name is not on the second list."

Ghandi wanted to say: *I warned you that changing the transit records could prove to be a dangerous move.* Instead, he shrugged and said: "So Calvin's mistake in recognizing that Susan Quint woman may have severely jeopardized us."

"Yes, even though at this juncture, Susan Quint herself may be the least of our worries. We have Gillian to consider now. Theophrastus suspects, and I concur, that the traitor may even possess the ability to deduce that Calvin is Paratwa, and perhaps even conclude that my Ash Nar is a tripartite."

An uneasy feeling took hold of Ghandi. Deep inside, he could feel the microbes begin their furious dance, coursing up and down his arms and legs, burrowing into his chest, making his heart beat faster. His feet, still locked around the bottom of the chair, began to quiver uncontrollably. The inside of his flesh seemed to be electrified.

Sappho stared at him dispassionately. And suddenly he knew.

"You want something from me," he blurted out, barely able to remain in his seat. "That's why you're talking to me, after twenty-five years of silence!"

"It has always been your belief that when you've outlived your usefulness to the Ash Ock, we would destroy you. Correct?"

He felt as if the microbes were jolting answers out of him, forcing him to utter truths that he had never before directly acknowledged. "You'll order Calvin to kill me!"

Sappho shook her head; a gesture of sadness that the eyes did not emulate. "You still believe that the Ash Ock desire decimation of humans. That is not our purpose. We kill only when necessary."

"And what about Calvin?" Ghandi challenged. "What about the infection of the cylinders?"

"The spreading of Theophrastus's skygene to every single Colony will bring about a lasting peace, with the least number of casualties. You are intelligent enough to realize that. As to my Ash Nar . . ." She shrugged. "Calvin was created and trained to be a warrior. That is his function. When the Colonies are ours, I plan to make him the head of E-Tech Security, in a greatly expanded role. He will be responsible for the enforcement of our rule."

"You'll kill me," insisted Ghandi. "I know too much."

"Colette loves you."

He frowned.

"I must admit that her feelings, which have developed for you over these past twenty-five years, were not an aspect of our original plan. It was merely fate which brought you and your Costeau shuttle to Denver that day; most any ship and crew would have sufficed. But you came and Colette developed true and deep feelings for you. She will not betray you.

"Emotions bind, Corelli-Paul. As for your knowing too much about us, that is a problem which will be rendered obsolete when the Colonies have been conquered."

Ghandi swallowed. "Colette . . . she's your tway. If you gave an order, she would obey."

Sappho shrugged. "That is the way of the Ash Ock. The tways yield to the wishes of the monarch." She gazed silently at him for a moment. "Colette will obey. And so must you."

"What do you want?" he muttered.

"Nothing at the moment, Corelli-Paul. However, we need time to complete the infection of the Colonies. If the Czar and Gillian manage to learn of tway Calvin, either through their own resources or through Susan Quint's sudden emergence from concealment, then CPG itself could be threatened. Calvin *could* go into hiding, still carry out Order of the Birch massacres, eliminating the skygene couriers. But it has been through the corporate auspices of CPG—actually our subsidiary, Venus Cluster—that we have been able to spread the skygene suitcases to so many Colonies. That function must continue unabated until every cylinder registers a positive reaction.

"And if it is ascertained that the E-Tech Security records from the massacre do not match the transit records, then E-Tech itself may fall under greater suspicion. Edward

Huromonus's action/probe could then turn upon the highest levels of E-Tech. That means that Doyle Blumhaven himself could come under scrutiny. And if enough pressure is brought upon Blumhaven, he could crack, and reveal his illicit connections with CPG. Naturally, that too cannot be permitted.

"Our conspiracy is beginning to unravel. The Czar and Gillian are closing in on us from one direction, Edward Huromonus's action/probe from another, and Susan Quint is a wild card, hanging over our heads. We must not be caught in the middle, not yet. Right now, time is our enemy. Meridian will arrive in the Colonies in a little over a month. Until then, CPG Corporation must remain, at the very least, partially operational. And the skygene infections must continue at their current rate if we are to make the deadline."

Sappho rose, and stood before him. "All these years I have remained silent in your presence because Colette so desired. She knew how much you feared me and she did not wish to see you needlessly suffer. I ordered her to seduce you only once—that day in Denver, twenty-five years ago. Since then, her feelings for you have been real, and she has consciously tried to spare you, as much as possible, from Ash Ock complexities. She has looked out for you, Corelli-Paul. Never forget that."

He sighed. "I know."

Sappho closed her eyes. Ghandi thought he detected a faint shudder running through her body.

"Colette?" he asked tentatively.

The eyes opened and there was warmth there again, and what he sensed as a deep compassion.

"My love," she whispered, slithering onto his lap. Ghandi found himself hugging his wife as if she were the only real thing in the universe. A tremor passed through him. Dancing microbes faded to nothingness as he burrowed his face into her bosom.

"I wish we could just . . . go away," he blurted out.

"She is my monarch, Corelli-Paul. I must obey her. And so must you. It is the only way."

*How can I trust her?* Ghandi wondered. *How can I know for certain that your monarch won't betray me?*

Colette hugged him tightly.

*I grow old and I grow stupid.*

Her hands wound around him. Fingers caressed.

*And now, even my third demon could once more arise,* he thought bitterly. *Now maybe I will even have to kill for you again.*

Demon three: the sin that offered no redemption. Ghandi remembered back, twenty-five years ago, to that icy windswept Denver boulevard, standing outside Colette/Sappho's shuttle—her starship—as she ordered his needbreeder-hypnotized crewmates into the vessel. The four Costeaus had finished transferring all the items of value over to Ghandi's ship: the maniac, asleep in his two stasis capsules; the prototype for Theophrastus's skygene machines; crates of data bricks, including the sunsetter; and miscellaneous boxes containing a variety of high-tech implements.

"It is the only way," Colette had urged, as they stood in their spacesuits, watching the Captain close the outer hatch, sealing himself and Ghandi's other three crewmates into their own tomb. And then she had handed Ghandi the small disk containing the trigger. At first he had protested:

"I can't do it, Colette. I can't!"

"Bring us together, Corelli-Paul," she had pleaded. "Bind our aspirations into a chain that dare not be broken. Show me that I can trust you always."

He had depressed the trigger before he could talk himself out of it.

*If only I had turned away. If only I had not seen the flash of white light through the portholes as the incineration device ignited, filling the inside of her starship with flames fierce enough to burn through metal. If only the Captain had not appeared in the window*

*for that fraction of a second, his countenance a mask of agony as his
plastic helmet visor melted onto his face . . .*

Ghandi shuddered with the memory.

"It is all right, my love," Colette whispered, stroking his
forehead. "Everything will be all right."

*No,* he thought sadly. *It can never again be all right. It can
only be bearable.*

"Did you know," offered Timmy, "that the Ontario Cloister was founded almost three hundred years ago?"

Susan lay stretched out on the sandy beach, half-
heartedly listening to her new companion's words while
her senses bathed in pleasing odors and rhythmic sounds.
Ocean-tainted waves gently splattered against a small jag-
ged cliff a hundred yards to their left; swirling breezes
brought a briny smell from the East, via the St. Lawrence
River's connection to the Atlantic.

"The Cloister was founded a hundred and fifty years
ago," Susan corrected, recalling the history lesson that
Lester Mon Dama had given her during their shuttle trip
down.

Timmy chuckled and wrapped his gray robe tighter at
the neck. His massive form squatted beside her, huge butt
displacing pounds of wet sand, looking like one of those
near-extinct animals she had once seen in the Preserve on
the Colony of Valley Lehigh. She could not recall the animal's exact name. Hippy Potamus, or something like that.

"Poor young lady," he said with a wide grin. "Too much
time in the Colonies for you, I'm afraid. Facts all mixed
up."

Susan sighed. It was her fifth time in his company; she had joined him out here on the beach every day since their first meeting, though she could not have said why. She supposed there was something relaxing about being in his presence. Timmy had a way of talking about things that challenged everyday notions. Being with him for any length of time was like being taken on a journey through a strange world.

*Far away from my own.*

No problems, no worries. And that aspect of Timmy's company was really very nice, along with the general isolation of being on the planet, the sense that time was passing more slowly down here, or perhaps not even passing at all.

She rolled over on her stomach, hoping for another of what Timmy called "sweep reversal layers" to yank away the cloud cover, expose her skin to a brief—but intensely satisfying—blast of sun. Today, she had stripped down to her shorts, feeling no sense of embarrassment at being half-naked in Timmy's presence. There was something almost fatherly about him. Besides that, she somehow sensed a woman's bare breasts had not excited Timmy for a very long time.

"Three hundred years," insisted Timmy, and Susan just rolled her head dreamily, not caring.

"The Church of the Trust," he explained, "did assume control of the Ontario Cloister about a hundred and fifty years ago. But some of the buildings were here before that. This was an authentic Church three hundred years ago, back in the days before the Apocalypse."

"I'm glad to know that," she sighed.

"It's important that you should know," said Timmy, hesitating. "The individuals . . . the ones who founded this Cloister . . . it's possible that they might return."

Susan frowned and propped her face up into folded palms. "What are you talking about?"

"It is said that this Cloister was a meeting place for the

Paratwa. It is said that the Ash Ock sometimes came here."

She sat up, instinctively wrapping her arms across her bosom, an action having nothing to do with any sudden onslaught of modesty. Shivers were racing through her.

"The Paratwa," Timmy solemnly continued, "may want their home back."

She forced a smile. "That's ridiculous. Even if they come back, why would they give a damn about some silly little religious sanctuary?"

He just stared out across the lake.

"Timmy," she chided. "You went away there."

His double chin dissolved into a hearty smile. "Yes, Susan, even I do it on occasion. But remember, going away is not a good thing. When you lose touch, you enable others to take advantage of you. You give enemies the opportunity to fill in that space that you have left vacant."

"But we're not enemies," she offered.

Timmy did not respond. He just kept staring out over the water.

She shrugged. "I think I should go back now. I don't think there're going to be any sunbursts today."

"You never know," he said, returning his attention to her. "Sometimes the clouds peel away, even when it looks so dark that you think there's going to be a thunderstorm."

"Did you ever see a real Earth thunderstorm?"

"Not for a very long time." He raised his arm and wagged a fat finger at the massive tower of the revivifier, about a quarter of a mile away. At this distance, the tarnished red giant completely dominated the interconnected buildings of the Cloister squatting behind it. "The revivifier has odd effects on local atmospheric conditions. The prerequisites for a thunderstorm can't take place here."

"Then where did you see a T-storm?" she asked.

"I used to travel around a bit . . . when I was younger. I saw a few storms down in the Kentucky area. I even saw a twister once, at very close range, out in one of the western states."

"A twister?"

"A tornado."

She did not recognize that term either, but the whole matter did not seem important. What *did* seem important was that Timmy had travelled to other locations on the planet. During a conversation the other day, he had seemed to suggest that the immediate area of the Cloister had been his lifelong home. "I thought you said you'd never been away from here?"

"Did I?"

"I distinctly remember."

"You're mistaken."

She felt a swell of anger. "You're lying. The other day, you said that—"

He swept his closed hand upward, thrust a palm full of sand into her face.

"Bastard!" she cried, roaring to her feet, spitting the grainy particles back onto the beach.

"Remember yesterday's lesson," he said sternly. "Allow your anger to assume a shape, and it will inhibit your natural body-thought. Allow your fury to reign, as you did just now, and you become vulnerable to—"

"You could have gotten it in my eyes!" she spluttered.

He laughed. "Yes, I forgot. You can't take either of your eyes out for cleaning . . ."

"That's not funny," she said sternly.

Timmy's jowls folded into a frown. The effort looked forced.

"I'm leaving now," she warned. "And don't look for me tomorrow. I've had enough of your stupid games."

"Sit down," he ordered.

Susan plopped herself back down on the sand. She shook her head, confused. She *had* wanted to leave. But Timmy did not want her to go. And now she was passively obeying his wishes.

*What's the matter with me? Have I suddenly turned into a masochist?*

"Susan, you must learn to control your anger. You don't have to repress it—emotional outlets have to be maintained—but you must not permit strong feelings to warp your body-thought."

"And just how do I do that?" she snapped.

"When you feel rage, or any strong emotion, beginning to wash over you, allow the emotion to function as a signal. Become conscious of it. With practice, you can detect the precursors of any outburst. That is all that it takes. In time, your body-thought will do the rest. Strong feelings will be aligned with your body-thought, not against it."

She thought about his words for a moment, feeling her anger beginning to dissipate in the process. She scowled.

"But I *want* to be angry with you! You're always throwing things at me!"

He scooped another handful of sand. She regarded him warily.

"Good," he said with a smile. "See, that wasn't so hard. You're still a bit mad at me, yes?"

"Yes."

"But not so mad that you blind yourself to the possibility that I may throw more sand in your face."

She nodded slowly.

He opened his palm. Sand trickled onto the beach.

Susan studied him: the round face, aflame with fat; the scalloped bangs of gray hair, the encroaching double chin. For the first time, she noticed that his right eye—the removable one—bore a thin film of moisture, as if it were suspended in a liquid.

"Are other parts of your body . . . wetware?"

He smiled faintly. "No, I'm afraid that the rest of me is merely aging flesh—one hundred percent natural organics."

Susan found herself growing angry again, but not at Timmy. *I'm angry at myself, for feeling so . . . confused.* She shook her head. Not confused, that was not exactly right. It was something else, something about being with Timmy that made her feel . . .

"You look frustrated," he offered.

Yes, that was it: frustrated. She suddenly found her thoughts racing toward new junctures, new possibilities.

"You're more than just a caretaker here at the Cloister, aren't you?"

Timmy shrugged. "I make sure that what's broken gets fixed, what's loose, gets tightened—"

"—what's twisted, gets straightened," she finished wearily. "Yes, Timmy, I know about those things. But I also spoke with an old priest last night and he told me that you are—"

"Odd, but tolerable."

"Pardon?"

"Odd, but tolerable. That's what I hear many of them say about old Timmy."

She sighed. "Actually, this priest said—"

"A description worthy of any man."

"Stop interrupting. This old priest said that you ask too many questions and you know too many answers. He said that the reason you're so big is that you're packed full of secrets." She drew a deep breath, feeling like she had just gotten something important off her chest.

Timmy chuckled, but his effort sounded forced.

"I think that a few of those secrets concern me," she prodded.

"Do they now?"

Something in his tone frightened her. But she forced herself to continue.

"I believe that you know all about me. I think that Lester Mon Dama told you about my troubles—about the Honshu massacre, the Paratwa . . . about everything."

For a moment, she thought that he was not going to respond. He stared at her keenly and his wetware eye seemed to pulse slightly, like a slow camera lens adapting to changes in light. Then: "Yes, Susan, I know all about you. Lester Mon Dama talked to me."

She nodded, relieved that things were coming out into the open.

"Lester felt that you needed a companion," Timmy explained.

"Oh." She felt a bit disappointed. "Do you know when Lester's due to return?"

"I think that Lester Mon Dama will not come to the planet again. This is the time of the Paratwa, the time that everyone has been anticipating for these many years." Timmy's eyes grew distant; a droplet emerged from the wetware eye, ran down his cheek. It appeared to be an artificial release of some kind, not a real tear.

"You're going away again," she warned, but he did not seem to hear.

"A time of the Paratwa," he continued, gazing out over the lake. "A time when the Colonists must face their future."

His attention abruptly returned to her and he spoke like a man possessed. "Did you know that for the past fifty-six years, your entire culture has been preparing for this? Do you have any idea of the psychological provisions that have been assimilated, consciously and unconsciously, by your society? On the conscious side, citizens representing all professional aspects of Colonial life—including religious leaders like Lester—have been trained to make the turmoil of the Paratwa return more bearable.

"Even so, your society has paid an enormous cost. Few could really accept the notion that their future—and their childrens' future—might end in slavery to a master race. And as it has been with all imminent confrontations throughout history, people have been catalyzed into two basic response patterns. They prepare to fight or they prepare to flee."

Susan stared at him, astonished by his sudden outpouring. It was so uncharacteristic.

"There are two million Guardians," Timmy continued gravely, "waiting at the outer reaches of our solar system, the vanguard of those who would fight. But there are many millions more who have turned inward, retreated beneath the haze of self-indulgence, denying even the possibility of the coming storm."

*He speaks like a member of the Order of the Birch.*

"They have fled into the degeneracy of their own souls," Timmy proclaimed, as if quoting some great passage. And with that, the strained passion suddenly departed from his face and the familiar, easygoing smile returned. "Running away does not build character, Susan."

She shook her head, not knowing what to say.

"Do you fight or do you flee, Susan Quint?"

"Who are you?" she whispered.

"Who are *you*?" His palm scooped a fresh ball of sand but she snapped a hand across his wrist before he could release it.

"Excellent, Susan! You thwarted the attack before it occurred. You are learning."

"Learning what?" she demanded, her anger returning in a fierce torrent. She did not release his wrist. "Who the hell are you? What do you want with me?"

"Excellent. Barely contained fury, yet fully attuned to body-thought. A natural fight response."

She twisted his wrist but he just smiled, ignoring the pain.

"And what about you?" she challenged angrily. "You don't even have to bother making a decision about fighting or fleeing. You're down here in your own little world, far from the reality of the Colonies. Whatever happens, it probably won't affect your status. And whether this Cloister was a Paratwa place or not, I sincerely doubt whether they're going to be too overly concerned about wanting it back. Ontario is not exactly Irrya."

"It's certainly not," he said ominously.

"And what's that supposed to mean?"

"I'll tell you if you let go of my wrist."

She released her grip, but remained alert. He still had a fistful of sand.

"The Earth, Susan, is a more valuable place than most people assume. This world is humanity's past, as well as its future."

"Now you sound like a Church of the Trust recruiter."

He chuckled. "I told you before. It's a silly religion. And too inflexible to survive for many more years. No, Susan, I speak now as a loyalist to the human race. The Earth is important. And I suspect that when the Paratwa return, it is the planet which they will ultimately covet, not the Colonies. The Earth offers roots. The Colonies do not."

Susan sighed. Perhaps Timmy did not realize just how much of the Church of the Trust doctrine he had absorbed over the years. She stood up and gazed toward the buildings of the Cloister. Her anger had disappeared again and she had a sudden desire to be alone, to rest. "I'm tired."

"Of course," he said graciously.

"May I go now?"

"Yes."

As she headed away, he called after her.

"Susan?"

"What?"

"I believe that tomorrow will be a special day for you. I believe that the time has come for you to become. I'll meet you out here right after lunch."

"Maybe," she replied, knowing that she would indeed keep their rendezvous no matter how much she thought about not doing it. *What's happening to me?*

"I think that you are the one, Susan. Tomorrow we shall learn for certain."

It was all so confusing. Frustrating.

"Tomorrow, Susan, I may give you something even better than a sunburst."

Gillian, flanked by Martha and Buff, entered the spacious lobby and headed for the central security desk. Halfway there, his attention was drawn to a pair of floating holos—a naked man and woman, icons of baby-flesh perfection—dissolving out of the far wall to embark on a choreographed hip-wiggling dance across the tile floor. From the opposite side of the lobby emerged a quartet of ruby red serving platters, each bathed in a steaming cloud of attractive smokeshape. One tray bore a melange of rich-looking pastries, another was heaped with gold and silver jewelry, and the other two overflowed with neatly folded exotic garb—complementary sets of male and female attire. Prancing servants met ruby red platters near the center of the vast space, melted into a laser-crisp geyser of orange light that soared thirty feet into the air. Holographic mutation brought clarity as the geyser slithered into a set of fiery vertical letters: VENUS CLUSTER.

"I think I used to have one of those in my day room," quipped Buff.

"You never had a day room," clarified Martha.

"Yeah, but if I did, I would have had an expensive holo in it."

"May I direct you?" asked the gray-haired security man, as they arrived at the central desk.

"Indeed, you may," Gillian announced, mimicking the formal mannerisms he had observed yesterday on one of Venus Cluster's commercial spots. "I am Troy Spencer De Fevre, good lord willing, and I am here for an eleven-thirty appointment with one of the vice presidents of your company: Mister Cochise."

The security man nodded politely and then scanned his monitor. "Yes, Mister De Fevre, here we are. And you are representing Valsacko Industries?"

"Indeed, at last perusal, I certainly am. I am their legal counsel, intercolonially bonded, and I am here with the full blessing of the Lord and Lady Valsacko themselves." For their visit here, Inez Hernandez had again utilized her numerous connections to fabricate a cover story.

The security man glanced at another monitor and then favored Gillian with a tense smile. "And your two companions, Mister De Fevre?"

"Why my bodyguards, naturally!"

The security man seemed relieved. "Yes, sir. That explains the weapons my scanners are picking up. I'm afraid that I must ask your bodyguards to either disarm or leave the building."

"Of course," said Gillian, idly wondering whether the guard's detection gear was capable of identifying the outlines of a Cohe wand. Not that it mattered. Gillian's Cohe was still safely back at the lion's retreat. There had been no sense in taking unnecessary chances.

"Venus Cluster does not permit guns and such on the premises," continued the guard.

"An admirable policy, good sir. Well, ladies?"

Martha, glaring coldly at the security man, stepped back a pace. For just an instant, Gillian thought that she was not going to comply. But then she smiled and inserted her hands in her wide jacket pockets and slowly withdrew the needlegun from her left side pouch. She laid it on the desk.

The guard's face twitched into a smile. "Thank you, ma'am. And now your thruster."

Martha's other hand emerged from her right pocket, gripping a rare triple-tube thruster. The security man raised his eyebrows. The thruster was attached to her body—two thin coils of wire snaked out from beneath the gun and slithered into a tiny implant junction on her wrist.

"A PAL box," murmured the guard.

Martha unsnapped the two cables from her arm and handed him the unit. The security man gingerly placed it beneath his desk.

Gillian hid his concerns. *A PAL Box—E-Tech-banned sync hardware—able to align a gun trigger directly to a human nervous system.* He hoped the guard would not report her.

Buff favored her partner with an annoyed glare, then removed a standard thruster, a miniature sandram, two slender throwing knives, and some sort of projectile gun from beneath her jacket.

"Starting a war?" asked the security man, still smiling, but looking about as tense as a cat confronting a rabid dog.

"Such show-offs!" uttered Gillian, hoping to dispel some of the guard's uncertainties about the excessive armaments. He emitted a loud sigh. "Sure, they're streetsmart and hard as nails, but just try to get them to take out the garbage!"

The guard stared at him, confused. Gillian had heard the amusing phrase the other day, uttered by one of the Colonies' most popular freelancers during a news report. Obviously, the security man did not tune to the same channels.

He tried another tack. "Well, I'm really not complaining, you see. The Lord and Lady Valsacko are sticklers for protection and goodness knows, we're all glad for it these days. Order of the Birch massacres, Paratwa coming back from outer space, and who knows what else!" He leaned over the desk and spoke conspiratorially. "And not to mention these damn Costeaus, and please don't tell me about how mainstreamed they are!"

His last remark struck a nerve. The security man's face dissolved into a collaborative scowl. "Yeah, those damn pirates, we ought to shuttle them all down to the planet. Give 'em Earth. That's where they belong."

"Absolutely!" agreed Gillian, glancing at Martha and Buff, and deciding that it was time to change the subject.

"Good sir, I notice that your building is blessed with convators." He pointed to a pair of larger-sized portals next to the regular elevator shafts. "Since I am, unfortunately, seventeen minutes early for my appointment, I wonder if we might utilize one?"

The security man shook his head. "Sorry. The convators are normally reserved in advance."

Something in the guard's tone caught Gillian's attention. "Yes, I believe I understand. A fee is involved. Good sir, we would certainly be willing to pay for usage."

The security man glanced around the empty lobby, then nodded. "Cash cards only and no receipt."

"Naturally."

It took only a moment to agree on the proper amount. Gillian placed the bribe on the desk and then headed across the lobby. One of the larger portals slid open and they entered conference elevator number one.

Buff looked astonished. "Extra yes! It's bigger than my apartment!"

The convator spread out before them, twenty feet wide and at least thirty feet long. A twelve station meeting table occupied the main area, with each station boasting senso-adjust chairs, double-port terminals, a forty-four hose liquid refreshment system and an extendable dining tray. Walls and ceiling were covered in a seamless coat of dark fur—a solitary mass of organic matter—gently writhing and pulsating as if it had been disturbed by their entrance. Brown-pelt neurofab: one of the latest and hottest items on the ever-turbulent Irryan social scene.

In addition to the lobby entrance, there were two other closed doors at the far end of the room.

"Toilet cubicle and control room?" wondered Buff.

As if in response to her question, the first door slid back

and a young male emerged. Gillian recognized his getup as that of a twenty-first century corporate attendant: patched blue jeans, frayed leather jacket, and open-faced Bell motorcycle helmet.

"Good day, Mister De Fevre," he said warmly. "I'm Jocko, your CV escort. I've programmed the convator for a fifteen minute trip so that you can maintain your appointment with Mister Cochise. However, due to the very short duration of your transfer, I regret that I cannot offer you more than a few basic con services."

"Those will suffice," said Gillian. "Tell me, Jocko, is this CV surveillance-secured?"

"Absolutely, sir! I just swept it myself not ten minutes before your arrival. Venus Cluster insists on cleanliness at all times."

"Thank you, Jocko." Gillian was wearing his meshwire tracking system and he too had scanned the chamber upon entering. There were no detectable bugs. But it did not hurt to get confirmation. He believed the escort was telling the truth.

"Sir, I might point out that the neurofab on the west wall can be made transparent. In about ten minutes, we'll pass by the building's main atrium. You'll be able to over-look downtown Irrya, including a rarely seen perspective of the Irryan Senate chambers—"

Thank you, Jocko, but I believe we'd prefer privacy."

"Very good, sir. Will there be anything else?"

Gillian faked hesitation. "As a matter of fact, Jocko, there is. Today will be my first meeting with Mister Cochise and it is despicably imprecise of me that I failed to do more than a basic data check." He placed his hands on his hips and emitted a loud sigh. "My own fault—no use sobbing in shame about it. Still, I was wondering if you might be of some help, Jocko. Good lord willing, you might be able to tell me a bit about what Mister Cochise is like."

Jocko smiled. "Certainly, sir."

"My blessings, young sir. I'm boundlessly relieved."

Buff rolled her eyes.

"Now, Jocko, my first question. Is Mister Cochise an easy man to get along with?"

The escort nodded enthusiastically. "Oh, yes sir. Mister Cochise is a fair-minded individual and very thoughtful. Last Rue Day, the entire staff received gifts from his office."

"Indeed," uttered Gillian, having to think for a moment about what that particular holiday represented. Then he remembered: *Rue Day—the perennial acknowledgment/celebration of Earth's abandonment in the year 2099.*

"As a company vice-president," Gillian continued, "I imagine Mister Cochise uses these convators quite often."

"Yes, sir."

"Tell me, Jocko, in your opinion, is he one of those 'hands-on' company vice-presidents or is he the type of man who usually delegates his authority?"

Jocko shrugged. "I'm afraid I wouldn't know that sort of thing, sir."

"Indeed. Just one more question, Jocko. Are there any new people who have come to work with the company lately . . . say, exec level transfers within the past year or so? To be perfectly frank, Jocko, after these legal matters with Mister Cochise are resolved, I'm thinking about restructuring some of my own finances, perhaps make some personal investments in your firm. And Jocko, I'll let you in on a little secret. In the business world, the newest boy on the block is usually the hungriest. That's the person Troy Spencer De Fevre wants to deal with."

The escort shook his head. "No, sir. There've been no incoming execs recently. Venus Cluster doesn't seem to have a whole lot of turnover. Except for Mister Cochise, of course."

Gillian released a genuine frown. "What do you mean? I was under the impression that Mister Cochise has been with the company for nearly eight years."

"Yes, sir, he has. But Mister Cochise only came to our Irryan headquarters about six months ago. Before that, he worked out of one of our auxiliary training facilities in the L5 Colonial cluster."

"He was a vice-president of the company and he didn't work out of the company HQ? That's a bit unusual."

"I wouldn't know, sir. That's just the way things were done around here."

"How often did Mister Cochise visit headquarters in these prior years?"

"Well, sir, I've only been with Venus Cluster about two and a half years. But from what I've heard, Mister Cochise never came here."

"Never?" exclaimed Gillian.

"Yes, sir. They say that he didn't much care for Irrya. I guess that finally someone upstairs decided that it was time for him to be transferred to the home office."

"Indeed," said Gillian quietly, wondering how Nick could have missed such a questionable facet of Cochise's history. A grim suspicion took shape. *Maybe he didn't miss it.*

"Will there be anything else, sir?" inquired the escort.

"No, Jocko, but thank you. You've been very helpful. I'll call you if our desires change."

Jocko politely tipped his racing helmet and then returned to his control room. Gillian faced Buff. "Check the other door."

She nodded and moved to obey.

Gillian sat down, thinking: *What's Nick up to?* Ostensibly, the main purpose of their visit here was merely to give them the opportunity to get a good look around the inside of these headquarters, perhaps permit Gillian's unique gestalt abilities to spot abnormalities in Venus Cluster's operational ambience. The meeting with the vice president was of secondary importance.

*But now it turns out that this Cochise has a very suspicious past. And Nick must have known about it when he arranged our meeting.*

Anger flashed through him. He considered cancelling

the appointment and returning immediately to the lion's retreat to confront the midget.

Martha eased into the chair beside Gillian and typed something into her refreshment terminal. A shot glass appeared beneath one of the hoses and a stream of Bowie-Arf—a cinnamon-flavored stimulant—filled it. She swivelled and propped her legs across Gillian's lap. The shot glass touched her lips.

"Cheers," she whispered, downing it with one gulp.

He rubbed his hand across her bare ankles, momentarily forgetting his anger, remembering last night, when she had come to him, naked and willing. And silent, uttering not so much as a sound, not even at the height of their passion. Yet her lust had been so intense that she had seemed to be swarming all over him, like some catlike creature overdosed on no-grog, unable to remain still for even an instant. Intercourse would have been impossible had he not finally pinned her to the bed.

"I didn't notice your PAL box last night," he said quietly.

Martha leaned forward, extending her arm, showing him the junction plate near the pulse of her right wrist. Gillian examined the tiny flesh-colored square—the visible face of the implanted metal cube. "It doesn't look very recent."

"I was eleven." She shrugged. "My father wanted me to have it."

Gillian thought he detected a hint of bitterness in her tone. "Ever think of having it removed?"

"It's a part of me now."

"Lavatory's clear," proclaimed Buff, returning to the table. She planted hands on hips and stood before him. "What's next, *Mister De Fevre*?"

"Are you both wearing your crescent webs?"

The Costeaus nodded.

Gillian realized he had come to a decision. Absently, he flicked his tongue across the intricate rubber pads attached

to his own bicuspids and molars—the activation circuitry
for his defensive energy web, the hardware of which was
strapped around his waist. He would keep to the plan, and
meet with Venus Cluster's vice president.

*And later I'll have it out with Nick, once and for all.*

Martha removed her legs from Gillian's lap and regarded him curiously. Buff pressed her heavy butt against
the table, folded her arms, and scowled.

"You think there's going to be trouble?" quizzed the
black woman.

Gillian shrugged. "Probably not. But I read Nick's report last night on this company VP, and there's no mention that Mister Cochise has been serving *in absentia* for the
past seven and half years. Pretty unusual, wouldn't you
say?"

"Not really," said Buff. "A lot of businesses have very
peculiar operating procedures. Especially Irryan-based
ones."

Martha toyed with her wrist implant. "A strange cylinder full of strange people."

"Just stay alert," he instructed.

Buff gave an old-fashioned salute. "Extra yes!"

"Funny what you can learn from a convator escort,"
said Martha, staring at him curiously. Then she smiled a
secret smile. "Want to know what Nick told us this morning?"

"Would it matter if I didn't want to know?"

"Your little partner told us who you *really* are."

"And just who am I?" Gillian asked quietly.

"You're the surviving tway of the Ash Ock Paratwa,
Empedocles."

He did not even try to hide his astonishment. "Nick *told*
you that?"

"Right after breakfast. And he told us to tell you."

Gillian shook his head, confused. *What's Nick up to?*

Deep inside, he sensed Empedocles beginning to stir.
*The more turmoil I experience, the more alert you become.* And Gil-

lian found himself wondering just how much of an influence Empedocles was exerting over his thoughts at this very moment. *Do you sense the possibility of the interlace? Is that what calls out to you? Are you hoping to manipulate me into the whelm?*

Manipulation—it seemed to form the very bedrock of Gillian's life. *Nick works me from the outside and Empedocles works me from the inside, like a pair of dueling pros.*

A strange tingle crept along the back of his neck. He had the oddest feeling that Empedocles was laughing. And then the tingle touched the base of his spine, and the echo of amusement turned to familiar pain.

*Catharine. If only you were still alive, a separate presence. If you still walked and breathed and could touch me, not only from the inside out, but from the outside in. If you were more than just a shadow creature, a mouthpiece for the lusts of our monarch . . .*

*If we were still tways, Catharine, able to be together and apart, then we could comprehend. We would know. We would possess the clarity to perceive not only Empedocles's strategies, but Nick's as well.*

"Is it my turn tonight?" quizzed Buff, forcing Gillian's attention back into the room.

He shook his head, confused.

"Martha and I are partners," said the black Costeau. "We always like to share. I'd like to try twayfucking."

Martha smiled sweetly.

"Just stay alert," said Gillian, ignoring their banter. He remained silent for the rest of the convator ride, until Jocko emerged from the control room. "Mister De Fevre, our CV will be docking with Mister Cochise's office in about forty seconds. I trust you had a pleasant trip."

"Very enlightening."

The convator rumbled softly, then seemed to spin slowly clockwise. It was the first real sense of motion Gillian had felt since entering. A muffled sound of pressure equalizers echoed in the distance and then the door opened into a wide brightly colored corridor flanked by a pair of vivid green desks. The one on the left was occupied by a young woman.

"Mister De Fevre?" she asked.

"Indeed, yes."

The secretary smiled politely. "Mister Cochise will see you immediately."

"Thank you." He turned to the Costeaus. "Dears, why don't you see if darling Jocko can be persuaded into holding the CV for us." He grinned at the young secretary. "Regular elevators are so upsetting."

She touched a key on her desk and a portion of the wall behind her slid open. Gillian waited until Martha and Buff ambled back into the convator before proceeding through the portal.

The door closed quietly behind him. Gillian was immediately struck by the dead silence inside the vice president's sanctum.

*A soundproofed chamber. No desk. Two long benches parallel to one another, each covered in bright red cushions. Plain gray walls, unmarred by the typical displays of paintings or rare prints. No visible windows. No detectable electronics, not even a simple terminal.*

Cochise stood in the far corner with his hands folded in front of his crotch. He was shorter than Gillian—maybe five-feet-six—and he wore a sleeveless gray muscle shirt, pin-striped white trousers, and shiny black boots. Whipcord muscles snaked across his bare upper arms. A bronze Rob'n'hood archer's cap lay perched delicately atop his skull, hiding all but the fringes of his closely cropped red hair. Dark pupils regarded Gillian silently for a moment. Then a warm smile filled his face as he came forward.

"Welcome, Mister De Fevre."

The words had a strange quality about them, as if each syllable was being uttered from a pronunciation guide, like a perfectionist attempting a foreign language for the first time. Gillian, for reasons he could not ascertain, found his senses instantly soaring to their hyperalert state, blanking

out all thoughts and concerns, synchronizing to the immediacy of the moment.

"My home is your home," uttered Cochise.

"Thank you," said Gillian, returning the smile. Deep
inside, he sensed Empedocles probing, hungering for additional data. Cochise's odd demeanor had put his monarch
on the alert as well.

"I am told," continued Cochise, "that the Lord and
Lady Valsacko provided you with two bodyguards. They
must think most highly of you."

Gillian sensed an air of challenge in those words. He
bowed his head, ostensibly in acknowledgment of the compliment, but actually to hide his growing concern. *What
have I stumbled into here? Who the hell is this man?* He could almost feel the hair standing up along the back of his neck.

"Please have a seat," offered Cochise, pointing to one of
the red cushioned benches.

Gillian sat down. The seat was extremely soft and the
bench was slightly lower than a normal chair. Insight
flowed across awareness.

*He has a juvenile look about him. But this austere office suggests
a deliberate ignorance of physical amenities, a maturity of purpose. A
strong contradiction.*

"So, Mister De Fevre," Cochise began, "to business. I
was just reviewing your file. Your employers have a long-
standing multiservant contract with us. For years, Venus
Cluster had provided the Valsackos with some of our company's finest—and most expensive—domestics. Our top of
the line model—the *luxuriator.*"

Cochise pouted and stepped over the circle of benches.
"But now, rather abruptly, the Lord and Lady claim that
some of our people are . . . how shall we say . . . removing
artistic dainties from the immediate premises?"

"They're stealing from the Lady's classic shoe collection," clarified Gillian, recalling the details of the cover
story. But even as he spoke, he fought an almost desperate
impulse to roar to his feet. *I'm seated. He's still standing. I'm*

*at a disadvantage.* He recognized his urge as a natural combat instinct.

"I'm shocked," said Cochise, bending his cheeks into a frown.

"It is shocking," agreed Gillian, focusing on Cochise's eyes now, trying to see past that phony melange of expressions, trying to perceive deeper intentions, baser emotions.

Abruptly, Cochise turned sideways, displaying his left profile. "What is to be done, Mister De Fevre? Naturally, Venus Cluster wishes to avoid the rambling oddities of the law."

*The rambling oddities of the law.* The words sang to Gillian's subconscious, and he sensed Empedocles analyzing, using the essence of a gestalt far more powerful than Gillian's own to rip into the phrase, seeking disguised permutations of meaning, phonetic displacements, intricate patterns that would reveal the truth behind this bizarre individual.

Cochise rubbed his palms together and then abruptly sat down on the other bench, facing Gillian. "I am deeply distraught over this incident. Venus Cluster takes pride in our people. *Luxuriators* especially are well screened."

"Mistakes occur," offered Gillian, feeling no more at ease now that Cochise was seated than he had been when the man was standing.

Cochise folded his hands on his lap, palms down. "You do understand that most of these types of problems—when they occasionally plague us—do *not* involve the vice president of the company. Naturally, the Lord and Lady Valsacko's outstanding social standing requires downgrading/correction from the highest echelon." A deep smile settled on his face. "How may Venus Cluster live up to its name?"

*Downgrading/correction.* Another phrase bubbling with tonal eccentricities, wailing to be comprehended. Again, Gillian sensed Empedocles analyzing this latest input.

Cochise hunched forward. Gillian, in response to the sudden movement, instinctively twisted his right wrist and gently compressed his knuckles. It was another combat impulse: Had Gillian been wearing a slip-wrist holster, the Cohe wand would have been launched straight into his palm.

Cochise observed Gillian's subtle motion. A momentary frown crossed the vice president's face. Then he smiled.

Their eyes met. And Gillian knew.

*I'm sitting across from a tway! Cochise is Paratwa!*

From deep within, he sensed the consciousness of Empedocles mushrooming, becoming an electrified, writhing conglomeration of forces, desperate for full consciousness, for unity. A terrifying feeling of unreality washed over Gillian, as if the symbols of his environment were being unraveled from the normal apparatus of physical perception—like a tree being stripped of its leaves, reduced to a bare tangle of twisted branches.

To Cochise's left, a golden bubble took shape, burning fiercely, and within it, Catharine appeared, her wild brown hair lacing the air, the delicate elfin face straining for solidity. Her mouth opened. Her voice whispered: *Bring us together, Gillian. Bring on the whelm.*

Cochise began to rise from his bench.

Gillian's desire for unity ripened, became an unbearable need; the whelm was almost upon him. But beyond that desire lay a cloud of darkness, a groping energy that he recognized as the interior manifestation of his own fear. He probed into that dark cloud, seeking an answer: *Why am I so terrified of the whelm?*

With an abruptness that took his breath away, the dark cloud ripped in two. Gillian was expecting to behold some terrible thing, but there was nothing behind the cloud— nothing but more darkness. And then his own gestalt came to life, turning inward, focusing on that interior symbolism, translating raw emotional resonances into abstract patterns of thought. A flash of golden light. Clarity.

*It's not the whelm that terrifies me—it's not the arising of Empedocles that brings on such dread!*

At last he understood.

*I'm not afraid of what I'll become if I allow the whelm. It's what we'll become—Empedocles and I!*

Cochise was on his feet now, his body deliberately relaxed, ready for action. The tway was observing Gillian calmly, but with a curious intensity.

Gillian's monarch had been right all along. *There is a way for us to be united forever.* Gillian and Empedocles—eternally interlaced in a monstrous surrender of personality, melded together in a whelm that could never be broken; tway and monarch, slowly synthesizing, until neither existed as a discrete presence, but only as a grotesque melange of consciousness—not tway, nor Paratwa, but something else, something nightmarish.

*So obvious,* thought Gillian. *How could I have not seen it?* But that question had an even simpler answer. *Empedocles prevented me from seeing the truth. He knew I would not surrender to such a fate.*

Catharine's eyes pleaded with him. Empedocles begged: *It is the only way, Gillian. Your long years of torment will end. At last, you will know inner peace. We will be together always. We will transcend.*

"No!" he screamed, hurtling out of his chair, jerking his arm forward, slamming his fist toward Cochise's jugular.

An instant of time, slashed open. Cochise's face erupting into a wild continuum of emotion: shock, delight, fury. And then the tway was wrenching sideways and Gillian's fist was meeting empty air.

Gillian clamped his jaw shut, igniting his crescent web just in time. Cochise's right boot slashed upward, aiming for Gillian's kidney. The energy field turned the blow. The tway's foot, still in motion, arched up across the protective barrier, then slid down the other side. The action put Cochise off balance.

Gillian slammed his open palm up under the tway's jaw. The Rob'n'hood archers cap flew from Cochise's head as he stumbled and fell backward across the bench.

Gillian dove after him, crashed down on top of the tway, his knee thrust forward into Cochise's groin for the crippling blow. But there was no sensation of hard contact. Instead, it felt as if Gillian had just rammed his knee into a thick soft pillow.

*Squash armor!* Cochise wore micro energy webs, protecting his vital organs.

Gillian still had the advantage. He continued his forward motion and brought his left elbow down onto the tway's face. But Cochise saw it coming and twisted his neck. Gillian's forearm glanced off the tway's cheek.

For a fraction of an instant, their eyes locked. Gillian saw the hatred, heard the virgin hiss of a creature who had never before experienced such punishment.

And suddenly—unnaturally—a heavy glistening sweat was pouring off of Cochise's body, as if the tway was actually oozing oil from his pores. Gillian found himself sliding across Cochise's chest and onto the floor.

*Son of a bitch!* Off balance, Gillian nailed the carpet with his right knee, feeling that portion of his web compress. He waited until his weight was centered, then used his knee as a pivot point and pirouetted one hundred and eighty degrees, roaring to his feet in a low crouch, crescent web arched forward, ruefully aware that he was now on the defensive, that this lone tway was no easy foe.

Cochise was retreating toward the far wall. On his hands and knees, the tway slithered madly across the floor, his whole body oozing the slippery fluid, leaving a shiny trail across the carpet like some bizarre human slug. Gillian's hyperalert consciousness analyzed the tway's defense, concluding that the pore oil trick had to be a one-shot gambit, utilized for precisely the reason that Cochise had activated it: to escape a hand-to-hand combat situation where the tway lacked tactical advantage.

Gillian hesitated. And out of that hesitation Catharine reappeared, her shadow presence floating in the air directly above Cochise's snaking form. She gazed at Gillian, her eyes shining brightly, lovingly—each eye a tiny pool of gold surrounded by an ocean of dark water. Her mouth opened. Empedocles spoke.

*The whelm, Gillian! Release yourself. Release me! Together we can take him!*

Twin electric currents—desire and fear—tore through Gillian.

*Bring us together!* screamed Empedocles. *Bring us together before this tway destroys you!*

"No!" Gillian shouted, using all the energies at his command to hinder the whelm, to fight the raging inner streams that sought coalescence.

Cochise, sliding out of control in his own fluids, crashed into the bare wall. In one twisting motion the tway vaulted upright, showering the office in a spray of the thick pore oil. Dripping palms slapped against the wall, fingers madly seeking.

Gillian's first thought was that the tway sought escape, that his writhing hands searched for the opening controls to a hidden door. But no portal appeared. Instead, Cochise's palms suddenly made contact with hidden switches. Two small serving platters popped out of the wall, one on each side of him. The tway's eyes lit up with murderous delight.

*The whelm!* shrieked Empedocles. *Do it now!*

Slimy hands grabbed a small knife from each platter. Weird cartoon images flickered madly—twin maelstroms of unstable color and form. Gillian recognized the weapons, though he had not actually seen such blades since his training with Meridian, ages ago.

Flash daggers. Cochise was the tway known as Slasher.

The assassin lunged forward, whipping the erratic shafts of light through the air like ancient scythes across a field of wheat. To Slasher's right, the shadow image of Catharine kept pace, coming at Gillian with the same intensity as the killer, her elfin face swelling with desire.

Gillian gritted his teeth with newfound determination.

*No, Empedocles—you may not arise. Go away or I swear to you—
I'll let him kill me!*

Slasher twisted sideways. The right-handed blade
plunged forward. For just an instant, Empedocles seemed
to teeter on the edge of Gillian's will, a mad and frustrated
presence. And then the image of Catharine dissolved.
Empedocles withdrew back into the deepest reaches of Gillian's being.

Slasher's blade, abruptly doubling in length, slashed at
the exposed left portal of Gillian's web. Gillian twisted
sideways. Flash dagger met energy screen and a volley of
hissing red sparks exploded across the office as the dueling
fields came together.

The words of his former teacher rushed through Gillian's awareness. *Constantly analyze your opponent's tactics,* Meridian would say, during those endless days and nights of
combat training. *Don't waste valuable micromoments between par-
ries and thrusts. During every step of the battle, allow your enemy to
instruct you.*

Gillian analyzed. *Slasher is wearing squash armor and boasts
two flash daggers. But he wears no crescent web or else it would have
been ignited at the moment of my attack. I have no offensive armaments, but I do have the most powerful defensive body-screen ever de-
vised.*

Slasher leaped backward and to the right, seeking a new
position. Then he lunged forward again, his left blade
thrusting at Gillian's unprotected hip. Gillian perceived the
trickery. He waited until the last possible moment, then
jerked his right hip out of the way. Cartoon knife and invisible web again met in a torrent of red tracers. Slasher's
right-handed dagger—the real threat—came whipping
down at Gillian's other flank.

Gillian leaped sideways. The tip of the pulsating flash
dagger missed his exposed left hip by inches.

*That was too close. I can't survive a long assault. Sooner or later,
one of his blades will get through my web.* Gillian acknowledged
another concern. *Right now, it's one on one. But Slasher's other*

*tways could be racing toward this office right now. Time is on his side as well.*

Slasher, as if suddenly becoming cognizant that he had the advantage, backed away from the combat arena. His face blurred into a wicked smile and his hands dropped to his sides. Flash daggers contracted to their normal length—sizzling barrels of light aimed at the floor. The tway laughed.

"They told me you were dangerous," he mocked.

"You should listen to your Ash Ock masters," parried Gillian, thinking: *He's stalling. Is another tway—or tways—coming?*

"They call you *the traitor*. But most of us are amused when we hear the tales of your petty exploits. They say: *Kascht moniken keenish.*"

Gillian felt Empedocles stir, as if those strange words meant something to him.

Slasher paused, watching him carefully. Then he laughed. "You should have died a long time ago. But better late than never."

A faint shiver went through Gillian—combat fear. And he thought: *I have to act now. I have to take this bastard down—and quickly—before his other tways arrive.*

With a deliberate grimace of panic showing on his face, Gillian turned and ran toward the featureless wall where the entrance portal lay hidden. Scraping his fingers desperately across the sound-proofing fabric, he pretended to be searching for the hidden door controls. He closed his eyes and recalled the words of his teacher.

*Listen with your entire being,* Meridian would urge. *Learn to fight without actually seeing your enemy. Eyesight is a potent mechanism, but with training, your ears and other senses can grow just as powerful.*

In the silence of Cochise's office, Gillian listened. He heard the faint patter of Slasher's boots, the shortened lapses between footfalls, and he knew that the tway was accelerating across the office, coming at him from the rear.

Raw data translated into an image of the assassin—a concrete gestalt. He waited until the tway was almost on top of him, and then he compressed his upper body against the wall and lashed out with his right foot.

The heel of his boot caught Slasher in the chest, and the force of the blow stopped him in midcharge. The assassin grunted. Arms flailed wildly; cartoon knives ripped at the air—icons of frustrated energy, unable to reach their prey. The tway fell to his knees, gasping for breath.

*If I'm lucky, he's got a collapsed lung.* Gillian did not wait to find out. He raced over to the twin red benches and ran his hands beneath them, hoping that he had guessed correctly.

He had. Door controls were mounted beneath both seats. Gillian pressed a relay and the portal entrance reappeared. He took one last look at Slasher—on his knees, eyes bright with pain, flash daggers still whipping back and forth—and then Gillian was racing out into the hallway. Behind him, the door snapped automatically shut.

The secretary's eyes widened with surprise as Gillian dashed up to her desk. "What's wrong—"

He grabbed her wrist and yanked her out of her chair. She screamed. Martha and Jocko appeared in the still-open door of the convator.

"Jocko, we're leaving!" yelled Gillian, dragging the secretary past them and into the CV. "Get us to ground floor! Quickly!"

Jocko just stood there, gaping. Buff appeared behind him.

"Let's go," Gillian snapped. "Pretend the building's on fire."

Buff went into action. She grabbed Jocko's arms, wrenched them behind his back, and marched him toward the control room.

Jocko squirmed painfully. "I can't move this CV without permission—"

He howled as Buff twisted his arm. "Jocko," the Costeau

warned pleasantly, "if you don't get this convator moving real quick, I'm going to take off your helmet—with your head still in it."

Gillian grabbed the secretary by the back of the neck. "Did you trigger any security alerts?"

The young woman began to cry. Gillian shook her. "Answer me! Did you trip any alarms?"

"No," she sobbed. "Don't hurt me—please!"

"Martha, tie her up and stick her in the lavatory."

Martha grabbed the secretary and led her away. The CV docking door slammed shut. A moment later, Gillian was almost knocked off his feet as the convator jerked violently to the left.

"Christ!" yelled Martha.

"Sorry," came Buff's voice from the control room. "You want speed, you get a rough ride." She emerged leading Jocko by the elbow. The escort looked pale.

"How long?" asked Gillian.

"Forty seconds till we dock with the lobby," said Buff. "I had Jocko program the emergency exit routine."

The CV tilted to the left. Gillian gripped the table for balance. "Jocko, an exit routine, that will send a signal to security?"

The escort gave a nervous nod. "I . . . think so."

"Buff, put him in the lavatory too." Gillian leaped onto the conference table and shifted his left leg through the weak side portal of his still-active crescent web. One of the mounted refreshment stations was in his way. He gave the unit three sharp kicks and it ripped loose from its mooring, tumbling away from the table in a spray of electrical sparks. A broken hose blasted a liquid stream ten feet across the room, soaking a two-foot-square patch of brown-pelt neurofab. Organic tissue parted, began slithering away from the wet spot.

Gillian moved to the end of the table furthest from the docking door. He crouched low, in a sprinter's position.

Martha and Buff finished locking their captives in the lavatory.

Gillian pointed to the door: "Security people—or worse—will be waiting for us. Follow me through as fast as you can. Get to the security desk and get your weapons."

"The lion is *not* going to like this," muttered Buff.

"Less than ten seconds," said Martha calmly.

The CV abruptly dropped down and to the right. Gillian felt his stomach rise in response to the wild motion. Then came a final sharp twist to the left and the convator jerked to a sudden halt. Gillian stared at the door.

At the instant the pressure seal parted, he lunged forward, sprinting the length of the table in four quick strides. He dove off the end and hurtled out into Venus Cluster's lobby, his arms and legs tucked inside the web, a flying sphere of compressed energy.

*Two security men, bearing pistols.* The guards barely had time to open their mouths in astonishment before Gillian slammed into them. Their three bodies tumbled wildly out into the lobby.

Gillian slid to a stop six feet in front of the central security desk, slightly bruised but essentially unhurt. He stood up. From somewhere behind him, he heard a series of shouts; pedestrians, scattered throughout the hall, were dashing around in panic. But right now, Gillian's most important concern was the gray-haired security guard, who was nervously aiming a thruster pistol at Gillian from behind his console.

"Don't move!" ordered the guard, apparently failing to notice that Gillian wore an active crescent web.

Gillian drew a couple of needed breaths, noting out of the corner of his eye that the other two security men were still on the deck, one unconscious, the other on his back, writhing in pain. Martha and Buff were twenty feet away, racing toward them.

Gillian asked the guard: "What about my friends?" and then pointed his arm at the rapidly approaching Costeaus.

The security man turned his head. Gillian lunged forward, snatched the thruster from his hand, and punched him in the mouth. Eyes glazed over and the guard fell back into his seat.

"Neat trick," said Buff, grimacing with exertion.

Martha vaulted over the security console and retrieved their weapons. Buff stuffed the throwing knives inside her jacket and handed her thruster to Gillian. She placed the odd-looking projectile weapon in her left hand and balanced the sandram in her right.

Gillian, feeling better now that he was armed, scanned the lobby. The floating holo display—naked man and woman—was just dissolving out of the far wall to embark on yet another choreographed dance across the tiles. The remainder of living pedestrians were frantically dashing toward the front and side exits.

"Let's go," Gillian urged, pointing to one of the lateral doors.

But just as he was about to move, one of the regular elevators dumped another pair of armed security men into the lobby. And from the main entrance, four E-Tech Security officers—two male and two female—dashed into the building. Faint red auras, glistening around their crisp blue uniforms, advertised crescent webs. All four carried thrusters.

"You are under arrest!" shouted their leader, a female lieutenant. "Do not move. Drop your weapons and deactivate your webs. Put your hands on top of your heads."

From their right flank, the two Security men from the elevator, also armed with thrusters, approached warily.

"Well, *Mister De Fevre*?" asked Buff softly. "What now?"

Behind the security console, Martha began to hum a melody. A faint smile touched Buff's lips. Gillian understood. Martha had attached to her PAL box, was utilizing a personalized combination of natural tonal patterns to realign the gun trigger with her nervous system.

"I'm ready," whispered Martha.

"Sing!" ordered Gillian, diving across the floor, firing at the closest E-Tech officer. From the corner of his eye he saw Martha's arm snap straight out, gun wailing, the triple-tube thruster a blur of motion as it swivelled back and forth in her palm, direct-drive neural trigger firing on multiple targets, scoring hits with uncanny accuracy. The E-Tech officers, protected by their webs, were nonetheless buffeted like saplings in the throes of a raging storm.

Buff's projectile weapon barked once and a blinding sheet of white light spilled into the front of the lobby. A floor-hugging sheet of transparent flame, eight feet wide and seemingly with a life of its own, began leaping from one E-Tech officer to the next—a fiery pencil trying to connect the dots. As the unnatural flame touched each crescent web, the outlines of the energy fields glistened brightly, like sickle-shaped vases wetted by soapy water.

The transparent flame quickly died away, but as it did, the four E-Tech officers began hopping madly, as if their feet were on fire. Gillian had never before seen anything like it.

Buff let loose a triumphant shout as the E-Tech squad—en masse—raced out of the building.

Gillian pivoted right at the same instant as Martha, their weapons seeking fresh targets. But the two security men had had enough, and were running back toward the safety of the elevators. Obviously, dealing with crazed combatants and high-tech weaponry fell outside their job descriptions.

"The side exit," Gillian urged. "Quickly!"

The three of them hid their weapons and raced out onto the bright and narrow Irryan street, slowing to a brisk walk as they melted into a dense lunchtime crowd. This was a pedestrian thorofare, free of cars: just fast-moving throngs of humanity, intertwining as they struggled toward their various destinations.

Gillian heard distant sirens, but he knew they were still far enough away to be no threat. The E-Tech Security people who had confronted them in the lobby must have been relatively close to have arrived so quickly. Their misfortune.

"Jesus, Gillian," whispered Buff, "this is *crazy*. What in the hell is going on?"

"We're not out of this yet," he warned. "Watch your backs. There are two more tways."

He glanced at Martha, saw that she was walking stiffly, her eyes panning back and forth like a scanner, and Gillian knew that she was still sync-locked to the PAL box, still in combat mode.

"The lion is *not* going to like this," lamented Buff. "And I have a feeling—"

The hideous wail of a thruster—firing with impossible speed—chopped her off. Gillian whirled.

*Shooter.*

He was a hundred feet away, marching up the middle of the street, the peak of his front crescent web shining weirdly under Irrya's intense noonday sun, clearly visible above the heads of the crowd. He was shoving his way through the crush, indiscriminately blasting pedestrians.

*Bastard!* cursed Gillian, knowing that Shooter was killing people in the hopes of drawing out Gillian. And the tway's energy screen should have been invisible under this sunlight, but Shooter must have juiced the web's powerpak, forcing incandescence in the hope that Gillian would see, would counterattack.

Screams filled the air. Gillian raised his thruster skyward and fired two blasts.

Shooter changed direction, began marching toward them.

Gillian ducked low. "Buff, get ready with that flame weapon of yours."

"I can't!" she hissed. "There're unprotected people out here. The salene will kill anyone not wearing a web!"

The random movement of the crowd abruptly transmuted into a framework of order as survival instincts surfaced and people got out of the way. A rank opened between Shooter and Gillian. Both fired at the same instant.

Modulated packets of energy—thruster blasts—hammered the front of Gillian's web. He leaned forward, desperately trying to stay balanced against the pummeling blows, but with twenty blasts per second hitting his web, it was hopeless. Swept off his feet, he tumbled backward into Buff.

Shooter kept marching forward, weapon wailing, and Gillian felt himself rolling along the street, almost totally out of control, a bowling pin propelled down an endless aisle by the unyielding force of the spray thruster. Twisting madly, he managed to keep his front crescent in line with the invisible blasts, desperately aware that the tactic would not save him for much longer.

From Shooter's left, Martha leaped out of the crowd, weapon arm perpendicular to her body—a steel shaft with hardwired armament—alternating thruster tubes discharging three blasts per second.

Shooter's web absorbed a couple of hits and then his own thruster arm whipped toward the new threat, firing into the crowd where Martha had emerged, knocking unprotected people off their feet, instantly killing many of them. Martha, battered by a series of direct hits, was catapulted back into the screaming conflux.

Gillian, taking advantage of the brief distraction, managed to scramble upright and fire a solitary blast at the assassin before Shooter's devastating weapon again turned upon him. But this time only a short spray compressed the front of Gillian's crescent.

Martha was on her feet again, marching forward, firing point blank, ponytails whipping behind her, face burning with Costeau fury. This time, Shooter turned to unleash his full wrath upon her. His thruster wailed, pounding Martha under an impossibly intense deluge.

"No!" shouted Buff, arm whipping over her head, releasing a slender knife, sending the blade toward its target. But the knife merely bounced harmlessly off Shooter's web.

Even as Martha tumbled across the pavement, she kept her arm outstretched, neuro-synchronized gun blasting away at Shooter's leading crescent. But he just kept coming, brutally spraying her protective web until at last her body jerked sideways, exposing unshielded flesh.

She made no outcry, at least none that Gillian could hear. She just closed her eyes and shuddered as Shooter's energy cannon pulverized skin and bone.

Buff shrieked—like a tway experiencing the deathshock of her other half—and then the black Costeau was racing up the street toward her partner. Something whizzed over Gillian's head.

Three miniature jets—E-Tech Security assault crafts—soared out of centersky, zeroing in on the disturbance. The crowd stampeded wildly and the clear firefield between Gillian and Shooter abruptly disappeared in a morass of aimless humanity. Buff, still trying to reach Martha, was turned away by the thick wave of people.

Gillian grabbed her arm. "Come on! We've got to get out of here!"

"No!" Buff cried, tears streaming down her face. "I've got to help her—"

"She's gone. She's dead." He shook her, gently but firmly. "We have to save ourselves now."

Buff's eyes pleaded. "I have to help her."

The jets descended, their red tracking lasers sweeping across the crowd, scanning for armed targets.

"No more time," Gillian hissed, dropping the thruster and yanking Buff toward the gleaming rectangular entrance of an exotic vegetable retailer. "We've got to get out of sight before those trackers pick us up."

Buff came to her senses. She wiped her eyes with the back of her sleeve. "All right—go!"

They ran into the store, ignoring startled clerks and customers, raced toward the back, toward the mandated fire exit. A deserted alley. Through a shipper's entrance and into another building.

"A few more blocks," said Gillian, breathing hard. "That should get us far enough away from the primary search area."

Buff, grimacing with exertion, managed a nod.

And even as Gillian ran, he sensed the patterns of Empedocles, pale distant shadows around a crackling fire, temporarily controlled, but waiting for another chance to come to the forefront. *You won't give up after one defeat,* Gillian thought bitterly. Empedocles was not finished. He would continue to pursue any path that might ultimately lead them both to that hideous melange of consciousness.

"But not today," Gillian whispered.

They were in the CPG boardroom, Colette and Ghandi arguing about the activation status of their profarming division, Calvin plopped at the opposite end of the table, his legs sprawled across a seat, loose khaki flak jacket unbuttoned at the collar. The maniac looked more bored than usual: one hand toyed with the stars 'n' stripes emblem sewn on his right sleeve while the other flip-flopped lazily across the pseudomahogany table.

Ghandi responded to Colette's latest question with a shrug. "We can start moving these megatons of hardware down to the surface with only three days' notice. That includes practically everything—harvesters, planters, compost stations, atmospheric revivifiers, the works. Within six months, two hundred and fifty profarming communities can be in place. You know that."

Colette raised her eyebrows. "Then I fail to see what your objections are."

"There are distinct problems," Ghandi reasoned. "First off, CPG does not have the support systems to back up such an enormous undertaking."

"Irrelevant," said Colette. "When the Colonies are under Paratwa control, the support systems will be acquired. Next objection?"

"Trained personnel. For your reseeding project to succeed in such a short time, I estimate that we'll need over one hundred and twenty thousand profarmers. That's almost double the number of existing workers in that specialty."

Colette paused. "Theophrastus will be bringing advanced training tools back to the Colonies—induction tutors and some very sophisticated mnemonic software which will drastically shorten training and apprenticeship periods. Also, many of the latest breeds of Paratwa are skilled in the complexities of profarming—the Ash Joella, in particular. And our human support units will also be able to share the burden."

Ghandi held back a frown. *Human support units—the descendents of the original Star-Edge crews, who had been overwhelmed by the Paratwa centuries ago.* He often wondered what they were like, these people who had lived their entire lives under Paratwa domain. *Do they have any real freedoms, or are they more like the slaves of the ancient world?* Colette mentioned them frequently, but never in much detail.

"What else, my love?"

Ghandi hesitated. The final problem cut to the heart of the matter. He broached his concerns slowly. "I don't quite understand why this new generation of crops that your people are bringing back must be grown strictly on the Earth. Why not utilize at least some of the existing profarming Colonies? If that were done, then the support unit and personnel inadequacies could be more readily solved."

"Intricate growth parameters," replied Colette quickly, as if wanting to end the entire discussion. "These new crops require vast amounts of space for maximum yield. Their proliferation would be severely stunted within the artificial confines of the cylinders."

Calvin yawned.

"All right," said Ghandi, acquiescing. "I suppose that these profarming communities can be set up within the allotted time-frame."

"They *must* be set up," Colette clarified. "Within six months of the Irryan Council's formal surrender, I expect to see the first harvest."

Ghandi said nothing. He still did not understand just what was so important about such a rapid reseeding of the Earth—"Ecospheric Turnaround," overnight, as it were. Colette's vague explanation that Paratwa control over the Colonial population could be more easily maintained by transferring the primary food sources to the planet made little sense.

He sighed. What the Ash Ock wanted, the Ash Ock would get. Ghandi had no choice but to accept Colette's latest dictates, and to regard them as just another puzzle in a long line of Paratwa mysteries. Eventually, he would gain enough knowledge of this profarming scheme to figure things out for himself.

"What are the newest intercolonial figures on acceptance of planetary reinhabitation?" asked Colette.

Ghandi checked his terminal. "Forty-three point two-eight-six percent of the population now favor an eventual return to the Earth. That's another gain; up nearly half a point in the past four weeks."

Colette smiled. "Excellent. I wasn't expecting a gain right now, not with all the turmoil. The announcement of Meridian's return and the accelerated pace of the Birch murders were expected to function as negative elements in this regard. The mere fact that we've registered a gain indicates that CPG's campaign is proving extremely effective."

Ghandi nodded, glanced at his terminal screen. "Yes, and in particular, the latest series of commercial spots—those espousing the values of a return to surface life—are generating strong ratings."

"Good. See if you can get our gut-ad department to expand on the theme, develop an even stronger line of pro-Earth commercials. But this time, we'll simply market the motif itself. Let some of our hidden subsidiaries sell customized versions of the pro-Earth storyline to as many nonfamily corporations as possible. We don't want it to appear that CPG has suddenly become promoter *extraordinaire* for a planetary homecoming. The Czar—and perhaps others—will likely analyze this latest trend. They might begin to wonder why CPG is so strongly in favor of a return to the planet."

"That's wise," agreed Ghandi, typing a note on his monitor. "Also, I think that CPG should . . ."

He trailed off as Calvin abruptly rose from the table. The maniac's cheeks withered into a tight scowl and he extended his arms in front of him, palms outthrust, as if he was preparing to push away some invisible object.

Ghandi sighed. "Calvin, I suggest that you—"

"Shh!" hissed Colette, gripping Ghandi's arm.

Calvin took one more slow step backward, then suddenly let out a terrifying screech—anger interfused with unmitigated anguish. The maniac's fingers compressed into fists. His eyes closed and his body slithered into a low crouch.

He seemed to rock back and forth for a moment, and then his arms were whipping violently from side to side, spraying senseless arrays of green holotronic letters and numerals in the space above the boardroom table. Shrieks filled the conference room and Ghandi stared wordlessly at his wife, wondering what in the hell was going on.

Colette remained perfectly still and something in her

manner persuaded Ghandi to adopt a similar pose. With frozen fascination, he returned his attention to the bizarre performance.

For a time, Calvin kept up the rhythmless rocking motion, looking like a C-ray ignor trying to learn to dance—body willing, but intellect too underdeveloped to coordinate sophisticated movements. And then the tway shuddered uncontrollably, and let loose another piercing scream that sent shivers up Ghandi's spine.

In motion now, marching two steps in one direction, pivoting, marching two steps back, boyish face crystallized in a raging grimace, expelling grunts as if he were some sort of shellshocked ape. And Ghandi finally began to comprehend. *Something is happening to his other tways, Ky and Jy.*

The exhibition ended as abruptly as it had begun. Calvin leaned against the table, breathing heavily, a trail of clear spittle dripping from the corner of his mouth. Ghandi glanced at the wall clock. The tway had been pantomiming for close to five minutes.

Colette rose from her seat. "Calvin, vocalize."

The tway whipped his left arm through the air, spraying another furious maelstrom of misshapen green letters the length of the boardroom. Ghandi could just make out fragments of a sentence: ATTACK ... CLUSTER ... KY ... E-TECH ... STREET ...

"Calvin!" snapped Colette. "Control the interlace."

The maniac gripped the edge of the table and squeezed so hard that Ghandi thought he would crush the grained plastic: Calvin seemed literally to be forcing the tension out of his body. At last, he released his vise-like grip and straightened to his full six-foot stature. But his face remained locked in a murderous scowl.

"We're waiting," urged Colette.

Calvin jerked his left arm up, palm outward. Sharp-edged holotronic letters burned into focus.

KY WAS ATTACKED IN HIS VENUS CLUSTER

OFFICE BY A SINGLE MALE. PROBABILITY HIGH THAT THE ASSAILANT WAS GILLIAN. KY INJURED, JY ARRIVED MOMENTARILY AND ENGAGED IN STREET COMBAT WITH THE ASSAILANT AND TWO FEMALE COMPANIONS. ONE FEMALE KILLED. TRAITOR AND OTHER FEMALE ESCAPED. JY FORCED TO DISENGAGE FROM BATTLE FOLLOWING THE ARRIVAL OF STRONG E-TECH SECURITY CONTINGENT. NUMEROUS CIVILIAN CASUALTIES.

Ghandi's mouth fell open in shock. He had fantasized about Gillian being set loose upon the maniac, but he had never believed it would actually happen.

A delicate shiver raced through Colette and then she was gone. The cold alien light appeared in his wife's eyes. Her voice dropped in timbre and pitch.

"How badly is Ky injured?" demanded Sappho.

Some of the fury seemed to depart from Calvin's face as he recognized the presence of his monarch/mistress.

A SEVERE BLOW TO THE CHEST. NO BROKEN RIBS BUT MASSIVE TISSUE DAMAGE. KY IS MOVING UNDER HIS OWN POWER AND HAS MANAGED TO EXIT THE BUILDING.

"How long can you bear the pain?"

Calvin's cheeks withered into an expression that was almost a sneer. I CAN TOLERATE THE PAIN FOR AS LONG AS YOU WISH.

"Good. I want Ky to avoid any of the immediate emergency treatment centers. E-Tech may place them under surveillance. Have Ky proceed directly to a private docking terminal—use CPG's Retro-Gamma facility in the Central district." She turned to Ghandi. "Corelli-Paul, please make the necessary arrangements to have Ky shuttled to one of our off-Colony relaxation centers for treatment."

Ghandi accessed his terminal to carry out her commands,

all the while thinking: *Are we in immediate danger? Will CPG be paid a visit by Gillian and his cronies?*

Sappho continued her questioning. "Calvin, how certain are you that it was the traitor?"

The maniac closed his eyes and threw his head back, and Ghandi knew that Calvin was reviewing the parameters of the attack, in that curious Ash Nar fashion. Finally:

IT WAS DEFINITELY GILLIAN. MOTOR/ MOTION CHARACTERISTICS FIT THE PROFILE THAT MERIDIAN TRAINED ME TO RECOGNIZE.

"Did Gillian immediately recognize you as Paratwa?"

DIFFICULT TO ASCERTAIN. HE WAS SUSPICIOUS, BUT I DON'T BELIEVE HE WAS CERTAIN UNTIL WE HAD ACTUALLY CONVERSED FOR SOME MOMENTS.

"Why didn't you utilize the needbreeder?" wondered Ghandi.

Calvin glared at him. Sappho raised her eyebrows, urging the tway to respond.

THERE WAS NO TIME. THE TRAITOR ATTACKED WITHOUT WARNING.

Sappho nodded. "And it is quite possible that Gillian would be immune to needbreeders." She turned to Ghandi. "What we've feared has occurred. The Czar must have identified Venus Cluster—and Ky's alter ego, Cochise—as being connected to the Order of the Birch massacres. As of this moment, Venus Cluster is useless to us." She turned back to Calvin.

"I assume that Ky was able to activate the self-destruction module before he exited the premises."

YES. HIS OFFICE WILL BE DESTROYED MOMENTARILY. INVESTIGATORS WILL FIND NO TRACES OF THE NEEDBREEDER. UNFORTUNATELY, THREE SKYGENE MACHINES THAT KY CURRENTLY HAD STORED THERE WILL ALSO BE LOST.

"Those can be replaced," said Sappho. "Our main

problem now is that the remainder of the skygene infections will have to be accomplished directly through the auspices of CPG. The next group of couriers must be brought here. We'll utilize our own needbreeder, the one disguised in the entrance hall."

Ghandi frowned. "Is that wise? For all we know, Gillian and his people have already identified Venus Cluster as a CPG-owned subsidiary. Hypnotizing the couriers right outside our own boardroom will put us at an even greater risk—"

"Do you have a better suggestion?"

Ghandi shook his head, uncertain of just how far he could go in contradicting Colette's monarch.

Sappho reiterated: "The skygene infection program *must* continue on schedule. The risks must be assumed. We shall operate under the assumption that Gillian and the Czar have not yet connected Venus Cluster with CPG even though they may eventually do so. Nevertheless, the project cannot be stopped. Every Colony must be infected by the time Meridian arrives."

"Of course," uttered Ghandi, his tone subservient but his head swarming with possibilities.

Until now, the entire skygene project had remained concentrated at Venus Cluster, CPG's secretly owned subsidiary. Months ago, one of the Ash Nar twins—Ky—had been installed as an officer of the company. From his vice presidential post, Ky was able to recruit suitable couriers from among the many inter-colonial travellers who flowed through the doors of Venus Cluster's Irryan headquarters.

Upon locating a courier, Ky would manipulate that individual into his executive office. Ky's needbreeder would be activated and a short time later, one temporarily hypnotized subordinate would emerge from Venus Cluster carrying a small suitcase, with instructions on what to do when he arrived at the targeted Colony.

Each suitcase contained a living skygene and its support machinery. Each skygene was capable of releasing a deadly aerobic virus—a lighter-than-air mutagen—that could spread through the sealed atmosphere of a medium-sized Colony within hours. The skygene virus, when breathed, was one hundred percent fatal to mammals. According to Colette, the skygene's mutagenic abilities dictated that there could be no cure. Once in the bloodstream, an average human being would die within days.

Each hypnotized skygene courier was responsible for secretly transporting one of the deadly suitcases to his home Colony and hiding the unit there. Each suitcase contained a coded trigger which—if and when remotely activated—would release the virus.

There were complications, however. The delicate and complex nature of each individual skygene machine dictated a significantly high failure rate. Therefore, each unit had to be tested immediately prior to activation.

The Ash Ock solution to that problem was brutally simple. Each needbreeder-driven servant, still totally unconscious of his actions, removed and ingested a minute tissue sample of the skygene organism. Next, the victim would place a call to tway Calvin, and inform the Ash Nar whether or not the skygene had tested positive in his or her own bloodstream. In the vast majority of cases, the tests themselves were not fatal as long as each victim ingested only a small dose; the ingestion merely caused a variety of cold and flu symptoms within the victim. But regardless of the test's outcome, the needbreeder slave was scheduled to die.

Calvin arranged for some of the victims to meet him at a certain time and place, and—gathering together a group of the hypnotized couriers—disguised their murders within the larger framework of an Order of the Birch massacre. Other victims were killed individually: A variety of "accidents" and "suicides" ensured that the courier deaths were spread over a wide arena, thus helping to negate suspicions.

And if a particular courier tested negative, indicating a

faulty skygene, Ky simply made arrangements for a second victim to transport another suitcase to that particular Colony. Eventually, all two hundred and seventeen cylinders would be infested with successfully tested skygene machines, poised to release their viruses and destroy their human populations.

That meant, of course, that at least two hundred and seventeen couriers had to be executed.

Ghandi shook his head, still amazed at the intricate ruthlessness of the scheme. But, hopefully, few of the skygene suitcases would ever have to be triggered. The Irryan Council, once they understood how futile their situation was, were expected to quickly surrender to the Paratwa.

"Calvin," continued Sappho, "you and Jy will have to accomplish the next scheduled Birch massacre without your injured tway. Do you foresee Ky's absence as creating any special problems?"

Calvin ambled across the room in that perversely delicate manner of his, arms slithering from side to side, legs wobbling as if his knees were about to crumble out from under him. He halted in front of his mistress.

THE MASSACRES WILL CONTINUE AS PLANNED. The tway knelt at Sappho's side and gently lifted the cuff of her pants, exposing her bare ankle. His tongue licked at her flesh. Sappho petted the back of his neck.

"I know," she soothed. "You cannot bear that he still lives. I promise—you will have your revenge upon the traitor."

Calvin turned to Ghandi with a dark smile.

"Corelli-Paul," said Sappho, "you recall our discussion the other day?"

Ghandi nodded, swallowing a sudden spasm of fear.

"With Venus Cluster gone, CPG Corporation *must* remain fully operational. Should enemy eyes turn upon us before the infection program has been completed, drastic measures will become necessary." Sappho rubbed her fingers across Calvin's cheek. "In the event CPG falls under suspicion, we must provide our enemy with a suitable shadow to chase. You will be that shadow, Corelli-Paul. It is you who will be called upon to make the great sacrifice, to become the public scapegoat."

"What sacrifice?" he asked, feeling the microbes begin their furious little dance.

Sappho perceived his quiet struggle. "Sometimes, Corelli-Paul, life is not easy. But the alternative to life is always much harder. Please remember that."

The threat was clear. "I'll do as you wish," Ghandi heard himself whisper, as the microbes roared up his spine: tiny shards of metal, cutting into muscles and bone, cutting into his very being.

"I know that you will," said Sappho.

"Do you feel trapped?" asked Timmy. "Do you feel as if your situation in life has conspired to keep your true soul repressed? Deep inside, do you sense the real Susan Quint lying dormant?"

They were out on the beach again, sitting side by side on the damp sand, alone, further away from the low buildings of the Cloister than ever before. The day remained heavily overcast. Susan knew that there would be no sunbursts.

"Do you ever wonder what it would feel like to suddenly wake up?" wondered Timmy. "And *not* be confused. *Not* be frustrated."

*No sunbursts*, Susan thought, churning the disappointment over in her mind. If the clouds would only part, even for a few seconds. Just a brief flash of that delicate heat, the glistening brightness, the shadows so crisp that you felt you could pick them up, move them as if they were real physical objects.

Timmy sighed with exasperation. "You're not paying attention."

"So throw something at me."

As always, their conversation had begun innocently. But today it had degenerated even more rapidly into a twisting, senseless interplay: Timmy challenging her, prying and pushing, wanting something, yet unwilling to clarify his desires.

"I'm tired, Timmy." *I'm tired of you.*

She kept her attention on him, just in case he *did* decide to throw something at her. But he just stared dispassionately, his jowled face lost in thought, the wetware eye moist, shimmering.

He broke into a sudden smile. "You need a change of pace!"

She shrugged.

"How about a swim?" he asked.

"The water's too polluted."

"That's true. I'll stay on the beach. You go in."

"Very funny."

With effort, Timmy shifted his weight on the sand. Knees compressed and his legs seemed ready to buckle out from under his massive frame, but he managed to stand up. "All right, Susan, I believe that Lake Ontario beckons. I promised yesterday that today would be a special day for you, and I like to remain true to my word. It is time for your baptismal. It is time for you to become."

"Become what?" she wondered dreamily.

"Susan," he announced sternly, "I want you to go into the water."

She compelled herself to laugh at the absurdity of his request. "I don't think so, Timmy."

*"Kascht moniken keenish,"* he uttered.

Unpleasant sounds, she remembered thinking, almost words, but not quite, more like the guttural outpouring of some sleeping animal, caught in the turmoil of a dark dream. Foolish sounds, devoid of meaning yet endowed with a curious quality, something quite indescribable.

*Plasma flowing through my pores,* she thought, aware that her attempted translation merely skimmed across the surface of meaning, like a child trying to describe some adult posture, a three-year-old explaining the intricacies of the Socratic teaching method.

And then the plasma seemed to be inside her skin, flowing freely, and she kept thinking of an inner wetness, a liquid breaching some part of her that had never known moisture. The wetness rose within her. She felt oddly transparent, like a vial being filled with colorless fluid.

It did not feel bad and it did not feel good. The experience was so utterly novel that no preconceived mental fabrications existed to provide bias.

*I feel with the freshness of a child.*

And abruptly, she became aware that her pants were wet.

The odd sensations left her, vanishing down some nerve pathway, dissolving into memories. She felt her face reddening with embarrassment as she realized that Timmy would take notice of her childish accident.

She turned around to hide the front of her wet shorts. But somehow, Timmy had moved. He now stood in front of her, yet at an unbelievable distance away—at least fifty feet. Understanding brought a cold chill. Timmy had not moved. He was standing at the same spot on the beach as before.

*And I am in the water.*

She had not wet her pants at all. In fact, she was up to her waist in the gentle waves of Lake Ontario.

A feeling of confusion overtook her and for an instant, she felt like she was going to faint. She closed her eyes, tightly, hoping that when she opened them again, things would be all right, things would be normal.

But she was still in the water.

"How's the temperature?" he yelled gleefully. "Should be pretty warm this time of year."

"You hypnotized me," she mumbled.

"Not hypnosis. Something else. Come on out—it's not good to stay in that dirty water for too long."

She waded back onto the beach, walked to within twenty feet of him. *Close enough.*

Timmy smiled. "Enjoy your baptismal?"

She regarded him warily. "No."

"Remember to take an extra-long detox shower tonight. That water's still heavily polluted—"

"What do you want from me?" It was a simple direct question, she thought. It should earn a simple direct answer.

"I just wanted you to feel the water—"

"What do you want from me?" she repeated, more forcefully.

He just kept grinning. "Are you angry with Timmy?"

"Yes!"

"Good. I'd rather see you angry than dreamy and unconcerned. Just remember not to allow—"

"—Not to allow my anger to interfere with my body-thought," she snapped. "Yes, I remember your *lessons*. But I'm sick of them, and I'm sick of you and your tricks. I'm sick of this whole damn planet and I want these absurd games to end! Now!"

"Good, Susan. I'm pleased by your reaction."

She lost control. "Bastard!" she screamed, reaching down, scooping up a handful of sand, hurling the grained particles toward him. From twenty feet away, her attack remained largely symbolic: The spray of sand fell harmlessly to the beach, ten feet short of its target.

"Excellent!" Timmy exclaimed. "Real and honest fury,

completely attuned. I was beginning to think that my poor little orphan girl was not capable of such emotion."

Something snapped inside her.

Motion. Her long legs plowing across the beach, running hard, straight toward him, every micro motion perceptible, her body soaring with clarity. It was as if she was hurtling along a razor-thin pathway, where thought and action flowed together, perfectly balanced, like in the Honshu terminal, like in her Irryan apartment, when the two E-Tech investigators had tried to kill her. But there was a difference; on those two occasions, fear had sent her racing along that razor. Now, fury drove her forward.

Debris. On the sand. Her eyes scanning, seeking a weapon, but watching Timmy at the same time, watching his face, alert for any emotional signals, however faint, that might portend resistance.

But he just stood there, a study in passivity.

A weapon on the sand—an eighteen inch cylinder of thick plastic, some long-abandoned piece of construction material, grimy with age. A slight shift in direction—the razor-path obediently shifting within her to compensate—and then her arm was sweeping downward, snatching the weapon from the sand, spinning it over her head, a deadly propeller, ready to create havoc.

Timmy's left eye opened wide.

She was five feet away from him, coming on strong, and suddenly his fat body dissolved with fear, and his arms flew up in front of his face, quivering.

"Don't hurt me!" he screamed.

Some of Susan's rage vanished, diminished by an onslaught of pity for the frightened and pathetic creature who cowered before her. She stopped a pace in front of him and lowered the makeshift weapon.

Timmy collapsed to his knees. "Please!" he begged, twining his fingers into the ancient symbol for prayer. "Don't hurt me."

"Goddamn you!" she yelled, throwing the stick back toward the lake. "Just who in the hell do you think you are!"

In that instant, he struck.

She barely had time to register the fist, slamming upward from the folds of his thick gray robe, knuckles shimmering red under the transparent field of an attack gauntlet.

The fisted energy web smashed into her guts and she doubled over with the pain, on the verge of vomiting her breakfast onto the sand. Something swept across her ankles—his other arm—and then her feet were flying out from under her and she was gazing upward at smog-filled skies. Her butt slammed onto the beach first, followed an instant later by her head and middle back. Dizziness blurred vision.

And then Timmy's massive form was on top of her and she thought: *He's going to rape me.* His fist, power-enhanced by the energy web, pressed under her jaw, forcing the back of her head further into the sand. Something sharp and cool pressed into her aching midsection.

His head descended. Mere inches separated their faces and she could no longer focus properly. Yet still, she had the impression that his artificial right eye was leering at her.

Hot breath blew across her mouth. "Don't move," he warned, pressing the sharp object into her stomach so ferociously that she feared her skin would suddenly rip open and the blade plunge through.

"Do I have your attention?" he asked.

She tried to nod her head but could not; the attack gauntlet compressed her neck so tightly that even the barest movement was impossible.

"Good," he said, reading her eyes. "Now, Susan, tell me what you've learned."

The fist pulled away, permitting her mouth to open. "Let me up," she whispered.

The knife pierced her. She gasped.

"The blade's inside you now," he explained calmly. "It's known as a bab knife—extremely sharp along all four edges, but very thin. Minuscule tissue damage has taken place thus far. If I remove the blade cleanly, you'll heal fairly rapidly, without a scar.

"However, this particular bab knife has been equipped with a rather gross version of a rhythm detector. If you make any sudden movements, those four tiny edges will sense it. They'll begin to vibrate. The bab will literally yank itself out of its handle and burrow straight through your body. I doubt if it will kill you; in fact, I've experienced it myself once, and obviously, I'm still here." A grim smile folded his flesh, outlining the cheekbones, as if they were tiny plateaus emerging from the rest of his face. "But believe me, Susan, a bab knife cutting straight through your body is an incredibly painful experience."

She felt her lungs convulsing, a panicked gasp for extra air. The blade seemed to stab deeper into her midsection. Her lips quivered, fighting terror. "What . . . do . . . you . . . want?"

"I'm training you. That much should be obvious. Pain techniques are perhaps not the best teaching methods, but they do have the advantage of being the fastest. And unfortunately, time does not allow for gentler ways. It's taken six sessions of stimulation just to awaken your real fury— one of only a handful of emotions that can serve to link body, spirit, and intellect. And now I am using that temporary linkage—that pathway extending into the deepest roots of your being—with the hopes of fully awakening you. Now, once again, Susan: What have you learned?"

*Don't panic!* screamed some inner voice. *Stay calm. Stay in control.*

She forced her breathing into a steady rhythm. The bab knife seemed to become motionless; a deep splinter, but not unbearable. As long as she did not move.

"I'm waiting," said Timmy, his words crackling with impatience. "I must warn you, Susan, there's another way for the bab to burrow through your body. With the push of a button, I can disengage the blade from the handle, and it will cut through you automatically. In other words, both of us have the power to cause you unbearable agony. You can do it to yourself by trying to move. Or I can do it to you."

She thought: *Someone from the Cloister has to see what's happening! Someone has to help!* But she knew they were too far away. From this distance, any observers would probably conclude that old Timmy was just having fun with the same young woman who had willingly accompanied him onto the beach every afternoon for the past six days.

Terror began to overwhelm her. The thought of that blade cutting through her body was almost too much to bear.

*Don't panic!* came the inward voice once again. *Give him what he wants. Then get away from here!*

She swallowed her fear. "I've learned . . . I've learned that I should listen to you . . . that I should obey your wishes . . ."

His cheeks bent into a grimace. "One more stupid answer like that, Susan, and I swear that I will release the bab! Now speak to me truthfully. What have you learned?"

Tears welled in her eyes. "I've learned that I can't trust anyone!"

"Clarify that," he ordered. "Be specific."

"I have to rely on my own instincts—"

"What are your instincts telling you—right now?"

"To . . . get away."

"But you can't get away. I'm not done with you, orphan girl."

His last words did it. A fresh wave of fury suddenly washed over her, drowning her fear. "You're a maniac!" she hissed. "That's what my instincts are telling me! They're telling me that I should have ripped your goddamn head off when I had the chance!"

Timmy's face seemed to glisten, ablaze with excitement.

"Give me more, Susan! Speak to me! Tell me who you are!" He twisted the knife and she gasped as a wave of pain flashed across her midsection. But there was something else as well, something beneath the pain; a strange sensation spreading out from the blade to envelop her entire body. She felt herself tingling from head to toe.

"Come to life," urged Timmy. "Emerge!"

And then her inner voice—that odd little aspect of her being that psychplan counsellors over the years had always explained away as a harmless byproduct of her complex neurosis, that voice that was always there when she was in trouble, urging and directing her, saving her life in Honshu, rescuing her from the murderous E-Tech officers in her apartment—that voice spoke again. But this time she recognized the words as her own.

"I know who I am," she gasped, aglow with wonder.

An inner wall vanished, torn away by the mere effort of conscious acknowledgment. That strange tingling sensation, radiating outward from the bab knife, brought ripples of her true self, expanding blossoms from the core of her being, the vanguard of the real Susan Quint.

She felt awash in revelation. Ecstasy. For the first time in ages, she felt totally in touch with herself, totally synchronized with the flowing majesty of her own soul, the elan vital.

*I am my body-thought.*

She became conscious of the bab knife, piercing the flesh over her stomach, and now she could even sense the four distinct razor edges of the blade, and the warm flow of blood as it coagulated along the outer edges of the puncture. The knife had not penetrated very far—a mere half-inch—and it was only her conceptualizing of future pain that had produced such dread.

*Fear what is, not what might be.*

The thought soothed her even more. And she began to perceive the needle in a new way, not merely as a focal point of pain, but as a real and living aspect of Timmy's will. And she understood his intentions, seeing the bab as a tool, a surgical instrument. There was an ancient science she had once read about—acupuncture. She wondered if he was a practitioner.

It did not matter. *I am my body-thought.* That was of overriding importance. And there was something else.

*I can take the pain.*

Pain was a grounding source, a direct organic conduit linking mind/emotion/body, and ultimately, folding that tripartite reality of human consciousness into the tapestry of life itself.

She gazed upon Timmy, aware that he was waiting, and she saw that his left eye held guarded excitement. But the right one, the fabricated orb, contained no emotion. It was a machine, absorbing and translating details, but ultimately disconnected to the flow of life. It was not a part of Timmy's body-thought, and never would be.

A dead eye. It was so very obvious that she felt a bit surprised that she had failed to make such an observation earlier.

"I'm still waiting," said Timmy, and the words seemed to flow from his mouth, bubbling with barely contained needs and desires.

"Your expectations betray you," she said calmly.

His left eye opened wide.

Susan took a slow deep breath, preparing herself for agony. "It's your choice now," she explained. "Either release me or use the knife."

She felt the blade withdraw, the gauntlet retreat from beneath her chin. Timmy rolled away from her quickly, as if he expected a violent reaction now that she was free. But she saw no reason to hurt him.

"May I examine your wound?" he asked gently, and she registered real kindness in his voice, real concern.

"No. I'll take care of it when we go back." She sat up in the sand and crossed her legs beneath her. A hesitant breeze touched her cheeks, and she heard its melody—a whispering whine, a chorus of the wind. Her tongue tasted the muted flavor of sea brine. Flesh up and down her bare arms seemed to tingle, the skin registering even the faint change of temperature between the warmer sand beneath and the cooler air above. Not since childhood had she felt so physically alive, so gloriously attuned to her surroundings. And inside . . .

A clarity of feeling, a freedom from the emotional seesaw that had seemed to drive her from the low points of pain and despair to the dreamy heights of loveless passion. She almost laughed, thinking how utterly ridiculous her preoccupation with the Clark Shuttle Service VP had been.

And finally, a clarity of intellect, a metamorphosis encompassing her entire being, focusing the power of her will into a clear stream, bubbling outward from the needs of her body to become a raging waterfall, gaining sustenance from its very turmoil, until finally flowing into an ocean of infinite knowledge.

*I am my body-thought.* She felt awe-struck—reverent of the very concept of life itself.

And that clarity of intellect provided answers even as it generated questions. She faced Timmy.

"It was no accident that we met."

He smiled. "Of course not. Do you know what mnemonic cursors are?"

"No."

"Tiny organic nodules—secret command programs residing in the deepest reaches of the mind. A mnemonic cursor was implanted within your genetic matrix when you were still a fetus, injected into your mother's womb during her earliest weeks of pregnancy. She never knew, of course. Your parents had absolute faith in their priests. And when Lester Mon Dama suggested a specific doctor, your parents naturally agreed."

Susan shook her head, thoughts churning. "So Lester

Mon Dama is a part of . . . this." *This what?* she thought. *This conspiracy encompassing my entire life?*

"There are code words . . . phrases," continued Timmy. "These serve as keys—opening circuits directly into your subconsciousness. The particular mnemonic cursor that resides in you contains a graduated set of these code triggers. One after another, these mnemonic phrases led you to me.

"Think back, Susan. The first mnemonic phrase? Can you recall what it was?"

She thought for a moment. Then: "Lester Mon Dama!" Even as she uttered the priest's name, a warm feeling coursed outward from her neck, spreading all the way to her loins. Pleasant thoughts accompanied the warm glow: Safety. Goodness. Helpfulness.

Timmy smiled at her reaction. "*Lester Mon Dama*—the first code phrase, the first emotional trigger. You were compelled to think of the priest if and when you reached a certain critical threshold of confusion and frustration."

She remembered. "I was in that bass cabaret, on the outskirts of North Epsilon. I was feeling very helpless. I didn't know who to turn to for help."

"Yes. Your circumstances forced you to recall Lester's name and then seek him out."

"And it happened once before," Susan murmured, aglow with the insight. "When I was eleven, when my parents died—back then I also sought out Lester Mon Dama."

"Yes. But back then you were too young to be of use. Lester did not take the next step. He let you go."

*Too young to be of use.* The words sent a faint chill through her. But she felt no bitterness, no anger at such manipulation, although she realized that such feelings could arise later on. For now, however, she was simply overwhelmed by curiosity. Scattered pieces of her life—fragments of a puzzle—were in the process of being reassembled.

She nodded. "But this time I did fit into your plans."

"Yes. So Lester uttered the second trigger phrase."

"Seek sanctuary," Susan murmured. Everything seemed so obvious now that she felt amazed at not being able to comprehend these things sooner.

*"Seek sanctuary,"* Timmy repeated. "Lester used that mnemonic key to unlock your emotions even further. You were compelled to trust the priest, desire him. In that frame of mind, Lester found it easy to persuade you to visit the Cloister.

"The first two mnemonic triggers brought you to me. Once you were in my presence, however, I was able to utilize a more direct method of control."

He pointed to his right eye—the artificial one. "This wetware orb contains an optic projector—a subliminal coding device that flashes messages that your own eyes cannot see—sort of like an invisible morse code enabling my very thoughts to activate your mnemonic cursor. This gave me the ability to control you in a number of ways, not the least of which was making certain that you felt the urge to join me out here on the beach every day."

She shook her head, stunned. "And when you made me go into the water, you uttered this very odd—"

*"Kascht moniken keenish,"* said Timmy, and Susan felt a weird tremor pass through her entire body, and she sensed that those harsh sounds possessed a power even greater than the other trigger codes.

"That phrase," continued Timmy, "is from a root language—a phonetic, protolingual tongue that was created to speak directly to *any* mnemonic cursor, no matter whom that cursor is implanted within. A language that even the emotions are unable to fathom, for it appeals directly to the syntactic substrata of the human reptilian brain, where an implanted cursor usually resides. A language of pure vocalization, capable of surging into the deepest levels of the psyche."

"You can make me do whatever you want?" she challenged.

"No. All mnemonic cursors have limits, even when the

root language is used to enhance a particular verbal suggestion or enforce a command. And there is another logic inherent to all mnemonic cursors. For the most part, their power remains inversely proportional to the consciousness of the controlled subject." Timmy grinned. "In other words, the more attuned you are to your body-thought, the less power a mnemonic cursor can exert over you."

Susan nodded silently, absorbing his words. Her next question was obvious.

"Why, Timmy? Why? All this trouble . . . all this manipulation . . ."

"Body-thought!" he exclaimed, his left eye flashing with excitement. "Body-thought so swift that a normal throw of a stone from ten feet away can't touch you. There exists a great power within your very cells, the power to move like the wind. And until you blundered into that Honshu massacre over two weeks ago, that power had remained almost totally latent."

Susan whispered, "I'm a genejob." It was the only possible explanation.

"Yes. When your parents conceived you, your genetic structure was normal. But while in your mother's womb, your fetus was given a series of injections which altered your genetic makeup. Your entire neuromuscular system received modifications that accelerated your reaction time—endowed Susan Quint with the potential to equal even the swiftness of a Paratwa. Your mnemonic cursor was simply a part of those genetic enhancements.

"You are indeed, in the popular idiom, a genejob. You are not, however, the only one. In fact, you were just one of *hundreds* of female fetuses that Lester Mon Dama, through the auspices of his priesthood, arranged to be brought to one of our doctors over a five-year period. The mothers were all devoted followers of the Church of the Trust. Unsuspecting. They all received injections. Their unborn children were all *enriched*.

"And all those modified fetuses are today young women.

In fact, Susan, you are not even the first of them to grow conscious of her power in some way, thus triggering her mnemonic cursor and compelling her to seek out Lester. But you are the first who truly appears suitable for our plans."

*Our doctors,* she thought. *Our plans.* "Who are you?" she demanded. "What do you want of me?"

He turned away for a moment, gazing out over the lake with what she took to be a peaceful expression. But when he faced her again, his countenance had hardened.

"Susan—you now speak from the confidence of your body-thought, and you must always remember that that is a power that can never be denied. But you are also driven by deep-seated needs, driven in a way that none of the other young women whom Lester brought to me could even remotely match. You are fueled by your own pain and that pain makes you into a fiercely burning star. Suffering has opened depths within you that most human beings remain forever unconscious of.

"I am the roots of your life, Susan Quint. I am the man whose genetic matrix was injected into your fetus. I am, in very real terms, your third parent."

"My third parent," she whispered.

He turned away from her again, and his finger pointed out over the water, tracking a pair of imported white herring gulls as they skimmed across the quivering surface. "See those birds? They are examples of natural body-thought—creatures interlaced to the purity of the moment. They could not be otherwise, for they lack the mechanisms of human-style consciousness, the ability to separate their needs from their wants. They are unaware of their own racial heritage. They cannot know that their ancestors were saved from extinction by humans, granted haven in the Colonies, and that they are the first of their species in over a quarter of a millennium to again soar over this lake."

The gulls raced high into the air, disappearing behind the hulk of the revivifier. When Timmy continued, a forlorn echo of sadness seemed to trail his words. "A long time ago, Susan, I was like them. But then the transmutation came upon me and I was made different. I was changed . . . beyond the mortal imagination of even my own profoundest *conceptions* of change. Now I am something else." An odd smile crossed his face. "Now I am the free-bird.

"Once upon a time, Susan, before there was Timmy, there was *the other*. He was just like me, yet he was unlike me. And until his final days, he lived in a world of apparent freedom. Like you, Susan, and like the gulls, he remained unaware of the larger sphere of consciousness that surrounded him, controlling and influencing all aspects of his existence."

Timmy's words grew bitter. "And then came the betrayal. And his brothers, whom he had trusted so implicitly, forced *the other* into transmutation. And *the other* was destroyed." The pupil of Timmy's natural eye dilated; his face twisted into a grimace as flesh recalled ancient pain. The wetware orb remained motionless.

"Once, Susan, I was of the mighty. Once, I could be both singular and plural. Once I was Aristotle, Ash Ock Paratwa of the royal Caste."

She just stared at him, finally overwhelmed by the very magnitude of his revelations. "What happens now?" she heard herself ask.

"Life, Susan. Life and consciousness. And a journey beyond your dreams."

One of the guards leaned his head into the open door of the lion's private study. "Sir, they've arrived."

"Have them come in," ordered the lion, his gaze drifting from the flower garden, visible through the slab glass wall, to Nick. The midget sat on the edge of the meeting table, his tiny fingers pattering nervously against the compressed lunar shale, his boots—a foot short of the floor—kicking back and forth in steady cadence, like a pair of dueling pumps powering some ancient machine.

"Are you sure you want to be here?" the lion asked.

A lazy grin settled on Nick's face. "That's the third time you've hit me with that question."

The lion sighed. "I know. But his condition . . . we really don't know . . ."

Nick shrugged. "Would there be any point in trying to hide from him?"

"I suppose not."

Two guards, armed with thruster rifles, entered the study. Gillian walked a pace behind them. Buff brought up the rear.

The lion nodded to the guards and they shouldered their weapons and exited, closing the door behind them.

"I'm glad you're unharmed," began the lion, watching Gillian closely, looking for some sign that Empedocles had arisen, or that Gillian's own emotions had been stirred into a dangerous turmoil. But his face revealed nothing. *Cold,* thought the lion. *Inaccessible.*

Buff stopped right inside the doorway and folded her thick arms across her bosom. She was easy to read; pain etched a clear story across her face. The handle of a gun was visible beneath her open jacket.

The lion moved toward her, shaking his head in genuine sadness. "I am truly sorry about Martha."

"Yes," murmured Buff, turning away, avoiding his gaze. "I never dreamed it would turn out like this."

Gillian crossed the room to stand before Nick. "Aren't you going to welcome us back?"

The midget stared up at him. "Rough day, huh?"

"You could call it that."

"I suppose I owe you an explanation."

"You owe me nothing," said Gillian, and the lion had no trouble reading the emotion in those words. Hatred. And barely contained.

"You feel betrayed," said the lion, thinking back to his own childhood—age twelve—to a time when he had desperately needed a friend, to a time when Gillian had been there.

A bitter laugh filled the study.

"You have a right to feel the way you do," the lion continued. "Nick and I knew about Cochise—at least we suspected. But we thought that the best course of action was not telling you." He shook his head. "Or perhaps it was just the easiest course. I truly don't know."

Nick shrugged. "I did what I had to do, Gillian. Your condition . . . you were in bad shape. And we weren't sure about Cochise . . . it was just a hunch. I made a decision to the best of my abilities, based on intuition and the available facts. I make no excuses for it."

"An honest answer?" snapped Gillian. "That's something new for you, isn't it?"

Nick did not reply. Gillian turned back to the lion.

"How many were killed, out there on the street?"

"Early E-Tech reports suggest at least a dozen fatalities," said the lion. "The freelancer channels are reporting higher figures."

"Do they know who was responsible?"

The lion nodded. "Shooter was seen, of course, but he disappeared shortly after heavy E-Tech Security forces began to arrive. You're the only one who saw Slasher and he's vanished as well. Also, the latest reports indicate that there was some kind of explosion in Slasher's—Cochise's—office, which caused massive destruction to that entire floor of Venus Cluster. The final death toll will undoubtedly be higher.

"E-Tech Security is searching for you and Buff. Naturally, they have descriptions, but they still don't know who you are." The lion sighed. "But once they identify Martha, they'll begin putting things together. And that 'Lord and Lady Valsacko' cover story won't hold up for very long. It's possible that Inez—"

"You didn't answer my question," interrupted Gillian. "Do they know who was responsible?"

The lion hesitated. "Shooter and Slasher—"

"Wrong answer."

"I was responsible," Nick said quietly. "That's what he wants to hear. I'm the one he feels the urge to blame."

Another harsh laugh escaped Gillian. "Urge to blame? Who the hell do you think you are? You've used me for so long that you can't even imagine that I might be offended by it."

Nick sighed. "I did what I had to do—"

"But not any more," promised Gillian. "Not to me. You'll have to find others to twist and manipulate. We're finished."

The midget's eyes narrowed. "And just who is it that is announcing his independence?"

"You know who I am."

"Give me a clue."

"Don't push it," Gillian warned. "You sent me to a meeting with a man whom you knew to be the tway of this assassin. And you sent me *unarmed*, you little bastard!"

Nick drew a deep breath. "There was no choice. Your Cohe wand would probably have been discovered at the security desk. But I didn't send you in there blind. I researched Venus Cluster and I made the best possible decision under a very difficult and complex set of circumstances."

Gillian shook his head. "You can't even imagine that you screwed up, can you?"

"I told you I take full responsibility," growled Nick. "You're alive, so don't feed me this crap. I sent you to a meeting with a man whom I suspected could be the tway of a Paratwa assassin because you were so messed up inside that you couldn't see straight anymore. I gave you the opportunity to wake up. You needed action—"

The movement was almost too quick for the lion to register—Gillian's right arm blurred and then Nick was hoisted violently up off the table, his squat neck crushed by Gillian's fingers, his own tiny hands clutching for his throat, trying to break the choking bond.

"Is this what you want?" hissed Gillian.

"Let him go!" ordered the lion.

Another blur as Gillian twisted sideways, rammed Nick into the wall, held him there, two feet off the floor, their faces level with one another, only inches apart, two sets of eyes burning in mutual hatred.

"Gillian!" the lion shouted.

The door opened and the two Costeau guards raced into the room with rifles unslung. Buff whipped out her salene and rammed the barrel up under the first guard's chin.

"Not your problem," warned Buff, her finger on the trigger. "And I'm in a real bad mood."

The guards were well trained. And they were Costeaus. They turned calmly to the lion, waiting for direction.

"Leave us," snapped the lion, not waiting to see whether the guards obeyed. He moved quickly, laying a hand on Gillian's shoulder, squeezing, feeling the rigid whipcord muscles compress between his fingertips.

Nick was turning red under the choking grip. But the midget's eyes remained frozen on Gillian: twin pools of fury, unafraid, eyes that said: *Do what you will—I'll give you no satisfaction.*

"Gillian, release him," said the lion calmly. "This will accomplish nothing."

"Don't bet on it," Gillian hissed, squeezing even harder. Nick's eyes bulged wide.

The lion shifted his hand to the back of Gillian's neck. He gripped a chunk of skin between thumb and forefinger and pinched sharply.

"Remember that pinch," whispered the lion, leaning forward so that his mouth was almost against Gillian's ear. "Remember the man who used that pinch to bring a small boy back to his senses. Remember that man's words.

"He said to me: 'I don't want to hurt you, Jerem. But I won't allow you to be a scuddie.' That man saved me from a horrible fate. And a few days later, he saved my very life."

Gillian turned to the lion, saw the deep passion scribed across the aged face, remembered the terrified young boy in the Sirak-Brath apartment, the boy whom he had helped. To Gillian, the event had occurred only weeks ago; to Jerem Marth, a lifetime had elapsed.

He released his iron grip on Nick's neck. The midget sank to his knees and fell back against the wall, chest heaving desperately as his lungs strained for oxygen.

At the doorway, Buff and the two guards remained frozen in a tableau of potential violence. The lion spoke calmly. "Buff, please put away your weapon and permit my people to bring a doctor."

Buff lowered the salene. The guards departed.

Gillian spoke quietly. "You've a good memory for an old man, Jerem."

"My past serves me well."

Gillian pointed to Nick. "Be careful of him in the future. There lies a man without scruples."

Nick continued to gasp for air.

"You'll be leaving," concluded the lion.

"Yes."

"Where will you go?"

Gillian shrugged. "I don't know. I really only came back to . . . get my things. My Cohe wand, in particular." He stared at the lion. "Are we going to have more problems?"

"It's your weapon. And if I said no, would it stop you? But there's been enough senseless violence for one day."

"Yes, there has."

The lion turned to Buff. "You'll be going with him?"

"I can no longer be of use to the lion of Alexander."

The lion nodded. "Serve Gillian well."

"I serve Martha," whispered the Costeau.

"So be it." The lion gazed out upon his flower garden, at the patch of rose bushes, petals blue and gray mostly, colors beginning to diffuse under Irrya's late afternoon sunlight. A gentle sadness crept over him. *He's going away again, leaving me, as he did fifty-six years ago.* The intrinsic selfishness of the feeling conveyed a touch of guilt.

"I'm sure we'll see each other again," offered Gillian, understanding the lion's silence.

"Perhaps." The lion did not believe it. *We may come face to face again, we may even speak. But in truth, there have been too many years placed between us. We can never again see each other as we once did.* And he realized that in touching Gillian, in reaching out across the decades for that common memory, the raw power of his ancient obsession finally had met its match.

*I am an old man, weighted with souvenirs of a time long gone. I will bear these feelings for the rest of my days, but they are, and will forever remain, mere emotional icons—markers on a path once tread.* He found himself smiling. *My past has finally caught up to me.*

"Before I go," said Gillian, "I do have . . . a favor to ask."

"Of course."

"If something should happen to me, Jerem . . . if I should become someone—*something*—an entity that you no longer recognize as Gillian . . ." He hesitated, struggling for the words, struggling to make clear that unnatural melding of consciousnesses that Empedocles so desired, but which Gillian still could comprehend only in the broadest and vaguest terms.

The lion frowned. "You're talking about your monarch?"

"I'm talking about Gillian going away and never coming back. Ever again."

The lion was not certain just what he was trying to say.

"If that should happen to me," Gillian continued quickly, "and you're sure that I can't be brought back . . ."

The lion raised his eyebrows. "Yes?"

"Send your Costeaus out to find me."

The lion shook his head, still confused. "To bring you back."

"No. Not to bring me back."

"I think . . . that I understand." The lion swallowed. "I will do what my feelings tell me is appropriate."

"Spoken like a true Costeau." Gillian managed a smile. "Live up to the name, Jerem Marth."

"I will try."


The lion found Nick in the computer room, seated in front of the console, his legs drawn up tightly against his squat body, his neck girdled by a ragged swatch of white fabric. The equipment remained inactive, the screens opaque, the room itself dimmed to the barest level of illumination. Gillian and Buff had departed hours ago.

"Evolving new strategies?" asked the lion.

"Ever wake up to find yourself wondering just what in the hell it is that you've been doing with your life?"

The lion nodded.

"Good for you," said Nick softly. "'Cause I haven't. Not in the twentieth century, nor in the twenty-first. Not fifty-six years ago. Not today. I always know what I'm doing with my life. I always know where I'm going."

The lion sat down beside him. "That sounds like a curse."

"More like a crippled leg, maybe. It makes you walk a bit different from everyone else. Makes you stand out in a crowd. Makes you more aware of the millions who aren't crippled. Lets you see them more clearly, more objectively. You stand apart. You're able to judge character, perceive motivations, understand why they are the way they are."

"You're going to miss him," said the lion.

Nick sighed. "It's not too often that you find another cripple who stumbles along the same way that you do. It makes you believe in destiny."

"It makes you believe in humanity."

Nick drew a deep breath. "Yeah. That too."

The lion found himself gazing at the blank monitors. "That meeting we had last week, with Gillian, Inez, and Adam. I remember you saying something about having a bad feeling . . . like we're heading into a battle that we've already lost. Do you still believe that?"

"Maybe."

The lion hesitated. "If the Paratwa should conquer us, what would you do? I mean, assuming you survived, could you adapt to living under their domain?"

"No."

"I feel the same way."

For a long moment, they sat there, staring at the blank screens. Finally, Nick reached forward and depressed a set of keys. The system hummed to life; the monitors burst into sheets of color. The lion stood up and headed for the door.

Nick said, "I don't doubt my actions, Jerem. I *can't* doubt them. I try not to hurt people. But I do what must be done."

The lion said nothing. He left the room, thinking about a time long ago and a future that might not be.

Turn the page for an exciting glimpse
of the third and final work of
Christopher Hinz's *Paratwa* series,

# THE PARATWA

Available in paperback
from Tor Books
December 1995

—from *The Rigors*, by Meridian

*It was the time of our emergence. It was the time of the first coming, when the Earth was still vital and the Ash Ock were fresh as today's memory; in retrospect, a fragile era, but one where life itself seemed aglow with all manner of possibility, where we Paratwa felt destined to rule the Earth, to rule the stars. It was a time when each of us sizzled under the spell of our own unique simultaneities, relishing the genetic fates that had cast our souls into two bodies instead of one. It was a time when our binary spirits seemed molded by the essence of some primordial ubiquity, our bodies glazed to perfection, our minds burnished by the hands of an immortal poet.*

*It was a time of the Ash Ock, the royal Caste—those five unique creations whose sphere of influence exploded outward from that secret jungle complex deep in the Brazilian rain forest, enveloping the world, uniting us, directing our disparate Paratwa breeds into a swarm of binary elegance that, for those brief fragile years, seemed unstoppable.*

*It was a time of innocence. It was a time that could not last.*

*Some of us began to perceive the underlying dynamics of Ash Ock power, to comprehend their subtle manipulations, to hear the distinctive growls of five exquisite motors beneath five exquisite hoods. The mirror that the Ash Ock had held before each of us, which had reflected only our virtues, splintered under the roar of those engines; our worship of their godlike prowess yielded to mere admiration, appreciative yet tempered by the knowledge that those of the royal Caste remained mortal, despite their incredible magic. And that magic, partially swollen by our own needs and desires, gave birth to a child swaddled in the robes of scientific superiority. The poet departed, never to return.*

*It was a time of terrible betrayal.*

*As the Star-Edge fleet—under the clandestine guidance of Theophrastus—prepared to escape from an Earth drowning under the fury of the Apocalypse, some of us began to learn the real secrets of the Ash Ock. And that juncture marked the beginning of a cynicism that spread through our ranks with the swiftness of a biological plague. By the time the Star-Edge fleet had cleared the boundaries of the solar system, Sappho and Theophrastus were almost faced with open revolt, for many of the Paratwa had trouble adjusting to the indignity of these ultimate truths.*

*But Ash Ock patience helped all of us persevere. The crisis passed. An even greater vista of conceptualization was now open to us, and we were invited to perceive the universe from new and dizzying heights. Most of us lost our cynicism. Those few who did not kept their doubts to themselves.*

*Theophrastus proclaimed:* "Never forget that you represent the vanguard of the second coming."

"And never forget that you serve the *true* Paratwa," *Sappho added.* "Your lives now intertwine with the destiny of the chosen."

*History texts were subtly altered; the roles of the other three Ash Ock—Codrus, Aristotle, and Empedocles—were lessened to those of supporting players.*

*Codrus was really the first of the royal Caste to fall from Ash Ock grace. His tways, like the tways of Empedocles, were of mixed* sexes—male and female. Even in those early days, when we were still emerging from the landscape of humans, when Theophrastus had not yet infiltrated the Star-Edge project, bending it to his own designs, Sappho had begun to suggest—subtly—that dual-gendered Paratwa were inherently flawed. For a while, even I fell for her elegant craftiness, though eventually I came to see such illogic as a refraction of my own male/male prejudice.

Still, I understood some of Sappho's negativity toward the others of her breed. Codrus often displayed the most blatant weaknesses, misconstruing Ash Ock formulations for precise truths, falling into that intellectual trap of regarding the mind as the ruler of the body. Those facets of reality that Codrus failed to grasp became DATA to be processed, information that simply remained undigested by his networks. Eventually, Codrus's inability to fathom the depths led Sappho to regard him like the child of her royal family, his tways forever loyal and anxious to please, yet his monarchial consciousness incapable of reaching its destined maturity. He was ultimately precluded from all Ash Ock intricacies, and it was arranged that he be left behind when the Star-Edge fleet departed. Until his death at the hands of the Costeaus, centuries later, Codrus remained blissfully ignorant, a true intellectual pauper.

Aristotle, for a time, also remained unaware of the greater concerns, although Aristotle's ignorance was not of his own making, for in many ways, he was the equal of Sappho: shrewd and cunning, with a natural aptitude for the intricate methodology of politics. Aristotle's male/male interlace seemed to know—instinctively—how to utilize others to amplify his own desires; he played the human race as a preinformation-age grandmaster played chess.

In the earliest years of Ash Ock ascendancy, I was the servant of Aristotle, and I grew to admire and respect the sophistication of his agile mind. For a time, I actually came to like him, especially after he had introduced me to Empedocles, youngest of the five, male/female tways whose infectious lust for all manner of experience rivaled even my own. In truth, I loved those years that we spent training Empedocles, helping to mold our young warrior into an elegant bastion of Ash Ock authority, ready to assume his place in the sphere of the royal Caste, to become the champion of all of Earth's Paratwa.

*And for a time in those early years, I even doubted Sappho's wisdom in keeping Aristotle—and thus Empedocles—ignorant of the greater reality. In Codrus's case, I understood. But I felt that Aristotle and Empedocles should be given full access to Sappho's knowledge—the secret knowledge—which at that time she shared only with Theophrastus and a few trusted lieutenants: Gol-Gosonia, myself, a handful of others.*

*Eventually, however, I came to see that Sappho was correct in keeping Aristotle in the dark, for that monarch's plans within plans began rivaling the complexity of even her own intrigues. The simple fact was: Aristotle was too much like Sappho. There could be but one ruler, and Sappho—by virtue of birthright alone—would be sole proprietress of our destiny.*

*Nevertheless, the day when I betrayed Aristotle—and doomed Empedocles in the bargain—remains the most regretted day of my life.*

Gillian felt eager for another fight. The darkness of Sirak-Brath seemed an ideal place for one.

He followed Buff and the smuggler through the alley separating a pair of low-tech industries—a nuke breeder and a manufacturer of organic soak-dye—the dank passage cutting between the towering buildings like a thin wafer sliced from a monstrous loaf. From the wet floor of the alley, the dirty vacuformed walls—slabs of reinforced plastic veneered in ancient brickface—soared over two hundred feet up into the night sky. Shadowy forms interconnected the two buildings: a plethora of structural support shafts, conduits, and soggy flexpipes. There were no windows.

A sliver of pale, yellowish gray light was exposed at the

peaks of the artificial canyon, and that illuminated snippet should have revealed the distant slabs of the Colony's cosmishield glass, and beyond, the darkness of space. But the thirty-eight-mile-long orbiting cylinder had managed, over the two and a half centuries of its existence, to acquire one of pre-Apocalyptic Earth's nastier habits: air pollution. During peak manufacturing periods, the smog became so dense that Sirak-Brath's atmospheric circulators could not remove it faster than it was being generated.

Buff turned to the smuggler. "How much farther?"

In the dim light of the alley, she was the shorter and thinner of the two figures. Weeks of hiding out with Gillian in a Costeau exercise cone had enabled Buff to shed nearly fifty pounds. She remained stocky, but there was little fat; upper arms bulged with muscle, and her legs now boasted a strength and agility that she had never known at her former weight.

The smuggler grunted. His name was Impleton, and he pointed ahead and whispered words that seemed to dissolve in the dense air, even as Gillian leaned forward, straining to hear. But Buff had understood; the black Costeau's firm nod provided assurance that Impleton's response gave no cause for alarm.

Gillian's last visit to Sirak-Brath had been over half a century ago, and tonight's smog seemed much worse than any he remembered from that first sojourn, in 2307. Back then, the periodic onslaughts of dirty air had not seemed so conspicuous, the haze so impenetrable. He would have expected that during his fifty-six years of stasis sleep, legitimate technical improvements would have contributed to making the air invisible again.

But despite the imminent threat of the returning Paratwa starships—a threat whose closing horizon lately had spawned bitter tensions throughout the populace of the Irryan Colonies—day-to-day scientific and technical advancements were still under the control of E-Tech, the powerful institution whose tenets essentially served to limit the degree of change. E-Tech's two-and-a-half-century-old ideal—to prevent wild permutations in the social structure, like those that had decimated the Earth during the Apocalypse of 2099—made it difficult for a Colony to alter the status quo. Sirak-Brath's smog served to illustrate the downside of E-Tech's otherwise noble cause.

Sirak-Brath had other problems as well. It was popularly considered to be the black sheep of the Irryan Colonies—the cylinder denizens of the other two hundred and sixteen orbiting space islands could point to with disdain. No matter how bad your home Colony might be in a particular respect, Sirak-Brath was probably worse. The industrial cylinder boasted the highest crime rates, the dirtiest streets, and the most consistently corruptible politicians. Many non-mainstreamed Costeaus, black marketeers, and high-tech smugglers called it home.

The alley began to curve to the left, and a soft breeze brought an oppressive odor of untreated sludge. Gillian glanced over his shoulder, saw the pale remaining light from the side street, nearly two blocks away, slowly compress into nothingness, and the heavy barred gate, through which Impleton had led them into this service corridor, disappear. Now, only the smog-reflected light from above remained to guide their footsteps.

Gillian closed his eyes, listened to the night: the dull omnipresent hum of heavy machinery, distant sirens of local patroller or E-Tech Security vehicles en route to fresh crime sites, their own footsteps, flapping across the wet pavement, an occasional echo of a human voice, amplified to prominence by the acoustic qualities of this artificial canyon. Sounds that were recognizable aspects of Sirak-Brath. Sounds that carried no threat of danger.

But there was still time.

The alley continued its steady curve to the left, on a sweeping tangent, until finally they were walking perpendicular to their original direction. Fresh bright light appeared up ahead; the canyon walls peeled back to reveal a cul de sac where nuke breeder joined organic soak-dye manufacturer, their common bulkhead a monolithic eruption of greasy pipes and spiraling twill tubes. It was power distribution machinery combined with an overworked pollution control grid. The entire conglomeration had been designed to serve both industries and probably others as well, whose sterns would be butting against the far side of the towering mech-wall.

Buff and Impleton became crisp silhouettes as they headed into the light, the fresh illumination provided by a series of globed lamps positioned ten feet above the dank floor. Buff's hairless pate, cosmetically scarred by a series of twisting blue and red lines—the delicate handiwork of luminescent crayons—began to shine. In the daytime, the black Costeau often wore a hat, but when a Colony's mirrors rotated into darkness, she exposed her shaved skull and the shiny photoluminescent streaks.

Blue lines and red lines, crisscrossing the crown of her head, all freshly painted each morning, as important to Buff as any other aspect of her daily grooming. Blue lines and red lines, each bound by the faint perimeter of her natural hairline, each glowing, like a nest of wet snakes. Buff was of the clan of the Cerniglias, but the painted streaks remained universal Costeau symbols. Blue for mourning. Red for vengeance. With Costeaus, the two colors often went together.

Buff had painted herself every morning for nearly a month and vowed to continue the ritual until she found the Paratwa assassin—the one who had been terrorizing the Irryan Colonies for the past five months. The one whose tripartite self—*three* discrete physical bodies controlled by a solitary, telepathically interlaced consciousness—remained unique among known Paratwa breeds. The one whose brutal massacres, throughout the orbiting cylinders, had been linked to the imminent return of the Paratwa starships.

The one who had killed her friend Martha.

Impleton—fat, pale-skinned, wearing a knee-length pink corselet coat—craned his neck and muttered something to Buff. She paused at the entrance to the bottleneck, waited for Gillian to catch up.

"He says Faquod's not here yet."

Gillian went hyper alert. Senses, normally diluted by a wide range of environmental stimuli, focused; muscles prepped for instantaneous response. His tongue slithered along the tiny rubber pads attached to his bicuspids and molars—the activation circuitry for the hidden crescent web hardware strapped around his waist. One snap of the jaw and the defensive field would ignite, form a near-invisible sheath along the front and rear contours of his six-foot frame, a barrier capable of deflecting projectile and energy weapons alike. And hidden in the sleeve covering his right forearm, gripped securely in a slip-wrist holster, lay a pale egg with a tiny needle protruding from one end.

His Cohe wand: a device infinitely rare and highly illegal, the original weapon of the Paratwa assassins from the days before the decimation of Earth, over two-and-a-half centuries ago. The Cohe was devilish to control, requiring years of training to become proficient in its more subtle capabilities. But once mastered, it was a weapon that bore no equal.

Impleton sucked in his gut and said loudly, "Faquod, he will be along shortly."

Two other figures were poised in the bottleneck. To Gillian's right, a well-groomed man with a sawed-off beard leaned against the wall, one hand tucked under his black coat. And across the alley, seated on a four-foot-high ledge, was a blond-haired muscle boy, grinning like a scuddie. The youth was stripped to the waist. Bulging pectorals bore tattoos of ancient motorized cycles and the cryptic phrase, *I'm a Harley in Heat*, was printed neatly above his navel.

Buff scowled. "You said he'd be waiting here for us."

The smuggler rolled his eyes. "Faquod, he does as he pleases."

The muscle boy laughed. Gillian approached the youth while casually scanning the mech-wall, already fairly certain of what he would find on it. He was not disappointed.

About twenty feet up, squeezed amid the filthy spirals of relay tubes and monstrous conduits, sat a hunched figure with a thruster rifle. It was a fairly good hiding place, though not good enough to escape Gillian's detection. Although he had met Impleton only yesterday, their brief encounter had provided enough raw data to establish a psych profile of the swarthy black marketeer. Gillian had known that bold deceit would be Impleton's fashion; the presence of an armed backup, out of sight, fit the smuggler's profile like a glove.

Impleton licked his lips. "These high-tech playthings you desire . . . Faquod, he says that they are not easy to come by. Faquod says they will not be cheap."

Gillian halted two paces away from the grinning muscle boy and leaned over the four-foot ledge that the tattooed smuggler sat upon. On the other side of the wall, a vertical drop plunged fifteen feet into a plodding river of sludge covered by a fine-meshed net. The harsh odor of untreated sewage, far more potent than it had been in the alley, assailed his nostrils. Gillian suspected that the open sewage channel was illegal.

"Very expensive," continued Impleton, his fat cheeks squirming as if his mouth were stuffed with unchewed food. "Faquod—he will want at least half the money in advance, I am sure."

"You told us that already," Buff replied calmly.

"You have the money?"

"Not with us, of course." Buff sighed. "You don't think we're that foolish, do you?"

Gillian leaned against the ledge and relaxed his muscles, body poised for action. He was now fairly certain that

Impleton was lying. *Faquod's not coming. We've been set up for a knockdown. They're planning to rob us. Maybe kill us as well.* He found himself secretly smiling as he began to consider ways to extend the duration of the upcoming fight. It was important for him to be able to relish every moment.

The smuggler with the black coat and sawed-off beard carefully withdrew a small thruster from his pocket. He made no threatening gestures, keeping the weapon aimed at the ground.

Impleton yawned. "My men . . . they're very excitable. I told them they would be paid tonight. I hope they will not be disappointed."

"Yeah," agreed Buff, with a sharp glance at Gillian, "I certainly hope no one gets pissed."

The fat smuggler stroked his chin. "I think that maybe you have some of the money, anyway. Down payment money. Sign of good faith. You give it to us. We give it to Faquod."

Buff scowled. "You bring Faquod. Then we'll talk about money."

Impleton's pudgy face attempted a smile. "Your way . . . it is not good for business. Faquod . . . he likes to know that there is trust, that there is openness."

Gillian felt his chest begin to tingle—the onslaught of the familiar desperate excitement that now directly preceded his fights. Buff referred to his eagerness for confrontation—for violence—as "full-body hard-on," and she was probably not far from the truth. Over the past month, his increasing desire to engage in combat had developed strange sexual overtones. Fighting had mutated into a distinct mode of self-expression; violence and lust had become intertwined.

But Gillian knew that at its core, the fighting remained a way for him to keep his turbulent inner forces at bay, a way to temporarily relieve the tremendous mental/emotional pressure that relentlessly strove to devolve his consciousness. He fought not only because it felt good but because it helped to maintain his sanity.

He turned to Buff. "We're wasting our time. These scuddies have been lying to us. I don't think they're smart enough even to know Faquod."

Impleton sneered. "Not smart? Smarter than you, maybe. Smart enough not to wander into an alley with strangers, maybe."

Gillian let out a harsh laugh, heard it echo up the canyon walls, heard his own heart beating with excitement, with the urgency of wild desire. A fresh assault of malodorous sewage drifted up from the sludge river. He inhaled deeply. The odor should have repulsed him, should have carried with it a hundred connotations: childhood naughtiness, genetically determined distaste, a manifest of internal responses, learned and innate. But it smelled good. The whole night smelled good.

He spun to face Impleton. "You're right. You should never allow yourself to be alone with strangers. It's not smart. It's not safe."

The smuggler with the sawed-off beard raised his thruster and pointed it at Buff. She held up her hands, pleading restraint.

"Look," she said softly, "we really don't want any trouble." She glared at Gillian. "We just want to meet Faquod."

"Then you pay," said Impleton. "Meeting Faquod . . . that is a privilege."

Gillian pointed his finger at the muscle boy, four feet away. "Can this ignor fight? Whenever I see someone like this, I'm reminded of the value of contraceptives. If his parents had only known."

"Oh shit," muttered Buff.

Muscle boy lost his smile. Saw-beard tightened his grip on the thruster and glanced at Impleton, waiting for orders. Impleton's mouth squirmed. The fat smuggler released a loud belch.

The belch was a signal. Muscle boy hopped down from the ledge and took a step toward Gillian. "I'm going to—"

His words ended in a choking gasp as Gillian's right foot lashed out, slammed into his belly. Muscle boy doubled over in pain.

Saw-beard pivoted, aimed his thruster at Gillian. He was far too late. Gillian, biting down hard, ignited his defensive web, heard the near-invisible crescents—front and rear—hum softly as they came to life. Saw-beard fired. Gillian, braced against the ledge, was hit by the discrete blast of energy, feeling it as a gentle nudge against his front crescent.

*A single-tube thruster,* thought Gillian. *A one-second recharge interval before it can be used again.*

All the time in the world.

Gillian flexed his right wrist and compressed his knuckles, launching the Cohe wand from its slip-wrist holster into his waiting palm. He squeezed the egg.

The twisting black beam whipped up the side of the mech-wall, the leading fifteen to twenty inches of the hot particle stream disintegrating everything in its path, the remainder of the beam merely a trail of harmless light. The fourth smuggler, perched twenty feet above the alley, screamed as twill tubes, relays, and conduits exploded, showering him beneath a mix of hot liquids and pressurized gases. Live wires arced; the alley's gloom vanished in a sizzling display of electrical madness. The smuggler— along with a melange of exploding flares—was jolted from the mech-wall, his arms flailing wildly, thruster rifle flying from his grasp, his crescent web turning the color of red wine as it soared to full power, trying to neutralize the thrashing high-voltage cables.

The smuggler was still in midair when Gillian twisted his wrist and turned the Cohe's deadly energy on Saw-beard. For an instant, the black beam seemed to coil in upon itself, lancing into an expanding spiral as it hurtled high into the air. Gillian squeezed the egg harder and jerked his wrist; the Cohe's deadly energy stream performed a U-turn, plunged toward the ground. Saw-beard opened his mouth in astonishment as the Cohe's devastating energy sliced off the barrel of his thruster.

Gillian released pressure on the egg-shaped wand. The black beam vanished just as the plummeting smuggler slammed onto the floor of the alley.

Muscle boy, still clutching his guts, reached into his pants pocket. Gillian jerked forward, extended his left foot through the weak side portal of his web, and slammed his heel into muscle boy's chest. The tattooed smuggler grunted hard, collapsed to his knees.

*Get up,* Gillian urged, feeling the excitement race through his body, unrestrained, as if his inner skin were being tickled, as if there were feathers in his bloodstream. His breath came in short intense gasps and he could feel tremendous waves of heat coursing up and down his chest. Full-body flush. Full-body hard-on.

"Cohe wand," whispered Impleton, the words echoing his fright. Buff grabbed the smuggler by the neck and yanked him forward so violently that he fell to his knees.

Saw-beard dropped the useless remnant of his weapon and backed away, his eyes wide with fear. The man from the mech-wall remained prone on the floor of the alley, moaning softly.

Gillian stared at muscle boy. "Get up!" He slithered into a combat crouch, turned sideways toward the tattooed smuggler, ready to lash out with hand or foot through the web's portals.

Muscle boy raised his head. A defeated face met Gillian's. Hard contours had been transformed into quivering patches of fear, humiliation. There was no more fight left in him. Eyes like those of a beaten puppy stared up at Gillian, begging forgiveness.

"No!" Gillian screamed, lunging forward, grabbing muscle boy's ankle and elbow, lifting the terrified smuggler overhead. With one violent twist, he sent him cartwheeling over the ledge. Muscle boy's shriek lasted until the youth plowed into the net-covered sludge river, fifteen feet below. There was a loud muffled splash, and then steaming gray geysers sprayed Gillian, bringing with them fresh wafts of the foul odor.

Gillian felt cheated; the fight had ended too soon. His left sleeve was damp with sludge, and he rammed the garment against his nostrils, sucked in the odor, wanting it to overpower him, hoping sensory overload would occupy consciousness, take his mind away from the reality of his damaged psyche. But the smell was a poor substitute for the cathartic power of violence. In a rage, he started toward Impleton.

The fat smuggler was on his knees, quaking in fear, his head pivoting wildly between Gillian and Buff. "Won't tell what I saw!" he pleaded. "Please . . . won't tell—"

Gillian grabbed the front of Impleton's coat and rubbed the protruding needle of his Cohe into the thick flesh of Impleton's neck.

"Won't tell," repeated the terrified smuggler, his voice dropping to a whisper, his eyes blinking like a set of short-circuiting status lights.

"Let's talk about Faquod," suggested Buff.

Impleton, with an overly vigorous nod of his head, managed to scratch himself on the needle of the Cohe.

"Oww!" he screamed.

"Calm down," ordered Buff. "And maybe you'll survive this night."

"Faquod," urged Gillian. "Where is he?"

The smuggler's lips began to quiver, uncontrollably, until finally the words exploded from his mouth.

"You're a Paratwa!" His eyes panned back and forth between Gillian and Buff. "You're tways!"

Buff laughed. "And you're a shitpile with maggots for neurons! Now talk! We want to find Faquod!"

Ten feet away, Saw-beard started to inch forward. Gillian glared at him. It was enough of a warning. Saw-beard froze in midstride.

"Don't want to die," whimpered Impleton.

"Faquod!" shouted Buff. "Where is he?"

Gillian pressed the Cohe's needle tip deep into a fold of flesh on the smuggler's neck, until it almost broke the skin.

"Fin Whirl in centersky," babbled Impleton. "Fin Whirl—tomorrow night. Faquod—he is always there. He never misses it."

Gillian glanced at Buff. "You know where this place is?"

"Yeah, I know where Fin Whirl is." A deep frown settled on her face. "Where else?" she asked Impleton. "Where else can we find him?"

"Don't know," whispered Impleton, his eyes begging. "It's truth! Fin Whirl—that's all I know."

Gillian leaned down, pressed his mouth against the smuggler's ear. "If you're lying, I'll come back for you. I'll slice off your head and put it in my trophy case."

"Fin Whirl," cried the smuggler. "It's truth—I swear!"

"Fin Whirl's a big place," pressed Buff. "Where exactly?"

"He has a private booth—BS-four."

Gillian believed him. He nodded to Buff, and she laid her palm on Impleton's forehead. The smuggler jerked once. His eyes glazed over, and he fell forward into her arms, unconscious. She let him slide off her body onto the damp paving and opened her palm, exposing the tiny white neuropad attached to the skin. She crooked her finger at Saw-beard.

He came quickly, almost eagerly, obviously finding a few hours of deep sleep via synaptic scrambling preferable to any further encounter with Gillian's Cohe wand.

"You may as well be comfortable," suggested Buff, pointing to Impleton's prone form. Saw-beard sat down beside his partner and rested the back of his head on Impleton's ample gut. Buff gave a quick touch with the neuropad. Saw-beard's eyes glazed over as he entered induced sleep.

"Let's go," said Gillian.

They began to jog up the alley, around the bend, retracing their path, toward the huge gate that Impleton had keyed open for them, toward the sanctuary of the street. Their boots splashed against puddles, spraying the canyon walls with the foul conglomeration of liquids, like twin-rotored boats leaving overlapping wakes.

"What's Fin Whirl?" asked Gillian, picking up the pace. It felt good to run hard, run fast, keep the body stimulated.

"I don't think you should go there," said Buff, the distaste in her voice easily discernible.

"We have to."

Buff did not reply. She was a Costeau, and she would do what was necessary. They had been partners for over a month now, ever since that Venus Cluster debacle in Irrya. Their near-fatal encounter with Slasher and Shooter—two tways of the vicious tripartite assassin who had been ravaging the Colonies—had provided a commonality of cause. Buff needed to avenge the death of her friend Martha; Gillian needed to keep his inner turbulence under control.

"What's Fin Whirl?" he repeated.

"It's a place where games are played ... dangerous games." She paused. "I don't think you should go there."

They reached the end of the alley, jogged to a halt in front of the massive service gate. Gillian found the control panel on the left wall, pressed the button. Silently, the gate slid open.

They emerged onto the narrow side street, deserted except for an old man seated on a stoop across the way, his head encased in a metallic shroud—a ree-fee—a self-powered programmable holo, providing a sensual experience as rich as the wearer's darkest fantasies. The man was muttering to himself:

"Now, silky—onto the floor. Onto your knees. Give us

what we've been asking for. Ground it, silky. Ground it good. Make it earth, silky. Make it wet as the world. . . ."

Behind them, the gate closed automatically. They headed quickly up the street toward one of the main boulevards, three blocks away, to a place where Sirak-Brath began to lose its shadows, where its fantasies became accessible to all.

"Is Fin Whirl an entertainment complex?" probed Gillian. "A fantasy club?"

"It's no fantasy. It's very real."

"But a place of enjoyment, nonetheless?"

Buff grimaced. "I don't think you should go there."

The message decoded itself. On screen, the weird blending of darting icons—spheres, triangles, bubbling spirals—erupted into words and sentences.

PERPS A WHITE MALE AND BLACK FEMALE. NO POSITIVE ID, BUT WEAPON USED ON SMUGGLERS DEFINITELY A COHE WAND. INTERVIEW WITH INJURED SMUGGLER SUGGESTS THAT MALE DISPLAYED EAGERNESS FOR CONFLICT. PERPS WERE OSTENSIBLY TRYING TO CONTACT A HIGH-TECH WEAPONS DEALER NAMED FAQUOD. PROBABILITY EXTREMELY HIGH THAT PERPS WERE GILLIAN AND BUFF.

# BEST OF SF FROM TOR

☐ 53016-0 *THE SHATTERED SPHERE*   $5.99
             Roger MacBride Allen   $6.99 Canada

☐ 53022-5 *THE STARS ARE ALSO FIRE*   $5.99
             Poul Anderson   $6.99 Canada

☐ 52213-3 *TROUBLE AND HER FRIENDS*   $4.99
             Melissa Scott   $5.99 Canada

☐ 55255-5 *THE GOLDEN QUEEN*   $5.99
             Dave Wolverton   $6.99 Canada

☐ 52047-5 *EON*   $6.99
             Greg Bear   $7.99 Canada

---